Remember When

Remember When

Nora Roberts

and

J.D. Robb

PIATKUS

Copyright © 2003 by Nora Roberts

First published in Great Britain in 2003 by
Judy Piatkus (Publishers) Ltd of
5 Windmill Street, London W1T 2JA
email info@piatkus.co.uk

First published in the United States in 2003
by G. P. Putnam's Sons

The moral right of the author has been asserted

*A catalogue record of this book is
available from the British Library*

ISBN 0 7499 0660 X

Typeset by Palimpsest Book Production Limited,
Polmont, Stirlingshire
Printed and bound in Great Britain by
MPG Books Ltd, Bodmin, Cornwall

To Mary Kay McComas,

who doesn't play a musical instrument,
but who is the best of pals

Part One

Covetous of others' possessions,
he was prodigal of his own.

SALLUST

Who in the world am I?
Ah, that's the great puzzle!

LEWIS CARROLL

Chapter One

A heroic belch of thunder followed the strange little man into the shop. He glanced around apologetically, as if the rude noise were his responsibility rather than nature's, and fumbled a package under his arm so he could close a black-and-white-striped umbrella.

Both umbrella and man dripped, somewhat mournfully, onto the neat square of mat just inside the door while the cold spring rain battered the streets and sidewalks on the other side. He stood where he was, as if not entirely sure of his welcome.

Laine turned her head and sent him a smile that held only warmth and easy invitation. It was a look her friends would have called her polite shopkeeper's smile.

Well, damnit, she *was* a polite shopkeeper – and at the moment that label was being sorely tested.

If she'd known the rain would bring customers into the store instead of keeping them away, she wouldn't have given Jenny the day off. Not that she minded business. A woman didn't open a store if she didn't want customers, whatever the weather. And a woman didn't open one in Small Town, U.S.A., unless she understood she'd spend as much time chatting, listening and refereeing debates as she would ringing up sales.

And that was fine, Laine thought, that was good. But if Jenny had been at work instead of spending the day painting her toenails and watching soaps, Jenny would've been the one stuck with the Twins.

Darla Price Davis and Carla Price Gohen had their hair tinted the same ashy shade of blond. They wore identical slick blue raincoats

3

and carried matching hobo bags. They finished each other's sentences and communicated in a kind of code that included a lot of twitching eyebrows, pursed lips, lifted shoulders and head bobs.

What might've been cute in eight-year-olds was just plain weird in forty-eight-year-old women.

Still, Laine reminded herself, they never came into Remember When without dropping a bundle. It might take them hours to drop it, but eventually the sales would ring. There was little that lifted Laine's heart as high as the ring of the cash register.

Today they were on the hunt for an engagement present for their niece, and the driving rain and booming thunder hadn't stopped them. Nor had it deterred the drenched young couple who – they'd said – had detoured into Angel's Gap on a whim on their way to D.C.

Or the wet little man with the striped umbrella who looked, to Laine's eye, a bit frantic and lost.

So she added a little more warmth to her smile. 'I'll be with you in just a few minutes,' she called out, and turned her attention back to the Twins.

'Why don't you look around a little more,' Laine suggested. 'Think it over. As soon as I—'

Darla's hand clamped on her wrist, and Laine knew she wasn't going to escape.

'We need to decide. Carrie's just about your age, sweetie. What would *you* want for your engagement gift?'

Laine didn't need to transcribe the code to understand it was a not-so-subtle dig. She was, after all, twenty-eight, and not married. Not engaged. Not, at the moment, even dating particularly. This, according to the Price twins, was a crime against nature.

'You know,' Carla piped up, 'Carrie met her Paul at Kawanian's spaghetti supper last fall. You really should socialize more, Laine.'

'I really should,' she agreed with a winning smile. *If I want to hook up with a balding, divorced CPA with a sinus condition.* 'I know Carrie's going to love whatever you choose. But maybe an engagement gift from her aunts should be something more personal than the candlesticks. They're lovely, but the dresser set's so feminine.'

4

She picked up the silver-backed brush from the set they were considering. 'I imagine another bride used this on her wedding night.'

'More personal,' Darla began. 'More—'

'Girlie. Yes! We could get the candlesticks for—'

'A wedding gift. But maybe we should look at the jewelry before we buy the dresser set. Something with pearls? Something—'

'Old she could wear on her wedding day. Put the candlesticks *and* the dresser set aside, honey. We'll take a look at the jewelry before we decide anything.'

The conversation bounced like a tennis ball served and volleyed out of two identical coral-slicked mouths. Laine congratulated herself on her skill and focus as she was able to keep up with who said what.

'Good idea.' Laine lifted the gorgeous old Dresden candlesticks. No one could say the Twins didn't have taste, or were shy of heating up their plastic.

She started to carry them to the counter when the little man crossed her path.

She was eye to eye with him, and his were a pale, washed-out blue reddened by lack of sleep or alcohol or allergies. Laine decided on lost sleep as they were also dogged by heavy bags of fatigue. His hair was a grizzled mop gone mad with the rain. He wore a pricey Burberry topcoat and carried a three-dollar umbrella. She assumed he'd shaved hurriedly that morning as he'd missed a patch of stubbly gray along his jaw.

'Laine.'

He said her name with a kind of urgency and intimacy that had her smile turning to polite confusion.

'Yes? I'm sorry, do I know you?'

'You don't remember me.' His body seemed to droop. 'It's been a long time, but I thought . . .'

'Miss!' the woman on her way to D.C. called out. 'Do you ship?'

'Yes, we do.' She could hear the Twins going through one of their shorthand debates over earrings and brooches, and sensed an impulse buy from the D.C. couple. And the little man stared at her with a hopeful intimacy that had her skin chilling.

5

'I'm sorry, I'm a little swamped this morning.' She sidestepped to the counter to set down the candlesticks. Intimacy, she reminded herself, was part of the rhythm of small towns. The man had probably been in before, and she just couldn't place him. 'Is there something specific I can help you with, or would you like to browse awhile?'

'I need your help. There isn't much time.' He drew out a card, pressed it into her hand. 'Call me at that number, as soon as you can.'

'Mr . . .' She glanced down at the card, read his name. 'Peterson, I don't understand. Are you looking to sell something?'

'No. No.' His laugh bounced toward hysterical and had Laine grateful for the customers crowded into the store. 'Not anymore. I'll explain everything, but not now.' He looked around the shop. 'Not here. I shouldn't have come here. Call the number.'

He clamped a hand over hers in a way that had Laine fighting an instinct to jerk free. 'Promise.'

He smelled of rain and soap and . . . Brut, she realized. And the aftershave had some flicker of memory trying to light in her brain. Then his fingers tightened on hers. 'Promise,' he repeated in a harsh whisper, and she saw only an odd man in a wet coat.

'Of course.'

She watched him go to the door, open the cheap umbrella. And let out a sigh of relief when he scurried out into the rain. *Weird* was her only thought, but she studied the card for a moment.

His name was printed, Jasper R. Peterson, but the phone number was handwritten beneath and underscored twice, she noted.

Pushing the card into her pocket, she started over to give the traveling couple a friendly nudge, when the sound of screeching brakes on wet pavement and shocked screams had her spinning around. There was a hideous noise, a hollow thud she'd never forget. Just as she'd never forget the sight of the strange little man in his fashionable coat slamming against her display window.

She bolted out the door, into the streaming rain. Footsteps pounded on the pavement, and somewhere close was the crunching sound of metal striking metal, glass shattering.

'Mr. Peterson.' Laine gripped his hand, bowed her body over his in a pathetic attempt to shield his bloodied face from the rain. 'Don't move. Call an ambulance!' she shouted and yanked off her jacket to cover him as best she could.

'Saw him. Saw him. Shouldn't have come. Laine.'

'Help's coming.'

'Left it for you. He wanted me to get it to you.'

'It's all right.' She scooped her dripping hair out of her eyes and took the umbrella someone offered. She angled it over him, leaned down closer as he tugged weakly on her hand.

'Be careful. I'm sorry. Be careful.'

'I will. Of course I will. Just try to be quiet now, try to hold on, Mr. Peterson. Help's coming.'

'You don't remember.' Blood trickled out of his mouth as he smiled. 'Little Lainie.' He took a shuddering breath, coughed up blood. She heard the sirens as he began to sing in a thin, gasping voice.

'Pack up all my care and woe,' he crooned, then wheezed. 'Bye, bye, blackbird.'

She stared at his battered face as her already chilled skin began to prickle. Memories, so long locked away, opened. 'Uncle Willy? Oh my God.'

'Used to like that one. Screwed up,' he said breathlessly. 'Sorry. Thought it'd be safe. Shouldn't've come.'

'I don't understand.' Tears burned her throat, streamed down her cheeks. He was dying. He was dying because she hadn't known him, and she'd sent him out into the rain. 'I'm sorry. I'm so sorry.'

'He knows where you are now.' His eyes rolled back. 'Hide the pooch.'

'What?' She leaned closer yet until her lips almost brushed his. 'What?' But the hand she had clutched in hers went limp.

Paramedics brushed her aside. She heard their short, pithy dialogue – medical codes she'd grown accustomed to hearing on television, could almost recite herself. But this was real. The blood washing away in the rain was real.

She heard a woman sobbing and saying over and over in a strident voice, 'He ran right in front of me. I couldn't stop in time. He just ran in front of the car. Is he all right? Is he all right? Is he all right?'

No, Laine wanted to say. He's not.

'Come inside, honey.' Darla put an arm around Laine's shoulders, drew her back. 'You're soaked. You can't do anything more out here.'

'I should do something.' She stared down at the broken umbrella, its cheerful stripes marked with grime now, and drops of blood.

She should have settled him down in front of the fire. Given him a hot drink and let him, warm and dry himself in front of the little hearth. Then he'd be alive. Telling her stories and silly jokes.

But she hadn't recognized him, and so he was dying.

She couldn't go in, out of the rain, and leave him alone with strangers. But there was nothing to be done but watch, helplessly, while the paramedics fought and failed to save the man who'd once laughed at her knock-knock jokes and sung silly songs. He died in front of the shop she'd worked so hard to build, and laid at her door all the memories she thought she'd escaped.

She was a businesswoman, a solid member of the community, and a fraud. In the back room of her store, she poured two cups of coffee and knew she was about to lie to a man she considered a friend. And deny all knowledge of one she'd loved.

She did her best to steady herself, ran her hands through the damp mass of the bright red hair normally worn in a shoulder-sweeping bob. She was pale, and the rain had washed away the makeup, always carefully applied, so freckles stood out on her narrow nose and across her cheekbones. Her eyes, a bright Viking blue, were glassy with shock and grief. Her mouth, just a hair too wide for her angular face, wanted to tremble.

In the little giltwood mirror on the wall of her office, she studied her reflection. And saw herself for what she was. Well, she would do what she needed to do to survive. Willy would certainly understand that. Do what came first, she told herself, then think about the rest.

She sucked in a breath, let out a shudder, then lifted the coffee. Her hands were nearly steady as she went into the main shop and prepared to give false testimony to Angel's Gap's chief of police.

'Sorry it took so long,' she apologized as she carried the mugs to where Vince Burger stood by the little clinker fireplace.

He was built like a bear with a great shock of white-blond hair that stood nearly straight up, as if surprised to find itself on top of the wide, comfortable face. His eyes, a faded blue and fanned with squint lines, were full of compassion.

He was Jenny's husband, and had become a kind of brother to Laine. But for now she reminded herself he was a cop, and everything she'd worked for was on the line.

'Why don't you sit down, Laine? You've had a bad shock.'

'I feel sort of numb.' That was true enough, she didn't have to lie about everything. But she walked over to sip her coffee and stare out at the rain so she wouldn't have to meet those sympathetic eyes. 'I appreciate your coming in to take my statement yourself, Vince. I know you're busy.'

'Figured you'd be more comfortable.'

Better to lie to a friend than a stranger, she thought bitterly. 'I don't know what I can tell you. I didn't see the actual accident. I heard . . . I heard brakes, screams, an awful thud, then I saw . . .' She didn't shut her eyes. If she shut them, she'd see it again. 'I saw him hit the window, like he'd been thrown against it. I ran out, stayed with him until the paramedics came. They were quick. It seemed like hours, but it was only minutes.'

'He was in here before the accident.'

Now she did close her eyes, and prepared to do what she had to do to protect herself. 'Yes. I had several customers this morning,which proves I should never give Jenny a day off. The Twins were in, and a couple driving through on their way to D.C. I was busy when he came in. He browsed around for a while.'

'The woman from out of town said she thought you knew each other.'

'Really?' Turning now, Laine painted a puzzled expression on her face, as a clever artist might on a portrait. She crossed back, sat on one of the two elbow chairs she'd arranged in front of the fire. 'I don't know why.'

'An impression,' Vince said with a shrug. Always mindful of his size, he sat, slow and careful, in the matching chair. 'Said he took your hand.'

'Well, we *shook* hands, and he gave me his card.' Laine pulled it out of her pocket, forced herself to keep her attention on Vince's face. The fire was crackling with warmth, and though she felt its heat on her skin, she was cold. Very cold. 'He said he'd like to speak with me when I wasn't so busy. That he might have something to sell. People often do,' she added, offering Vince the card. 'Which is how I stay in business.'

'Right.' He tucked the card into his breast pocket. 'Anything strike you about him?'

'Just that he had a beautiful topcoat, and a silly umbrella – and that he didn't seem like the sort to wander around small towns. Had city on him.'

'So did you a few years ago. In fact . . .' He narrowed his gaze, reached out and rubbed a thumb over her cheek. 'Still got some stuck to you.'

She laughed, because it's what he wanted. 'I wish I could be more help, Vince. It's such an awful thing to happen.'

'I can tell you, we got four different witness statements. All of them have the guy running straight out into the street, dead in front of that car. Like he was spooked or something. He seem spooked to you, Laine?'

'I wasn't paying enough attention. The fact is, Vince, I basically brushed him off when I realized he wasn't here to shop. I had customers.' She shook her head when her voice broke. 'It seems so callous now.'

The hand Vince laid over hers in comfort made her feel foul. 'You didn't know what was coming. You were the first to get to him.'

'He was right outside.' She had to take a deep gulp of coffee to wash the grief out of her throat. 'Almost on the doorstep.'

'He spoke to you.'

'Yes.' She reached for her coffee again so their hands parted. 'Nothing that made much sense. He said he was sorry, a couple of times. I don't think he knew who I was or what happened. I think he was delirious. The paramedics came and . . . and he died. What will you do now? I mean, he's not from around here. The phone number's New York. I wonder, I guess I wonder if he was just driving through, where he was going, where he was from.'

'We'll be looking into all that so we can notify his next of kin.' Rising, Vince laid a hand on her shoulder. 'I'm not going to tell you to put it out of your mind, Laine. You won't be able to, not for a while. I'm going to tell you that you did all you could. Can't do more than all you could.'

'Thanks. I'm going to close up for the day. I want to go home.'

'Good idea. Want a ride?'

'No. Thanks.' It was guilt as much as affection that had her rising on her toes to press a kiss to his cheek. 'Tell Jenny I'll see her tomorrow.'

His name, at least the name she'd known, was Willy Young. Probably William, Laine thought as she drove up the pitted gravel lane. He hadn't been her real uncle – as far as she knew – but an honorary one. One who'd always had red licorice in his pocket for a little girl.

She hadn't seen him in nearly twenty years, and his hair had been brown then, his face a bit rounder. There'd always been a spring in his step.

Small wonder she hadn't recognized him in the bowed and nervy little man who'd come into her shop.

How had he found her? *Why* had he?

Since he'd been, to her knowledge, her father's closest friend, she assumed he was – as was her father – a thief, a scam artist, a small-time grifter. Not the sort of connections a respectable businesswoman wanted to acknowledge.

And why the hell should that make her feel small and guilty?

She slapped on the brakes and sat, brooding through the steady whoosh of her wipers at the pretty house on the pretty rise.

She loved this place. Hers. Home. The two-story frame house was, strictly speaking, too large for a woman on her own. But she loved being able to ramble around in it. She'd loved every minute she'd spent meticulously decorating each room to suit herself. And only herself.

Knowing, as she did, she'd never, ever have to pack up all her belongings at a moment's notice to the tune of 'Bye Bye Blackbird' and run.

She loved being able to putter around the yard, planting gardens, pruning bushes, mowing the grass, yanking the weeds. Ordinary things. Simple, *normal* things for a woman who'd spent the first half of her life doing little that was normal.

She was entitled to this, wasn't she? To being Laine Tavish and all that meant? The business, the town, the house, the friends, the *life*. She was entitled to the woman she'd made herself into.

It wouldn't have helped Willy for her to have told Vince the truth. Nothing would have changed for him, and everything might have changed for her. Vince would find out, soon enough, that the man in the county morgue wasn't Jasper R. Peterson but William Young, and however many aka's that went with it.

There'd be a criminal record. She knew Willy had done at least one stint alongside her father. 'Brothers in arms,' her father had called them, and she could still hear his big, booming laugh.

Because it infuriated her, she slammed out of the car. She made the house in a dash, fumbled out her keys.

She calmed, almost immediately, when the door was closed at her back and the house surrounded her. Just the quiet of it, the scents of lemon oil rubbed into wood by her own hand, the subtle sweetness of spring flowers brought in from her own yard stroked her frayed nerves.

She set her keys in the raku dish on the entry table, pulled her cell phone out of her purse and plugged it into the recharger. Slipped out of her shoes, out of her jacket, which she draped over the newel post, and set her purse on the bottom step.

Following routine, she walked back to the kitchen. Normally, she'd have put on the kettle for tea and looked through the mail she'd picked up from the box at the foot of the lane while the water heated.

But today, she poured a big glass of wine.

And drank it standing at the sink, looking through the window at her backyard.

She'd had a yard – a couple of times – as a kid. She remembered one in . . . Nebraska? Iowa? What did it matter, she thought and took a healthy gulp of wine. She'd liked the yard because it had a big old tree right in the middle, and he'd hung an old tire from it on a big thick rope.

He'd pushed her so high she'd thought she was flying.

She wasn't sure how long they'd stayed and didn't remember the house at all. Most of her childhood was a blur of places and faces, of car rides, a flurry of packing up. And him, her father, with his big laugh and wide hands, with his irresistible grin and careless promises.

She'd spent the first decade of her life desperately in love with the man, and the rest of it doing everything she could to forget he existed.

If he was in trouble, again, it was none of her concern.

She wasn't Jack O'Hara's little Lainie anymore. She was Laine Tavish, solid citizen.

She eyed the bottle of wine and with a shrug poured a second glass. A grown woman could get toasted in her own kitchen, by God, especially when she'd watched a ghost from the past die at her feet.

Carrying the glass, she walked to the mudroom door, to answer the hopeful whimpering on the other side.

He came in like a cannon shot – a hairy, floppy-eared cannon shot. His paws planted themselves at her belly, and the long snout bumped her face before the tongue slurped out to cover her cheeks with wet and desperate affection.

'Okay, okay! Happy to see you, too.' No matter how low her mood, a welcome home by Henry, the amazing hound, never failed to lift it.

She'd sprung him from the joint, or so she liked to think. When she'd gone to the pound two years before, it had been with a puppy in mind. She'd always wanted a cute, gamboling little bundle she'd train from the ground up.

But then she'd seen him – big, ungainly, stunningly homely with his mud-colored fur. A cross, she'd thought, between a bear and an anteater. And she'd been lost the minute he'd looked through the cage doors and into her eyes.

Everybody deserves a chance, she'd thought, and so she sprung Henry from the joint. He'd never given her a reason to regret it. His love was absolute, so much so that he continued to look adoringly at her even when she filled his bowl with kibble.

'Chow time, pal.'

At the signal, Henry dipped his head into his bowl and got serious.

She should eat, too. Something to sop up some of the wine, but she didn't feel like it. Enough wine swimming around in her bloodstream and she wouldn't be able to think, to wonder, to worry.

She left the inner door open, but stepped into the mudroom to check the outside locks. A man could shimmy through the dog door, if he was determined to get in, but Henry would set up the alarm.

He howled every time a car came up the lane, and though he would punish the intruder with slobber and delight – after he finished trembling in terror – she was never surprised by a visitor. And never, in her four years in Angel's Gap, had she had any trouble at home, or at the shop.

Until today, she reminded herself.

She decided to lock the mudroom door after all, and let Henry out the front for his evening run.

She thought about calling her mother, but what was the point? Her mother had a good, solid life now, with a good, solid man. She'd earned it. What point was there in breaking into that nice life and saying, 'Hey, I ran into Uncle Willy today, and so did a Jeep Cherokee.'

She took her wine with her upstairs, with the dog dancing happily at her heels. She'd change, take Henry for a long walk in the rain, then fix herself a little dinner, take a hot bath, have an early night.

She'd close the book on what had happened that day.

Left it for you, he'd said, she remembered. Probably delirious. But if he'd left her anything, she didn't want it.

She already had everything she wanted.

Max Gannon slipped the attendant a twenty for a look at the body. In Max's experience a picture of Andrew Jackson cut through red tape quicker than explanations and paperwork and more levels of bureaucracy.

He'd gotten the bad news on Willy from the motel clerk at the Red Roof Inn where he'd tracked the slippery little bastard. The cops had already been there, but Max had invested the first twenty of the day for the room number and key.

The cops hadn't taken his clothes yet, nor from the looks of it done much of a search. Why would they on a traffic accident? But once they ID'd Willy, they'd be back and look a lot closer.

Willy hadn't unpacked, Max noted as he took stock of the room. Socks and underwear and two dress shirts were still neatly folded in the single Louis Vuitton bag. Willy had been a tidy one, and he'd loved his name brands.

He'd hung a suit in the closet. Banker gray, single-breasted, Hugo Boss. A pair of black Ferragamo loafers, complete with shoe trees, sat neatly on the floor.

Max went through the pockets, felt carefully along the lining. He took the wooden trees out of the shoes, poked his long fingers into the toes.

In the adjoining bath, he searched Willy's Dior toiletry kit. He lifted the tank lid on the toilet, crouched down to search behind it, under the sink.

He went through the drawers, through the suitcase and its contents, flipped over the mattress on the standard double.

It took him less than an hour to search the room and verify Willy had left nothing important behind. When he left, the space looked as tidy and untouched as it had when he'd entered.

He considered giving the clerk another twenty not to mention the visit to the cops, then decided it might put ideas in his head. He climbed into his Porsche, switched on Springsteen and headed to the county morgue to verify that his strongest lead was on ice.

'Stupid. Goddamn, Willy, I figured you for smarter than this.'

Max blew out a breath as he looked at Willy's ruined face. *Why the hell did you run?* And what's in some podunk town in Maryland that was so important?

What, Max thought, or who?

Since Willy was no longer in the position to tell him, Max walked back out to drive into Angel's Gap to pick up a multi-million-dollar trail.

If you wanted to pluck grapes from the small-town vine, you went to a place where locals gathered. During the day, that meant coffee and food, at night, alcohol.

Once he'd decided he'd be staying in Angel's Gap for at least a day or two, Max checked into what was billed The Historic Wayfarer's Inn and showered off the first twelve hours of the day. It was late enough to pick door number two.

He ate a very decent room-service burger at his laptop, surfing the home page provided by the Angel's Gap chamber of commerce. The Nightlife section gave him several choices of bars, clubs and cafes. He wanted a neighborhood pub, the kind of place where the towners knocked back a beer a the end of the day and talked about each other.

He culled out three that might fit the bill, plugged in the addresses for directions, then finished off his burger while studying the printout map of Angel's Gap.

Nice enough place, he mused, tucked in the mountains the way it was. Killer views, plenty of recreational choices for the sports enthusiast or camping freak. Slow enough pace for those who wanted to shake the urban off their Docksides, but with classy little pockets of culture – and a reasonable drive from several major metro areas should one be inclined to spend the weekend in the Maryland mountains.

The chamber of commerce boasted of the opportunities for

hunting, fishing, hiking and other manner of outdoor recreation –
none of which appealed to the urbanite in Max.

If he wanted to see bear and deer in their natural habitat, he'd
turn on The Discovery Channel.

Still, the place had charm with its steep streets and old buildings solid in their dark red brick. There was a nice, wide stretch
of the Potomac River bisecting the town, and the interest of the
arching bridges that spanned it. Lots of church steeples, some with
copper touches gone soft green with age and weather. And as he
sat, he heard the long, echoing whistle of a train signaling its
passing.

He had no doubt it was an eyeful in fall when the trees erupted
with color, and pretty as a postcard when the snow socked in. But
that didn't explain why an old hand like Willy Young had gotten
himself mowed down by an SUV on Market Street.

To find that piece of the puzzle, Max shut down his computer,
grabbed his beloved bomber jacket and headed out to go bar
hopping.

Chapter Two

He bypassed the first choice without bothering to stop. The forest of Hogs and Harleys out front tagged it as a biker bar, and not the sort of place where the customers talked town business over their brew.

The second took him less than two minutes to identify as a college den with strange alternative music piped in, and a couple of earnest types playing chess in a corner while most of the others performed standard mating rituals.

But he hit it on the third.

Artie's was the sort of place a guy might take his wife to, but not his side piece. It was where you went to socialize, to bump into friends or grab a quick one on the way home.

Max would've made book that ninety percent of the customer base knew each other by name, and a good chunk of them would be related.

He sidled up to the bar, ordered Beck's on tap and scoped out his surroundings. ESPN on the bar tube, sound muted, snack mix in plastic courtesy baskets. One very large black guy working the stick, and two waitresses handling the booths and four-tops.

The first waitress reminded him of his high-school librarian, which made him think she'd seen it all and wasn't too pleased with the view. She was short, heavy at the hip and on the high side of forty. There was a look in her eye that warned him she wouldn't tolerate lip.

The second was early twenties and the flirty type. She showed off a nicely packed body with a snug black sweater and painted-on jeans. She spent as much time tossing her curly blond hair as she did scooping up empties.

From the way she lingered at her stations, shooting the breeze, Max bet she was a fount of information, and the sort that liked to share.

He bided his time, then sent her a winning smile when she stopped by the bar to call in an order. 'Busy tonight.'

She shot a winning smile right back at him. 'Oh, not too bad.' She shifted her weight, swiveled her torso toward him in a body-language invitation to talk. 'Where you from?'

'I move around a lot. Business.'

'You got southern boy in your voice.'

'Caught me. Savannah, but I haven't been home in a while.' He held out a hand. 'Max.'

'Hi, Max. Angie. What kind of business brings you to the Gap?'

'Insurance.'

Her uncle sold insurance and he sure as hell didn't decorate a bar stool like this one. Six-two, most of it leg, and a well-toned one-ninety, if she was any judge. And Angie considered herself a damn good judge of her eye candy.

There was a lot of streaky brown hair the humidity had teased into waves around a sharp, narrow face. The eyes were tawny brown and friendly, but there was an edge to them. Then there was that hint of dreamy drawl, and the slightly crooked eyetooth that kept his smile from being perfect.

She liked a man with an edge, and a few imperfections.

'Insurance? Could've fooled me.'

'It's just gambling, isn't it?' He popped a pretzel into his mouth, flashed the grin again. 'Most people, they like to gamble. Just like they like to believe they're going to live forever.' He took a sip of his beer, noted she glanced at his left hand. Checking for a wedding ring, he assumed. 'They don't. I heard some poor bastard got creamed right on Main Street this morning.'

'Market,' she corrected, and he made himself look puzzled. 'Happened this morning on Market Street. Ran right out in front of poor Missy Leager's Cherokee. She's a mess about it, too.'

19

'That's rough. Doesn't sound like it was her fault.'

'It wasn't. Lots of people saw it happen, and there wasn't a thing she could've done. He just ran right out in front of her.'

'That's hard. I guess she knew him, too. Small town like this.'

'No, nobody did. He wasn't from here. I heard he was in Remember When – I work there part-time – right before. We sell antiques and collectibles and stuff. I guess maybe he was browsing on through. Awful. Just awful.'

'It sure is. You were there when it happened?'

'Uh-uh. I wasn't working this morning.' She paused, as if conducting a quick debate on whether she was glad or sorry to have missed it. 'Don't know why anybody'd run out in the street that way. It was raining pretty bad. I guess he didn't see the car.'

'Bad luck.'

'I'll say.'

'Angie, you waiting for those drinks to serve themselves?'

It was from the librarian and had Angie rolling her eyes. 'I'm getting 'em.' She winked at Max, then hefted her tray. 'See you around?'

'You bet.'

By the time Max walked back into his hotel room, he had a good handle on Willy's movements. He'd checked into his motel at around ten the night before, paid cash for a three-night stay. He wouldn't be getting a refund. He'd had a solo breakfast at the coffee shop the next morning, then drove in his rental car to Market Street and parked two blocks north of Remember When.

Since, at this point, Max couldn't put him in any of the other shops or businesses in that section, the most logical reason for parking that distance from his assumed destination, in the rain, was caution. Or paranoia.

Since he was dead, caution was the safer bet.

So just what had Willy wanted with an antique shop in Angel's Gap that had him making tracks from New York – and doing everything he could to cover those tracks?

A drop point? A contact?

Once again, Max booted up his computer and brought up the

town's home page. In a couple of clicks, he linked to Remember When. Antiques, estate jewelry, collectibles. Bought and sold.

He scribbled the shop name on a pad and added *Fence?,* circling the question twice.

He read the operating hours, phone and fax numbers, e-mail address, and the fact that they claimed to ship worldwide.

Then he read the proprietor's name.

Laine Tavish.

It wasn't one on his list, but he checked anyway. No Laine, he verified, no Tavish. But there was Elaine O'Hara. Big Jack's only daughter.

Lips pursed, Max leaned back in the desk chair. She'd be . . . twenty-eight, twenty-nine now. Wouldn't it be interesting if Big Jack O'Hara's little girl had followed in her daddy's larcenous footsteps, had changed her name and snuggled herself away in a pretty mountain town?

It was, Max thought, a puzzle piece begging to fit.

Four years of living in Angel's Gap meant Laine knew just what to expect when she opened Remember When in the morning.

Jenny would arrive, just a hair late, with fresh doughnuts. At six months pregnant, Jenny rarely went twenty minutes without a craving for something that screamed sugar and fat. As a result, Laine was viewing her own bathroom scale with one eye closed.

Jenny would complement the doughnuts with a thermos of the herbal tea she'd become addicted to since conception and demand to know all the details of yesterday's event. Being married to the chief of police wouldn't stop her from wanting Laine's version to add to already accumulated data.

At ten sharp, the curious would start to wander in. Some, Laine thought as she filled the cash register with change, would pretend to be browsing, and others wouldn't bother to disguise the hunt for gossip.

She'd have to go through it all again. Have to lie again, or at least evade with the pretense that she'd never before seen the man who called himself Jasper Peterson.

It had been a long time since she'd had to put on a mask just to get through the day. And it depressed her how easy a fit it was.

She was ready when Jenny rushed in five minutes late.

Jenny had the face of a mischievous angel. It was round and soft, pink and white, and had clever hazel eyes that tilted up just a tad at the outside corners. Her hair was a curling black mass, often, as it was today, bundled any which way on top of her head. She wore an enormous red sweater that stretched over her pregnant belly, baggy jeans and ancient Doc Martens.

She was everything Laine wasn't – disordered, impulsive, undisciplined, an emotional whirlwind. And exactly the sort of friend Laine had pined for throughout childhood.

Laine considered it one of those golden gifts of fate that Jenny was in her life.

'I'm *starving*. Are you starving?' Jenny dumped the bakery box on the counter, ripped open the lid. 'I could hardly stand the *smell* of these things on the two-minute walk from Krosen's. I think I started to whimper.' She stuffed the best part of a jelly-filled into her mouth and talked around it. 'I worried about you. I know you said you were okay when I called last night, just a little headache, don't want to talk about it, blah, blah, blah, but Mommy worried, sweetie.'

'I'm okay. It was awful, but I'm okay.'

Jenny held out the box. 'Eat sugar.'

'God. Do you know how long I'll have to work out to chip this off my ass?'

Jenny only smiled when Laine caved and took a cream-filled. 'You've got such a pretty ass, too.' She rubbed her belly in slow circles as she watched Laine nibble. 'You don't look like you got much sleep.'

'No. Couldn't settle.' Despite every effort not to, she looked through the display window. 'I must've been the last person he spoke to, and I brushed him off because I was busy.'

'Can you imagine how Missy's feeling this morning? And it's no more her fault than yours.' She went to the back room, moving in the waddle/march she'd developed in the sixth month of her

22

pregnancy and came back with two mugs. 'You'll have some tea to go with your sugar hit. You're going to need both to fortify you for the onslaught when we open. Everybody's going to want to come by.'

'I know.'

'Vince is going to keep it quiet until he's got more figured out, but it's going to get out, and I figure you've got a right to know.'

Here it comes, Laine thought. 'Know what?'

'The guy's name? It wasn't the name on the card he gave you.'

'I'm sorry?'

'It wasn't the name he had on his driver's license or credit cards either,' Jenny continued excitedly. 'It was an alias. His name was William Young. Get *this*. He was an ex-convict.'

She hated hearing the man she remembered so fondly called an ex-con, as if it was the sum of him. And hated herself for doing nothing to defend him. 'You're kidding? That little man?'

'Larceny, fraud, possession of stolen goods, and that's just convictions. From what I wormed out of Vince, he was suspected of a lot more. Like a career criminal, Laine. And he was in here, probably casing the joint.'

'You're watching too many old movies, Jenny.'

'Come *on*! What if you'd been alone in here? What if he had a gun?'

Laine dusted sugar off her fingers. 'Did he have a gun?'

'Well, no, but he could have. He could've robbed you.'

'A career criminal comes all the way to Angel's Gap to rob my store? Man, that website really works.'

Jenny struggled to look annoyed, then barked out a laugh. 'Okay, so he probably wasn't planning on knocking over the joint.'

'I'm going to take exception if you keep calling my shop a joint.'

'But he had to be up to something. He gave you his card, right?'

'Yes, but—'

'So *maybe* he was hoping to sell you stolen merchandise. Who'd look in a place like this for hot goods? Like I told Vince, he probably did a job recently, and maybe his usual fence dried up or something, so he had to find a way to turn the goods, and fast.'

'And of all the antique stores in all the world, he walks into mine?' She laughed it off, but there was a twist in her gut as she wondered if that was indeed the reason Willy had come to her door.

'Well, he had to walk into one, why *not* yours?'

'Ah . . . because this isn't a TV movie of the week?'

'You have to admit it's strange.'

'Yes, it's strange, and it's sad. And it's also ten o'clock, Jen. Let's open and see what the day brings.'

It brought, as expected, the gossip hounds and gawkers, but Jenny was able to exchange theories with a few customers while she rang up genuine sales. It was cowardly, but Laine decided to take the yellow feather and escape into the back with the excuse of paperwork while Jenny handled the shop.

She'd stolen barely twenty minutes of solitude when Jenny poked her head in. 'Honey, you've *got* to see this.'

'Unless it's a dog that can juggle while riding a unicycle, I need to update this spreadsheet.'

'It's better.' Jenny jerked her head toward the shop, stepping back with the door open.

Since her curiosity was piqued, Laine slipped out after her. She saw him, holding a green Depression glass water glass up to the light. It seemed entirely too delicate, too feminine, for a man wearing a battered bomber jacket and worn hiking boots. But he didn't fumble it as he set it down and picked up its mate for a similar study.

'Mmmm.' Jenny made the same sound she made when contemplating jelly doughnuts. 'That's the kind of long drink of water a woman wants to down in one big slurp.'

'Pregnant married women shouldn't slurp at strange men.'

'Doesn't mean we can't appreciate the scenery.'

'Mixing metaphors.' She elbowed her friend. 'And staring. Wipe the drool off your chin and go make a sale.'

'You take him. I gotta pee. Pregnant woman, you know.'

Before Laine could object, Jenny nipped into the back. More amused than irritated, Laine started across the room. 'Hi.'

She had her friendly merchant smile in place when he turned, and his eyes locked on hers.

She felt the punch dead center of the belly, with the aftershocks of it radiating down to her kneecaps. She could almost feel cohesive thought drain out of her brain, replaced by something along the lines of: Oh. Well. Wow.

'Hi back.' He kept the glass in his hand and just looked at her.

He had tiger eyes, she thought dimly. Big, dangerous cat eyes. And the half smile on his face as he stared at her had what could only be lust pooling at the back of her throat. 'Um . . .' Fascinated by her own reaction, she let out a half laugh, shook her head. 'Sorry, mind was wandering. Do you collect?'

'Not so far. My mama does.'

'Oh.' He had a mama. Wasn't that sweet? 'Does she stick to any particular pattern?'

He grinned now, and Laine cheerfully allowed the top of her head to blow off. 'She doesn't – in any area whatsoever. She likes . . . the variety of the unexpected. Me too.' He set the glass down. 'Like this place.'

'Excuse me?'

'A little treasure box tucked away in the mountains.'

'Thank you.'

And so was she, unexpected, he thought. Bright – the hair, the eyes, the smile. Pretty as a strawberry parfait and a hell of a lot sexier. Not in the full-out, warmly bawdy way the brunette had struck him, but in a secret, I'll-surprise-you way that made him want to know more.

'Georgia?' she asked, and his left eyebrow lifted a fraction.

'Tagged.'

'I'm good with accents. Does your mother have a birthday coming up?'

'She stopped having them about ten years ago. We just call it Marlene's Day.'

'Smart woman. Those tumblers are the Tea Room pattern, and in fairly short supply. You don't often see a set of six like this, and in perfect condition. I can give you a nice price on the complete set.'

He picked one up again but continued to look at her. 'I get to haggle?'

25

'It's required.' She stepped closer to lift another glass and show him the price on the bottom. 'As you can see, they're fifty each, but if you want the set, I'll give them to you for two seventy-five.'

'I hope you don't take this the wrong way, but you smell really good.' It was some smoky fragrance you didn't notice until it had you by the throat. 'Really good. Two and a quarter.'

She never flirted, *never* flirted with customers, but found herself turning toward him, standing just a little closer than was strictly business and smiling into those dangerous eyes. 'Thanks, I'm glad you like it. Two-sixty, and that's a steal.'

'Throw in the shipping to Savannah and have dinner with me and we've got a deal.'

It had been too long, entirely too long, since she'd felt that little thrill swim through the blood. 'Shipping – and a drink, with the option for dinner at a later time and place. It's a good offer.'

'Yeah, it is. Seven o'clock? They've got a nice bar at the Wayfarer.'

'Yes, they do. Seven's fine. How would you like to pay for this?'

He took out a credit card, handed it to her.

'Max Gannon,' she read. 'Just Max? Not Maxwell, Maximillian, Maxfield.' She caught the slight wince and laughed. 'Maxfield, as in Parrish.'

'Just Max,' he said, very firmly.

'All right then, Just Max, but I have a couple of very good framed Parrish posters in the next room.'

'I'll keep that in mind.'

She walked away and behind the counter, then laid a shipping form on it. 'Why don't you write down the shipping information. We'll have this out this afternoon.'

'Efficient, too.' He leaned against the counter as he filled in the form. 'You've got my name. Do I get yours?'

'It's Tavish. Laine Tavish.'

He kept his smile easy as he looked up. 'Just Laine? Not Elaine?'

She didn't flick an eyelash. 'Just Laine.' She rang up the sale and handed him a pretty gold-foiled gift card. 'We'll include this, and gift wrap, if you'd like to write a message to your mother.'

She glanced over as the bells rang, and the Twins came in.

'Laine.' Carla made a beeline for the counter. 'How are you holding up?'

'I'm fine. Just fine. I'll be right with you.'

'We were worried, weren't we, Darla?'

'We certainly were.'

'No need.' With something like panic, she willed Jenny to come back in. The interlude with Max had driven the grief and the worry over Willy out of her mind. Now, it was flooding back. 'I'll get those things I have on hold for you as soon as I'm finished here.'

'Don't you rush.' Carla was already angling her head so she could read the destination on the shipping form. 'Our Laine prides herself on good customer service,' she told Max.

'And certainly delivers. Ladies, you are a two-scoop treat for the eyes.'

They blushed, in unison.

'Your card, Mr. Gannon, and your receipt.'

'Thank you, Ms. Tavish.'

'I hope your mother enjoys her gift.'

'I'm sure she will.' His eyes laughed into hers before he turned to the Twins. 'Ladies.'

The three women watched him walk out. There was a prolonged beat of silence, then Carla let out a long, long breath and said simply, 'My, oh my.'

Max's smile faded the minute he was out on the street. He had nothing to feel guilty about, he told himself. Having a drink with an attractive woman at the end of the day was a normal, pleasant activity, and his inalienable right as a healthy, single man.

Besides, he didn't believe in feeling guilty. Lying, prevaricating, pretense and guile were all part of the job. And the fact was he hadn't lied to her – yet.

He walked a half a block down where he could stand and look back at the spot where Willy had died.

He'd only lie to her if she turned out to be part of this. And if she was, she was going to get a lot worse than a few smooth lies.

What worried him was the not knowing, the not intuiting. He had

27

a sense about these things, which was why he was good at his work. But Laine Tavish had blindsided him, and the only thing he'd felt was that slow, sugary slide of attraction.

But big blue eyes and sexy smile aside, the odds were she was in it up to her pretty neck. He always went with the odds. Willy had paid her a visit and ended up splattered on the street outside her shop. Once he knew why, he was one step closer to the glittery end of the trail.

If he had to use her to get there, those were the breaks.

He went back to his hotel room and took the receipt from his pocket, carefully dusted it for prints. He had good ones of her thumb and forefinger. He took digital pictures and sent them to a friend who'd run them without asking irritating questions.

Then he sat down, flexed his fingers and went to work on the information highway.

He plowed through a pot of coffee, a chicken sandwich and really good apple pie while he worked. He had Laine's home address and, between the phone and the computer, the information that she'd bought her home and established her building on Market four years before. Previously, she'd listed a Philadelphia address. A bit more research located it as an apartment building.

With methods not strictly ethical, he spent more time peeling away the layers of Laine Tavish and began to get a picture. She'd graduated from Penn State, with her parents listed as Marilyn and Robert Tavish.

Funny, wasn't it? Max thought, tapping his fingers on the desk. Jack O'Hara's wife was, or had been, Marilyn. And wasn't that just a little too coincidental?

'Up to your pretty neck,' he murmured and decided it was time for more serious hacking.

There were ways and there were ways to eke out tidbits of information that led to more tidbits. Her business license had been, according to law, clearly displayed in her shop. And that license number gave him a springboard.

Some creative finessing netted him the application for the license, and her social security number.

He stuck with it, using the numbers, intuition and his own insatiable curiosity to track down the deed to her house through the county courthouse, and now he had the name of her lender should he want to break several laws and hack his way to her loan application.

It would be fun because God knew he *loved* technology, but it would serve more purpose to find out where she'd come from rather than where she was now.

He went back to the parents, began a search that required a second pot of coffee from room service. When he finally pinpointed Robert and Marilyn Tavish in Taos, New Mexico, he shook his head.

Laine didn't strike him as a flower of the West. No, she was East, he thought, and largely urban. But Bob and Marilyn, as he was thinking of them, had a link to something called Roundup, which turned out to be a western barbecue joint, and they had a web page. Everyone did, Max thought.

There was even a picture of the happy restaurateurs beside an enormous cartoon cowboy with lariat. He enlarged and printed out the picture before flipping through the site. The attached menu didn't sound half bad, and you could order Rob's Kick-Ass Barbecue Sauce through the site.

Rob, Max noted. Not Bob.

They looked happy, he thought as he studied the photo. Ordinary, working class, pleased as punch to own their own business. Marilyn Tavish didn't look like the former wife – and suspected accomplice – of a career thief and con artist who'd not only gotten delusions of grandeur, but had somehow pulled it off.

She looked more like the type who'd fix you a sandwich before she went out to hang up the wash.

He noted Roundup had been in business eight years, which meant they'd started the place while Laine had been in college. Playing a hunch, he logged onto the local Taos paper, dipped into the archives and looked for a story on the Tavishes.

He found six, which surprised him, and went back to the first, in which the paper had covered the restaurant opening. He read it

29

all, paying close attention to personal details. Such as the Tavishes had been married for six years at that point, and had met, according to the report, in Chicago, where Marilyn had been a waitress and Rob worked for a Crystler dealership. There was a brief mention of a daughter who was a business major in college back East.

Rob had always wanted to own his own place, blah blah, and finally took up his wife's dare to do something with his culinary talents besides feed their friends and neighbors at picnics.

Other stories followed Rob's interest in local politics and Marilyn's association with a Taos arts council. There was another feature when Roundup celebrated its fifth anniversary with an open-air party, including pony rides for kids.

That story carried a picture of the beaming couple, flanking a laughing Laine.

Jesus, she was a knockout. Her head was thrown back with the laugh, her arms slung affectionately around her mother and step-father's shoulders. She was wearing some western-cut shirt with little bits of fringe on the pockets, which – for reasons he couldn't fathom – made him crazy.

He could see a resemblance to her mother now that they were side by side. Around the eyes, the mouth.

But she'd gotten that hair, that bright red hair, from Big Jack. He was sure of it now.

The timing worked, too well. Marilyn O'Hara had filed for divorce while Jack was serving a short stretch, courtesy of the state of Indiana. She'd taken the kid and moved to Jacksonville, Florida. Authorities had kept their eye on her for a few months, but she'd been clean and had worked as a waitress.

She'd bumped around a bit. Texas, Philadelphia, Kansas. Then she'd dropped out of sight, off the radar, a little less than two years before she and Rob tied the knot.

Maybe she'd wanted to start fresh for herself, for the kid. Or maybe it was just a long con. Max was making it his mission to find out.

30

Chapter Three

'What am I doing? This isn't something I do.'

Jenny peered over Laine's shoulder at their dual reflections in the bathroom mirror. 'You're going to have a drink with a great-looking man. Why that isn't something you do is best discussed with a therapist.'

'I don't even know who he is.' Laine set down the lipstick she held before applying it. 'I hit on him, Jen. For God's sake, I hit on him in my own shop.'

'A woman can't hit on a sexy guy in her own shop, where can she? Use the lipstick.' She glanced down to where Henry was thumping his tail. 'See, Henry agrees with me.'

'I should just call the inn, leave a message for him, tell him something came up.'

'Laine, you're breaking my heart.' She picked up the lipstick. 'Paint,' she ordered.

'I can't believe I let you talk me into closing a half hour early. I can't believe how easy it was for you to talk me into it. Coming home to change – it looks obvious, doesn't it?'

'What's wrong with obvious?'

'I don't know.' Laine used the lipstick, studied the tube. 'I'm not thinking straight. It was that moment, that *ka-boom* moment. I just wanted to yank off his shirt and bite his neck.'

'Well, go to it, honey.'

With a laugh, Laine turned around. 'I'm not following through. A drink, okay. It'd be rude not to show up, wouldn't it? Yes, it would be rude. But that's it. After that, common sense will once more rule the day, and I'll come home and close the door on this very strange interlude.'

She held her arms out. 'How do I look? Okay?'

'Better.'

'Better than okay is good. I should go.'

'Go ahead. I'll put Henry out in the mudroom. You don't want to smell like dog. I'll lock up for you.'

'Thanks. Appreciate it. And the moral support. I feel like an idiot.'

'If you decide to . . . extend the evening, just give me a call. I can come back and get Henry. We'll have a sleepover.'

'Thanks again, but I'm *not* going to extend the evening. One drink. I figure an hour tops.' She gave Jenny a light kiss on the cheek, then, risking eau de Henry, bent down to kiss the dog's snout. 'See you tomorrow,' she called as she dashed for the stairs.

It had been silly to drive all the way home just to drive back to town, but she was glad she'd been silly. Though even Jenny hadn't been able to talk her into slipping into a little black dress – talk about obvious – she felt more polished out of her work clothes. The soft sweater in forest green was a good color, and just casual enough not to send the wrong signal.

She had no idea what sort of signal she wanted to send. Yet.

There was a little bubble of panic when she walked into the hotel. They hadn't actually confirmed they were meeting for drinks. It had all been so off the cuff, and so out of character for her. What if he didn't show or, worse, happened into the bar while she was waiting and looked surprised – chagrined – annoyed?

And if she was this nervous about something as simple as a drink in a classy, public bar, she'd definitely let her dating tools rust.

She stepped in through etched-glass doors and smiled at the woman working behind the black oak bar.

'Hi, Jackie.'

'Hey, Laine. What can I get you?'

'Nothing yet.' She scanned the dimly lit room, the plush red sofas and chairs. A few businessmen, two couples, a trio of women starting a girls' night out with a fancy drink. But no Max Gannon.

She chose a table where she wouldn't actually face the door but could observe it. She started to pick up the bar menu just to do something with her hands, then decided it might make her look bored. Or hungry. God.

Instead, she took out her cell and used it to check for messages on her home answering machine. There weren't any, of course, since she'd only walked out the door twenty minutes earlier. But there were two hangups, a couple minutes apart.

She was frowning over that when she heard him speak.

'Bad news?'

'No.' Both flustered and pleased, she disconnected, then dropped the phone into her purse. 'Nothing important.'

'Am I late?'

'No. I'm irritatingly prompt.' It surprised her that he sat beside her on the little sofa rather than across the table in the chair. 'Habit.'

'Did I mention you smell great?'

'Yes, you did. I never asked what you were doing in the Gap.'

'Some business, which I've managed to extend a few more days. Due to local attractions.'

'Really.' She wasn't nervous anymore, and wondered why she had been. 'We have a number of them. There are some wonderful trails through the mountains if you like to hike.'

'Do you?' He brushed his fingers over the back of her hand. 'Like to hike.'

'I don't make much time for it. The store keeps me busy. And your business?'

'Fills the day,' he said, and glanced up when the waitress stopped by their table.

'What can I get you?'

She was new, and not someone Laine recognized. 'Bombay martini, straight up, two olives. Iced.'

'That sounds perfect. Make it two. Did you grow up here?' he asked Laine.

'No, but I imagine it would be nice to grow up here. Small-town enough without being Mayberry, close enough to the city without being crowded. And I like the mountains.'

She remembered this part of the first-date ritual. It hadn't been *that* long. 'Do you still live in Savannah?'

'New York primarily, but I travel a lot.'

'For?'

'Business, pleasure. Insurance, but don't worry, I'm not selling.'

The waitress brought the glasses and shakers on a tray and poured the drinks at the table. She set down a silver bowl of sugared nuts, then slipped discreetly away.

Laine lifted hers, smiled over the rim. 'To your mother.'

'She'd like that.' He tapped his glass to hers. 'How'd you come to running an antique store?'

'I wanted a place of my own. I always liked old things, the continuity of them. I don't mind paperwork, but I didn't want to work in an office all day.' Comfortable now, she settled back with her drink, shifting her body so they could continue the flirtatious eye contact along with the small talk. 'I like buying and selling, and seeing what people buy and sell. So I put all that together and opened Remember When. What kind of insurance?'

'Corporate, mainly. Boring. Family in the area?'

Okay, she thought, doesn't want to talk about his work, particularly. 'My parents live in New Mexico. They moved there several years ago.'

'Brothers, sisters?'

'Only child. You?'

'I've got one of each. Two nephews and a niece out of them.'

'That's nice,' she said and meant it. 'I always envy families, all the noise and traumas and companionship. Competition.'

'We've got plenty of that. So, if you didn't grow up here, where did you?'

'We moved around a lot. My father's work.'

'I hear that.' He sampled a nut, kept it casual. 'What does he do?'

'He . . . he was in sales.' How else to describe it in polite company. 'He could sell anything to anyone.'

He caught it, the hint of pride in her voice, the contrast of the shadow in her eyes. 'But not anymore?'

34

She didn't speak for a moment, using a sip of her drink as cover until she worked out her thoughts. Simple was best, she reminded herself. 'My parents opened a little restaurant in Taos. A kind of working retirement. With work the main feature. And they're giddy as kids about it.'

'You miss them.'

'I do, but I didn't want what they wanted. So here I am. I love the Gap. It's my place. Do you have one?'

'Maybe. But I haven't found it yet.'

The waitress stopped by. 'Another round?'

Laine shook her head. 'I'm driving.'

He asked for the check, then took Laine's hand. 'I made reservations in the dining room here, in case you changed your mind. Change your mind, Laine, and have dinner with me.'

He had such wonderful eyes, and that warm bourbon-on-the-rocks voice she loved listening to. Where was the harm?

'All right. I'd love to.'

He told himself it was business and pleasure and there was never anything wrong with combining the two as long as you remembered your priorities. He knew how to steer conversations, elicit information. And if he was interested in her on a personal level, it didn't interfere with the work.

It wouldn't interfere with the work.

He was no longer sure she was neck-deep. And his change of mind had nothing, absolutely nothing to do with the fact that he was attracted to her. It just didn't play the way it should have. Her mother tucked up with husband number two in New Mexico, Laine tucked up in Maryland. And Big Jack nobody knew just where.

He couldn't see how they triangulated at this point. And he read people well, well enough to know she wasn't marking time with her shop. She loved it, and had forged genuine connections with the community.

But it didn't explain Willy's visit, or his death. It didn't explain why she'd made no mention of knowing him to the police. Not that innocent parties were always straight with the cops.

Weighing down the other side of the scale, she was careful to edit her background, and had a smooth way of blending her father and stepfather so the casual listener would assume they were the same man.

No mention of divorce when they spoke of family. No mention of moving all over the country during her childhood. And that told him she knew how to hide what she wanted to hide.

Though he regretted it, he pushed Willy's ghost into the conversation. 'I heard about the accident right outside your place.' Her knuckles, he noted, whitened for a moment on her spoon, but it was the only sign of internal distress before she continued to stir her after-dinner coffee.

'Yes, it was awful. He must not have seen the car – with the rain.'

'He was in your shop?'

'Yes, right before. Just browsing. I barely spoke to him as I had several other customers, and Jenny, my full-time clerk, had the day off. It was nobody's fault. Just a terrible accident.'

'He wasn't a local?'

She looked directly into his eyes. 'He was never in my shop before. I suppose he might've come in just to get out of the rain for a few minutes. It was a nasty day.'

'Tell me about it. I was driving in it. Seems I got into town only a couple hours after it happened. Heard different versions of it every place I stopped the rest of the day. In one of them, I think it was at the gas pump, he was an international jewel thief on the lam.'

Her eyes softened with what he could only judge as affection. 'International jewel thief,' she murmured. 'No, he certainly wasn't that. People say the oddest things, don't they?'

'I guess they do.' For the first time since he'd taken the job, he believed that Laine Tavish aka Elaine O'Hara had absolutely no clue what her father, William Young and a so far unidentified third party had pulled off six weeks before.

He walked her out to her car and tried to think how he could, and might have to, use her as a lever. What he could tell her, and what he wouldn't if and when the time came.

36

It wasn't what he wanted to think about with the chill of the early spring evening blowing at her hair, sending her scent around him.

'Chilly yet,' he commented.

'It can stay cool at night right up into June, or turn on a dime and bake you before May's out.' He'd be gone before the nights grew warm. It would be smart to remember that. It would be sensible.

She was so damn tired of being sensible.

'I had a nice time. Thanks.' She turned, slid her hands up his chest, linked them around his neck and pulled his mouth down to hers.

That's what she wanted, and screw being sensible. She wanted that punch, that rush, that immediate flash in the blood that comes from a single dangerous act. She lived safe. The second half of her life had been nothing if not safe.

This was better. This hot and shocking clash of lips, of tongue, of teeth was better than safe. It pumped life into her, and made her remember what it was to just take.

How could she have forgotten what a thrill it was to leap and look later?

He'd known she'd surprise him. The minute he'd clamped eyes on her, he'd known. But he hadn't expected her to stagger him. It wasn't a come-on kiss, or a silky flirtation, but a full-on, sexual blast that rocked him back and shot the libido into overdrive.

One minute she had that compact and curvy body plastered to his like they were a couple of shipwreck survivors, then there was a little cat-in-cream purr in her throat and she was pulling away slowly – an elastic and endless move that he was too dazed to stop.

She rubbed her lips together. Sexy, wet lips. And smiled.

'Good night, Max.'

'Hold it, hold it, hold it.' He slapped a hand on her car door before she could open it. Then just left it there as he wasn't confident of his balance.

She was still smiling – soft lips, sleepy eyes. She had the power now, all of it, and they both knew it. How the hell had that happened?

'You're going to send me up there.' He nodded toward the hotel, the general direction of his room. 'Alone? That's just mean.'

'I know.' Her head angled a bit to the side as she studied him. 'I don't want to, but I have to. That's just going to have to hold us both.'

'Let's have breakfast. No, a midnight snack. Screw it, let's go have a brandy now.'

She laughed. 'You don't want a brandy.'

'No. It was a thinly disguised euphemism for wild and crazy sex. Come inside, Laine.' He ran a hand over her hair. 'Where it's warm.'

'I really, really can't, and it's a damn shame.' She opened the car door, glancing over her shoulder, deliberately provocative, as she slid inside. 'Henry's waiting for me.'

His head snapped back as if she'd sucker punched him. 'Whoa.'

Suppressing a bubble of laughter, she slammed the door, waited just a beat, then rolled down the window. 'Henry's my dog. Thanks for dinner, Max. Good night.'

She was laughing as she drove away, and couldn't remember the last time she'd felt so alive. They'd be seeing each other again, she was absolutely sure of it. Then they'd see . . . well, what they'd see.

She turned the radio up to blast and sang along with Sheryl Crow as she drove, just a bit too fast. The recklessness felt good, a sexy fit. Lusty little chills danced over her skin as she bumped up her lane and parked in the secluded dark outside her house. There was a nice kicky breeze whisking along through the barely budded trees and a pretty half-moon that added its light to the old amber glass lantern she'd left glowing on the porch.

For a moment, she sat in the car, in the music and moonlight, and replayed every move and touch and taste of that brain-draining kiss.

Oh yeah, she was definitely going to get another taste of Max Gannon, transplanted Georgia boy with the tiger eyes.

She was still singing as she strolled up her path. She unlocked her front door, tossed her keys into their bowl, slid her cell phone into the recharger, then all but skipped into the living room.

38

The heady sexual buzz flipped into shock. Her couch was turned over, its cushions shredded. The cherry wood armoire she used as an entertainment center stood wide open, and empty. The trio of African violets she'd rooted from leaves and babied into lush plants had been dumped out of their pots, and the soil scattered. Tables had been overturned, drawers emptied, and framed prints she'd arranged on the walls were tossed on the floor.

For a moment she stood, frozen in the inertia of denial. Not possible. Not her house, not her things, not her world. She broke through it with a single thought.

'Henry!'

Terrified, she bolted for the kitchen, ignoring the debris of her possessions that littered the hall, the mess of glassware and staples that covered the kitchen floor.

Tears of relief stung her eyes as she heard the frantic answering barks as she charged toward the mudroom door. The instant she flung open the door she was covered by trembling, frightened dog. She went down with him, her shoes skidding on spilled sugar, to clutch him against her as he struggled to crawl into her lap.

They were all right, she told herself over the frantic pounding of her heart. That's what mattered most. They were okay.

'They didn't hurt you. They didn't hurt you,' she crooned to him while tears tracked down her cheeks, while she ran her hands over his fur to check for injuries. 'Thank God they didn't hurt you.'

He whimpered, then bathed her face as they tried to calm each other down.

'We have to call the police.' Shivering herself, she pressed her face into his fur. 'We're going to call the police, then see how bad it is.'

It was bad. In the few hours she'd been gone, someone had come into her home, stolen her property and left a manic rubble in his wake. Small treasures broken, valuables gone, her personal things touched and examined then taken or discarded. It bruised her heart, shattered her sense of safety.

Then it just pissed her off.

She'd worked her way up to anger before Vince arrived. She

preferred anger. There was something powerful about the rage that was building inside her, something more useful than her initial shock and fear.

'You're okay?' It was Vince's first question as he took her arms, gave them a quick, bolstering rub.

'I'm not hurt, if that's what you mean. They were gone before I got home. Henry was in the mudroom. He couldn't get out, so they left him alone. Jenny. I left Jenny here, Vince. If she'd still been here when—'

'She wasn't. She's fine. Let's deal with what is.'

'You're right. Okay, you're right.' She drew a deep breath. 'I got home about ten-thirty. Unlocked the front door, walked in, saw the living room.' She gestured.

'Door was locked?'

'Yes.'

'Broken window here.' He nodded to the front facing window. 'Looks like that's how they got in. Got your stereo and components, I see.'

'The television in the media room upstairs, the little portable I used in the kitchen. Jewelry. I've just taken an overview, but it looks like they took electronics and small valuables. I've got a couple of good Deco bronzes, several other nice pieces, but they left those. Some of the jewelry they took is the real deal, some of it junk.' She shrugged.

'Cash?'

'A couple hundred that I kept in my desk drawer. Oh, and the computer I used here at home.'

'Made a goddamn mess out of it, too. Who knew you'd be out tonight?'

'Jenny, the man I met for drinks – we ended up having dinner, too. He's at the Wayfarer. Max Gannon.'

'Jenny said you just met him, in the shop.'

Heat tingled its way up her neck. 'It was just a drink and a meal, Vince.'

'Just saying. We're going to go through everything. Bunch of cops tromping around in here, you might want to go to our place, stay the night.'

40

'No, but thanks. I'll stick.'

'Yeah. Jenny said you would.' He gave her shoulder a pat with his big hand and walked to the door as he heard the radio car pull up. 'We'll do what we do. You might want to start working up a list of what's missing.'

She spent the time in the sitting room upstairs with Henry curled tight at her feet. She wrote down what she'd already seen was missing, answered questions as Vince or one of the other cops stopped in. She wanted coffee, but since what she'd stocked was on her kitchen floor, she settled for tea. And drank a potful.

She knew her feelings of violation, fear, anger were all classic reactions, just as the sheen of disbelief that kept layering over them. It wasn't that crime was nonexistent in the Gap. But this sort of break-in, the malicious destruction of it, certainly wasn't typical.

And to Laine, it seemed very, very personal.

It was after one in the morning before she was alone again. Vince offered to leave an officer outside, but she'd refused. Though she'd gratefully accepted his offer to board up the broken window.

She checked, then double-checked the locks, with Henry keeping close on her heels as she moved around the house. Anger was trickling back, wiping away the fatigue that had begun to drag at her while the police worked. She used it, and the resulting energy, to set her kitchen to rights.

She filled a waste can with broken crockery and glassware, and tried not to mourn the lost pieces of colorful Fiestaware she'd collected so carefully. She swept sugar, coffee, flour, salt, loose tea, then mopped the biscuit-colored tiles.

Energy was leaking out of her system by the time she trudged upstairs. One look at her bed – the mattress stripped and dragged onto the floor, the turned-out drawers of her lovely mahogany bureau, the gaping holes in the old apothecary chest she'd used as a jewelry case, brought the grief back.

But she wouldn't be driven out of her own room, out of her own home. Gritting her teeth, she hauled the mattress back into place. Then got out fresh sheets, made the bed. She rehung clothes that had been pulled out of her closet, folded more and tucked them neatly into drawers.

It was after three before she crawled into bed, and breaking her own rule, she patted the mattress and called Henry up to sleep beside her.

She reached for the light but hesitated, then drew her hand away. If it was cowardice and a foolish security blanket to sleep with a light on, she could live with that.

She was insured, she reminded herself. Nothing had been taken, or broken, that couldn't be replaced. They were just things – and she made her living, didn't she, buying and selling things?

She burrowed under the blankets with the dog staring soulfully into her eyes. 'Just things, Henry. Things don't matter all that much.'

She closed her eyes, let out a long sigh. She was just drifting off when Willy's face floated into her mind.

He knows where you are now.

She sat straight up in bed, her breath coming in short pants. What did it mean? *Who* did it mean?

Willy shows up one day, out of the blue, after nearly twenty years, and ends up dead on the doorstep of her shop. Then her house is burgled and vandalized.

It had to be connected. How could it not be? she asked herself. But who was looking for what? She didn't have anything.

Chapter Four

Half-dressed, his hair still dripping from his morning shower, Max answered the knock on his hotel room door with one and only one thought on his mind: coffee.

The disappointment was one thing. A man learned to live with disappointments. Hadn't he slept alone? Finding a cop at his door was another. It meant nimbling up the brain without the God-given and inalienable right of caffeine.

He sized up the local heat – big, fit, suspicious – and tried on a cooperative if puzzled smile. 'Morning. That doesn't look like a room service uniform, so I'm guessing you're not here to deliver my coffee and eggs.'

'I'm Chief Burger, Mr. Gannon. Can I have a minute of your time?'

'Sure.' He stepped back, glanced at the room. The bed was unmade, and steam from the shower was still drifting into the room through the open bathroom door.

The desk looked like the hotel room desk of a busy businessman – laptop, file folders and disks, his PDA, his cell phone – and that was fine. He'd taken the precaution, as he always did, of closing down all files and stashing any questionable paperwork.

'Ah . . .' Max gestured vaguely to the chair. 'Have a seat,' he invited and walked to the closet to pull out a shirt. 'Is there some problem?'

Vince didn't sit; he didn't smile. 'You're acquainted with Laine Tavish.'

'Yeah.' A lot of little warning bells went off and echoed with questions, but Max just pulled on the shirt. 'Remember When. I bought a present for my mother at her place yesterday.' He put a shadow of concern in his voice. 'Something wrong with my credit card?'

'Not that I'm aware of. Miss Tavish's residence was broken into last night.'

'Is she all right? Was she hurt?' He didn't have to feign concern now as those alarm bells shot through him. The hands that had been busily buttoning his shirt dropped to his side. 'Where is she?'

'She wasn't on the premises at the time of the break-in. Her statement indicates she was with you.'

'We had dinner. Damnit.' As coffee was no longer paramount on his list, Max cursed at the knock. 'Hold on a minute.' He opened the door to the cute little blonde who stood by the room service cart.

'Morning, Mr. Gannon. Ready for breakfast?'

'Yeah, thanks. Just . . . put it anywhere.'

She caught sight of Vince as she rolled in the cart. 'Oh, hi, Chief.'

'Sherry. How you doing?'

'Oh . . . you know.' She angled the cart and tried not to look overly curious as she shot glances at both men. 'I can go down, get another cup if you want coffee, Chief.'

'Don't you worry about it, Sherry. I had two before I left the house.'

'Just call down if you change your mind.' She pulled the warming cover off a plate, revealing an omelette and a side of bacon. 'Um . . .' She held out the leather folder to Max, waited while he signed the bill. 'Hope you enjoy your breakfast, Mr. Gannon.'

She walked out, casting one last look over her shoulder before she shut the door.

'Go ahead,' Vince invited. 'No point letting those eggs get cold. They make a nice omelette here.'

'What kind of break-in was it? Burglary?'

'Looked that way. Why was Miss Tavish with you last night?'

Max sat, decided to pour the coffee. 'Socializing. I asked her to have a drink with me. She agreed. I hoped to be able to extend that to dinner, and since she was agreeable to that after we had a drink – down in the lounge here – we went into the dining room.'

'You always make dates with women when you buy presents for your mother?'

'If it worked that well, I'd be buying my mama a lot more presents.' Max lifted his cup, drank and met Vince's eyes over the rim. 'Laine's a very attractive, very interesting woman. I wanted to see her, socially. I asked. I'm sorry she's got trouble.'

'Somebody got in and out of her place during the time she was in town here, socializing with you.'

'Yeah, I get that.' Max decided he might as well eat, and forked up some omelette. 'So you're wondering if I go around hitting on pretty women in shops, then setting them up for a burglary while I charm them over dinner. That's a stretch, Chief, since I never set eyes on Laine before yesterday, don't – as yet – know her residence or if she's got something worth stealing in it. Be smarter, wouldn't it, to hit the shop? She's got a lot of nice merchandise in it.'

Vince simply watched Max eat, said nothing. 'Couple of good thick glasses over there,' Max said after a moment, 'if you want some of this coffee after all.'

'I'll pass. What's your business in Angel's Gap, Mr. Gannon?'

'I'm with Reliance Insurance, and I'm here doing some field-work.'

'What kind of fieldwork?'

'Chief Burger, you can contact Aaron Slaker, CEO of Reliance, and verify my association with the company. He's based in New York. But I'm not at liberty to discuss the details of my work without my client's permission.'

'That doesn't sound like insurance work to me.'

'There's all kinds of insurance.' Max opened a little jar of strawberry jam and spread some on a triangle of toast.

'You got identification?'

'Sure.' Max rose, walked over to the dresser and took his driver's license out of his wallet. He passed it to Vince, then took his seat again.

'You don't sound like New York City.'

'Just can't drum the Georgia out of the boy.' He was just irritated enough to exaggerate his drawl and make it a challenge. 'I don't steal, Chief. I just wanted to have dinner with a pretty woman. You go ahead and call Slaker.'

Vince dropped the license beside Max's plate. 'I'll do that.' He started for the door, turned with his hand on the knob. 'How long do you plan to be in town, Mr. Gannon?'

'Till the job's done.' He scooped up more egg. 'Chief? You were right. They do a really good omelette here.'

Even when the door shut behind Vince, Max sat and ate. And considered. A cop being a cop, Burger would run him, and the run would turn up his four years on the force. And his investigator's license. Small towns being small towns, that little tidbit would get back to Laine before too long.

He'd decide how to play that when it had to be played. Meanwhile there was the matter of the break-in. The timing was just a little too good to be serendipity. And it told him he wasn't the only one who thought the very attractive Miss Tavish had something to hide.

It was all a matter of who was going to find it first.

'Don't worry about anything,' Jenny assured Laine. 'Angie and I can handle things here. Are you sure you don't want to just close the store for the day? Vince said your place is a wreck. I could come over and help you out.'

Laine switched the phone to her other ear, scanning her home office and thinking about the very pregnant Jenny dragging chairs and tables into place. 'No, but thanks. I'd feel better knowing you and Angie have the shop. There's a shipment coming in this morning, a pretty big one from the auction in Baltimore.'

And, damnit, she wanted to be there, getting her hands on all those lovely things. Admiring them, cataloguing them, arranging them. A good deal of the enjoyment came from setting up new stock in her place, and the rest came from watching it walk out the door again.

46

'I need you to log in the new stock, Jen. I've already done the pricing, that's in the file. There's a Clarice Cliff lotus jug, with a tulip design. You want to call Mrs. Gunt and let her know we have it. The price we agreed on is seven hundred, but she'll want to negotiate. Six seventy-five is firm. Okay?'

'Gotcha.'

'Oh, and—'

'Laine, relax. It's not my first day on the job. I'll take care of things here, and if anything comes up I can't handle, I'll call you.'

'I know.' Absently, Laine reached down to pet the dog, who was all but glued to her side. 'Too much on my mind.'

'Small wonder. I hate the thought of you handling that mess on your own. You sure you don't want me to come? I could bop over at lunchtime. Angie can handle the shop for an hour. I'll bring you something to eat. Something loaded with fat and wasted calories.'

Angie *could* handle the shop, Laine considered. She was good and getting better. But Laine knew herself. She'd get more done if she worked alone without conversation or distraction.

'That's okay. I'll be all right once I get started. I'll probably be in this afternoon.'

'Take a nap instead.'

'Maybe. I'll talk to you later.' When she hung up, Laine stuck the little portable phone in the back pocket of her baggy jeans. She knew herself well enough to be sure she'd find half a dozen reasons to call the shop during the day. Might as well keep a phone handy.

But for now, she needed to focus on the matter at hand.

'"Hide the pooch,"' she murmured. Since the only pooch she had was Henry, she had to assume Willy had been delirious. Whatever he'd come to tell her, to ask of her, to give her, hadn't been done. He'd thought someone was after him, and unless he'd changed his ways, which was highly unlikely, he'd probably been right.

A cop, skip tracer, a partner in crime who hadn't liked the cut? Any or all of the above was a possibility. But the state of her house told her the last option was the most likely.

Now, whoever had been looking for him, was looking at her.

She could tell Vince . . . what? Absolutely nothing. Everything she'd built here was dug into the foundation that she was Laine Tavish, a nice, ordinary woman with a nice, ordinary life with nice, ordinary parents who ran a barbecue place in New Mexico.

Elaine O'Hara, daughter of Big Jack of the charming and wily ways – and yard-long yellow sheet – didn't fit into the pretty, pastoral landscape of Angel's Gap. Nobody was going to come into Elaine O'Hara's place to buy a teapot or a piecrust table.

Jack O'Hara's daughter couldn't be trusted.

Hell, she didn't trust Jack O'Hara's daughter herself. Big Jack's daughter was the type who had drinks in a bar with a strange man and ended up knocking said man on his excellent ass with a steamy, soul-deep kiss. Jack's daughter took big, bad chances that had big, bad consequences.

Laine Tavish lived normal, thought things through and didn't make waves.

She'd let the O'Hara out for one brief evening, and look what it had gotten her. An exciting, sexy interlude, sure, and a hell of a mess at the end of it.

'It just goes to show,' she murmured to Henry, who demonstrated his accord by thumping his tail.

Time to put things back in order. She wasn't giving up who she was, what she'd accomplished, what she planned to accomplish, because some second-rate thief believed she had part of his last take.

Had to be second-rate, she thought as she gathered up the loose stuffing from the once pretty silk throw pillows she'd picked out for the George II daybed. Uncle Willy never traveled in the big leagues. And neither, despite all his talk, all his dreams, had Big Jack.

So, they'd trashed her place, come up empty and took easily fenced items in lieu.

That, Laine thought, would be that.

Of course, they'd probably left prints all over the damn place. She rolled her eyes, sat on the floor and started stacking scattered paperwork. Dim bulbs were a specialty when Uncle Willy was involved in a job. It was likely whoever'd broken in, searched, stolen, would have a record. Vince would trace that, identify them, and it was well within the realm of possibility that they'd get picked up.

It was also in that realm that they'd be stupid enough to tell the cops why they broke in. If that came down, she'd claim mistaken identity.

She'd be shocked, outraged, baffled. Acting the part – whatever part was necessary – was second nature. There was enough of Big Jack in her veins that running a con wouldn't be a stretch of her skills.

What was she doing now, Laine Tavish of Angel's Gap, but running a lifetime con?

Because the thought depressed her, she pushed it aside and immersed herself in refiling her paperwork. Immersed enough that she nearly jumped straight off the floor when she heard the knock on the front door.

Henry bolted out of his mid-morning snooze and sent out a furious spate of throaty, threatening barks – even as he slunk behind Laine and tried to hide his bulk in the crook of her arm.

'My big, brave hero.' She nuzzled him. 'It's probably the window guy. No eating the window guy, right?'

As a testament to his great love and devotion, Henry went with her. He made growling noises and stayed one safe pace behind.

She was wary enough herself after the break-in to peek out the window before unlocking the door. Her brain, and her blood, did a little snap and sizzle when she saw Max.

Instinctively she looked down, in disgust, at her oldest jeans, her bare feet, the ancient gray sweatshirt. She'd yanked her hair back in a short tail that morning and hadn't bothered with makeup.

'Not exactly the look I wanted to present to the man I considered getting naked with at the first reasonable opportunity,' she said to Henry. 'But what're you gonna do?'

She pulled open the door and ordered herself to be casual. 'Max. This is a surprise. How'd you find me?'

'I asked. You okay? I heard about . . .' He trailed off, his gaze

49

tracking down to her knees. 'Henry? Well, that's about the home-liest dog I've ever seen.' A big grin split his face when he said it, and it was hard to take offense as he crouched down to dog level and aimed the grin at the dog.

'Hey, big guy, how's it going?'

Most, in Laine's experience, were at least initially intimidated by the dog. He *was* big, he *was* ugly, and when he was growling in his throat, he sounded dangerous. But Max was already holding a hand out, offering it for a sniff. 'That's some bad face you've got there, Henry.'

Obviously torn between terror and delight, Henry inched his snout forward, took some testing whiffs. His tail whapped the back of Laine's knees before he collapsed, rolled and exposed his belly for a rub.

'He has no pride,' Laine stated.

'Doesn't need any.' Max became the newest love of Henry's life by giving the soft belly a vigorous rub. 'Nothing like a dog, is there?'

First there'd been lust, she thought, naturally enough. Then interest and several layers of attraction. She'd been prepared – or had been trying to prepare – to shuffle all those impulses aside and be sensible.

Now, seeing him with her dog, she felt the warming around the heart that signaled – uh-oh – personal affection. Add that to lust and attraction and a woman, even a sensible woman, was sunk. 'No, there really isn't.'

'Always had a dog at home. Can't keep one in New York, not the way I travel around. Doesn't seem right.' His hand slid up to rub Henry's throat and send the dog into ecstasy.

Laine very nearly moaned.

'That's the downside of city living for me,' Max added. 'How'd they get around him?'

'I'm sorry?'

He gave Henry a last thumping pat, then straightened. 'I heard about the break-in. Big dog like this should've given them some trouble.'

Down, girl, Laine ordered herself. 'Afraid not. One, he was shut in the mudroom. That's his place when I'm out. And second, well . . .' She looked down at Henry, who was slavishly licking Max's hand. 'He doesn't exactly have a warrior's heart.'

'You okay?'

'As good as it gets, I suppose, the morning after you come home and find somebody's trashed your house and stolen your property.'

'You're pretty secluded back here. I don't guess anyone saw anything.'

'I doubt it. Vince, the police chief, will ask, but I'm the only house back on this lane.'

'Yeah, I met the chief. Another reason I came by was to make sure you didn't think I asked you to dinner to get you out of the house so this could happen.'

'Well, of course not. Why would . . .' She followed the dots. 'Vince. I hope he didn't make you uncomfortable.'

'It's his job. And now I see I've put the same suspicion in your head.'

'No, not . . .' But she was trying it on. 'Not really. It's just been a very strange week. I think I've dealt with Vince twice on a professional level since I moved here. Now it's been twice in a matter of days. He must've come by your hotel room this morning. I'm sorry.'

'Just routine. But coming home and finding your house has been burgled isn't.' He reached out, touched her cheek. 'I was worried about you.'

The warmth pumped up a few degrees. She told herself it wasn't a good fit – Willy Young and Max Gannon in league. And that if Max was of the ilk, she'd know.

Like, she believed, recognized like.

'I'm okay. Jenny and Angie will work the shop today while I put the house back into shape.' She gestured toward the living room. 'I've barely made a dent. Good thing I like to shop, because that'll be stage two.'

He stepped around her, looking into the room himself.

It could be taken for a spate of vandalism accompanying a

51

burglary. But to Max's eyes it looked like what it was: a fast, nasty search. And if they'd gotten what they were after, he didn't think Laine would be calmly clearing up the debris and talking about shopping.

Nobody was that cool.

On the tail of that thought, he imagined her coming home alone, in the dark, and opening her house to this. Small wonder she had shadows under her eyes and the pale look of a woman who'd spent a sleepless night.

'They did a number on you,' he murmured.

'Not the usual thing in the Gap. When I lived in Philadelphia, I worked with a woman who went home one night, found her apartment broken into. They cleaned her out *and* spray-painted obscenities on the walls.'

He looked back at her. 'So it could be worse?'

'It can always be worse. Listen, I've put the kitchen back together and made a quick morning run to the store so there's coffee. You want?'

'I always want.' He walked to her. She looked so fresh. All that bright hair pulled back from that pretty face, her eyes only bluer with the shadows haunting them. She smelled like soap, just soap. The innocent charm of freckles was sprinkled over her nose.

'Laine, I'm not looking to get in your way, but . . . let me help you.'

'Help me what?'

He wasn't sure, but he knew he meant it, that the offer was unqualified. He looked at her, and he wanted to help. 'For a start, I can help you put your house back together.'

'You don't have to do that. You must have work—'

'Let me help.' He cut off her protest simply by taking her hand. 'I've got time, and the fact is, if I went on my way, I'd worry about you and I'd never get anything done anyway.'

'That's awfully sweet.' And she knew she was a goner. 'That's really very sweet.'

'And there's this one other thing.' He took a step forward, into her, which put her back up against the wall. Still, when his mouth came down, the kiss was slow and smooth, almost dreamy. She felt her knees unlock and go halfway to dissolve before he lifted his head. 'If I didn't do that, I'd be thinking about doing it. Figured we'd get more done if I got it out of the way first.'

'Good.' She ran her tongue over her bottom lip. 'Finished?'

'Not hardly.'

'That's good, too. Coffee,' she decided before they started rolling around on the floor of the disordered room instead of setting it to rights. 'I'll just get that coffee.'

She walked back toward the kitchen, with the dog prancing happily beside her. It helped, for the moment, to keep busy. Grinding beans, measuring coffee into the French press. He'd gotten her nerves up again, she realized. He was just leaning against the counter, watching her. That long body relaxed, but those eyes focused. Something about him made her want to rub up against him like a cat begging to be stroked.

'I have to say something.'

'Okay.'

She got down two of the mugs that had survived the kitchen rampage. 'I don't usually . . . Hold on, let me figure out how to say this without sounding incredibly stupid and ordinary.'

'I don't think you could sound either. Ever.'

'Boy, you really push the right buttons. All right.' She turned to him while the coffee steeped. 'It's not my habit to make dates, even casual ones, with a man I've just met. With a customer. In fact, you're the first.'

'I've always liked being first.'

'Who doesn't? And while I enjoy the company of men, and the benefits thereof, I also don't, as a rule, wrap myself around one after dinner like sumac around an oak.'

He was certain he'd remember the moment she had for a long time. It would probably come back to him on his deathbed as a major highlight of his life and times. 'Would I be the first there, too?'

'At that level.'

'Better and better.'

'You want cream? Sugar?'

'Just black's good.'

'Okay then, to continue. I also don't – and this has been a pretty hard-and-fast rule of thumb – contemplate sleeping with a man I've only known for twenty-four hours, give or take.'

He was scratching Henry between the ears, but he never took his eyes off her face. 'You know what they say about rules.'

'Yes, and though I agree with what they say, I don't break them lightly. I'm a firm believer in the need for structure, Max, in rules and lines. So the fact that I'm considering breaking a rule, crossing a line, makes me nervous. It'd be smarter, safer, more sensible if we backed away a bit, at least until we get to know each other better. Until we give things a chance to develop at a more reasonable and rational pace.'

'Smarter,' he agreed. 'Safer. Sensible.'

'You have no idea how hard I've worked to live by those three attributes.' She laughed a little, then poured the coffee. 'And the problem here is I've never been as attracted to anyone as I am to you.'

'Maybe I'm a little looser when it comes to rules and lines, and not as worried about being sensible in certain areas.' He took the mug she offered, then set it on the counter. 'But I know I've never looked at another woman and wanted her the way I want you.'

'That's not going to help me be smart.' She picked up her coffee, stepped back. 'But I need some order. Let me put my house back together, as best I can, and we'll see where things go.'

'Hard to argue with that. We share some of these domestic chores, we ought to get to know each other.'

'Well, it's one way.' He'd be a distraction, she concluded. A lot more of a distraction than Jenny and a lunchtime Big Mac.

But what the hell.

'Since I've got some muscle on hand, let's start with the living room. The sofa's pretty heavy.'

In Remember When, business was brisk. Or at least browsing was. It hadn't taken long for word to get out about Laine's latest trouble, or to bring out the curious to pump for more details. By one, with the new shipments logged, tagged and displayed, sales rung up and gossip exchanged in abundance, Jenny pressed a hand to the ache in her lower back.

'I'm going to take lunch at home where I can put my feet up for an hour. Will you be all right on your own?'

'Sure.' Angie held up a protein bar and a bottled, low-fat Frappucino. 'Got my lunch right here.'

'You don't know how sad it makes me, Ange, to hear you call that lunch.'

'Weighed in at one-nineteen this morning.'

'Bitch.'

While Angie laughed, Jenny got her purse from behind the counter and her sweater from the hook. 'I'm going to nuke left-over pasta primavera and finish it off with a brownie.'

'Now who's the bitch?' She gave Jenny's belly a pat, hoping as always to catch the baby kicking. 'How's it going in there?'

'Night owl.' She stuck a loose bobby pin back in her messy topknot. 'I swear the kid wakes up and starts tap dancing every night about eleven, and keeps it up for hours.'

'You love it.'

'I do.' Smiling now, Jenny tugged on the sweater. 'Every minute of it. Best time of my life. Be back in an hour.'

'Got it covered. Hey, should I call Laine? Just check on her?'

'I'll do it from home,' Jenny called back as she walked to the door. Before she reached it, it opened. She recognized the couple, searched around in her mental files for the name. 'Nice to see you. Dale and Melissa, right?'

'Good memory.' The woman, thirtyish, gym-fit and stylish, smiled at her.

'And as I recall, you were interested in the rosewood armoire.'

'Right again. I see it's still here.' Even as she spoke, she walked to it, ran her hand over the carving on the door. 'It keeps calling my name.'

'It's such a beautiful piece.' Angie strolled around the counter. 'One of my favorites.' The truth was she preferred the modern and streamlined, but she knew how to pitch. 'We just got another rose-wood piece today. It's a gorgeous little davenport. Victorian. I think they're made for each other.'

'Uh-oh.' Laughing, Melissa squeezed her husband's arm. 'I guess I have to take a look at least.'

'I'll show you.'

'I was just on my way out, if you don't need me . . .'

'We're fine.' Angie waved Jenny away. 'Isn't it beautiful?' she said, aiming her pitch at Melissa as she ran a fingertip down the glossy writing slope. 'It's in wonderful condition. Laine has such a good eye. She found this in Baltimore a few weeks ago. It arrived only this morning.'

'It's wonderful.' Leaning down, Melissa began opening and closing the small side drawers. 'Really wonderful. I thought a davenport was a kind of couch.'

'Yeah, but this kind of little desk is called that, too. Don't ask me why; that's Laine's territory.'

'I really love it, whatever it's called. Dale?'

He was fingering the price tag, and sent her a look. 'I've got to think about getting both, Melissa. It's a pretty big chunk.'

'Maybe we can chip it down a little.'

'We can work on that,' Angie told her.

'Let me take another look at the armoire.' She walked back over, opened the doors.

Knowing how to pace a sale, Angie hung back while Dale joined his wife and they began a whispered consultation.

The doors were closed again, opened again, drawers were pulled out.

'Do we get what's inside, too?' Dale called out.

'I'm sorry?'

'Box in here.' He took out the package, shook it. 'Is it like the prize in the cereal box?'

'Not this time.' With an easy laugh, Angie crossed over to take the box. 'We had a big shipment come in this morning,' she began. 'And we were pretty busy on top of it. Jenny must've gotten distracted and set this in there.'

Or had she? Things had been hopping for an hour or two. Either way, Angie considered it a lucky break the drawer had been opened before the piece was missed.

'We're just going to talk this over for a few minutes,' Melissa told her.

'Take your time.' Leaving them to it, Angie went back to the counter. She unwrapped the package and studied the silly china dog. Cute, she thought, but she didn't understand why anyone paid good money for animal pieces.

She found soft, fuzzy stuffed animals more companionable.

This was probably Doulton or Derby or one of those things Laine was still trying to teach her.

Since, from little snatches of conversation, Melissa seemed to be wearing Dale down all on her own, Angie gave them a little more space by walking the statue over to one of a few displays of figurines and bric-a-brac to try to identify the type and era.

It was like a game to her. She'd find it in the file, of course, but that would be cheating. Identifying pieces in the shop was very like identifying character types in the bar. If you spent enough time at it, it got so you knew who was who and what was what.

'Miss?'

'Angie.' She turned, grinned.

'If we took both, what sort of a price could you give us?'

'Well . . .' Delighted with the prospect of greeting Jenny with news of a double, she set the china dog down and went over to bargain with the customers.

In the excitement of closing the deal, arranging for delivery, ringing up the sale, she didn't give the little dog another thought.

Chapter Five

Max learned quite a bit about Laine over the next few hours. She was organized, practical and precise. More linear-minded than what he'd expected from someone of her background. She looked at a task, saw it from beginning to end, then followed it through the steps to completion. No detours, no distractions.

And she was a nester. His mother had the same bent, just loved feathering that nest with pretty little – what did his father call them? – gimcracks. And like his mother, Laine knew exactly where she preferred every one of them.

But unlike his mother, Laine didn't appear to have a sentimental, almost intimate attachment to her things. He'd once seen his mother weep buckets over a broken vase, and he himself had felt the mighty heat of her wrath when he'd shattered an old decorative bowl.

Laine swept up shards of this, pieces of that, dumped broken bits into a trash can with barely a wince. Her focus was on returning order to her space. He had to respect that.

Though it was a puzzlement to him how the daughter of a drifter and a grifter executed a one-eighty to become a small-town homebody, the fact that puzzles were his business made it, and her, only more interesting.

He liked being in her nest, being in her company. It was a given that the sizzle between them was going to complicate things along the way, but it was tough not to enjoy it.

He liked her voice, the fact that it managed to be both throaty and smooth. He liked that she looked sexy in a sweatshirt. He liked her freckles.

He admired her resilience in the face of what would have devastated most people. And he admired and appreciated her flat-out honesty about her reaction to him and what was brewing between them.

The fact was, under other circumstances, he could see himself diving headfirst into a relationship with her, burning his bridges, casting caution to the wind or any number of clichés. Even given the circumstances, he was poised to make that dive. He couldn't quite figure out if that was a plus or a minus.

But side benefit or obstacle to the goal, it was time to get back in the game.

'You lost a lot of stuff,' he commented.

'I can always get more stuff.' But she felt a little tug of sorrow at the wide chip in the Derby jug she'd kept on the dining room server. 'I got into the business because I like to collect all manner of things. Then I realized I didn't need to own them so much as be around them, see them, touch.'

She ran her finger down the damaged jug. 'And it's just as rewarding, more in some ways, to buy and sell, and see interesting pieces go to interesting people.'

'Don't dull people ever buy interesting pieces?'

She laughed at that. 'Yes, they do. Which is why it's important not to become too attached to what you plan to sell. And I love to sell. Ka-ching.'

'How do you know what to buy in the first place?'

'Some's instinct, some's experience. Some is just a gamble.'

'You like to gamble?'

She slid a glance over and up. 'As a matter of fact.'

Oh yeah, he thought, he was poised and rolling up to his toes on the edge of the cliff. 'Want to blow this joint and fly to Vegas?'

She arched her eyebrows. 'And if I said sure, why not?'

'I'd book the flight.'

'You know,' she said after a moment's study, 'I believe you would. I think I like that.' The O'Hara in her was already on her way to the airport. 'But unfortunately, I can't take you up on it.' And that was the Tavish. 'How about a rain check?'

'You got it. Open-ended.' He watched her place a few pieces that had survived the break-in. Candlesticks, an enormous pottery bowl, a long flat dish. He had a feeling she'd put them precisely where they'd been before. There would be comfort in that. And defiance.

'You know, looking around at all this, it doesn't seem like a simple break-in. If that can be simple when it's your place. It sure doesn't strike me as a standard grab-and-run. It feels more personal.'

'Well, that goes a long way to relieving my mind.'

'Sorry. Wasn't thinking. Actually, you don't seem particularly spooked.'

'I slept with the light on last night,' she admitted. 'Like that would make a difference. It doesn't do any good to be spooked. Doesn't change anything or fix anything.'

'An alarm system wouldn't hurt. Something a little more high-tech than the canine variety,' he added, looking down at where Henry snored under the dining room table.

'No. I thought about that for about five minutes. An alarm system wouldn't make me feel safe. It'd just make me feel like I had something to worry about. I'm not going to be afraid in my own home.'

'Let me just push this button a little more before we let it go. Do you think this could've been somebody you know? Do you have any enemies?'

'No, and no,' she answered with a careless shrug as she scooted the ladder-back chairs back to the table. But she heard Willy's words in her head: *He knows where you are.*

Who knew?

Daddy?

'Now I've got you worried.' He tipped her face up with a finger under her chin. 'I can see it.'

'No, not worried. Disconcerted, maybe, at the idea that I could have enemies. Ordinary shopkeepers in small Maryland towns shouldn't have enemies.'

He rubbed his thumb along her jaw. 'You're not ordinary.'

She let her lips curve as his came down to meet them. He had no idea, she thought, how hard she'd worked for nearly half her life to *be* ordinary.

His hands were sliding over her hips when her phone rang. 'You hear bells?' he asked.

She drew back with a little laugh and pulled the phone out of her pocket. 'Hello? Hi, Angie.' As she listened, she shifted the chipped jug a half inch on the server. '*Both* pieces? That's wonderful. What did . . . Uh-huh. No, you did exactly right. It's called a davenport because a small desk was designed for a Captain Davenport back in the 1800s and it stuck, I guess. Yes, I'm fine. Really, and yes, this certainly perks me up. Thanks, Angie. I'll talk to you later.'

'I thought a davenport was a couch,' Max said when she stuck the phone back in her pocket.

'It is, or a small sofa that often converts into a bed. It's also a small desk with a boxlike form with an upper section that slides or turns to provide knee space.'

'Huh. The things you learn.'

'I could teach you all sorts of things.' Enjoying herself, she walked her fingers up his chest. 'Want me to show you the difference between a canterbury and a commode?'

'Can't wait.'

She took his hand, drew him toward her little library, where she could give a short lesson in antiques while they put the room back in order.

When the tall, distinguished gentleman with the trim pewter mustache walked into Remember When, Jenny was contemplating what she might fix for dinner. Since it seemed she was hungry *all* the time, thinking about food was nearly as satisfying as eating it.

After Angie's big sale, the pace had slowed. She'd had a few browsers, and Mrs. Gunt had come on the run to see the lotus jug and snap it up. But for the next hour, she and Angie had been puttering, and the day took on a lazy tone that had her giving Angie an early out.

She looked over at the sound of the door, pleased that a customer would temporarily take her mind off pork chops and mashed potatoes.

'Good afternoon. Can I help you?'

'I think I'll just look around, if that's all right. What an interesting place. Yours?'

'No. The owner's not in today. Browse all you like. If you have any questions or need any help, just let me know.'

'I'll do that.'

He was wearing a suit nearly the same color as his mustache and the thick, well-cut head of hair. The suit, and subtle stripe of the tie, made her think money. His voice was just clipped enough to have her assuming North.

Her saleswoman's instinct told her he wouldn't mind a little conversation as he wandered. 'Are you visiting Angel's Gap?'

'I have business in the area.' He smiled, and it deepened the hollows of his cheeks, turned his eyes into a warm blue and made distinguished just a little sexy. 'Such a friendly town.'

'Yes, it is.'

'And so scenic. Good for business, I'd think. I have a shop of my own.' He leaned over to study the display of heirloom jewelry. 'Estate jewelry,' he said, tapping the glass. 'The buying and selling. Very nice pieces here. Unexpected, really, outside a metropolitan area.'

'Thank you. Laine's very particular about what we sell here.'

'Laine?'

'Laine Tavish, the owner.'

'I wonder if I haven't heard that name. Possibly even met her at one of the auctions. It's a relatively small pool we swim in.'

'You might have. If you're staying in town for a while, you could come back in. She's usually here.'

'I'll be sure to do that. Tell me, do you sell loose stones as well?'

'Stones?'

At Jenny's blank look he angled his head. 'I often buy stones – gemstones – to replace ones lost from an antique setting, or to duplicate an estate piece for a client.'

62

'Oh. No, we don't. Of course, the jewelry's just a small part of our stock.'

'So I see.' He turned, and those eyes scanned every inch of the main showroom. 'An eclectic mix, styles, periods. Does Ms. Tavish do all the buying?'

'Yes, she does. We're lucky to have someone like Laine in the Gap. The store's developed a good reputation, and we're listed in several guides to the area, and antique and collectible magazines.'

He wandered off, walking in the direction of a table set with porcelain figurines and small bronzes. 'So, she's not a local then.'

'You're not a local in the Gap unless your grandfather was born here. But no, Laine moved here a few years ago.'

'Tavish, Tavish . . .' He angled back around, narrowing his eyes, stroking his mustache. 'Is she a tall, rather lanky woman with very short blond hair. Wears little black glasses?'

'No, Laine's a redhead.'

'Ah well, hardly matters. This is a lovely piece.' He picked up an elegant china cat. 'Do you ship?'

'We certainly do. I'd be happy to . . . Oh, hi, honey,' she said when Vince walked in. 'My husband,' she said to the customer with a wink. 'I don't call all the cops honey.'

'I was heading by, thought I'd stop in to see if Laine was here. Check on her.'

'No, I don't think she's coming in today after all. Got her hands full. Laine's house was broken into last night,' she said.

'God, how awful.' The man lifted a hand to the knot of his tie, and the dark blue stone in his pinkie ring winked. 'Was anyone hurt?'

'No, she wasn't home. Sorry, Vince, this is Mr. . . . I never did get your name.'

'It's Alexander, Miles Alexander.' He offered a hand to Vince.

'Vince Burger. Do you know Laine?'

'Actually, we were just trying to determine that. I sell estate jewelry and wondered if I've met Ms. Tavish along the circuit. I'm sorry to hear about her trouble. I'm very interested in the cat,' he said to Jenny, 'but I'm going to be late for my afternoon appointment. I'll come back, and hopefully meet Ms. Tavish. Thanks for your time, Mrs. Burger.'

'Jenny. Come back anytime,' she added as he walked to the door.

When they were alone in the shop, Jenny poked Vince in the belly. 'You looked at him like he was a suspect.'

'No, I didn't.' He gave her a return, and very gentle, poke in her belly. 'I'm just curious, that's all, when I see a guy in a slick-looking suit hanging around the shop the day after Laine's house is broken into.'

'Yeah, he looked like a rampaging burglar all right.'

'Okay, what's a rampaging burglar look like?'

'Not like that.'

His name was Alex Crew, though he had proper identification in the name of Miles Alexander – and several other aliases. Now he walked briskly along the sloping sidewalk. He had to walk off his anger, his quietly bubbling rage that Laine Tavish hadn't been where he'd wanted to find her.

He despised being foiled, on any level.

Still, the walk was part business. He needed to get the lay of the land on foot, though he had a detailed map of Angel's Gap in his head. He didn't enjoy small towns, or the burgeoning green view of the surrounding mountains. He was a man for the city, its pace, its opportunities.

Its abundance of marks.

For rest and relaxation, he enjoyed the Tropics, with their balmy breezes, moon-washed nights and rich tourists.

This place was full of hicks, like the pregnant salesclerk – probably on her fourth kid by now – and her ex-high-school football hero turned town cop husband. Guy looked like the type who sat around on Saturday nights with his buddies and talked about the glory days over a six-pack. Or sat in the woods waiting for a deer to come by so he could shoot it and feel like a hero again.

Crew deplored such men and the women who kept their dinner warm at night.

64

His father had been such a man.

No imagination, no vision, no palate for the taste of larceny. His old man wouldn't have taken the time of day if it wasn't marked on his time sheet. And what had it gotten him but a worn-out and complaining wife, a hot box of a row house in Camden and an early grave.

To Crew's mind, his father had been a pathetic waste of life.

He'd always wanted more, and had started taking it when he crawled through his first second-story window at twelve. He boosted his first car at fourteen, but his ambitions had always run to bigger, shinier games.

He liked stealing from the rich, but there was nothing of the Robin Hood in him. He liked it simply because the rich had better things, and having them, taking them, made him feel like he was part of the cream.

He killed his first man at twenty-two, and though it had been unplanned – bad clams had sent the mark home early from the ballet – he had no aversion to stealing a life. Particularly if there was a good profit in it.

He was forty-eight years old, had a taste for French wine and Italian suits. He had a home in Westchester from which his wife had fled – taking his young son – just prior to their divorce. He also kept a luxurious apartment off Central Park where he entertained lavishly when the mood struck, a weekend home in the Hamptons and a seaside home on Grand Cayman. All of the deeds were in different names.

He'd done very well for himself by taking what belonged to others and, if he said so himself, had become a kind of connoisseur. He was selective in what he stole now, and had been for more than a decade. Art and gems were his specialties, with an occasional foray into rare stamps.

He'd had a few arrests along the way, but only one conviction – a smudge he blamed entirely on his incompetent and overpriced lawyer.

The man had paid for it, as Crew had beaten him to bloody death with a lead pipe three months after his release. But to Crew's mind

65

those scales were hardly balanced. He'd spent twenty-six months inside, deprived of his freedom, debased and humiliated.

The idiot lawyer's death was hardly compensation.

But that had been more than twenty years ago. Though he'd been picked up for questioning a time or two since, there'd been no other arrests. The single benefit of those months in prison had been the endless time to think, to evaluate, to consider.

It wasn't enough to steal. It was essential to steal well, and to live well. So he'd studied, developed his brain and his personas. To steal successfully from the rich, it was best to become one of them. To acquire knowledge and taste, unlike the dregs who rotted behind bars.

To gain entrée into society, to perhaps take a well-heeled wife at some point. Success, to his mind, wasn't climbing in second-story windows, but in directing others to do so. Others who could be manipulated, then disposed of as necessary. Because, whatever they took, at his direction, by all rights belonged exclusively to him.

He was smart, he was patient, and he was ruthless.

If he'd made a mistake along the way, it was nothing that couldn't and wouldn't be rectified. He *always* rectified his mistakes. The idiot lawyer, the foolish woman who'd objected to his bilking her of a few hundred thousand dollars, any number of slow-minded underlings he'd employed or associated with in the course of his career.

Big Jack O'Hara and his ridiculous sidekick Willy had been mistakes.

A misjudgment, Crew corrected as he turned the corner and started back to the hotel. They hadn't been quite as stupid as he'd assumed when he'd used them to plan out and execute the job of his lifetime. His grail, his quest. *His.*

How they had slipped through the trap he'd laid and gotten away with their cut before it sprang was a puzzle to him. For more than a month they'd managed to elude him. And neither had attempted to turn the take into cash – that was another surprise.

But he'd kept his nose to the ground and eventually picked up

O'Hara's scent. Yet it hadn't been Jack he'd managed to track from New York to the Maryland mountains, but the foolish weasel Willy.

He shouldn't have let the little bastard see him, Crew thought now. But goddamn small towns. He hadn't expected to all but run into the man on the street. Any more than he'd expected Willy to bolt and run, a scared rabbit hopping right out and under the wheels of an oncoming car.

He'd been tempted to march through the rain, up to the bleeding mess and kick it. Millions of dollars at stake, and the idiot doesn't remember to look both ways before rushing into the street.

Then she'd come running out of that store. The pretty redhead with the shocked face. He'd seen that face before. Oh, he'd never met her, but he'd seen that face. Big Jack had photographs, and he'd loved to take them out and show them off once he had a couple of beers under his belt.

My daughter. Isn't she a beauty? Smart as a whip, too. College educated, my Lainie.

Smart enough, Crew thought, to tuck herself into the straight life in a small town so she could fence goods, transport them, turn them over. It was a damn good con.

If Jack thought he could pass what belonged to Alex Crew to his daughter, and retire rich to Rio as he often liked to talk of doing, he was going to be surprised.

He was going to get back what belonged to him. Everything that belonged to him. And father and daughter were going to pay a heavy price.

He stepped into the lobby of the Wayfarer and had to force himself to suppress a shudder. He considered the accommodations barely tolerable. He took the stairs to his suite, put out the do not disturb as he wanted to sit in the quiet while he planned his next move.

He needed to make contact with Laine Tavish, and should probably do so as Miles Alexander, estate jewelry broker. He studied himself in the mirror and nodded. Alexander was a fresh alias, as was the silver hair and mustache. O'Hara knew him as Martin Lyle or Gerald Benson, and would have described him as clean-shaven, with close-cropped salt-and-pepper hair.

A flirtation might be an entrée, and he did enjoy female companionship. The mutual interest in estate jewelry had been a good touch. Better to take a few days, get a feel for her before he made another move.

She hadn't hidden the cache at her house, nor had there been any safe-deposit or locker key to be found. Otherwise he and the two thugs he'd hired for the job would have found them.

It might've been rash to burgle her place in such a messy fashion, but he'd been angry and so sure she had what belonged to him. He still believed she did, or knew where to find it. The best approach was to keep it friendly, perhaps romantic.

She was here, Willy was here – even if he was dead. Could Jack O'Hara be far behind?

Satisfied with the simplicity of the plan, Crew sat in front of his laptop. He brought up several sites on estate jewelry and began to study.

Laine woke in lamplight and stared blankly around her bedroom.

What time was it? What day was it? She scooped her hair back as she pushed herself up to peer at the clock. Eight-fifteen. It couldn't be a.m. because it was dark, so what was she doing in bed at eight at night?

On the bed, she corrected, with her chenille throw tucked around her. And Henry snoring on the floor beside the bed.

She yawned, stretched, then snapped back.

Max!

Oh my God. He'd been helping her clear out the worst of the guest room, and they'd talked about going out to dinner. Or ordering in.

What had happened then? She searched her bleary brain. He'd taken the trash downstairs – outside – and she'd come into her bedroom to freshen up and change.

She'd just sat down on the bed for a minute.

All right, she'd stretched out on the bed for a minute. Shut her eyes. Just trying to regroup.

And now she was waking up nearly three hours later. Alone.

He'd covered her up, she thought with a sappy smile as she brushed a hand over the throw. And had turned on the light so she wouldn't wake in the dark.

She started to toss the throw aside and get up, and saw the note lying on the pillow beside her.

You looked too pretty and too tired for me to play Prince Charming to your Sleeping Beauty. I locked up, and your fierce hound is guarding you. Get a good night's sleep. I'll call you tomorrow. Better, I'll come by and see you.
  Max

'Could he be more perfect?' she asked the still snoring Henry. Lying back, she pressed the note to her breast. 'You should immediately suspect perfection, but oh boy, I'm enjoying this. I'm so tired of being suspicious and cautious, and alone.'

She lay there another moment, smiling to herself. Sleeping Beauty wasn't sleepy anymore. In fact, she couldn't have been more awake or alert.

'You know how long it's been since I've done something really reckless?' She drew a deep breath, let it out. 'Neither do I, that's how long it's been. It's time to gamble.'

She sprang up, dashed into the bathroom to start the shower. On second thought, she decided, a bubble bath was more suited to the occasion she had in mind. There was time for one, and while it ran she'd look through her choices and pick something to wear most suited for seducing Max Gannon.

She used a warm freesia scent in the tub, then spent a full twenty minutes on her makeup. It took her nearly that long to decide whether to leave her hair down or put it up. She opted for up because he hadn't seen it that way yet, and fashioned a loose updo that would tumble at the slightest provocation.

This time, she went for the obvious and the little black dress. She was grateful for the shopping spree months before with the not-yet-pregnant Jenny that had netted them both some incredible lingerie.

Then, remembering that Jenny credited her current condition to that lingerie, Laine added more condoms to the ones she'd already tucked in her purse. It brought the total up to half a dozen, a number she giddily decided was both cautious and optimistic.

She slipped a tissue-thin black cashmere cardigan, a ridiculous indulgence she didn't get to wear nearly often enough, over the dress.

Taking one last study in the mirror, she turned to every angle. 'If he turns you down,' she stated, 'there's no hope for mankind.'

She whistled for the dog to follow her downstairs. After a dash into the kitchen to grab a bottle of wine, she took Henry's leash from the hook by the back door.

'Wanna go for a ride?' she asked, a question that always sent Max into leaps and dashes of wild glee and shuddering excitement. 'You're going to Jenny's. You're going to have a sleepover, and please, God, so am I. If I don't find an outlet for all this heat, I'm going to spontaneously combust.'

He raced to the car and back three times by the time she reached it and opened the door for him. He leaped in and sat grinning in the passenger seat while she strapped the seat belt over him.

'I'm not even nervous. I can't believe I'm not nervous when I haven't done this in . . . well, no point thinking of that,' she added as she got behind the wheel. 'If I think of that, I *will be nervous*. I really like him. It's crazy because I hardly know him, but I really like him, Henry.'

Henry barked, either in understanding or in joy as she started down the lane.

'It probably can't come to anything,' she continued. 'I mean, he lives in New York and I live here. But it doesn't have to come to anything, right? It doesn't have to mean undying love or lifetime commitment. It can just be lust and respect and affection and . . . lust. There's a whole lot of lust going on here, and there's nothing wrong with that.

'And I'm going to shut up before I find a way to talk myself out of this.'

It was nearly ten by the time she pulled up in Jenny's driveway.

Late, she thought. Sort of late to go knocking on a guy's hotel room door.

But just what was the proper time to go knocking on a guy's hotel room door?

Jenny was already coming out of the front door and down the walk. Laine released Henry's seat belt and waited for her friend to open the passenger door.

'Hi, Henry! There's my best guy, there he is. Vince is waiting for you.'

'I owe you,' Laine said as Henry raced madly for the house.

'Do not. Late date, huh?'

'Don't ask, don't tell.'

Jenny leaned in as far as her belly would allow. 'Are you kidding me?'

'Yes. I'll tell you everything tomorrow. Just do me one more favor?'

'Sure, what?'

'Pray, really hard, that there's something to tell.'

'You got it, but the fabulous way you look, those prayers are already answered.'

'Okay. Here goes.'

'Go get 'em, honey.' Jenny closed the door and stepped back, rubbing her belly as Laine drove away. 'The guy's toast,' she murmured, and went inside to play with Henry.

71

Chapter Six

It occurred to Laine that she looked like a woman on her way to an assignation. The little black dress, the sexy shoes, the bottle of wine tucked into the crook of her arm.

But that was okay. She *was* a woman on her way, she hopee to an assignation. The man involved just didn't know it yet. And if she ran into someone she knew, so what? She was an adult, she was single and unencumbered. She was entitled to a night of healthy, no-strings sex.

But she was relieved when she crossed the lobby of the Wayfarer without seeing a familiar face. She pressed the Up button on the elevator and caught herself doing a relaxation breathing technique she'd learned in a yoga class.

She stopped.

She didn't want to relax. She could relax tomorrow. Tonight she wanted that live-wire sizzle in the blood, the tingling stomach muscles, the dance of chills and heat along the skin.

She stepped into the car when the doors opened and pressed the button for Max's floor. As her elevator doors closed, the doors on the one beside hers opened.

Alex Crew stepped out.

At his desk, with the TV muttering in the background for company, Max reviewed his notes and wrote up his daily report. He left out a few things, it was true. There was no point in documenting that he'd played with the dog, kissed Laine, or that he'd tucked a blanket over her then stood watching her sleep.

None of that was salient information.

He did detail the extent of the damage to her property, her actions and reactions and his opinions on what he observed to be her current lifestyle.

Simple, small-town, successful. Knowledgeable about her profession, cozily dug into her hillside home and the community.

But where had she gotten the funds to buy that home, to start up her business? The business loan and the mortgage he'd accessed – not in a strictly legal manner – didn't quite add up. She'd put down sizable deposits – more than it logically seemed possible for a young woman who'd earned a steady but unremarkable salary since college.

And still not an exorbitant amount, he reflected. Nothing showy. Nothing that hinted there was a great big money tree somewhere dripping with millions.

She drove a good, middle-of-the-road car. American made and three years old. She had some nice pieces of art and furnishings in her home but she was in the business, so it wasn't remarkable.

Her wardrobe, what he'd seen, showed good classic taste. But it, too, wasn't exorbitant, and fit very neatly into the image of the single, successful antique merchant.

Everything about her fit that image, down to the ground.

She didn't live rich. She didn't look like an operator, and he could usually spot one. What was the point of buying a house in the woods, getting an ugly dog, opening a Main Steet, U.S.A., business if it wasn't what you wanted?

A woman with her attributes could be anywhere, doing anything. Therefore, it followed that she was doing exactly what she wanted to do.

And *that* just didn't add up either.

He was messed up about her, that was the problem. He tipped back in his chair, stared up at the ceiling. Every time he looked at her, his brain went soft on him. There was something about that face, the voice, Jesus, the *smell* of her, that was making a sap out of him.

Maybe he couldn't see her as an operator because he didn't want to see her that way. He hadn't been this twisted up in a woman since . . . Actually, he'd never been this twisted up in a woman.

Practically then, professionally then, he should back off a bit on the personal contact. Whether or not she appeared to be his best conduit to Jack O'Hara, he couldn't use her if he couldn't get over her.

He could make an excuse, leave town for a few days. He could establish a base nearby where he could observe and record. And use his contacts and connections, as well as his own hacker skills, to dig deeper into the life and times of Elaine O'Hara aka Laine Tavish.

When he knew more, he'd decide how to handle her and come back. But meanwhile, he'd have to maintain some objective distance. No more dinners for two, no more spending the day with her at home, no more physical contact that couldn't lead to anything but complications.

He would check out in the morning, give her a quick call to tell her he'd been called back to New York and would be in touch. Keep the lines open, but ease back on the personal front.

A man couldn't do his job efficiently if he was wandering around in a sexual haze.

Satisfied with the plan, Max got up. He'd pack most of his things tonight, maybe go down afterward for a nightcap, then try to sleep off the feelings for her that were building much too quickly and much too inappropriately inside him.

The knock on the door distracted him. They'd already done the turndown, little chocolate mints on the pillows included. He half expected to see an envelope sliding under the door. Though he preferred all communications via e-mail, his clients often insisted on a hard copy fax for instructions.

When nothing appeared, he walked over, glanced through the peep. And came within a breath of swallowing his own tongue.

What the hell was she doing at his door? And what was she wearing?

Jesus Christ.

He backed up, rubbed a hand over his face, his heart.

Professional instinct kicked in enough to have him hurrying back to the desk, shutting down his files, burying any hard paperwork, then doing a quick visual sweep for anything that might blow his cover.

He'd get her downstairs to the lounge, that's what he'd do. Get her down, in a public place, tell her he'd been called back, have a quick drink with her.

And move out. Move along. Move away.

He dragged a hand through his hair a couple of times, shook off the nerves. He worked up what he considered an easy, mildly surprised, mildly pleased expression and opened the door.

The full impact of her hadn't come through the peephole. Now the tongue he'd nearly swallowed rolled out again and all but plopped at his feet.

He couldn't quite focus on what she was wearing other than noticing it was black, it was short, and it displayed more curves than a Formula One race. Her legs were longer than he'd imagined, and ended in very high, very thin black heels.

All that fiery hair was scooped up somehow or other, and her eyes seemed bluer, brighter than ever. She'd slicked something dark and glossy and tantalizingly wet over her lips.

God help him.

'I woke up.'

'You did. You certainly did.'

'Can I come in?'

'Ah. Um.' It was as coherent as he could manage, so he just stepped back. And when she walked by him, the scent of her wrapped around his glands, and squeezed.

'I didn't get a chance to thank you, so I thought I would.'

'Thank you. Thank me,' he corrected and felt like an imbecile.

She smiled and, holding up the bottle of wine, wagged it slowly side to side. 'How do you feel about Merlot?'

'I feel pretty good about it.'

It took all her willpower not to laugh. Was there anything that made a woman feel more of a woman than having a man stare at her as if he'd been bewitched? She took a step toward him and was wonderfully flattered when he took one in retreat. 'Good enough to share?' she asked him.

'Share?'

'The wine.'

'Oh.' He'd had a couple of concussions in his day. They often gave the victim the same fuzzy, out-of-body sensation he was experiencing now. 'Sure.' He took the bottle she held out. 'Sure. Sure.'

'Well then.'

'Well?' There seemed to be some sort of time lag between his brain and his mouth. 'Oh, right. Ah, corkscrew.' He glanced toward the minibar, but she reached in her purse.

'Try this.' She offered him a corkscrew. One half of the handle was a naked woman, head to torso. The other was all leg.

'Cute,' he managed.

'Kitschy,' she corrected. 'I have a small collection. Nice room,' she added. 'A lot of bed.' She wandered to the window, eased the drapes apart a few inches. 'I bet the view's wonderful.'

'Oh yeah.'

Perfectly aware his gaze was on her, she continued to look out the window and slowly peeled off the thin sweater. She heard the abrupt clunk of the wine bottle against wood and was satisfied the dress had done its job. From his viewpoint, there wasn't much of it, just a lot of her naked back framed by a bit of snug black.

She wandered away, toward the bed, and plucked one of the mints from the pillow. 'Mmm, chocolate. Do you mind?'

The best he could do was a slow shake of his head. The cork came out of the bottle with a suprised pop and the words 'Oh my God' rushed into his mind as she unwrapped the little mint, bit slowly into it.

She gave a sexy little moan, licked her lips. 'I heard somewhere that money talks but chocolate sings. I like that.' She walked to him, held the second half of the mint to his lips. 'I'll share, too.'

'You're killing me.'

'Let's have some wine then, so you can die happy.' She sat on the edge of the bed, crossed her legs. 'Did I interrupt your work?'

'Reports. I'll get back to it.' *When I find my sanity,* he decided.

He poured wine, handed her a glass. And watched her watch him as she took the first, slow sip.

'It's been a while since anyone's tucked me in. I didn't mean to fall asleep on you, Max.'

'You had a rough night, a hard day.'

'Not as hard a day as I'd expected, thanks to you.'

'Laine—'

'Let me thank you. It was easier doing what needed to be done with you there. I like spending time with you.' She took another, longer sip. 'I like wanting you, and speculating that you want me.'

'Wanting you's squeezing the breath out of my throat, cutting off the oxygen to my brain. That wasn't the plan.'

'Ever want to say screw the plan and go with impulse?'

'All the time.'

She did laugh now, downed the wine and rose to pour another glass. After another sip, she walked to the door. 'I don't. Or rarely do. But you have to respect the exceptions that make the rule.'

She opened the door, hung the do not disturb sign on the outside knob. She closed the door, locked it, leaned back against it. 'If you don't like where this is going, better speak up.'

He took a deep gulp of wine himself. 'I have absolutely nothing to say.'

'That's good because I was prepared to get rough.'

He imagined the grin that split his face was big, and stupid. He didn't give a damn. 'Really?'

She started back toward him. 'I wasn't sure I'd be able to fight fair.'

'That dress isn't fighting fair.'

'Oh?' She took a last sip of wine, then set the glass aside. 'Then I should just take it off.'

'Let me. Please.' He trailed a fingertip along the milky white skin edged with black. 'Let me.'

'Help yourself.'

He forgot about practicality, professionalism. He forgot about the emotional and physical distance he'd decided would best suit his needs. He forgot about everything but the reality of her, the water-soft texture of her skin, the heady scent, the hot ripe taste of her mouth when he gripped her hips, pulled her close and kissed her.

She enveloped him – those textures, that scent, that taste until they were – she was – everything he could want or need or imagine.

It was a mistake. Taking her now, like this, was a mistake and edged very close to the forbidden. Knowing that only added an irresistible element of danger to the whole.

He tugged the dress away from her shoulder, set his teeth on flesh. And when her head fell back, he worked his way back toward the little purr in her throat.

'Something to be said about plans though,' he murmured, and bared her other shoulder. 'I've got all sorts of plans for you.'

'I was hoping.' She fumbled her hand back to where she'd dropped her purse on the bed. 'You're going to need this,' she said and pulled out a condom.

'At some point, we're also going to need a defibrillator and a fire extinguisher.'

'Promises, promises.'

He grinned. 'I could go seriously crazy over you.' He laid his lips on hers again, rubbed. 'Is this one of those peel-out-of-it deals? The dress, I mean.'

'Pretty much.'

'Hot damn, a personal favorite.' He worked slowly, drawing out the process with his mouth on hers until they were both ready to shudder. Then he drew back, took her hand so she could step out of the dress that pooled at her feet. And just looked at her.

She wore some sort of fascinating female construction of silk and lace that flirted over her breasts so they had little choice but to rise up, threaten to spill out. The black silk skimmed down her torso, nipping in her waist, molding over her hips to end in flirty little garters that held up sheer black stockings.

'I'm trying to think of something memorable to say, but it's really hard when all the blood's drained out of my head.'

'Give it a shot.'

'Wow.'

'That's what I was shooting for.' She reached out and began to unbutton his shirt. 'I like the way you look at me. I did right from the first time. I especially like the way you're looking at me now.'

'I see you even when I'm not looking. That's a first for me, and a little unnerving.'

'Maybe some people are supposed to see each other. Maybe that's why this is happening so fast. I don't care why.' She drew his shirt away, ran her hands up his chest, then locked them around his neck. 'I don't care,' she repeated and crushed her lips to his.

She only knew she wanted to go on feeling this way, to have these jolts of excitement shocking her system, to tremble with the shocking flood of anticipation. To know the power of having a man's, *this* man's, complete attention and desire.

She wanted to be reckless, to take exactly what she wanted in greedy gulps for once in her life, and to think only of the moment, of the pleasure, of the passion.

When he spun her around, she arched back against him, lifting her arms to hook them around his neck and gave his hands the freedom to run over her. Over lace, silk, flesh. He fed at her neck, at the curve of her shoulder while he touched her, aroused her. Her breath caught, released on a moan when his hand slid between her thighs. She pressed hers against his, rocked her hips and rose up on that hot wave of pleasure.

He imagined himself swinging her up, laying her on the bed to take the next stage with something approaching romance and finesse. But somehow they were tangled together on the neatly turned-down sheets in a desperate struggle to touch, to taste.

Her hair had spilled down, bright fire against the white. The scent of it, of her skin, dazed his senses until he wondered if he would ever take another breath without drawing her in.

'Do things to me.' Her mouth was wild hunger on his. 'Do everything to me.'

He was lost in a storm of needs and greed, drowning in the heat of them even as he feasted on her, and she on him. As she moved under him, over him, surrounded him, he was rougher than he meant to be in a desperate search for more.

Her lungs were screaming, her heart galloping to the point of pain. Her skin was so hot it seemed it might melt off her bones. And God, it was glorious.

His hands were so strong, his mouth so ravenous. She could revel in the sensation of being taken over, body and mind. He tugged and pulled at snaps, impossibly tiny hooks, made her laugh breathlessly when he fumbled and cursed. Made her gasp in shock when he drove into her and shot her over the edge.

It was she who demanded it all, now, now, *now*! And arched and opened, who cried out when he plunged inside her. Her vision blurred, her galloping heart stopped. Then everything, everything was clear as crystal, her heartbeat raging, her body racing as they took each other.

She could see his face, the lines and hollows, the shadow of the beard not shaved since morning, and his eyes, tiger eyes focused on hers. Then going darker, going opaque an instant before he buried his face in her hair and emptied into her.

Her body was drenched, saturated with pleasure, and her mind calm as a summer lake. She was trapped under his body, and delighted with herself and him. She could hear the ragged sound of his breathing. There was such satisfaction in knowing she'd caused that. Toying with his hair, she closed her eyes and let herself drift.

'You okay down there?' he murmured.

'I'm wonderful down here, thanks. You okay up there?'

'I may be paralyzed, but I'm feeling pretty good about it.' He turned his head so his lips brushed the side of her neck. 'Laine.'

Eyes still closed, she smiled. 'Max.'

'I have to say . . . I have to say,' he repeated as much for himself as her, 'this is something I never expected when I `. . . took this assignment.'

'I like surprises. I stopped liking them along the way, but I'm remembering why I always liked surprises. It's because they just happen.'

'If surprises deal with finding you at my door wearing a sexy black dress, I freaking love them.'

'If I did it again, it wouldn't be a surprise, it would be a repeat.'

'I can live with that. Where's Henry?'

'Henry?'

He pushed onto his elbows to look down at her. 'You didn't leave him at home, did you? After what happened last night.'

It wasn't heat flashing now, but a slow and lovely warmth sliding. He was worried about a dog. Her dog. Any man who'd worry about a dog when he was naked in bed with a woman shot straight to the top of her list of all-time heroes. She dragged his face down to hers so she could rain kisses over it.

'No, I didn't leave him alone. I took him to Jenny's. How can you be so perfect? I'm always looking for the flaws in everything, but you're just . . .' She pressed her lips to his in a long, noisy kiss. 'Absolutely perfect.'

'I'm not.' He didn't care for the twinge of guilt. It was a sensation he overcame or avoided. Worse, there was worry tangled with it. What would she think, how would she react when she found out just what his flaws were?

'I'm selfish and single-minded,' he told her. 'I—'

'Selfish men don't wander into antique stores looking for a gift for their mother, just because.'

The twinge became a pang. 'That was impulse.'

'See, a surprise. Didn't I just say I love surprises? Don't try to convince me you're not perfect. I'm too happy with you right now to think anything else. Uh-oh, now I've got you thinking.' She ran her hands down his back, gave his butt a friendly pat. 'Is she trying to turn this into more than fun and games?'

'That's not what I was thinking. And it already is more than fun and games.'

'Oh.' Her heart tripped, but she kept her eyes steady on his. 'Is it?'

'That's what I wasn't expecting, Laine.' He lowered his head, touched his lips to hers. 'Makes things a little more complicated.'

'I don't mind complications, Max.' She framed his face with her hands. 'We can worry about what this is, or isn't, what it's going to be, tomorrow, or we can enjoy it. And each other. The one thing

81

I know is when I woke up at home tonight, I was happy because I knew I wanted to be with you. I haven't felt that way in a long time.'

'Happy?'

'Satisfied, content, productive and happy enough. But not dance-around-the-house happy. So about the only thing you could tell me that would make this too complicated for me is that you've got a wife and a couple of kids in Brooklyn.'

'I don't. They're in Queens.'

She pinched him, hard, then wrestled him over onto his back. 'Ha ha. Very funny.'

'It's my ex-wife who lives in Brooklyn.'

She straddled him, tossed her hair back. 'You've been busy.'

'Well, you collect corkscrews. Some guys collect women. My current mistress is in Atlanta, but I'm thinking of branching out. You could be my Maryland tootsie.'

'Tootsie? It's always been one of my driving ambitions to be someone's tootsie. Where do I sign up?'

He sat up, wrapping his arms around her and just holding on. Complications, he thought. He couldn't begin to list them. So he'd just have to deal with them. So would she. But not tonight. Tonight he was going to take her at her word and just enjoy.

'Are you going to stay awhile? Stay awhile, Laine.'

'I thought you'd never ask.'

'Don't go.' The moment the words were out of Max's mouth, he realized he'd never said them to a woman before. Maybe it was sleep deprivation, sexual exhaustion. Maybe it was just her.

'It's after three in the morning.'

'Exactly. So come on back to bed. We'll just spoon up here and snooze for a couple hours, then order breakfast.'

'That sounds wonderful, but I'll need another one of those rain checks.' She wiggled into the dress, forgoing underwear. And erased all thoughts of snoozing from his mind.

'Then just come back to bed.'

'I have to go.' She chuckled, dancing out of reach when he made a grab for her. 'I need to go home, catch a couple hours' sleep, change, run back into town and pick up Henry, take him home, then go back into town to the shop.'

'If you stay here, you could pick up Henry on the way home and save yourself a trip.'

'And provide the gossip mill with enough grist to run it until next Christmas.' She was small-town enough, in the woman she'd created, to be concerned about such things. 'A woman strolls out of a hotel in the morning wearing this sort of dress, eyebrows raise. Especially in the Gap.'

'I'll lend you a shirt.'

'I'm going.' She stuffed her lingerie into her purse. 'But if you'd like to have dinner with me tonight . . .'

'Name the time and place.'

'Eight, my place. I'll cook.'

'Cook?' His eyes blinked slowly, twice, then seemed to glaze. 'Food?'

'No, I thought I'd cook up an insidious plot against the government. Of course food.' She turned to the mirror, pulled a tiny brush out of her bulging purse and swooped it through her hair. 'What do you like?'

He just stared at her. 'Food?'

'I'll think of something.' Satisfied she was as good as she was going to get, she dropped the brush back into the purse and crossed to him. She leaned over the bed, gave him a light kiss. 'See you later.'

He stayed where he was after she'd closed the door behind her. Stayed, staring at the door with the taste of her lingering on his lips.

None of it made any sense. Not what had happened between them, not what he felt for her, not who she was. Because his reading of her wasn't off. He was *never* this far off, and it had nothing to do with glands.

If Laine Tavish was mixed up in a multimillion-dollar heist, he'd eat his own investigator's license.

It didn't explain why William Young had come to see her. It

didn't explain why he was dead. It didn't explain why her house had been ransacked.

But there were explanations, and he'd ferret them out. He was good at it. Once he had, once he'd cleared her, satisfied his client, done the job, he'd tell her everything.

She'd probably be a little upset.

Get real, Gannon, he thought, she'd be completely pissed. But he'd bring her around.

He was good at bringing people around, too.

The best way to work through the mess he'd gotten into was to proceed with logic. Logically, Jack O'Hara's daughter Elaine had severed ties with him, changed her name, adjusted her background and started a life for herself. Everything pointed in that direction, including his own instincts.

That didn't mean Big Jack, Willy or any of their associates were unaware of her and her location. Didn't mean there wasn't occasional contact, or the attempt to contact.

And okay, her finances still struck him as dicey, but he'd work on that. A few thousand here or there to put a down payment on a house or start up a business was nothing. Not compared to a share of $28 million and change.

Willy may have tracked her down to ask her for help, a place to hide out, to deliver a message from her father. Whatever the purpose, he was dead as Moses now and couldn't be asked. And would never cash in on his share, either, Max mused.

Didn't that up the stakes considerably?

Laine didn't have anything at the house worth worrying about. There was no question of that. Even if whoever'd broken in had missed something, she wouldn't have left the house unattended for the night to play heat the sheets if she had something hidden there.

Logically, she didn't have anything. She'd been in Angel's Gap when the jewels were stolen. For Christ's sake, she'd barely finished her first decade when she was shuffled out of Big Jack's aegis and influence.

Regardless, to clear her, to cross her name off all lists, he had to cover all the bases. He had to take a good look around her shop.

84

The sooner he did it, the sooner they could move on. He checked the time, judged he had a good three hours before daylight.

Might as well get started.

Chapter Seven

It amazed him that anyone who shared DNA with a thief would secure their own business with standard locks and a rinky-dink alarm system any twelve-year-old with a Swiss army knife and a little imagination could circumvent.

Really, if this . . . thing of theirs turned into an actual relationship, he was going to have a serious sit-down with Laine about home and business security. Maybe a store in a town of this type and size didn't require riot bars, gates or surveillance cameras, but she hadn't even bothered with security lights, in or out. As for the door, it was pathetic. If he'd *been* a thief who didn't worry about finesse, a couple of good kicks would've done the job.

Her current excuse for a system made the nighttime B&E embarrassingly easy. He bypassed the alarm and picked the locks on the back door in case some insomniac decided to take a predawn stroll down Market Street. And he'd walked from the hotel, taking his time, circling the block on foot. Just because something was easy didn't mean you could afford to be careless about procedure.

The town was quiet enough so he could hear the rumble of a furnace when it kicked on inside a building. And the long, mournful whistle of a freight train that rose eerily out of the silence. There were no winos, no junkies, no homeless, no hookers or street people populating the night in what would be considered downtown Angel's Gap.

You had to wonder if you were actually in America or if you'd somehow stumbled into a postcard printed up by the local chamber of commerce.

It was, Max decided, mildly creepy.

The streetlights along the steep sidewalk were old-fashioned lantern style, and every one of them glowed. All the display windows in the storefronts were sheer glass. As with Remember When, there were no gates, no security bars.

Hadn't anyone ever thrown a brick through one and helped themselves before hotfooting it away? Or kicked in a door for a quick looting party?

It just didn't seem right.

He thought of New York at three twenty-seven a.m. There'd be action, or trouble, if you were inclined for either. There'd be both pedestrian and vehicular traffic and the stores would all be chained down for the night.

So was there more crime there on a per capita basis just because it was expected?

It was an interesting theory, and he'd have to give some thought to it when he had a little downtime.

But for now, alarm and locks dispatched, he eased open the rear door of Remember When.

In and out in an hour, tops, he promised himself. Then back to the hotel to catch a little sleep. When New York opened, he'd contact his client and report that all evidence pointed to the fact that Laine Tavish was not, knowingly, involved.

That would clear him, from his point of view, to explain things to her. Once he'd done that, and talked her out of being pissed off, he'd pick her brain. He had a feeling she'd be an excellent source in tracking Big Jack and the diamonds.

And in collecting his finder's fee.

Max shut the door quietly behind him. Reached down to switch on his penlight.

But instead of the narrow beam coming on, lights exploded inside his head.

He woke in dead dark with his head banging with all the gusto and violence of his young nephew slamming pot lids together. He managed to roll over to what he thought was his back. The way his head was pounding and spinning, he couldn't be sure.

He lifted a hand to check if that head was still face front and felt the warm wet running.

And that pushed temper through the pain. It was bad enough to get ambushed and knocked out, but it was a hell of another thing if he had to go to the damn ER and get stitches.

He couldn't quite clear his brain, but he pushed himself to a sitting position. Since the head he was now reasonably certain was still on the correct way seemed in danger of falling off his shoulders, he lowered it to his hands until he felt more secure.

He needed to get up, turn on a light. Take stock of himself and what the hell had happened. He wiped at the blood, opened his aching eyes and scowled at the open rear door.

Whoever'd hit him from behind was long gone. He started to get to his feet with the idea of taking a quick look around the place before following suit.

And the rear doorway was suddenly filled with cop.

Max took a long look at Vince Burger, and at the police-issue pointing in his direction and said, 'Well, shit.'

'Look, you can pop me for the B and E. It'll sting. I'll get around it, but it'll sting. But—'

'I did pop you for the B and E.' Vince kicked back in his desk chair and smiled humorlessly at Max, who sat cuffed to a visitor's chair in the office of the station house.

Didn't look so big city and cocky now, Vince thought, with the bandage on his temple and the sizable lump on his forehead.

'Then there's attempted burglary—'

'I wasn't stealing anything, damnit, and you know it.'

'Oh, so you just break into stores in the middle of the night to browse around. Like window shopping but on the inside.' He lifted an evidence bag, gave it a shake that rattled Max's burglar tools and personal data assistant. 'And you carry these around in case you have to do some small home repairs?'

'Look—'

'I can pop you on possession of burglary tools.'

'That's a goddamn PDA. Everybody's got a PDA.'

'I don't.'

'Surprise, surprise,' Max said sourly. 'I had reasons for being inside Laine's shop.'

'You break into all the shops and homes of women you date?'

'I never broke into her house, and it's pretty damn elementary, Watson, that whoever was in the store ahead of me, whoever cold-cocked me was the one who did. You're protective of her, I get that, but—'

'Damn right.' The good-old-boy's eyes went hard as cinders. 'She's a friend of mine. She's a good friend of mine, and I don't like some New York asshole messing with my friends.'

'I'm a Georgia asshole, actually. I just live in New York. I'm conducting an investigation for a client. A private investigation.'

'So you say, but I didn't find any license on you.'

'You didn't find any wallet either,' Max snapped back, 'because whoever knocked me out helped himself to it. Goddamnit, Burger—'

'Don't swear in my office.'

At wits' end, Max leaned his head back, closed his eyes. 'I didn't ask for a lawyer, but I'm going to beg you, I may even work up some tears along with it, for some fricking aspirin.'

Vince opened a desk drawer, took out a bottle. Maybe he slammed the drawer just for the satisfaction of seeing Max wince, but he heaved himself up and poured a cup of water.

'You know I'm what I say I am.' Max took the pills, downed them with the water and prayed for them to break Olympic records swimming into his bloodstream. 'You've run me. You know I'm a licensed investigator. You know I used to be a cop. And while you're wasting time and getting your jollies busting my balls, whoever was in her place has gone back to ground. You need—'

'You don't want to tell me what I need to do.' The voice was mild enough to have Max respecting the cold fury under it – particularly since he was cuffed to a chair. 'You told Laine all that? About the used to be a cop, going private, working on a case here in the Gap?'

Just his luck, Max decided, to run foul of the Norman Rockwell version of a hard-ass town cop. 'Is this about my relationship with Laine or about me being inside the shop?'

'Six of one to me. What's the case you're working on?'

'I'm not giving you any details on that until I talk to my client.' And his client was unlikely to be pleased he'd been busted slithering around the fine points of the law. Not that he'd slithered, but that he'd gotten caught. But that was another problem.

'Look, someone was in that shop when I walked in, and that same person tore up Laine's house. Laine's the one we need to be concerned about right now. You need to send a deputy out to her place and make sure—'

'Telling me how to do my job isn't going to make me feel any more kindly toward you.'

'I don't care if you want to ask me out to the prom. Laine needs protection.'

'You've been doing a good job of that.' Vince settled his weight on the edge of the desk, like, Max thought with a sinking heart, a man settling in for a nice, long chat. 'Funny how you show up from New York right after I end up with a guy from New York in the morgue.'

'Yeah, I'm still laughing about that one. Eight million people in New York, give or take,' Max said coolly. 'Seems reasonable a few of them would pass through here from time to time.'

'Guess I'm not feeling real reasonable. Here's what I see. Some guy walks out of Laine's shop, gets spooked and runs into the street, ends up dead. You show up, talk Laine into having dinner with you, and while you're moving on her, her house gets burgled and vandalized. Next thing you know, you're inside her shop at three-thirty in the morning carrying burglar tools. What are you looking for, Gannon?'

'Inner peace.'

'Good luck with that,' Vince said as they heard the quick march of footsteps down the hall.

Laine swung into the room. She wore sweats, and her hair was pulled back into a tail that left her face unframed. There were smudges from lack of sleep under her eyes, and those eyes were full of baffled concern.

'What's going on? Jerry came by the house, told me there was trouble at the shop and that I had to come right in and talk to you. What kind of trouble? What's—' She spotted the handcuffs and stopped short as she stared at them, then slowly lifted her gaze to Max's face. 'What is this?'

'Laine—'

'You're going to want to sit quiet a minute,' Vince warned Max. 'You had a break-in at the store,' Vince told her. 'Far as I could see there wasn't any damage. You'll have to take a look yourself to see if anything was taken.'

'I see.' She wanted to sit, but only braced a hand on the back of a chair. 'No, I don't. Why have you got Max cuffed?'

'I got an anonymous call that there was a burglary in progress at the location of your store. When I got there, I found him. Inside. He had a nice set of lock picks in his possession.'

She took a breath – air in, air out – and shifted her gaze to Max's face. 'You broke into my shop?'

'No. Well, yes, technically. But after someone else did. Someone who bashed me on the head, then called in the tip so I'd get rousted for this.'

She studied the bandage on his temple, but the concern had already chilled out of her eyes. 'That doesn't explain what you were doing there in the middle of the night.' *After I left your bed,* she thought. *After I spent the night in your bed.*

'I can explain. I need to talk to you privately. Ten minutes. Give me ten minutes.'

'I'd like to hear it. Can I talk to him alone, Vince?'

'I wouldn't recommend it.'

'I'm a licensed investigator. He knows it.' Max jerked a thumb at Vince. 'I have a case and a client, and I'm pursuing leads. I'm not free to say any more.'

'Then you'd be wasting all our time,' Vince pointed out.

'Ten minutes, Laine.'

An investigator. A case. In the time it took her to absorb the blow, she'd added her father into the mix. Hurt, anger and resignation rolled through her in a messy trio, but none of it showed. 'I'd appreciate the time, Vince. It's personal.'

'Figured as much.' Vince pushed to his feet. 'As a favor to you, then. I'll be right outside the door. Watch yourself,' he added to Max, 'or you're going to have a few new bruises to go with the old ones.'

Max waited until the door clicked shut. 'You've got very protective friends.'

'How much of the ten minutes do you want to waste on irrelevant observations?'

'Could you sit down?'

'I could, but I won't.' She walked over to Vince's Mr. Coffee machine. She needed something to do with her hands before she surrendered to impulse and pounded them into Max's face. 'What game are you running, Max?'

'I'm working for Reliance Insurance, and I'm skirting a line telling you that before I clear it with my client.'

'Really? But breaking into my shop after spending several hours having sex with me isn't a line you're worried about, apparently.'

'I didn't know. I didn't expect . . .' Fuck it, he thought. 'I can apologize, but it wouldn't make any difference to you, and wouldn't excuse the way this happened.'

'Well, there we are.' She drank coffee, bitter and black. 'We're on the same page on something, after all.'

'You can be pissed off at me if you want—'

'Why, thanks. I believe I will.'

'But you've got to get past it. Laine, you're in trouble.'

She lifted her eyebrows, stared deliberately at the handcuffs. '*I'm* in trouble?'

'How many people know you're Elaine O'Hara?'

She didn't bat an eyelash. He hadn't expected her to be quite that good.

'You'd be one, apparently. I don't choose to use that name. I changed to my stepfather's name a long time ago. And I fail to see how this is any of your business.' She sipped at the coffee. 'Why don't we get back to the part where about an hour after we were sliding around naked on each other, you were arrested for breaking into my place of business.'

Guilt swept over his face but gave her little satisfaction. 'One doesn't have anything to do with the other.'

With a nod, she set the coffee down. 'With answers like that we don't need our allotted ten minutes.'

'William Young died outside your store,' Max said as she took a step toward the door. 'Died, according to witness reports, all but in your arms. You must've recognized him.'

Her facade cracked minutely, and the grief eked through. Then she shored it up again. 'This sounds more like an interrogation than an explanation. I'm not interested in answering the questions of a man who lied to me, who used me. So you can start telling me what you're doing here and what you want, or I'll bring Vince back in and we'll get started on pressing charges.'

He took a moment. It was all he needed to confirm in his mind that she'd do exactly that. Shove him aside, lock the door, walk away. It was all he needed to understand he'd toss the job aside before he'd let that happen.

'I broke into your shop tonight so I could clear you, so I could report to my client this morning that you weren't involved, and so I could tell you the truth.'

'Involved in what? The truth about what?'

'Sit down for a damn minute. I'm tired of craning my neck.'

She sat. 'There. Comfy?'

'Six weeks ago, diamonds appraised at and insured by Reliance for twenty-eight point four million dollars were stolen from the offices of the International Jewelry Exchange in New York City. Two days later, the body of Jerome Myers, a gem merchant with offices in that location, was found in a New Jersey construction site. Through the investigation it's been determined this merchant was the inside man. It's also been determined he had a connection and an association with William Young and Jack O'Hara.'

'Wait a minute, wait a minute. You're saying you believe my father was involved in a heist with a take of over twenty-eight million? *Million*? That he had something to do with a murder? The first is ridiculous, the second impossible. Jack O'Hara dreamed big, but he's small time. And he never hurt anyone, not that way.'

'Things change.'

'Not that much.'

'The cops don't have enough to charge Jack or Willy, though they'd sure like to talk to them. Since Willy's not going to be talking to anybody, that leaves Big Jack. Insurance companies get really irritated when they have to pay out big-ass claims.'

'And that's where you come in.'

'I've got more of a free hand than the cops. And a bigger expense account.'

'And a bigger payoff,' she added. 'What's your take?'

'Five percent of the recovered amount.'

'So in this case, you bring back the twenty-eight-plus, you tuck away . . .' Her eyes narrowed as she did the math. 'A tidy one million, four hundred and twenty thousand in your piggy bank. Not bad.'

'I earn it. I've put a lot of hours in on this. I know Jack and Willy were in it, just like I know there was a third party.'

'Me?' She'd have laughed if she hadn't been so angry. 'So I, what, broke out my black catsuit and watch cap, bopped up to New York, stole millions in jewels, cut out my share, then came home to feed my dog?'

'No. Not that you wouldn't look hot in a catsuit. Alex Crew. The name ring any bells?'

'No.'

'Both the merchant and your father were seen with him prior to the heist. He's not small time, though this would be his biggest effort. In the interest of time, let's just say he's not a nice guy, and if he's looking at you, you're in trouble.'

'Why would he look at me?'

'Because you're Jack's daughter and Willy died minutes after talking to you. What did he tell you, Laine?'

'He didn't tell me anything. For God's sake, I was a kid the last time I saw him. I didn't recognize him until . . . I didn't know who he was when he came in. You're chasing the wrong tail, Max. Jack O'Hara wouldn't begin to know how to organize or execute a job like this – and if by some miracle he had a part in it, he'd be long gone with his share. That's more money than he'd know what to do with.'

'Then why was Willy here? What spooked him? Why were your home and business broken into? Whoever got in your house was looking for something. They were probably doing the same, or about to, when I interrupted them in the shop. You're too smart not to follow the dots.'

'If anyone's looking at me, it's probably because you led them here. I don't have anything. I haven't spoken to my father in over five years, and I haven't seen him in longer than that. I've made a nice life here, and I'm going to keep right on living it. I'm not going to let you, my father or some mythical third party screw that up.'

She got to her feet. 'I'll get you out of the cuffs, and out of this jam with Vince. In return you leave me the hell alone.'

'Laine—'

'Just shut up.' She rubbed a hand over her face, her first sign of fatigue. 'I broke my own rule and followed impulse with you. Serves me right.'

She went to the door, gave Vince a weary smile. 'I'm sorry about all this trouble. I'd like you to let Max go.'

'Because?'

'It's been a stupid misunderstanding, Vince, and largely my own fault. Max tried to convince me I needed a better security system at the store, and I argued that I didn't. We had a little tiff about it, and he broke in to prove me wrong.'

'Honey.' Vince lifted one of his big hands and patted her cheek. 'That's just bullshit.'

'I'd like you to write it up that way, if you have to write it up at all. And let him go. There's no point in charging him when he'll use his investigator's license, his rich client and their fancy lawyers to get it tossed anyway.'

'I need to know what this is about, Laine.'

95

'I know you do.' The sturdy foundation of her new life shook a bit. 'Give me a little time, will you, to sort it all through. I'm so damn tired right now, I can barely think straight.'

'All right. Whatever it is, I'm on your side.'

'I hope so.'

She walked out without another look, without another word for Max.

She wasn't going to break. She'd worked too hard, she'd come too far to break over a good-looking man with a dreamy southern accent. A charmer, Laine thought as she paced around her house.

She *knew* better than to fall for a charmer. What was her father but a charming, smooth-talking cheat?

Typical, she thought in disgust. Typical, typical and so embarrassingly predictable for her to fall for the same type. Max Gannon might do his lying and cheating on the legal side, but it was still lying and cheating.

Now everything she'd worked for was at risk. If she didn't come clean with Vince, he'd never really trust her again. Once she came clean . . . how could he trust her again?

Screwed either way, she thought.

She could pack up, move on, start over. That's what Big Jack did when things got rough. So she was damned if she'd do the same. This was her home, her place, her life. She wouldn't give it up because some nosy PI from the big city tramped over it and left her smudged.

And heartbroken, she admitted. Under the anger and anxiety, her heart was broken. She'd let herself *be* herself with him. She'd taken the big risk, and trusted him with herself.

He'd let her down. The men who mattered most to her always did.

She flopped down on the couch, which caused Henry to bump his nose against her arm in hopes of a good petting.

'Not now, Henry. Not now.'

Something in her tone had him whimpering in what sounded like sympathy before he turned a couple of circles and settled down on the floor beside her.

Lesson learned, she told herself. From now on the only man in her life was Henry. And it was time to close down the pity party and *think*.

She stared up at the ceiling.

Twenty-eight million in gems? Ridiculous, impossible, even laughable. Big, blustering Jack and sweet, harmless Willy pulling off the big score? Millions? And out of a New York landmark? No possible way. At least not if you went by history and skill and background.

But if you threw the believable out the window, you were left with the fantastic.

What if Max was right? What if the fantastic had happened, and he was right? Despite all the years between, she felt a quicksilver thrill at the possibility.

Diamonds. The sexiest of takes. Millions. The perfect number. It would have been the job of a lifetime. The mother of all jobs. If Jack had . . .

No, it still didn't play.

The affection inside her that wouldn't die for her father might let her fantasize that he'd finally, finally, hit it big. But nothing and no one would convince her Jack O'Hara had any part in a killing. A liar, a cheat, a thief with a very flexible conscience – okay, those attributes fit him like a glove. But to cause anyone physical harm? Not possible.

He'd never carried a weapon. The fact was, he was phobic about guns. She still remembered the story of how he'd done his first stretch, before she was born. He'd hit a cat while driving away from a B&E and not only stopped to check, but took the injured cat to a vet. The local cops spotted the car – stolen, of course – in the lot.

The cat recovered and lived a long, happy life. Big Jack did two to five.

No, he wouldn't have had any part in the murder of Jerome Myers.

But the con could be conned, couldn't he? Had he gotten roped into something that was bigger and badder than he'd believed?

Had someone dangled a shiny carrot and had him hopping along after it?

That she could believe.

So he'd sent Willy to tell her something, or give her something, but he'd died before he could do either.

But he'd tried to warn her. *He knows where you are now.*

Had he meant Max? Had he seen Max and panicked, ran into the street?

Hide the pooch? What the hell had he meant? Could Willy have placed some kind of dog figurine in the store? Laine tried to visualize the store after Willy's visit. She had personally arranged all the displays, and she couldn't think of a single thing out of place. And neither Jenny nor Angie had mentioned any strange items.

Maybe he'd meant 'pouch.' Maybe she'd misunderstood. You could put gems in a pouch. But he hadn't given her a pouch, and if he'd had a bag of gems hidden on him, or in his things, the authorities would have found it.

And this was all just stupid conjecture, based on the word of a man who'd lied to her.

She let out a huge breath. How could she pretend to hold honesty in such pompous hands when she was living a lie herself?

She had to tell Vince and Jenny everything. She supposed it went against her early childhood training to volunteer information to a cop, but she could overcome it. All she had to do was figure out how to tell them.

'Let's take a walk, Henry.'

The words acted like an incantation and popped the snoozing dog up as if his legs were springs. He bounced all the way to the front door. A walk would clear the cobwebs, she decided, give her time to figure out the best way to tell her friends.

She opened the front door so Henry could fly out like a cannonball. And saw Max's car parked at the end of her lane. He was behind the wheel, eyes shielded with dark glasses. But they must have been open and trained on the house as he stepped out of the car even before she'd shut the front door.

'What the hell are you doing here?'

'I said you're in trouble. Maybe I brought some of that trouble along with me, maybe it was already here. But either way, I'm keeping an eye on you, whether you like it or not.'

'I learned how to take care of myself about the same time I learned how to run a three-card-monte scam. So the only watchdog I need is Henry.'

As Henry was currently trying to climb a tree in pursuit of a squirrel, Max merely gave the dog a baleful stare. 'I'm sticking.'

'If you think you're going to collect your five percent by staking out my house, you're going to be disappointed.'

'I don't think you had anything to do with it. I did,' he added when she sneered and turned away to walk. 'When I first made you, I figured you had to have some piece of it. I did some checking on you, and things didn't add up right on either side, but I stopped looking at you for the job.'

'Thanks so very much. If that's so, why were you breaking into my shop?'

'My client wants facts, not feelings, though they give me a nice retainer largely based on my instinct track record. I've been through your house with you,' he said when her head turned sharply. 'A woman's hiding any portion of damn near thirty million in diamonds on the premises, she doesn't let some guy help her sweep her floors and take out the trash. Next step was to take a look around the shop, verify there was nothing there that linked you.'

'Missed a step, Max. I believe it has to do with a lot of naked bouncing on your hotel room bed.'

'Okay, let's run this. You see a halo?' He pointed a finger at the top of his head.

She felt a little bubble that might have been humor in her throat and ruthlessly swallowed it. 'No,' she said after a narrow-eyed stare. 'But wait . . . are those little horns?'

'Okay, give me a flat yes or no. A guy opens his hotel room door to an incredible-looking woman, a woman he's got all kinds of feelings for messing around in his head – and other parts of the body. The woman indicates – no, let's get it right – the woman states without qualification that she'd enjoy an evening of intimate physical contact. Does said guy close the door in her face?'

She stopped by a skinny stream running briskly from the spring rains. 'No. Now you give me one. Does a woman, upon learning that the guy she had this intimate physical contact with set her up, and lied about his purpose and his interest, then have the right to kick his lying ass black and blue?'

'Yeah, she does.' He took off the sunglasses, hooked one arm of them in the front pocket of his jeans. They both recognized the gesture for what it was.

Look at me. You have to see what I'm saying as much as hear it. Because it matters.

'She does, Laine, even when that interest twisted around, changed into something he'd never dealt with before and bit him on that ass. I think I fell in love with you last night.'

'That's a hell of a thing to say to me.'

'It's a hell of a thing to hear myself say to you. But I'm saying it. Actually, I think I tripped somewhere between hauling out your trash and vacuuming your sitting room, then I swung my arms around, working on my balance, and fell flat between rounds of intimate physical contact.'

'And I should believe that because?'

'You shouldn't. You should kick my ass, dust your hands off and walk away. I'm hoping you won't.'

'You've got a knack for saying the right thing at the right time. That's a damn handy skill – and suspect to me.' She turned away a moment, rubbed her arms warm.

'When it comes to the job I'll say whatever I need to say to get it done. This isn't about the job. I hurt you, and I'm sorry, but that was the job. I don't see how I could've played it any different.'

She let out a half laugh. 'No, I don't suppose so.'

'I'm in love with you. Hit me like a damn brick upside the head, and I still can't see straight. I don't know how I could've played that any different either, but it gives you all the cards, Laine. You can finish the hand, or toss it in and walk away.'

Up to her, she thought. Isn't that what she wanted? To make her

100

own choices, take her own chances. But what he hadn't said, and they were both smart enough to know it, was that holding all the cards didn't mean you wouldn't lose your shirt.

Tavish would cut her losses and fold. But O'Hara, she'd want the chance to scoop up that big, juicy pot.

'I spent the first part of my life adoring a man who couldn't spit out the truth if it was dancing the tango on his tongue. Jack O'Hara.'

She blew out a breath. 'He's just no damn good, but, Jesus, he makes you believe there's a pot of gold at the end of the rainbow. He makes you believe it because *he* believes it.'

She dropped her hands, turned to face Max. 'I spent the next part with a woman who was trying to get over him. Trying more for me than herself, which it took me a while to figure out. She finally succeeded. The next part I spent with a very decent man I love very much standing in as my father. A good, decent, loving man who will never give the same shine to my heart as that born liar can. I don't know what that makes me. But I've spent the last part of my life trying to be responsible and ordinary and comfortable. I've done a good job of it. You've messed that up for me, Max.'

'I know it.'

'If you lie to me again, I won't bother to kick your ass. I'll just dust my hands and walk away.'

'Fair enough.'

'I don't have the diamonds you're after, and I don't know anything about them. I don't know where my father is, how to contact him or why Willy came to see me.'

'Okay.'

'But if I figure it out, if what I figure leads you to that five percent, I get half.'

He stared at her a minute, then his grin moved slowly over his face. 'Yeah, pretty damn sure I fell for you.'

'We'll see about that. You can come in. I need to call Vince and Jenny, ask them to come out so I can confess my sins. Then we'll see if I still have friends, and a place in this town.'

Chapter Eight

She worried over it. Not just what to say, how to say it, but *where* to say it. Laine started to set up in the kitchen with coffee and the coffee cake she had in the freezer. But that was too informal, she decided, and too friendly when friendship was at stake.

Vince was a cop, she reminded herself. And Jenny a cop's wife. However tight they'd become over the past few years, the bonds of that relationship could unravel when she told them about her past. When she told them she'd lied to them right from the start.

The living room was better – and hold the coffee cake.

While she agonized if that was the proper setting, she got out her little hand vac and started on the sofa.

'Laine, what the hell are you doing?'

'Planting apple trees. What does it look like I'm doing? I'm getting the dog hair off the furniture.'

'Okay.'

He stuck his hands in his pockets, pulled them out, dragged them through his hair as she vacuumed, plumped pillows she'd restuffed, fussed with the angle of the chenille throw.

'You're making me nervous.'

'Well, excuse me.' She stepped back, inspected the results. Though she'd shoved most of the stuffing back in the cushions, arranged them damaged side down, the sofa still looked sad and pitiful. 'I have the chief of police and my closest friend coming by so I can tell them basically everything they think they know about me is a big, juicy lie; I've had two break-ins in the same number of days; my father's suspected of taking part in a twenty-eight-million-dollar burglary, with murder on the side and my couch looks like it was attacked by rabid ferrets. But I'm really sorry I'm making you nervous.'

'You forgot the part where you had a sexual marathon with the investigator assigned to the case.'

She tapped the vacuum against her palm. 'Is that supposed to be funny? Is that supposed to be some warped attempt to amuse me?'

'Pretty much. Don't hit me with that thing, Laine. I've already got a mild concussion. Probably. And relax. Changing your name and editing your background isn't a criminal offense.'

'That's not the point. I lied to them every day. Do you know why so many scams work? Because after the marks realize they've been taken, they're too embarrassed to do anything about it. Someone's made a fool out of them, and that's just as tough a hit as losing money. More, a lot of the time.'

He took the hand vac and set it on the table, so he could touch her. So he could cup his hands on her shoulders, slide them up until his thumbs brushed her cheeks.

'You weren't looking to make fools out of them, and they're not your friends because of your all-American-girl background.'

'I could run a bait and switch by the time I was seven. Some all-American girl. I should change.' She looked down at the sweats she'd pulled on when the deputy had come by the house to wake her. 'Should I change?'

'No.' Now he laid his hands on her shoulders, rubbing until she lifted her head and met his eyes. 'You should stay just the way you are.'

'What do you think you're falling for, Max? The small-town shopkeeper, the reformed grifter, the damsel in distress? Which one of those trips up a guy like you?'

'I think it's the sharp redhead who knows how to handle herself, and gives in to the occasional impulse.' He lowered his head to press his lips to her forehead. He felt her breath hitch, a sob that threatened and was controlled. 'There are a lot of sides to her. She loves her dog, worries about her friends, she's a little anal on the

103

organization front, and I've heard she cooks. She's practical, efficient and tough-minded – and she's amazing in bed.'

'Those are a lot of opinions on short acquaintance.'

'I'm a quick study. My mama always said, "Max, when you meet the woman, you'll go down like you've been poleaxed."'

A smile twitched at her lips. 'What the hell does that mean?'

'Hell if I know, but Marlene's never wrong. I met the woman.'

He drew her in, and she let herself take the warmth and comfort of him, the sturdiness of being held against a strong man. Then she made herself pull away.

She didn't know if love meant leaning on someone else, but in her experience, that sort of indulgence often sent the leaner and the leanee down to the mat.

'I can't think about it. I can't think about it, or what I feel about it. I just need to take the next step and see where I land.'

'That's okay.'

She heard Henry's crazed barking, and a moment later the sound of tires crushing gravel. There was a quick dip in her belly, but she kept her shoulders straight. 'They're here.' She shook her head before Max could speak. 'No, I have to gear up. I have to handle this.'

She walked to the door, opened it and watched Jenny play with Henry.

Jenny looked over. 'Must be true love,' she called out, then started toward the house. 'Getting me out of bed and over here before eight in the morning must be a sign of true friendship.'

'I'm sorry it's so early.'

'Just tell me you have food.'

'I . . . I have a coffee cake, but—'

'Sounds great. What are you having?' She gave her big, barking laugh, then shut it down when she saw Max. 'I don't know what I think about you being here. If you're some big-city detective, why didn't you say so?'

'Jenny.' Laine laid a hand on her friend's arm. 'It's complicated. Why don't you and Vince go in the living room and sit down?'

'Why don't we just sit in the kitchen? It's closer to the food.' And rubbing circles on her belly, Jenny started back.

'Okay then.' Laine took a deep breath, closed the door behind Vince. 'Okay.'

She followed them back. 'This might be a little confusing,' she began, talking as she set out the pot of herbal tea she'd made for Jenny. 'I want to apologize first off. Just say I'm sorry, right off the bat.'

She poured coffee, cut slices of cake. 'I haven't been honest with you, with anyone.'

'Sweetie.' Jenny stepped over to where Laine stood meticulously arranging the cake on a garnet glass dessert plate. 'Are you in trouble?'

'I guess I am.'

'Then we'll fix it. Right, Vince?'

Vince was watching Laine. 'Why don't you sit down, Jen. Let her say what she needs to.'

'We'll fix it,' Jenny said again, but she sat, bored through Max with a steely stare. 'Is this your fault?'

'It's not,' Laine said quickly. 'It's really not. My name's not Laine Tavish. It is . . . I changed it, legally, and I've used it since I was eighteen, but it's not the name I was born with. That's Elaine O'Hara. My father's name is Jack O'Hara, and if Vince was to do a background check on him, he'd find my father has a long and varied sheet. It's mostly theft, and cons. Scams.'

Jenny's eyes went round and wide. 'He doesn't run a barbecue place in New Mexico?'

'Rob Tavish, my stepfather, does. My father got popped—' Laine cut herself off, sighed. How quickly it comes back. 'Jack was arrested and sent to prison for a real-estate scam when I was eleven. It wasn't the first time he'd been caught, but this time my mother had had enough. She was, I realized later, worried for me. I just worshiped my father, and I was doing considerably well, considering my age, at following in his footsteps.'

'You ran con games?'

There was as much fascination as shock in Jenny's tone, and it made Laine smile a little. 'Mostly I was just the beard, but yes, I did. Picking pockets was turning into my specialty. I had good hands, and people don't look at a little girl when they realize their wallet's been lifted.'

'Holy cow,' was all Jenny could say.

'I liked it. It was exciting, and it was easy. My father . . . well, he made it such a *game*. It never occurred to me that when I took some man's wallet, he might not be able to pay the rent that month. Or when we bilked some couple out of a few thousand in a bogus real-estate deal, that might've been their life savings, or a college fund. It was fun, and they were marks.'

'And you were ten,' Max added. 'Give the kid a break.'

'You could say that's what happened. I got a break. The direction I was heading in convinced my mother to change her life, and mine. She divorced my father and moved away, changed her name, got a straight job waiting tables. We moved around a lot the first few years. Not to shake my father loose – she wouldn't have done that to him. She let him know where we were, as long as he kept his word and didn't try to pull me back into the game. He kept his word. I don't know which of the three of us was more surprised by that, but he kept his word. We moved around to keep the cops from rousting us every time . . .'

She trailed off, managed a sickly smile in Vince's direction. 'Sorry, but when you've got a rep for scams and theft, even by association, the locals tend to look you over. She wanted a fresh start, that's all. And a clean slate for me. It wasn't easy for her. She loved Jack, too. And I didn't help. I liked the game and didn't appreciate having it called, or being separated from my father.'

She topped off cups of coffee, though she'd yet to touch her own. 'But she worked so hard, and I started to see something in her, the pride and the satisfaction she got from earning her way. The straight way. And after a while, we weren't moving every time we turned around anymore. We weren't packing up in the middle of the night and slipping out of apartments or hotel rooms. And she kept her promises. Big Jack was long on the promises

106

but came up short on keeping them. When my mother said she was going to do something, she did it.'

No one spoke when she went to the refrigerator and took out a pitcher of water with lemon slices. She poured a glass, drank to wet her dry throat.

'Anyway, things changed. She met Rob Tavish, and things changed again, for the better. He's a wonderful man, crazy about her, and he was good to me. Sweet and kind and fun. I took his name. I made myself Laine Tavish because Laine Tavish was normal and responsible. She could have a place of her own, and a business of her own, and a life of her own. Maybe it wouldn't have all those wild ups she'd ridden on during the first part of her life, but it wouldn't have all those scary downs, either. That seemed just fine. So anytime you asked me about my background, or growing up, I fabricated whatever seemed to fit Laine Tavish. I'm sorry. That's all. I'm sorry.'

There was a long moment of silence. 'Okay, wow.' Jenny goggled at Laine. 'I'm going to have a lot of follow-up comments and questions after my head stops spinning, but the first thing I have to ask is how all this – and there's a lot of this – applies to you being in trouble.'

'There's probably a quote somewhere about not being able to escape the past, or cover it over. William Young.' She saw Vince nod slowly and knew he was putting some of it together.

'The man who was killed when he ran out into the street,' Jenny prompted.

'Yes. He used to run with my father. They were close as brothers, and hell, he lived with us half the time. I called him Uncle Willy. I didn't recognize him when he came in. I swear that, Vince. It's been years since I've seen him, and it just didn't click. It wasn't until after the accident and he . . . God, he was dying.'

She drank more water, but this time her hand trembled lightly. 'He looked so sad when I didn't recognize him, when I basically brushed him off. Then he was lying there, bleeding. Dying. He sang part of this stupid song he and my father used to do as a duet. "Bye Bye Blackbird." Something they'd start singing when we

107

were loading up to skip out of a hotel. I realized who he was, and it was too late. I didn't tell you, and that's probably some sort of offense, but I didn't tell you I knew him.'

'Why did he come to see you?'

'He didn't get much of a chance to tell me. I didn't give him much of a chance,' she corrected.

'It's a waste of time to beat yourself up over that.' Max said it briskly, and had her swallowing tears.

'Maybe. Looking back, I know he was nervous, edgy, tired. He gave me his card – just as I told you – with a phone number written on it. I really thought he was in the market to sell something. After, I realized he wanted to talk to me about something.'

She stared into her empty glass, set it aside. 'I think my father must've sent him. One of Willy's best skills was blending. He was a small, nondescript sort of man. Jack's big and redheaded and stands out, so I think Jack sent him to tell me something or give me something. But he didn't have a chance to do either. He only said . . . he said, "He knows where you are now," and for me to hide the pouch. I think he said "pouch," it's the only thing that makes sense. Except it sounded like "pooch," but that's just silly.'

'What?' Max snapped the word like a whip. 'You're just getting around to telling me?'

In contrast, Laine's voice was mild as milk. 'That's right, and I really don't believe you're in any position to criticize timing. Insurance, my ass.'

'It *is* insurance, goddamnit. Where's the pouch? What did you do with it?'

Heat flamed into her cheeks, not from embarrassment but temper. 'He didn't give me a pouch, or anything else. I don't have your stupid diamonds. He was delirious, he was *dying*.' Despite all her determination, her eyes filled and her voice broke. 'He was dying right in front of me, and it was too late.'

'Leave her alone.' A mama bear protecting her cub, Jenny rounded on Max before she shifted to wrap her arms around Laine. 'You just leave her alone.'

While Vince patted Laine's shoulder in a show of support, his gaze was keen on Max's face. 'What diamonds?'

'The twenty-eight point four million in diamonds stolen from the International Jewelry Exchange in New York six weeks ago. The diamonds my client, Reliance, insured and would very much like to recover. The diamonds my investigation has led me to believe were stolen by Jack O'Hara, William Young and a third party I believe is one Alex Crew.'

'Holy shit,' Jenny whispered.

'I don't know anything about them,' Laine said wearily. 'I don't have them, I've never seen them, I don't know where they are. I'll take a polygraph.'

'But somebody thinks you have them, or access to them.'

Grateful for the support, Laine rested her head on Jenny's shoulder and nodded at Vince. 'Apparently. You can search the house, Vince. You and Max. You can search the shop. I'll authorize you full access to my phone records, bank records, anything you want. I'm only asking you to keep it quiet so I can just live my life.'

'Do you know where your father is?'

'I don't have a clue.'

'What do you know about this Alex Crew?'

'I've never heard of him. I'm still having a hard time believing Jack O'Hara was part of anything with this scope. He was loose change compared to this.'

'If you had to get ahold of your father, what would you do?'

'It's never come up.' Because they stung and burned, she rubbed her eyes. 'I honestly don't know. He's contacted me a few times over the years. Right after I graduated from college, I got a FedEx letter. Inside was a first-class ticket to Barbados, and vouchers for a week's stay at a suite in a luxury hotel. I knew it was from him, and almost didn't go. But hey, Barbados. He met me there. We had a great time. It's impossible not to have a great time with Jack. He was proud of me – the whole college graduate thing. He never held any hard feelings toward my mother or me for stepping out of his life. He popped up a couple more times. The last was before I moved here, when I was living in Philadelphia.'

'The New York business isn't mine,' Vince said. 'But your break-ins are – and William Young is.'

'He'd never hurt Willy, if that's what you're thinking. Not over ten times as much money. And he'd never come into my home and tear it up this way. He wouldn't do that to me. To anyone, for that matter. He loves me, in his way, he loves me. And it's just not his style.'

'What do you know about this Crew?' Vince asked Max.

'Enough to say Jack and Willy fell in with bad companions. The inside man on the New York job was a gem merchant. He was shot, execution style. His body was found in his burned-out car in New Jersey.'

His gaze flicked to Laine. 'We can link O'Hara to Myers, the gem merchant. But neither O'Hara's nor Young's history runs to violent crimes, or any sort of armed offense. Can't say the same for Crew – though he's never been convicted of murder, he's suspected of a few. He's smooth, and smart. Smart enough to know these stones are hot, hot enough to wait until they've cooled off some before trying to liquidate them or transport them out of the country. It could be somebody got greedy or impatient.'

'If this is Alex Crew, and he's trying to get to the stones or my father through me, he's doomed to disappointment.'

'That doesn't mean he's going to stop trying,' Max pointed out. 'If so, he's been in the area, and may still be in the area. He copped my wallet, so he knows who I am and why I'm here.' Absently, Max fingered the bandage on his temple. 'He'll have to think about that for a while. I've got copies of photographs. He likes to play with faces, change his looks, but if he's been around town, maybe one of you will recognize him.'

'I'll want copies for my men,' Vince put in. 'Cooperating with the New York authorities on a suspect believed to be in the vicinity. I'll keep Laine out of it as long as I can.'

'Good enough.'

'Thanks, Vince. Thank you.' Laine lifted her hands, let them fall.

'Did you think we were going to be mad at you?' Jenny asked her. 'Did you think this was going to affect our friendship?'

'Yes, I did.'

'That's a little bit insulting, but I'm cutting you a break because you look really tired. What about him?' She jerked her chin up toward Max. 'Are you forgiving him?'

'I guess I have to, considering the circumstances.'

'All right, I'll forgive him, too. God, I just realized, I've been too preoccupied with all this to eat. Just let me make up for that.' She took a slice of cake, bit in, then spoke around it. 'I think you should come stay with Vince and me until this is all cleared up.'

'I love you, Jenny.' Because she felt the tears threaten again, she rose so she could turn her back and get them under control under the guise of getting more coffee. 'And I appreciate the offer, but I need to be here, and I'll be fine. Max will be staying with me.'

She turned back just in time to see the surprise wing over his face. She only smiled as she brought the pot over to top off cups. 'Isn't that right, Max?'

'Yeah. Sure. I'll look out for her,' he told Jenny.

'Since you're the one with the mild concussion, why don't we just leave it that you'll be staying here. I need to go up and change for work. I have to open the shop.'

'What you need to do,' Jenny disagreed, 'is go upstairs and crawl into bed for a few hours. You can keep the shop closed one day.'

'I think the cops – public and private – would both say I need to keep it business as usual.'

'You do that. We'll be keeping a close eye on the shop and your house until we run this all down. I want those pictures,' Vince said to Max.

'I'll bring them by.'

Laine walked them to the door.

'I'm going to have tons of questions. We need to have a girls' night,' Jenny decided, 'so I can pump you. Did you ever do that shell thing? You know, the switcheroo?'

'Jenny.' Vince cast his eyes at the sky.

'Well, I want to *know,* for God's sake. Tell me later. How about the one with the three cards?' she called out as Vince pulled her toward the car. 'Later, but I want specific details.'

'She's something.' Max watched Vince load his wife into the car.

'Yeah, she's something else again. She's the luckiest thing that ever happened to me.' She waited until the car was out of sight before she closed the door. 'Well, that went better than I deserved.'

'You're doing better at forgiving me than you are at forgiving yourself.'

'You were doing a job. I respect the work ethic.' She gave a little shrug, turned toward the stairs. 'I need to pull myself together and get into town.'

'Laine? I figured we were going to go a few rounds when I told you I was going to stay out here. Instead, you tell me I'm staying out here. Why is that?'

She leaned against the railing. 'There are a few reasons. First, I'm not a sniveling coward, but I'm not brainless and brave. I have no intention of staying out here alone, so far from town, when someone who wishes me no good may come back. I'm not risking myself or my dog over someone else's rocks.'

'Sensible.'

'So, I get me a big-city PI who I assume, despite current evidence, can handle himself.'

He scowled at that and shifted his feet. 'I can handle myself just fine.'

'Good to know. Next, since I have a stake in seeing these gems are recovered, I prefer you at hand so I know exactly what you're doing about it. I can use seven hundred thousand dollars, just like the next guy.'

'Practical.'

'Last, I liked the sex and don't see why I should deprive myself of more of it. Easier to get you into bed if you're staying here.'

Since he didn't seem to be able to come up with a term for that one, she smiled. 'I'm going up to shower.'

'Okay,' he managed after she'd strolled upstairs. 'That explains that.'

*

Thirty minutes later, she came back down looking fresh as the spring morning in a short green jacket and pants. Her hair was scooped back at the temples with silver combs and left to fall straight toward her shoulders in that bright flood.

She walked up to Max and handed him a brass key ring. 'Front and back doors,' she told him. 'If and when you get home before me, I'd appreciate you letting Henry out, giving him some play time.'

'No problem.'

'If and when I cook, you do the dishes.'

'Deal.'

'I like a tidy house and have no intention of picking up after you.'

'I was raised right. Thank Marlene.'

'That should do it for now. I've got to go.'

'Hold it, those are your rules. Now here are mine: Take this number.' He pressed a card into her hand. 'That's my cell. You call me when you leave for home. If you're not coming straight home for any reason, you let me know that, too.'

'All right.' She slipped the card into her pocket.

'You call that number if anything happens, anything that bothers you. I don't care how minor it seems, I want to hear about it.'

'So, if I get one of those calls from a telemarketer, I let you know.'

'I'm serious, Laine.'

'All right, all right. Anything else? I'm running very late.'

'If you hear from your father, you tell me. You tell me, Laine,' he repeated when he saw her face. 'Divided loyalties aren't going to do him any good.'

'I won't help you put him in prison. I won't do that, Max.'

'I'm not a cop. I don't put people in prison. All I want is to recover the gems, collect my fee. And keep us all healthy while I'm at it.'

'You promise me you won't turn him in, no matter what, and I'll promise to tell you if I hear from him.'

'Done.' He held out a hand, shook hers. Then gave it a yank so she'd tumble into his arms. 'Now kiss me goodbye.'

113

'All right.'

She took a good grip on his hips, rose on her toes and met his mouth with hers. She took it slow, rocking into him, changing the angle to tease, using her teeth to challenge. She felt his hands tunnel through her hair, fingers tangling. When the heat rose inside her, when she felt it pumping off him, she slid her hands around, gave his butt a squeeze.

Her own pulse was tripping, but she enjoyed the sensation of being in control and turned her head so her lips were close to his ear.

'That oughta hold me,' she whispered, then drew away.

'Now I'll kiss you goodbye.'

She laughed and slapped a hand on his chest. 'I don't think so. Mark your place, then you can kiss me hello. I should be home by seven.'

'I'll be here.'

He went out with her, followed her into town and peeled off to go to his hotel.

He stopped by the desk to ask the clerk to make up his bill for checkout.

She scanned his face. 'Oh, Mr. Gannon, are you all right? Were you in an accident?'

'It was pretty much on purpose, but I'm fine, thanks. I'll be back down in a few minutes.'

He got in the elevator. He'd already decided to work on his notes and reports once he'd set up at Laine's. Might as well make himself comfortable. A man who traveled as often as he did knew how to pack quickly and with the least amount of fuss. He swung the strap of his garment bag over one shoulder, the strap of his laptop case over the other, and was walking out of the room fifteen minutes after he'd walked in.

Back at the desk, he glanced over his bill, signed the credit slip.

'I hope you enjoyed your stay.'

'I did.' He made a note of her name tag. 'One thing before I head out, Marti.' Bending, he pulled a file out of his laptop case, flipped through for the photos of Jack O'Hara, William Young and

114

Alex Crew. He laid them faceup on the desk. 'Have you seen any of these men?'

'Oh.' She blinked at him. 'Why?'

'Because I'm looking for them.' To this he added a thousand-watt smile. 'How about it?'

'Oh,' she repeated, but this time she looked down at the photos. 'I don't think so. Sorry.'

'That's okay. Anybody in the back? Maybe they could come out for a minute, take a look?'

'Sure, I guess. Mike's here. If you'll just wait a minute.'

He ran the same routine with the second clerk, minus the flirtatious smile, and garnered the same results.

After stowing his bags in the trunk of his car, he made the rounds. First stop, he took the photos to Vince, waited while copies were made. Then he hit the other hotels, motels, B and B's within a ten-mile radius.

Three hours later, the most tangible thing he had to show for his efforts was a raging headache. He popped four extra-strength ibuprofen like candy, then got a take-out sandwich at a sub shop.

Back at Laine's he generously split the cold cut sub with a grateful Henry and hoped that would be their little secret. With the headache down to an ugly throb he decided to spend the rest of the day unpacking, setting up some sort of work space and reviewing his notes.

He spent about ten seconds debating where to put his clothes. The lady had said she wanted him in bed, so it was only fair his clothes be handy.

He opened her closet, poked through the clothes. Imagined her in some of them, imagined her out of all of them. He noted that she apparently shared his mother's odd devotion to shoes.

After another short debate, he concluded that he was entitled to reasonable drawer space. Because rearranging her underwear made him feel like a pervert, he made a stack of his own in a drawer with a colorful army of neatly folded sweaters and shirts.

With Henry clipping after him, he surveyed Laine's home office, then her sitting room, then the guest room. The fancy little writing desk in the guest room wouldn't have been his first choice, but it was the best space available.

He set up. He typed up his notes, a progress report, read them both over and did some editing. He checked his e-mail, his voice mail, and answered what needed answering.

Then he sat at the pretty little desk, stared up at the ceiling and let theories ramble through his mind.

He knows where you are now.

So, who was he? Her father. If Willy knew where Laine was, odds were so did Big Jack. But from what Laine had said, Jack had kept tabs on her off and on all along. So the phrase didn't work. He knows where you are *now*. The arrow in Max's mind pointed to Alex Crew.

There was no violence in O'Hara's history, but there was in Crew's. O'Hara didn't look good for the two taps to the back of the diamond merchant's head. And no reason, going by that history, for Willy to run scared of his old pal Jack O'Hara.

More likely, much more likely, he'd run from the third man, the man Max was convinced was Alex Crew. And following that, Crew was in the Gap.

But that didn't tell Max where Willy had put the stones.

He'd wanted to get them to Laine. Why in the hell would Willy, or her father, want to put Laine in front of a man like Crew?

He batted it around in his head, getting nowhere. Uncomfortable in the desk chair, he moved to stretch out on the bed. He closed his eyes, told himself a nap would refresh his brain.

And dropped into sleep like a stone.

Chapter Nine

It was his turn to wake with a blanket tucked around him. As was his habit, he came out of sleep the same way he went into it. Fast and complete.

He checked his watch and winced when he saw he'd been under for a solid two hours. But it was still shy of seven, and he'd expected to be up and around before Laine got back.

He rolled out of bed, popped a couple more pills for the lingering headache, then headed down to find her.

He was several paces from the kitchen when the scent reached out, hooked seductive fingers in his senses and drew him the rest of the way.

And wasn't she the prettiest damn thing, he thought, standing there in her neat shirt and pants with a dishcloth hooked in the waistband while she stirred something that simmered in a pan on the stove. She was using a long-handled wooden spoon, keeping rhythm with it, and her hips, to the tune that bounced out of a mini CD player on the counter.

He recognized Marshall Tucker and figured they'd mesh well enough in the music area.

The dog was sprawled on the floor, gnawing at a hank of rope that had seen considerable action already from the look of it. There were cheerful yellow daffodils in a speckled blue vase on the table. An array of fresh vegetables were grouped beside a butcher-block cutting board on the counter.

He'd never been much on homey scenes – or so he'd believed. But this one hit him right in the center. A man, he decided, could walk into this for the next forty or fifty years and feel just fine about it.

Henry gave two thumps of his tail then rose to prance over and knock the mangled rope against Max's thigh.

Tapping the spoon on the side of the pot, Laine turned and looked at him. 'Have a nice nap?'

'I did, but waking up's even better.' To placate Henry, he reached down to give the rope a tug, and found himself engaged in a spirited tug-of-war.

'Now you've done it. He can keep that up for days.'

Max wrenched the rope free, gave it a long, low toss down the hallway. Scrambling over tile then hardwood, Max set out in mad pursuit. 'You're home earlier than I expected.'

She watched him walk to her, her eyebrows raising as he maneuvered her around until her back was against the counter. He laid a hand on either side, caging her, then leaned in and went to work on her mouth.

She started to anchor her hands on his hips, but they went limp on her. Instead she went into slow dissolve, her body shimmering under the lazy assault. Her pulse went thick; her brain sputtered. By the time she managed to open her eyes, he was leaning back and grinning at her.

'Hello, Laine.'

'Hello, Max.'

Still watching her, he reached down to give the rope Henry had cheerfully returned another tug. 'Something smells really good.' He leaned down to sniff at her neck. 'Besides you.'

'I thought we'd have some chicken with fettuccine in a light cream sauce.'

He glanced toward the pot, and the creamy simmering sauce. 'You're not toying with me, are you?'

'Why, yes, I am, but not about that. There's a bottle of pinot noir chilling in the fridge. Why don't you open it, pour us a glass.'

'I can do that.' He backed up, went another round with Henry, won the rope and tossed it again. 'You're actually cooking,' he said as he retrieved the wine.

118

'I like to cook now and then. Since it's just me most of the time, I don't bother to fuss very much. This is a nice change.'

'Glad I could help.' He took the corkscrew she offered, studied the little silver pig mounted on the top. 'You do collect them.'

'Just one of those things.' She set two amber-toned wineglasses on the counter. It pleased her to see the way he switched between sommelier duties and playing with the dog. To give him a break, she squatted down to get a tin from a base cabinet.

'Henry! Want a treat!'

The dog deserted the rope instantly to go into a crazed display of leaping, trembling, barking. Max could have sworn he saw tears of desperation in the dog's eyes as Laine held up a Milk-Bone biscuit.

'Only good dogs get treats,' she said primly, and Henry plopped his butt on the floor and shuddered with the effort of control. When she gave the biscuit a toss, Henry nipped it out of the air the way a veteran right fielder snags a pop-up. He raced away with it like a thief.

'What, you lace them with coke?'

'His name is Henry, and he's a Milk-Bone addict. That'll keep him busy for five minutes.' She pulled out a skillet. 'I need to sauté the chicken.'

'Sauté the chicken.' He moaned it. 'Oh boy.'

'You really are easy.'

'That doesn't insult me.' He waited while she got a package of chicken breasts from the refrigerator and began slicing them into strips. 'Can you talk and do that?'

'I can. I'm very skilled.'

'Cool. So, how was business?'

She picked up the wine he'd set beside her, sipped. 'Do you want to know how things went today in the world of retail, or if I saw anything suspicious?'

'Both.'

'We did very well today, as it happens. I sold a very nice Sheraton sideboard, among other things. It didn't appear that anything in the shop, or my office, or the storeroom was disturbed – except for a little blood on the floor in the back room, which I assume is yours.' She drizzled oil in the skillet, then glanced at him. 'How's your head?'

'Better.'

'Good. And I saw no suspicious characters other than Mrs. Franquist, who comes in once or twice a month to crab about my prices. So how was your day?'

'Busy, until naptime.' He filled her in while she lay the chicken strips in the heated oil, then started prepping the salad.

'I guess there are a lot of days like that, where you go around asking a lot of questions and not really getting any answers.'

'A no is still an answer.'

'I suppose it is. Why does a nice boy from Savannah go to New York to be a private detective?'

'First he decides to be a cop because he likes figuring things out and making them right. At least as right as they can be made. But it's not a good fit. He doesn't play well with others.'

She smiled a little as she went back to the salad. 'Doesn't he?'

'Not so much. And all those rules, they start itching. Like a collar that's too tight. He figures out what he really likes to do is look under rocks, but he likes to pick the rocks. To do that, you've got to go private. To do that and live well . . . I like living well, by the way.'

'Naturally.' She poured some wine in with the chicken, lowered the heat, covered the pan.

'So to live well, you've got to be good at picking those rocks, and finding people who live even better than you to pay you to poke at all the nasty business going on under them.' He snitched a chunk of carrot to snack on. 'Southern boy moves north, Yankees a lot of time figure he moves slow, thinks slow, acts slow.'

She glanced up from whisking salad dressing ingredients together in a small stainless steel bowl. 'Their mistakes.'

'Yeah, and my advantage. Anyway, I got interested in computer security – cyber work. Nearly went in that direction, but you don't get out enough. So I just throw that little talent in the mix. Reliance liked my work, put me on retainer. We do pretty well by each other all in all.'

'Your talents extend to table setting?'

'A skill I learned at my mama's knee.'

'Dishes there, flatware there, napkins in that drawer.'

'Check.'

She put water on for the pasta while he went to work. After checking the chicken, adjusting the heat, she picked up her wine again. 'Max, I've thought about this a lot today.'

'Figured you would.'

'I believe you'll do right by my father for a couple of reasons. You care about me, and he's not your goal. Recovering the stones is.'

'That's a couple of them.'

'And there's another. You're a good man. Not shiny and bright,' she said when he paused to look at her. 'Which would just be irritating to someone like me, because I'd keep seeing my own reflection bounced off someone like that, and I'd always come up short. But a good man, who might bend the truth when it suits, but keeps his word when he gives it. It settles my mind on a lot of levels knowing that.'

'I won't make a promise to you that I can't keep.'

'You see, that's just the right thing to say.'

While Laine and Max ate pasta in the kitchen, Alex Crew dined on rare steak accompanied by a decent cabernet in the rustic cabin he'd rented in the state park.

He didn't care for rustic, but he did appreciate the privacy. His rooms at the Wayfarer in Angel's Gap had abruptly become too warm to suit him.

Maxfield Gannon, he mused, studying Max's investigator's license while he ate. Either a free agent out for a bounty, or a private working for the insurance company. Either way, the man was an irritant.

Killing him would have been a mistake – though he'd spent a tempting and satisfying moment considering it as he'd stood over the unconscious detective, fuming over the interruption.

121

But even a yahoo police force such as those fumbling around that pitiful little town would be riled to action by murder. Better for his purposes if they continued to bumble about giving parking tickets and rousting the local youth.

Better, he mused as he sipped his wine, and easier by far to have taken the irritant's identification, to have placed an anonymous call. It pleased him to think of this Maxfield Gannon trying to explain to the local law just what he'd been doing inside a closed store at three-thirty in the morning. It should have knotted things up nicely for a space of time. And no doubt it sent a very clear message to Jack O'Hara through his daughter.

But it was annoying just the same. He hadn't been able to take the time to search the premises, and he'd had to change his accommodations. That was very inconvenient.

He took out a small leather-bound notebook and made a list of these additional debits. When he caught up with O'Hara – and of course he would – he wanted to be able to detail all these offenses clearly while he tortured the location of the remaining diamonds out of him.

The way the list was mounting up, he was going to have to hurt O'Hara quite a bit. It was something to look forward to.

He could add O'Hara's daughter and the PI to his payment-due list as well. It was a bonus, in the grand scheme, for a man who equated inflicting pain with power.

He'd been quick and merciful with Myers, the greedy and idiotic gem buyer he'd employed as an inside man. But then Myers hadn't done anything more than be stupid enough to believe he was entitled to a quarter of the take. And greedy enough to meet him alone, in a closed construction site, in the middle of the night when promised a bigger cut.

Really, the man hadn't deserved to live if you thought about it.

In any case, he'd been a loose end that required snipping. The trail would have led to him eventually. He'd have bragged to someone, or would have thrown money around, squandering it on tasteless cars or women or God knew what that class of people considered desirable.

122

He'd blubbered and begged and sobbed like a baby when Crew held the gun to his head. Distasteful display, really, but what could one expect?

He'd also handed over the key to the mailbox locker where he'd stashed the Raggedy Andy doll with a bag of gems in its belly.

Genius, really, he had to give O'Hara credit for that little touch. Tucking millions of dollars' worth of gems into innocuous objects, objects no one would look at twice. So when the alarms went off, the building locked down, the cops swarmed, no one would consider all those pretty stones were still inside, tucked into something as innocent as a child's doll. Then it was just a matter of retrieving the extraordinary within the ordinary while the search went on else-where.

Yes, he could give Jack credit for that amusing detail, but that hardly negated all the debits.

They could hardly be trusted to hold millions of dollars' worth of gems for the year they'd agreed to. How could he possibly trust thieves to keep their word?

After all, he'd had no intention of keeping his.

Besides, he wanted it all. Had always intended to take it all. The others had merely been tools. When a tool had served its purpose, you discarded it. Better, you destroyed it.

But they'd deceived him, slipped through his fingers and taken half the prize with them. And cost him weeks of time and effort. He had to worry that they'd be caught pulling one of the pitiful scams Big Jack was so fond of, and end up confessing to the heist and losing half his property.

They should be dead now. The fact that one of them continued to live, to breathe, to walk, to hide, was a personal insult. He never tolerated insults.

His plan had been simple and clean. Myers first, execution style to make it seem as if one of his gambling debts had caught up with him. Then O'Hara and Young, bumbling idiots. They should have been where he'd *told* them to be, but they were too *stupid* to follow instructions.

If they had, he'd have contacted them as he'd planned, planted seeds of worry over Myers's demise and arranged for a meet in a quiet, secluded location not unlike the one he was dining in now.

There, he could have dealt with them both with little effort as neither had the stomach to so much as carry a weapon. He'd have left enough evidence to link them to the New York job, and set the scene to look, even to the most moronic cop, like a matter of thieves falling out.

But they'd vanished on him. Scuttled his careful planning by attempting to go underground. Over a month now, it had taken over a month to finally pick up the trail and track Willy back to New York, only to miss him by inches and be forced to spend more time, more effort, more money to chase him to Maryland.

Then lose him to a traffic accident.

Shaking his head, Crew cut another bite of bloody steak. He'd never be able to collect directly from Willy now, so that account would be transferred to Big Jack – and the rest.

How to do it was the question, and the possibilities entertained him through the rest of his meal.

Did he go after the girl directly at this point, sweat her father's location and the whereabouts of the gems out of her? But if Willy had died before giving her any salient information, that would be a wasted effort.

Then there was this Maxfield Gannon to factor in. It might be wise to do a bit of research there, find out just what sort of man he was. One amenable to a bribe, perhaps? Obviously, he knew something about the girl or he wouldn't have been sneaking into her shop.

Or, and the thought struck him like an arrow in the heart, she had already cut a deal with Gannon. And that would be too bad, he thought slapping his fist on the table again and again. That would be too bad for all involved.

He wasn't going to settle for half. It was not acceptable. Therefore, he would find a way to get back the rest of his property.

The girl was the key. What she knew or didn't know was undetermined. But there was one simple fact: She was Jack's daughter, and the apple of his larcenous eye.

She was bait.

Considering this, he leaned back, tidily dabbed his mouth with his napkin. Really, the food was better here than one might think, and the quiet was soothing.

Quiet. Private. A nice little woodland getaway. He began to smile as he indulged himself in another glass of wine. Quiet and private, with no neighbors nearby to disturb if one was to have a discussion with . . . associates. A discussion that might become a bit heated.

He looked around the cabin, at the country dark pressing against the windows.

It might do very well, he thought. It might do very well indeed.

It was very odd waking up with a man in your bed. A man took up considerable room, for one thing, and she wasn't used to worrying about how she looked the minute she opened her eyes in the morning.

She supposed she'd get over the last part, if she continued to wake up with this man in her bed for any length of time. And she could always get a bigger bed to compensate for the first part.

The question was, how did she feel about sharing her bed – and wasn't that just a metaphor for her life? – with this man for any length of time? She hadn't had time to think it through, hadn't taken time, she corrected.

Closing her eyes, she tried to imagine it was a month later. Her garden would be exploding, and she'd be thinking about summer clothes, about getting her outdoor furniture from the shed. Henry would be due for his annual vet appointment.

She'd be planning Jenny's baby shower.

Laine opened one eye, squinted at Max.

He was still there. His face was squashed into the pillow, his hair all cute and tousled.

So, she felt pretty good about having him there a month from now.

Try six months. She closed her eyes again and projected.

Coming up on Thanksgiving. In her usual organized fashion – she didn't care *what* Jenny said, it wasn't obsessive or disgusting – she'd have her Christmas shopping finished. She'd be planning holiday parties, and how she'd decorate the shop and the house.

She'd order a cord of wood and enjoy lighting a fire every evening. She'd stock a few bottles of good champagne so she and Max could . . .

Uh-oh, there he was.

She opened both eyes now and studied him. Yeah, there he was. Popping right up in her little projections, lying right there beside her sleeping while Henry, her pre-alarm clock, was beginning to stir.

She had a feeling if she added six months to that projection and made it a year, he was still going to be there.

He opened his eyes, a quick flash of that tawny brown, and had her yelping in surprise.

'I could hear you staring.'

'I wasn't. I was thinking.'

'I could hear that, too.'

His arm shot out, hooked around her. She had a foolish little thrill tremble in her belly at the easy strength of him when he pulled her over and under him.

'I need to let Henry out.'

'He can wait a minute.' His mouth took hers so that thrill twisted into a throb.

'We're creatures of habit.' Her breath caught. 'Henry and me.'

'Creatures of habit should always be in the market to develop another habit.' He nuzzled her neck where her pulse pounded. 'You're all warm and soft in the morning.'

'Getting warmer and softer by the minute.'

His lips curved against her skin, then he lifted his head to look into her eyes. 'Let's see about that.'

He scooped his hands under her hips, lifted them. And slid inside her. Those bright blue eyes blurred.

126

'Oh yeah.' He watched her, watched her in the pale morning sunlight as he stroked. 'You're absolutely right.'

Henry whined and plopped his front paws on the side of the bed. He cocked his head as if trying to figure out why the two humans were still in there with their eyes closed when it was past time to let him out.

He barked once. A definite question mark.

'Okay, Henry, just a minute.'

Max trailed his fingertips over Laine's arm. 'Want me to do it?'

'You already did it. And thanks.'

'Ha ha. Do you want me to let the dog out?'

'No, we have our little routine.'

She got out of bed, which had Henry racing to the bedroom doorway, racing back, dancing in place while she got her robe out of the closet.

'Does the routine include coffee?' Max asked her.

'There is no routine without coffee.'

'Praise God. I'm going to grab a shower, then I'll be down.'

'Take your time. Are you sure you want to go out, Henry? Are you absolutely, positively sure?'

From the tone, and the dog's manic reaction, Max imagined the byplay was part of the morning ritual. He liked hearing the dog gallop up and down the steps, while Laine's laugh rolled.

He grinned all the way into the shower.

Downstairs, with Henry bouncing on all four legs, Laine unlocked the mudroom door. Per routine, she unlocked the outside door so Henry could fly through rather than wiggle through his doggie door, and so she could take a deep breath of morning air.

She admired her spring bulbs, bent down to sniff the hyacinths she'd planted in purples and pinks. Arms crossed, she stood and watched Henry make his morning circuit, lifting his leg on every tree in the near backyard. Eventually, he'd take a run into the woods, she knew, to see if he could scare up a few squirrels, flush some deer. But that little adventure would wait until he'd scrupulously marked his perimeter.

127

She listened to the birds chirp, and the bubble of her busy little stream. She was still warm from Max, still warm for him, and wondered how anyone could have a single worry on such a perfect and peaceful morning.

She stepped back in, closed the outside door. And was starting to hum when she walked back into the kitchen.

He stepped from behind the door and shot her heart into her throat. She was opening her mouth to scream when he laid a warning finger to his lips and had the sound sliding away.

Chapter Ten

It knocked the breath out of her so she stumbled back a step, hit the wall while her hand groped at her throat as if to decide whether to push the scream out or block it.

While he stood grinning at her, his finger still tapping on his lips, she sucked in a wheeze of breath and let it out with a single explosive whisper.

'Dad!'

'Surprise, Lainie.' He whipped his hand from behind his back and held out a drooping clutch of spring violets. 'How's my sweet baby girl?'

'Poleaxed' was a word Max had used. She now understood it perfectly. 'What are you *doing* here? How did you—' She stopped herself before asking him how he'd gotten in. Ridiculous question seeing as lifting locks was one of his favorite pastimes. 'Oh, Dad, what have you done?'

'Now, is that any way to greet your dear old dad after all this time?' He opened his arms wide. 'Don't I get a hug?'

There was a twinkle in his eyes, eyes as blue as her own. His hair – his pride and joy – was stoplight red and combed into a luxurious mane around his wide, cheerful face. Freckles sprinkled over his nose and cheeks like ginger shaken on cream.

He wore a buffalo check flannel shirt in black and red, and jeans, both of which she imagined he'd selected as a nod to the area, and both of which appeared to have been slept in. The boots he'd paired with them looked painfully new.

He cocked his head and gave her a dreamy, puppy-dog smile.

Her heart had no defense against it. She leaped into his arms, locking herself around him as he squeezed tight and spun into a few giddy circles.

'That's my girl. That's my baby. My Princess Lainie of Haraland.'

With her feet still a foot off the floor, she rested her head on his shoulder. 'I'm not six anymore, Dad. Or eight, or ten.'

'Still my girl, aren't you?'

He smelled like cinnamon sticks and had the build of a Yukon grizzly. 'Yes, I guess I still am.' She eased back, giving his shoulders a little nudge so he'd set her down. 'How did you get here?'

'Trains, planes and automobiles. With the last of it on my own two feet. It's a place you've got here, sweetie pie. Scenic. But did you notice, it's in the woods?'

It made her smile. 'No kidding? Good thing I like the woods.'

'Must get that from your mother. How is she?'

'She's great.' Laine didn't know why it always made her feel guilty when he asked, without rancor, with sincere interest. 'How long have you been here?'

'Just got in last night. Since I arrived at your woodland paradise late, figured you to be in dreamland, I let myself in. Bunked on your couch, which I should tell you is in sorry shape.' He pressed a hand to his lower back. 'Be a lamb, sweetie, and make your daddy some coffee.'

'I was just about . . .' She trailed off as the reminder of coffee cleared her head. *Max!* 'I'm not alone.' Panic trickled her throat. 'There's someone upstairs – in the shower.'

'I gathered that from the car in your drive, the fancy piece with New York plates.' He chucked her under the chin. 'You're going to tell me, I hope, that you had a slumber party with an out-of-town girlfriend.'

'I'm twenty-eight. I graduated from slumber parties with girlfriends to having sex with men.'

'Please.' Jack pressed a hand to his heart. 'Let's just say you had a friend spend the night. This is the sort of thing a father needs to take in stages. Coffee, darling? That's a good girl.'

'All right, all right, but there are things you need to know about . . . my overnight guest.' She got out her bag of beans, poured some into her grinder.

'I already know the most important thing. He's not good enough for my baby. Nobody could be.'

'This is so complicated. He's working for Reliance Insurance.'

'So, he's got a straight job, a nine-to-fiver.' Jack shrugged his broad shoulders. 'I can forgive that one.'

'Dad—'

'And we'll talk about this young man in just a bit.' He sniffed the air as she measured the coffee grounds into the filter. 'Best scent in the world. While that's doing what it's doing, could you fetch me the package Willy left with you? I'll keep an eye on the pot.'

She stared at him while all the thoughts, all the words, circled around in her head and coalesced into a single horrible certainty. He didn't know.

'Dad, I don't . . . He didn't . . .' She shook her head. 'We'd better sit down.'

'Don't tell me he hasn't been by yet.' The faintest flicker of irritation crossed his face. 'Man would get lost in his own bathroom without a map, but he's had more than enough time to get here. If he'd turn his damn cell phone on I'd have gotten in touch, told him there was a change in plans. I hate to tell you, Lainie, but your uncle Willy's getting old and absent-minded.'

No easy way, she thought as the coffee spilled into the pot. No easy way. 'Dad, he's dead.'

'I wouldn't go that far. Just forgetful.'

'Dad.' She gripped his arms, squeezing while she watched the indulgent smile fade from his face. 'There was an accident. He was hit by a car. And he . . . he died. I'm sorry. I'm so sorry.'

'That can't be. That's a mistake.'

'He came into my shop a few days ago. I didn't recognize him.' She ran her hands along his arms now because they'd begun to tremble. 'It's been so long, I didn't recognize him. He gave me a number, asked me to call him. I thought he had something to sell,

131

and I was busy so I didn't pay much attention. Then he left, and just after, just seconds after, it seemed, there were these horrible sounds.'

Jack's eyes were filling, and hers did the same. 'Oh, Dad. It was raining, and he ran into the street. I don't know why, but he ran out, and the car couldn't stop. I ran out, and I . . . I realized who he was but it was too late.'

'Oh God. God. God.' He did sit now, lowering into a chair, dropping his head into his hands. 'He can't be gone. Not Willy.'

He rocked himself for comfort while Laine wrapped her arms around him, pressed her cheek to his. 'I sent him here. I told him to come because I thought it was . . . Ran out into the street?'

His head came up now. Tears tracked down his cheeks, and she knew he'd never been ashamed of them, or any big emotion. 'He wasn't a child who goes running into the street.'

'But he did. There were witnesses. The woman who hit him was devastated. There was nothing she could do.'

'He ran. If he ran, there was a reason.' He'd gone pale under the tears. 'You need to get what he gave you. Get it and give it to me. Don't tell anyone. You never saw him before in your life, that's what you say.'

'He didn't give me anything. Dad, I know about the stones. I know about the New York job.'

His hands were on her shoulders now with a grip strong enough she knew there'd be bruises. 'How do you know if he didn't give you anything?'

'The man who's upstairs. He works for Reliance. They insured the gems. He's an investigator.'

'An insurance cop.' He came straight out of the chair. 'You've got a cop in your shower, for the sake of Jesus!'

'He tracked Willy here, and he connected him to me. To you and me. He only wants to recover the stones. He's not interested in turning you in. Just give me what you have, and I'll take care of this.'

'You're sleeping with a cop? My own daughter?'

'I don't think this is the time to go into that. Dad, someone broke

132

into my house, into my shop because they're looking for the stones. I don't have them.'

'It's that bastard Crew. That murdering bastard.' His eyes were still wet and swimming, but there was fire behind them. 'You don't know anything, do you hear me? You don't know anything, you haven't seen me. You haven't spoken to me. I'll take care of this, Laine.'

'You can't take care of it. Dad, you're in terrible trouble. The stones aren't worth it.'

'Half of twenty-eight million's worth quite a bit, and that's what I'll have to bargain with once I find out what Willy did with his. He didn't give you anything? Say anything?'

'He told me to hide the pouch, but he didn't give me one.'

'Pouch? He took them out?'

'I just said he didn't give me a pouch. He was . . . fading, and it was hard to understand him. At first I thought he said "pooch."'

'That's it.' Some of the animation came back into his face. 'His share is in the dog.'

'The *dog*?' Genuine shock had her voice squeaking. 'You fed diamonds to a dog?'

'Not a real dog. God almighty, Lainie, what do you take us for?'

She simply covered her face with her hands. 'I don't know anymore. I just don't know.'

'It's in a statue of a dog, little black-and-white dog. Cops probably have his things. Cops probably have it and don't know what they've got. I can work with that.'

'Dad—'

'I don't want you to worry. No one's going to bother you again. No one's going to touch my little girl. Just stay quiet about it, and I'll handle the rest.' He gave her a hug, a kiss. 'I'll just get my bag and be gone.'

'You can't just go,' she protested as she hurried after him. 'Max says Crew is dangerous.'

'Max is the insurance narc?'

'Yes.' She glanced nervously toward the steps. 'No, he's not a narc.'

'Whatever, he's not wrong about Crew. Man doesn't think I know who he is,' Jack muttered. 'What he did. Figured I'd swallow his fake names and fairy story whole. Been in the game since I could talk, haven't I?' Jack slung a duffel over his shoulder. 'I should never have gotten tangled with him, but well, twenty-eight million, give or take, makes for strange bedfellows. Now I've gotten Willy killed over it.'

'You didn't. It's not your fault.'

'I took the job knowing who Crew was though he called himself Martin Lyle. Knowing he was dangerous and planning a double cross all along, I took the job. Willy came with me. But I'll fix it. I won't let anything happen to you.' He gave her a quick kiss on the top of her head, then moved to the front door.

'Wait. Just wait and talk to Max.'

'I don't think so.' He let out a snort at the idea. 'And do us both a favor, princess.' Now he tapped a finger to her lips. 'I was never here.'

She could hear him whistling 'Bye Bye Blackbird' as he set off at a jog. He'd always moved well for a big man. Before she knew it, he'd rounded the curve of her lane and was gone.

As if he'd never been there.

She closed the door, rested her forehead against it. Everything ached: her head, her body, her heart. There'd been tears in his eyes still when he trotted away. Tears for Willy. He'd grieve, she knew. He'd blame himself. And in that state, he might do something stupid.

No, not stupid, she corrected and wandered into the kitchen to pace aimlessly. Reckless, foolish, but not stupid.

She couldn't have stopped him. Even if she'd begged, pleaded, even if she'd turned on the tears herself. He'd have carried the weight of them when he walked away, but he'd have walked.

Yes, he'd always moved well for a big man.

She heard Max coming toward the kitchen and hurriedly reached into the cupboard for mugs.

'Right on time,' she said brightly. 'Coffee's just up.'

'Morning coffee's got to be one of life's best smells.'

She turned then, stared at him as his words echoed her father's in her mind. His hair was still damp from the shower. Her shower. He'd smell like her soap. He'd slept in her bed. He'd been inside her.

She'd given him all that. But after a ten-minute visit from her father, she was holding back trust, and truth.

'My father was here.' She blurted it out before she could question herself.

He set down the mug he'd just picked up. 'What?'

'He just left. Minutes ago. And I realized I wasn't going to tell you, wasn't going to say anything. I was going to cover for him. It's conditioning, I guess. Or partly. I love him. I'm sorry.'

'Jack O'Hara was here? He's been in the house, and you didn't tell me?'

'I'm telling you. I don't expect you to understand what a step this is for me, but I'm telling you.' She tried to pour coffee, but her hands were shaking. 'Don't hurt him, Max. I couldn't stand it if you hurt him.'

'Let's just back up a square here. Your father was here, in this house, and you cooked me dinner, went to bed with me. I'm upstairs making love to you and he's hiding out—'

'No! No! I didn't know he was here until this morning. I don't know when he got here, let himself in. He slept on the couch. I let Henry out, and when I walked into the kitchen again, there he was.'

'Then what the hell are you apologizing to me for?'

'I wasn't going to tell you.'

'For what, three minutes? Jesus Christ, Laine. You put that kind of honesty bar up for us, I'm going to keep rapping my head on it. Give me a break.'

'I'm very confused.'

'He's been your father for twenty-eight years. I've been the guy in love with you for about two days. I think I can cut you some slack. Okay?'

She let out a shuddering breath. 'Okay.'

'That's the end of the slack. What did he say, what did he want, where did he go?'

'He didn't know about Willy.' Her lips trembled before she managed to press them together. 'He cried.'

'Sit down, Laine, I'll get the coffee. Sit down and take a minute.'

She did what he asked as everything that had been aching was now shaking. She sat, stared at her hands while she listened to liquid hitting stoneware. 'I think I might be in love with you, too. It's probably an awkward time to mention that.'

'I like hearing it.' He set the mug in front of her, then sat. 'Whatever the time.'

'I'm not playing you, Max. I need you to know that.'

'Baby, I bet you're good at it. Considering. But you're not that good.'

The cocky tone was just what was needed to dry up threatening tears. She looked at him then with a definite flash of amused arrogance. 'Oh yeah, I am. I could swindle you out of your life savings, your heart, your pride, and make you believe it was your idea to hand them over with a bow on top. But since it looks like the only thing I'm interested in is your heart, I'd rather it really be your idea. Jack could never play it straight with my mother. He loved her. Still does, for that matter. But he could never play it straight, even with her. So they didn't make it. If you and I go into this, I want the odds in our favor.'

'Then let's start by figuring out how to handle your father.'

She nodded and picked up the coffee he'd brought her. She would be steady, and she would be straight. 'He sent Willy here to give me a share of the take. For safekeeping, from what I can gather. You should know that if that had gone through, I'd have taken the stones, then passed them back to him. I'd have given him considerable grief about it, but I'd've done it.'

'Blood's thick,' Max acknowledged.

'From what I can gather, he got worried because Willy didn't call him – and his, Willy's, cell phone's been off. So he changed the plan, came here to pick up the dog.'

'What dog?'

'See, it was a pooch, not a pouch. Or, the pouch is in the pooch. God, it sounds like a bad comedy routine. But I didn't get the pooch with the pouch, so my father figures the cops scooped it up with Willy's effects. And he believes Crew – he verified Crew, by the way – tracked Willy here, just like you did, and that's what spooked Willy and had him running into the street.'

'There's not enough coffee in the world,' Max murmured. 'Go back to the dog.'

'Oh, it's not an actual dog. It's a figurine of a dog. It's one of Jack's old gambits. Hide the take in something ordinary so it can be passed – and passed over by whoever's looking to get it back – until the heat's off. Once he hid a cache of rare coins inside my teddy bear. We strolled right out of the apartment building, chatted with the doorman and walked away with a hundred and twenty-five large inside Paddington.'

'He took you on a job?'

His very real shock had her lowering her gaze to her coffee mug. 'I didn't have what you'd call a standard childhood.'

Max closed his eyes. 'Where's he going, Laine?'

'I don't know.' She reached out, covered his hand with hers until their eyes met. 'I swear I don't know. He told me not to worry, that he'd take care of everything.'

'Vince Burger has Willy's effects?'

'Don't tell him, Max, please don't. He'll have no choice but to arrest Jack if he shows up. I can't have any part in that. You and I, we don't have a chance if I have a part in that.'

Thinking, he drummed his fingers on the table. 'I searched Willy's motel room. Didn't see any dog figure.' He brought the room back into his head, tried to see it section by section. 'Don't remember anything like that, but it's possible I passed over it, thinking it was just part of the room's decor. "Decor" being used in the loosest possible sense.'

'That's why it works.'

'All right. Can you talk Vince into letting you see Willy's effects?'

'Yes,' she said without hesitation. 'I can.'

'Let's start there. Then we'll go to Plan B.'

'What's Plan B?'

'Whatever comes next.'

It was a little distressing how easy it all came back. Maybe it was easier, Laine thought, since she didn't have to talk to Vince. But she was, essentially, still deceiving a friend and lying to a cop.

She knew Sergeant McCoy casually, and when she realized she'd be dealing with him, quickly lined up all the facts she knew about him in her head. Married, Gap native, two children. She was nearly sure it was two, and that they were both grown. She thought there was a grandchild in the picture.

She added to those with observation and instinct.

Carrying an extra twenty pounds, so he liked to eat. Since there was a bakery Danish on a napkin on his desk, his wife was probably trying to get him to diet, and he had to sneak his fixes with store bought.

He wore a wedding ring, his only jewelry, and his nails were clipped short. His hand was rough with calluses when it shook hers. He'd gotten to his feet to greet her and had done what he could to suck in his gut. She sent him a warm smile and noted the color that crept into his cheeks.

He'd be a pushover.

'Sergeant McCoy, it's nice to see you again.'

'Miz Tavish.'

'Laine, please. How's your wife?'

'She's fine. Just fine.'

'And that grandbaby of yours?'

His teeth showed in a doting smile. 'Not such a baby anymore. Boy's two now and running my daughter ragged.'

'Such a fun age, isn't it? Taking him fishing yet?'

'Had him out to the river last weekend. Can't sit still long enough yet, but he'll learn.'

'That'll be great fun. My granddaddy took me fishing a couple of times, but we had a serious difference of opinion when it came to worms.'

McCoy let out an appreciative guffaw. 'Tad, he loves the worms.'

'That's a boy for you. Oh, I'm sorry. Sergeant, this is my friend Max Gannon.'

'Yeah.' McCoy studied the bruised temple. 'Had you a little run in the other night.'

'It was all a misunderstanding,' Laine said quickly. 'Max came in with me this morning for a little moral support.'

'Uh-huh.' McCoy shook hands, because Max extended one, then glanced back at Laine. 'Moral support?'

'I've never done this sort of thing before.' She lifted her hands, looked fragile and frustrated. 'Vince might have mentioned that I realized I knew William Young. The man who was killed in that awful accident outside my shop?'

'He didn't mention it.'

'I just told him, and I guess it doesn't make any difference in the – in the procedure. It wasn't until after . . . until after that I remembered. He knew my father, when I was a child. I haven't seen him – William – since I was, oh, ten, I guess. I was so busy when he came into the shop.'

Her eyes went shiny with distress. 'I didn't recognize him, and I just didn't pay that much attention. He left me his card and asked me to call him when I had the chance. Then nearly as soon as he walked out . . . I feel terrible that I didn't remember, that I brushed him off.'

'That's all right now.' McCoy dug at box of tissues out of a drawer and offered it.

'Thanks. Thank you. I want to do what I can for him now. I want to be able to tell my father I did what I could.' Those things were true. It helped to work in truth. 'He didn't have any family that I know of, so I'd like to make whatever arrangements need to be made for burial.'

'The chief has his file, but I can check about that for you.'

'I'd appreciate that very much. I wonder if, while I'm here, I could see his things. Is that possible?'

'I don't see why not. Why don't you have a seat?' He took her arm, gently, and led her to a chair. 'Just sit down, and I'll go get them for you. Can't let you take anything.'

'No, no, I understand.'

As McCoy left the room, Max sat beside her. 'Smooth as butter. How well you know this cop?'

'McCoy. I've met him a couple of times.'

'Fishing?'

'Oh, that. He has a fishing magazine tucked under his case files on the desk, so it was a reasonable guess. I'm going to arrange for Uncle Willy's burial,' she added. 'Here, I think, in Angel's Gap, unless I can find out if there's somewhere else he'd rather . . .'

'I bet here would suit him fine.'

He rose, as did she, when McCoy returned with a large carton. 'He didn't have much. Looks like he was traveling light. Clothes, wallet, watch, five keys, key ring—'

'Oh, I think I gave him that key ring for Christmas one year.' She reached out, sniffling, then closed it into her fist. 'Can you imagine? He used it all these years. Oh, and I didn't even recognize him.'

Clutching the keys, she sat, wept.

'Don't cry, Laine.'

Max sent McCoy a look of pure male helplessness and patted Laine on the head.

'Sometimes they gotta.' McCoy went back for the tissues. When he stepped back up, Laine reached out, took three, mopped at her face.

'I'm sorry. This is just *silly*. It's just that I'm remembering how sweet he was to me. Then we lost contact, you know how it is? My family moved away, and that was that.'

Composing herself, she got to her feet again. 'I'm fine. I'm sorry, I'll be fine.' She took the manila envelope, dropped the keys back into it and slipped it back into the carton herself. 'Can you just tell me the rest? I promise, that won't happen again.'

'Don't you worry about it. You sure you want to deal with this now?'

'I do. Yes, thank you.'

'There's a toiletry kit – razor, toothbrush, the usual. He was carrying four hundred twenty-six dollars and twelve cents. Had

140

a rental car – a Taurus from Avis out of New York, road maps.'

She was looking through the items as McCoy detailed them from his list.

'Cell phone – nothing programmed in the phone book for us to contact. Looks like there's a couple of voice messages. We'll see if we can track those.'

They'd be from her father, she imagined, but only nodded.

'Watch is engraved,' he added when Laine turned it over in her hand. '"One for every minute." I don't get it.'

She gave McCoy a baffled smile. 'Neither do I. Maybe it was something romantic, from a woman he loved once. That would be nice. I'd like to think that. This was all?'

'Well, he was traveling.' He took the watch from her. 'Man doesn't take a lot of personal items with him when he's traveling. Vince'll be tracking down his home address. Don't worry about that. We haven't found any next of kin so far, and if we don't, seems like they'll release him to you. It's nice of you to want to bury an old friend of your father's.'

'It's the least I can do. Thank you very much, Sergeant. You've been very kind and patient. If you or Vince would let me know if and when I can make the funeral arrangements, I'd appreciate it.'

'We'll be in touch.'

She took Max's hand as they walked out, and he felt the key press his palm. 'That was slick,' he commented. 'I barely caught it.'

'If I wasn't a little rusty, you wouldn't have caught it. It looks like a locker key. One of those rental lockers. You can't rent lockers at airports or train stations, bus stations, that sort of thing anymore, can you?'

'No. Too small for one of those garage-type storage lockers, and most of those are combination locks or key cards anyway. It might be from one of those mailbox places.'

'We should be able to track it down. No dog though.'

'No, no dog. We'll check the motel room, but I don't think it's there, either.'

She stepped outside with him, took a fond look at the town she'd made her own. From this vantage point, high on the sloped street, she could see a slice of the river, and the houses carved into the rising hill on the other bank. The mountains climbed up behind, ringing their way around the sprawl of streets and buildings, the parks and bridges. They formed a scenic wall covered with the green haze of trees beginning to leaf, and the white flash of blooming wild dogwoods.

The everydayers, as her father had dubbed normal people with normal lives, were about their business. Selling cars, buying groceries, vacuuming the rug, teaching history.

Gardens were planted, or being prepared for planting. She could see a couple of houses where the Easter decorations had yet to be dispatched, though it was nearly three weeks past. Colorful plastic eggs danced in low tree limbs, and inflatable rabbits squatted on spring-green grass.

She had rugs to vacuum and groceries to buy, a garden to tend. Despite the key in her hand, she supposed that made her an everydayer, too.

'I'm not going to pretend some of that didn't stir the juices. But when this is over, I'll be happy to retire again. Willy never could, my father never will.'

She smiled as they walked to Max's car. 'My father gave him that watch. The key ring was just a ploy, but my dad gave Willy that watch for his birthday one year. I think he might have actually bought it, but I can't be sure. But I was with him when he had it engraved. "One for every minute."'

'Meaning?'

'There's a sucker born every minute,' she said, and slipped into the car.

Chapter Eleven

It was the same clerk at the desk of the Red Roof, but Max could see the lack of recognition in his eyes. The simplest, quickest way in to Willy's last room was to pay the standard freight.

'We want one-fifteen,' Max told him.

The clerk studied the display of his computer, checked availability and shrugged. 'No problem.'

'We're sentimental.' Laine added a sappy smile and snuggled next to Max.

Max handed over cash. 'I need a receipt. We're not that sentimental.'

With the key in hand, they drove around to Willy's section.

'He must've known where I live. My father did, so Willy did. I wish he'd just come to see me there. I can only think he knew somebody was right behind him – or was afraid someone was – and figured the shop was safer.'

'He was only here one night. Hadn't unpacked.' Max led the way to the door. 'Looked like enough clothes for about a week. Suitcase was open, but he hadn't taken anything out but his bathroom kit. Could be he wanted to be ready to move again, fast.'

'We were always ready to move again, fast. My mother could pack up our lives in twenty minutes flat, and lay it out again in a new place just as quick.'

'She must be an interesting woman. Takes mine longer than that to decide what shoes to wear in the morning.'

'Shoes aren't a decision to be made lightly.' Understanding, she laid a hand on his arm. 'You don't have to give me time to prepare myself, Max. I'm okay.'

He opened the door. She stepped into a standard motel double. She knew such rooms made some people sad, but she'd always found them one of life's small adventures for their very anonymity.

In such rooms you could pretend you were anywhere. Going anywhere. That you were anyone.

'As a kid we'd stop off in places like this, going from one point to another. I loved it. I'd pretend I was a spy chasing down some nefarious Dr. Doom, or a princess traveling incognito. My father always made it such a wonderful game.

'He'd always get me candy and soft drinks from the vending machines, and my mother would pretend to disapprove. I guess, after a while, she wasn't pretending anymore.'

She fingered the inexpensive bedspread. 'Well, that's a long enough walk down Memory Lane. I don't see any dog in here.'

Though he'd already done a search, and knew the police had been through the room, followed by housekeeping, Max went through the procedure again.

'Don't miss much, do you?' she said when he'd finished.

'Try not to. That key might be the best lead we've got. I'll check out the local storage facilities.'

'And what you're not saying is he could've stashed it in a million of those kind of places from here to New York.'

'I'll track it back. I'll find it.'

'Yes, I believe you will. While you're doing that, I'll go back to work. I don't like leaving Jenny there alone very long, under the circumstances.'

He tossed the room key on the bed. 'I'll drop you off.'

Once they were back in the car, she smoothed a hand over her pants. 'You'd have disapproved, too. Of the motel rooms, the game. The life.'

'I can see why it appealed to you when you were ten. And I can see why your mother got you out of it. She did what was right for you. One thing about your father . . .'

She braced herself for the criticism and promised herself not to take offense. 'Yes?'

'A lot of men in . . . let's say, his line, they shake off wives and kids or anything that resembles responsibility. He didn't.'

Her shoulders loosened, her stomach unknotted, and she turned to send Max a luminous smile. 'No, he didn't.'

'And not just because you were a really cute little redheaded beard with light fingers.'

'That didn't hurt, but no, not just because of that. He loved us, in his unique Jack O'Hara way. Thanks.'

'No problem. When we have kids, I'll buy them candy out of the vending machine, but we'll keep it to special occasions.'

Her throat closed down so that she had to clear it in order to speak. 'You do jump ahead,' she stated.

'No point in dragging your feet once you've got your direction.'

'Seems to me there's a lot of road between here and there. And a lot of curves and angles in it.'

'So, we'll enjoy the ride. Let's round one of those curves now. I don't need to live in New York if that's something you're chewing on. I think this area's just fine for raising those three kids.'

She didn't choke, but it was close. 'Three?'

'Lucky number.'

She turned her head to stare out the side window. 'Well, you sailed right around that curve. Have you considered slowing down until we've known each other, oh, I don't know, a full week?'

'People get to know each other faster in certain situations. This would be one of them.'

'Favorite childhood memory before the age of ten.'

'Tough one.' He considered a moment. 'Learning to ride a two-wheeler. My father running alongside – with this big grin, and a lot of fear in his eyes I didn't recognize as such at the time. How it felt, this windy, stomach-dropping rush when I realized I was pedaling on my own. Yours?'

'Sitting on this big bed in the Ritz Carlton in Seattle. It was a suite because we were really flush. Dad ordered this ridiculous room service meal of shrimp cocktails and fried chicken because

I liked them both, and caviar, which I hadn't yet acquired a taste for. There was pizza and hot fudge sundaes. An eight-year-old's fantasy meal. I was half sick from it, and sitting on the bed with probably a hundred in ones he'd given me to play with.'

She waited a beat. 'Not exactly from the same world, Max.'

'We're in the same one now.'

She looked back at him. He looked confident and tough, his clever hands on the wheel of the powerful car, his sun-streaked hair unruly from the breeze, those dangerous cat's eyes hidden behind tinted lenses.

Handsome, in control, sure of himself. And the butterfly bandage on his temple was a reminder he didn't always come out on top, but he didn't stay down.

Man of my dreams, she thought, *what am I going to do with you?*

'Hard to trip you up.'

'I already took the big stumble, sweetheart, when I fell for you.'

Laughing, she let her head fall back. 'That's sappy, but somehow it works. I must still have a weakness for a guy with a quick line.'

He pulled up in front of her shop. 'I'll pick you up at closing.' Leaning over, he gave her a light kiss. 'Don't work too hard.'

'This is all so strangely normal. A little pocket of ordinary in a big bunch of strange.' She reached out, feathered her fingertips over his bandage. 'Be careful, all right? Alex Crew knows who you are.'

'I hope we run into each other soon. I owe him one.'

The normal continued through most of the day. Laine waited on customers, packed merchandise to ship, unpacked shipments of items she'd ordered. It was the sort of day she usually loved, with plenty to do but none of it rushed. She was sending things off with people who enjoyed or admired them enough to pay for them, and finding things in the shipping boxes she'd enjoyed or admired enough to want in her shop.

Despite it, the day dragged.

She worried about her father and what reckless thing he might do while the grief was on him. She worried about Max and what could happen if Crew came after him.

She worried about her relationship with Max. Mentally examined, evaluated and dissected it until she was sick of herself.

'Looks like it's just you and me,' Jenny said when a customer left the shop.

'Why don't you take a break? Put your feet up for a few minutes.'

'Happy to. You do the same.'

'I'm not pregnant. And I have paperwork.'

'I am pregnant, and I won't sit until you sit. So if you don't sit down you're forcing a pregnant woman to stand on her feet and they're swollen.'

'Your feet are swollen? Oh, Jenny—'

'Okay, not yet. But they *could* be. They probably will be, and it'll be your fault. So let's sit.'

She nudged Laine toward a small, heart-backed divan. 'I love this piece. I've thought about buying it a dozen times, then remember I have absolutely no place to put it.'

'When you love a piece, you find a place.'

'So you always say, but your house doesn't look like an antique warehouse.' She ran her fingers over the satiny rose-on-rose stripes of the cushions. 'Still, if it hasn't sold in another week, I'm going to cave.'

'It'd look great in the little alcove off your living room.'

'It would, but then I'd have to change the curtains, and get a little table.'

'Naturally. And a nice little rug.'

'Vince is going to kill me.' She sighed, plopped her joined hands on the shelf of her belly. 'Okay, time for you to unload.'

'I've already unpacked the last shipment.'

'Emotionally unload. And you knew what I meant.'

'I wouldn't know where to start.'

'Start with what pops to the surface first. You've got a lot bobbing around under there, Laine. I know you well enough to see it.'

'You still think you know me after everything you've found out in the last couple of days?'

147

'Yeah, I do. So uncork it. What comes first?'

'Max thinks he's in love with me.'

'Really?' It wasn't as easy for her to come to alert as it once had been, but Jenny dug her elbows into the cushions and pushed her heavy body straighter. 'Did you intuit that, or did he say it? Right out say it?'

'Right out said it. You don't believe in love at first sight, do you?'

'Sure I do. It's all chemicals and stuff. There was this whole program on it on PBS. I think it was PBS. Maybe it was The Learning Channel. Anyway.' She waved that part aside. 'They've done all these studies on attraction and sex and relationships. Mostly, it boils down to chemicals, instincts, pheromones, then building on that. Besides, you know Vince and I met when I was in first grade. I went right home from school and told my mom that I was going to marry Vince Burger. Took us a while to get there. State law's pretty firm about six-year-olds getting hitched. But it sure was the right mix of chemicals from day one.'

She never tired of picturing it – gregarious Jenny and slow-talking Vince. And she always saw them with their adult heads on sturdy little kids' bodies. 'You've known each other all your lives.'

'That's not the point. Minutes, days, years, sometimes it's just a click, click.' Jenny snapped her fingers to emphasize. 'Besides, why shouldn't he be in love with you? You're beautiful and smart and sexy. If I were a man I'd be all over you.'

'That's . . . really sweet.'

'And you've got this interesting and mysterious past on top of it. How do you feel about him?'

'All sort of loose and itchy and feeble-minded.'

'You know, I liked him right away.'

'Jenny, you liked his ass right away.'

'And your point would be?' She snickered, pleased when Laine laughed. 'Okay, besides the ass, he's considerate. He bought his mother a gift. He's got that accent going for him, has a sexy job. Henry likes him, and Henry's a very good judge of character.'

'That's true. That's very true.'

'And he's not hung up with commitment phobia or he wouldn't have used the *l* word. Added to all that,' she said softly, 'he's on your side. That came across loud and clear. He's on your side, and that won him top points from the best-pal seats.'

'So I should stop worrying.'

'Depends. How is he in bed? Gladiator or poet?'

'Hmm.' Thinking back, Laine ran her tongue over her bottom lip. 'A poetic gladiator.'

'Oh *God*!' With a little shudder, Jenny slumped back. 'That's the best. Snap him up, girl.'

'I might. I just might. If we manage to get through all this without screwing it up.'

She glanced back as her door opened and the bells jingled. 'I'll get this. Sit.'

The couple was fortyish, and Laine pegged them as affluent tourists. The woman's jacket was a thin butter-colored suede, and the shoes and bag were Prada. Good jewelry. A nice, square-cut diamond paired with a channel-set wedding band.

The man wore a leather jacket that looked Italian in cut over nicely faded Levi's. When he turned to close the door behind him, Laine spotted the Rolex on his wrist.

They were both tanned and fit. Country club, she thought. Golf or tennis every Sunday.

'Good afternoon. Can I help you with anything?'

'We're just poking around,' the woman answered with a smile, and a look in her eye that told Laine she didn't want to be guided or pressured.

'Help yourself. Just let me know if you need anything.' To give them space, she walked to the counter, opened one of her auction catalogues.

She let their conversation wash over her. Definitely country club types, Laine thought. And made one of her little bets with herself that they'd drop five hundred minimum before heading out again.

If she was wrong, she had to put a dollar in the ginger jar in her office. As she was rarely wrong, the jar didn't see much action.

'Miss?'

149

Laine glanced over, then waved Jenny back before her friend could heft herself off the divan. She gave the female customer her merchant's smile and wandered over.

'What can you tell me about this piece?'

'Oh, that's a fun piece, isn't it? Chess table, circa 1850. British. It's penwork and ivory-inlaid ebony. Excellent condition.'

'It might work in our game room.' She looked at her husband. 'What do you think?'

'A little steep for a novelty piece.'

All right, Laine thought. She was supposed to bargain with the husband while the wife looked around. No problem.

'You'll note the double spiral pedestal. Perfect condition. It's really one of a kind. It came from an estate on Long Island.'

'What about this?'

Laine walked over to join his wife. 'Late nineteenth century. Mahogany,' she said as she ran a fingertip over the edge of the display table. 'The top's hinged, the glass beveled.' She lifted it gently. 'Don't you just love the heart shape?'

'I really do.'

Laine noted the signal the wife sent her husband. *I want both,* it said. *Make it work.*

She wandered off, and Laine gave Jenny the nod to answer any questions she might have over the collection of wineglasses she was eyeing.

She spent the next fifteen minutes letting the husband think he was cutting her price to the bone. She made the sale, he felt accomplished and the wife got the pieces she wanted.

Everybody wins, Laine thought as she wrote up the sale.

'Wait! Michael, look what I found.' The woman hurried to the counter, flushed and laughing. 'My sister loves this sort of thing. The sillier the better.' She held up a ceramic black-and-white dog. 'There's no price.'

Laine stared at it, the practiced smile still curving her lips while her pulse pounded in her ears. Casually, very casually, she reached out and took the statue. An icy finger pressed at the base of her spine.

150

'Silly's the word. I'm so sorry.' Her voice sounded perfectly natural, with just a hint of laughter in it. 'This isn't for sale. It's not part of the stock.'

'But it was on the shelf, right back there.'

'It belongs to a friend of mine. He must have set it down without thinking. I had no idea it was there.' Before the woman could object, Laine set it on the shelf under the counter, out of sight. 'I'm sure we can find something along the same lines that will suit your sister. And if we do, it's half off for the disappointment factor.'

The half off stilled any protests. 'Well, there was a cat figure. Siamese cat. More elegant than the dog, but still kitschy enough for Susan. I'll go take another look at it.'

'Go right ahead. Now, Mr. Wainwright, where would you like your pieces shipped?'

She finished the transaction, chatted easily, even walked her customers to the door.

'Nice sale, boss. I love when they keep finding something else, adding it on.'

'She was the one with the eye, he was the one with the wallet.' It felt a little like floating, but Laine got back to the counter, lifted the dog. 'Jenny, did you shelve this piece?'

'That? No.' Lips pursed, Jenny walked over to study it. 'Sort of cute, in a ridiculous way. A little flea market for us, isn't it? It's not Doulton or Minton or any of those types, is it?'

'No, it's not. I imagine it came in one of the auction shipments by mistake. I'll sort it out. Look, it's nearly five. Why don't you take off early? You covered for me for more than an hour this morning.'

'Don't mind if I do. I've got a craving for a Quarter Pounder. I'll swing by the station and see if Vince is up to dining at Chez McDonald's. I'm as close as the phone, you know, if anything else pops to the surface and you want to vent.'

'I know.'

Laine shuffled papers until Jenny gathered her things and headed out the door. She waited another five full minutes, doing busywork in case her friend doubled back for any reason.

Then she walked to the front, put up the closed sign, locked the door.

Retrieving the statue, she took it into the back room, checked those locks. Satisfied no one could walk in on her unexpectedly, she set the statue on her desk, studied it.

She could see the glue line now that she was looking for it, just a hint of it around the little cork shoved into the base. It was good work, but then Big Jack was never sloppy. Beside the cork was a faded stamp. MADE IN TAIWAN.

Yes, he'd have thought of little details like that. She shook it. Nothing rattled.

Clicking her tongue, she got out a sheet of newspaper, spread it on the desk. She centered the dog on it, then walked to the cabinet where she kept her tools. She selected a small ball-peen hammer, cocked her head, swung back her arm.

Then stopped.

And because she stopped, she realized, without a single doubt, she was in love with Max.

On a breath, she sat, staring at the dog as she set the hammer aside.

She couldn't do it on her own because she was in love with Max. That meant they would do it together. And so whatever came next together.

And that, she thought, is what her mother had found with Robert Tavish. What she'd never really had with Jack, for all the excitement and adventure. Her mother had been part of the team, and possibly the love of Jack's life. But at the core, they hadn't been a couple.

Her mother and Rob were a couple. And that's what she wanted for herself. If she was going to be in love with someone, she damn well wanted to be half of a couple.

'Okay then.'

She rose, got bubble wrap from her shipping supplies. She wrapped the cheap plaster dog as carefully, as meticulously as she would've wrapped antique crystal. Over layers of bubble wrap, she secured brown shipping paper, then nestled the package into a

152

tissue-lined shopping bag, along with a second item she'd taken from her stock and wrapped.

When the job was complete, she arranged for the shipping for her final sale of the day, then filed paperwork. At precisely six o'clock, she was at the front door waiting for Max.

He was fifteen minutes late, but that only gave her time to calm completely.

He'd barely pulled to the curb when she was walking out, locking the door.

'You're always on time, right?' he asked her when she got into the car. 'Probably more like always five minutes early.'

'That's right.'

'I hardly ever am, exactly on time, that is. Is this going to be a deal with us down the road?'

'Oh yes. You get this initial honeymoon period where I just flutter my lashes when you show up and don't say a word about your being late. After that, we'll fight about it.'

'Just wanted to check on that. What's in the bag?'

'A couple of things. Did you have any luck with the key?'

'That depends on your point of view. I didn't find the lock it fits, but I eliminated several it didn't.'

He drove up her lane, parked behind her car. 'How come Henry doesn't zip out his dog door when he hears a car drive up?'

'How does he know who it is? It could be someone he doesn't want to talk to.'

She got out, waited for him to pop the trunk. And beamed at the bucket of fried chicken.

'You bought me chicken.'

'Not only, but the makings for hot fudge sundaes.' He lifted the two bags. 'I thought about shrimp cocktail and pizza, but figured we'd both be sick. So just the Colonel and ice cream for you tonight.'

She set the shopping bag down, threw her arms around his neck and crushed her mouth to his.

'I can hit up the Colonel every night,' he said when he could manage it.

'It's those secret herbs and spices. They get me every time. I decided I love you.'

She watched the emotion swirl into his eyes. 'Yeah?'

'Yeah. Let's go tell Henry.'

Henry seemed more interested in the chicken, but settled for a quick wrestle and a giant Milk-Bone biscuit while Laine set the table.

'You can eat that sort of thing on paper towels,' Max told her.

'Not in this house.'

She fancied it up in a way he found sweet and female. Her colorful plates turned the fast-food chicken and tubs of coleslaw into a tidy celebration.

They had wine and candles and extra-crispy.

'Would you like to know why I decided I love you?' She waited, enjoying the meal, watching him enjoy it.

'Because I'm so handsome and charming?'

'That's why I decided to sleep with you.' She cleared the plates. 'I decided I might love you because you made me laugh, and you were kind and clever and because when I played the next-month game, you were still there.'

'The next-month game?'

'I'll explain that later. But I decided I must love you when I started to do something by myself, and stopped. Didn't want to do it by myself. I wanted to do it with you, because when two people make one couple, they do important things, and little things, together. But before I explain all that, I've got a present for you.'

'No kidding?'

'No, I take presents very seriously.' She took the first wrapped item out of her bag. 'It's a favorite of mine, so I hope you like it.'

Curious, he ripped the protective brown paper off, then broke into a huge grin. 'You're not going to believe this.'

'You have it already?'

'Nope. My mother does. Happens it's one of her favorites, too.'

It pleased her to hear it. 'I imagine she was fond of Maxfield Parrish's work or she wouldn't have named her son after the artist.'

154

'She has a few of his prints. This one's in her sitting room. What's it called again?'

'*Lady Violetta About to Make Tarts*,' Laine told him as they both studied the framed print of a pretty woman standing in front of a chest and holding a small silver pitcher.

'She's pretty hot. Looks a little like you.'

'She does not.'

'She's got red hair.'

'That's not red.' Laine tapped a finger against the model's reddish-gold hair, then tugged a lock of her own. '*This* is red.'

'Either way, I'm going to think of you every time I look at her. Thanks.'

'You're welcome.' She took the picture from him and laid it on the kitchen counter. 'All right, now for the explanation as to why I decided I was in love with you and decided to give you a present to commemorate it. This couple in my shop today,' she continued as she set the shopping bag on the table. 'Upper class, second- or third-generation money. Not wealthy but rich. They worked as a team, and I admire that. The signals, the rhythm. I like that. I want that.'

'I'll give you that.'

'I think you will.' She lifted the package out of the bag, retrieved scissors and went patiently to work on the wrap.

'While they were in the shop, buying some nice glassware, a gorgeous display table and a very unique chess table, the wife part of the team spotted this other piece. Completely *not* her style, let me tell you. But apparently her sister's. She got all excited, brought it to the counter while I was ringing up. She wanted it, but it wasn't priced. I hadn't priced it because I'd never seen it before.'

She saw the jolt of understanding run over his face. 'Christ, Laine, you found the pooch.'

She set the unwrapped statue on the table. 'Sure looks like it.'

Chapter Twelve

He picked it up to examine it, just as she had. Shook it, just as she had.

'It looks like an ordinary, somewhat tacky, inexpensive ceramic dog.' Laine gave it a quick tap with her fingers. 'And just screams Big Jack O'Hara to me.'

'You'd know.' He hefted it, as if checking weight while he looked at her. 'You didn't just bust it open and see for yourself.'

'No.'

'Big points for you.'

'Major, but if we stand here discussing it much longer I'm going to crack, scream like a maniac and smash it into lots of doggie pieces.'

'Then let's try this.' Even as she opened her mouth to protest, he smacked the statue smartly on the table. Its winsome head rolled off so that the big painted eyes stared up in mute accusation.

'Well.' All Laine could do was huff out a breath. 'I thought we might do that with a little more ceremony.'

'Quick is more humane.' He dipped his fingers into the jagged opening and tugged. 'Padding,' he said and had her wincing as he smashed the body on the table.

'I have a hammer in the mudroom.'

'Uh-huh.' He unwrapped the layers of cotton, pulled out the small pouch. 'I just bet this is a lot more upscale than anything I ever got out of a cereal box. Here.' He handed her the jewelry pouch. 'You do this part.'

'And major points right back at you.'

156

The buzz was there, that hum in the blood she knew came as much from holding something that belonged to someone else as it did from discovery. Once a thief, she thought. You could stop stealing, but you never forgot the thrill.

She untied the cord, pulled open the gathered top and poured a glittering rain of diamonds into her open palm.

She made a sound. Not unlike, Max noted, the one she made when he brought her to orgasm. And her eyes, when they lifted to his, were just a bit blurry. 'Look how big and shiny,' she murmured. 'Don't they make you just want to run out and dance naked under the moon?' When he lifted an eyebrow, she shrugged. 'Okay, just me then. You'd better take them.'

'I would, but you've got them clutched in your fist, and I'd rather not have to break your fingers.'

'Oh, sorry. Obviously, I still have to work on my recovery. Ha ha. Hand doesn't want to open.' She pried her fingers into a loose curl and let the diamonds drip out into Max's open palm. When he continued to stare at her with that lifted brow, she laughed and let the last stone drop.

'Just seeing if you were paying attention.'

'This is a new aspect of you, Laine. Something must be a little twisted in me because I like it. Maybe you could clean this mess up. I've got to go get a couple things.'

'You're taking them with you?'

He glanced back at the doorway. 'Safer for both of us that way.'

'Just so you know,' she called after him, 'I counted them, too.'

She heard him laugh and felt another click inside her. Somehow fate had tossed her the man who was perfect for her. Honest, but flexible enough not to be shocked or appalled by certain urges that still snuck up on her. Reliable, with a flicker of the dangerous about him to spice it up.

She could make this work, she mused as she swept the broken shards into the center of the newspaper. They could make this work.

He came back in, saw she'd put the dog's head on a lace-edged napkin, like a centerpiece. After a double take, he snickered.

'You're a strange and unpredictable woman, Laine. That sure suits me.'

'Funny, I was thinking the same about you, except for the woman part. What've you got there?'

'Files, tools.' He set the file folder down, opened it to a detailed description of the missing diamonds. Sitting, he took out a jeweler's loupe and a gem scale.

'You know what you're doing with those?'

'Take a case, do your homework. So, yeah, I know what I'm doing with them. Let's take a look.'

He spread the diamonds on the pouch, selected one. 'It's eye-clean.' He held it up. 'No inclusions or blemishes visible to my naked eye. How about yours?'

'Looks perfect.'

'This one's a full cut, weighing . . .' He laid it on the scale, calculating. 'Whew, a whopping sixteen hundred milligrams.'

'Eight gorgeous carats.' She sighed. 'I know a little about diamonds myself, and about math.'

'Okay, closer look.' Using a small pair of tongs, he lifted the stone and studied it with the loupe. 'No blemishes, no clouds or inclusions. Terrific brilliance and fire. Top of the sparkle chart.'

He set it to the side, on a small scrap of velvet he'd brought down with him. 'I can cross the eight-carat, full-cut, Russian white off my list.'

'It would certainly make a wonderful engagement ring. A little over the top, and yet, who cares?' His expression, one of mild horror mixed with hopeful amusement, made her laugh. 'Just kidding. Sort of. I'm going to pour us some wine.'

'Great.'

He chose another diamond, repeated the routine. 'So, does this talk about engagement rings mean you're going to marry me?'

She set a glass of wine by his elbow. 'That's my intention.'

'And you strike me as a woman who follows through on her intentions.'

'You're a perceptive man, Max.' Sipping her own wine, she ran a hand over his hair. 'Just FYI, I prefer the square cut.' Leaning down, she brushed her lips over his. 'A nice clean, uncluttered look, platinum setting.'

'So noted. Should be able to afford one considering the finder's fee on these little babies.'

'*Half* the finder's fee,' she reminded him.

He gave her hair a tug to bring her mouth back to his. 'I love you, Laine. I love every damn thing about you.'

'There are a lot of damn things about me, too.' She sat beside him while he worked. 'I should be scared to death. I should be racked with nerves over what's happening between you and me. I should be terrified knowing what it means to have those pretty shiny rocks on my kitchen table, aware that someone's already been inside my house looking for them. And could come back. I should be worried sick about my father – what he'll do, what Crew will do to him if he finds him.'

She took a contemplative sip of wine. 'And I am. Under here,' she said, with a hand on her heart. 'All those things are going on under here, but over it, and through it, I'm so happy. I'm happier than I've ever been in my life, or expected to be. The worry, the nerves, even the fear can't quite outweigh that.'

'Baby, I'm a hell of a catch. Nothing for you to be nervous about on that score.'

'Really? Why hasn't anybody caught you before?'

'None of them were you. Next, whoever – and we'll assume it was Crew – broke in, tore the place up looking for these didn't find them here. Not much sense in coming back to go over the same ground. Last, your father's managed to land on his feet all his life. I bet he's still got his balance and agility.'

'I appreciate the logic and common sense.'

She didn't look like she was buying any. He considered showing her the snub-nosed .38 strapped to his ankle, but wasn't sure if it would reassure her or scare her.

'You know what we've got here, Ms. Tavish?'

'What have we got here?'

'Just over seven million – or one quarter of twenty-eight point four million in diamonds – almost to the carat.'

159

'Seven point one million.' She said it in a reverent whisper. 'On my kitchen table. I'm sitting here, looking at them, and still I can't really believe he pulled it off. He always said he would. "Lainie, one day, one fine day, I'm going to make the big score." I swear, Max, most times he said it he was just conning himself. And now look at this.'

She picked up a stone, let it sparkle in her hand. 'All his life, he wanted that one, big, glittery take. He and Willy must've had the best time.' She let out a breath, set the stone back with the others. 'Okay, reality check. The sooner those are out of my house and back where they belong, the better.'

'I'm going to contact my client, make arrangements.'

'You'll have to go back to New York?'

'No.' He reached for her hand. 'I'm not leaving. We finish this out. Three-quarters of the pie is still out there. Where would your father go, Laine?'

'I don't know. I swear to you I don't have a clue. I don't know his habits and haunts anymore. I cut myself off from him because I wanted so much to be respectable. And still . . . God I'm such a hypocrite.'

She rubbed her hands over her face, dragged them back into her hair. 'I took money from him. Through college, a little here, a little there. There'd be an envelope stuffed with cash in my mailbox, or now and then a cashier's check made out to me. And after I gradu-ated, too. A little windfall out of the blue, which I dutifully banked or invested. So I could buy this house, start my business. I took it. I knew it wasn't from the goddamn tooth fairy. I knew he'd stolen it or bilked someone out of it, but I took it.'

'You want me to blame you for that?'

'I wanted to be respectable,' she repeated. 'But I took the money to build that respectability. Max, I wouldn't use his name, but I used the money.'

'And you rationalized it and justified it. I could do the same. But let's just cut through all that and agree that it's a very shaky area. Let's agree you don't take it anymore, and make it clear to him the next time you see him.'

160

'If I had a dollar for every time I tried to make it clear to him. Oh, that's right. I do. But I'll make it stick this time. I promise. Do me one favor?'

'Just ask.'

'Put those away somewhere and don't tell me where. I don't want him coming back and talking me into giving them to him. It's not out of the realm.'

Max slid the stones back into the pouch, tucked it in his pocket. 'I'll take care of it.'

'I want to help you get the rest of them. I want that for a few reasons. One, I guess it'll go a ways toward easing my conscience. Two, and more important, it's just the right thing to do. More important than that, I hope that recovering them, getting them back where they belong will protect my father. I couldn't stand for him to be hurt. And somewhere between the conscience and the right thing lies the two-and-a-half-percent finder's fee.'

He took her hand and kissed it. 'You know, you may have bought that respectability, but you must've been born with that style. I've got a few things to see to. Maybe you can see about warming up that fudge.'

'If I wait a bit, both of us get our evening chores done, we could have those sundaes in bed with extra whipped cream.'

'I believe I might just be the luckiest man alive at this point in time.' His cell phone beeped, making Laine chuckle when she heard the digitized opening riff 'Satisfaction.'

'Hold that thought,' he said, and answered. 'Gannon.' His face broke into a wide grin. 'Hey, Mama.'

Since he leaned against the stove instead of heading out of the room for privacy, Laine started to ease out. But he grabbed her hand, pulled her back.

'So, you liked the glasses. That makes me the good son, right? Your favorite.' He scowled, tucking the phone between his ear and shoulder so he could keep a hand on Laine and reach for his wine. 'I don't think it's fair to put your grandchildren in the mix. It's not like Luke went out specially and picked them out to suit you. Stay,' he said in a hushed aside to Laine, then

161

transferred the phone to his other hand when he released her.

'Yeah, I'm still in Maryland. On a job, Mama.' He paused, listening, while Laine puttered around the kitchen looking for something to do. 'No, I don't get tired of hotels and eating in restaurants. No, I'm not sitting here chained to my nasty computer and working too hard. What am I doing? Actually, I'm two-timing you with a sexy redhead I picked up the other day. There's talk of whipped cream later.'

Laine's shocked gasp only had him crossing his feet at the ankles.

'I am not making it up. Why should I? She's right here. Want to talk to her?' He tipped the phone slightly away from his ear. 'She says I'm embarrassing you. Am I?'

'Yes.'

'Guess you're right about that, Mama. Her name's Laine, and she's the prettiest thing I've seen in my life. How do you feel about redheaded grandchildren?'

He winced, held the phone out a good six inches. Across the room, Laine could hear the exclamations – but couldn't tell the tone of them.

'No problem. I've got another eardrum. Yeah, I'm crazy in love with her. I will. Of course I will. She won't. As soon as . . . We *will*. Mama, take a breath, will you? Yes, she makes me very happy. Really? I want you to hang up and call Luke right now. Tell him he's been shuffled into second place, and I'm your favorite son. Uh-huh, uh-huh. Okay. I love you, too. Bye.'

He clicked off, stuck the phone back in his pocket. 'I'm her favorite son. That'll burn Luke's ass. Anyway, I'm supposed to tell you that she can't wait to meet you, and we have to come down to Savannah ASAP so she can, and can have a little engagement party for us. Which in Marlene-speak means a couple hundred of her closest friends and family. You're not allowed to change your mind about me. And she'd like it very much if you'd call her tomorrow when she's calmed down so you can have a nice chat.'

'Oh my God.'

'She's prepared to love you because I do. Plus she's thrilled that I'm going to settle down and get married. Then there's you having

162

the good sense to see what a prize I am. You've got a big leg up with Marlene.'

'I feel a little sick.'

'Here.' He pulled his phone out again. 'Call your mama, then you can tell her and put me on the spot. We'll be even.'

She stared at the phone, stared at him. 'This is real.'

'Damn right.'

'You really want to marry me.'

'We're past the want to. I'm going to marry you. You don't follow through on this, Marlene will hunt you down and make your life a living hell.'

She laughed, took two running strides, then jumped into his arms. Hooked her legs around his waist and covered his mouth with hers. 'I've always wanted to visit Savannah.' She took the phone out of his hand, laid it on the counter behind him.

'What about your mother?'

'I'll call her later. There's a two-hour time difference, you know. So if I call her in two hours, it's really the same thing as calling her now. That way we can do something else for two hours.'

Since she was chewing on the lobe of his ear, he had a pretty good idea what the something else would be. Hitching her to a steadier position, he started out of the room. 'What about those evening chores?'

'Let's be irresponsible.'

'I like your thinking.'

She ran her tongue down his throat, up again. 'Can you make it all the way upstairs?'

'Honey, the way I'm feeling, I could make it all the way to New Jersey.'

She bounced lightly as he started up the stairs. 'We forgot the whipped cream.'

'Save it for later.'

She reached down to tug his shirt out of his waistband. 'Big talk.' Her hands snuck under the shirt, ran up the hard plane of his chest. 'Mmm, I love your body. I noticed it right away.'

'May I say, ditto.'

'But it wasn't the kicker.'

'What was?' he asked and turned into the bedroom.

'Your eyes. They looked into mine, and my tongue went thick, my brain went stupid. I thought . . . oh, yum, yum, yum.' She kept legs and arms hooked tight around him when he tumbled them into bed. 'Then when you asked me to dinner, I thought – in the far reaches of my mind I didn't quite acknowledge – that I'd have this rash, wild, impulsive affair with you.'

'I think you did.' He got busy undoing her blouse.

'Now I'm going to marry you.' Delighted, she pulled his shirt over his head and threw it aside. 'Max, I should tell you, I'd've slept with you if Henry didn't like you, but I wouldn't be marrying you if he objected.'

He lowered his mouth to her breast, bit gently. 'Fair's fair.'

She arched, absorbed, then riding on the thrill rolled over to reverse positions. 'I'd just sneak around behind his back and have sex with you. I'd feel bad about it, but I'd do it anyway.'

'You're such a slut.'

She threw back her head and hooted with laughter. 'Oh God! I feel wonderful.'

His hands ran up her sides, then in and over curves. 'You're telling me.'

'Max.' The sweetness seeped into her, had her brushing her hands through his hair, then cupping his face. 'I love you, Max. I'll be such a good wife.'

She was everything he wanted and hadn't known he was looking for. The whole of her, all those strange and lovely layers that formed her fit the whole of him as no one ever had, or ever would.

He drew her down to him, stroking her hair, her back, as love swarmed inside him. And when she sighed, the long, contented sound of it was like music.

Soft, so soft, her skin, her lips, so that the moment took on a dreamy hue that made it easy to be tender. He could cherish her here, and wondered if anyone ever had.

Instead of seeing her as competent or clever, as practical and smart, had anyone ever shown her she was precious?

He murmured to her, foolish things, romantic things as he eased her over to undress her. His hands skimmed over her as if she were more fragile than glass, more splendid than diamonds.

Her breath caught, another quiet little sigh as she let him take her over, as she sailed over smooth, gentle waves of pleasure. Under his hands she was pliant, willing to lay herself open for whatever he gave, or took.

Long, lush kisses that shimmered through the blood and sent pulses skipping. Slow, indolent caresses that sent warm thrills over the skin. She floated on the lazy river of sensation.

As that river rose, she felt the sleepy passion wake to roll through her in an endless swell. She arched to him, once again wrapping herself around him so they sat, locked together in the middle of the bed.

Mouths met more urgently, with breath quickening as the air went misty, as heart kicked against heart. Need welled inside her, throbbing like a wound, spreading like a fever.

She murmured his name, over and over, as she pushed him back, as she straddled him and cupped his hands to her breasts.

She took him inside her, captured him in all that velvet heat. Watching him through the shadows, her hair gleaming through them, her eyes impossibly blue.

Angling back, she offered him the lovely white line of her. He could feel the canter of her heart, the shivers along her skin, the taunt brace of it as she set to ride him.

Then she leaned forward, her hair raining down to curtain her face, and his. She anchored her hands on his shoulders, dug her fingers in. And drove him mad.

Her hips charged like lightning, shooting sparks of shock through his blood. The pleasure stormed through him now, whipped by her energy. She threw her head back, crying out when she clamped around him, convulsed around him.

Clinging to the edge, he reared up, banded her in his arms and, with his lips hot on her throat, let her drag him over with her.

*

165

He had to work. It wasn't the easiest transition with his body sated with sex and his mind veering constantly back to Laine. But the work was vital. Not just for his client, or for himself, but for Laine.

The sooner this portion of the diamonds was back where it belonged, the better for all concerned.

But that was hardly the end of it, or of her problems.

He didn't expect Crew would come back searching for them in the house, but neither did he expect the man to just cut his losses and walk away. He'd killed for those stones, and he wanted all of them.

He'd planned to have all of them from the beginning, Max concluded while he shuffled his notes into another pattern to wait for some new piece to fall into place.

No reason that made sense to have lured Myers out for a private meeting unless he'd planned to eliminate him and increase his take. He'd have picked his other partners off and slithered away with the full twenty-eight million.

Had they sensed it? Wouldn't someone who'd lived a life on the grift catch the smell of a scam? That was his bet, in any case. Either Jack or Willy had sensed a double cross, or been spooked by Myers's disappearance.

So they'd gone into the wind.

And had both ended up here, assuming Laine would be the perfect place to hide the stones until they could liquidate them and vanish for good.

He'd kick Jack O'Hara's sorry ass for that later.

They'd led Crew right to Laine's doorstep. The stones were secure, but not in the way they'd planned. And Willy was dead, Laine a target.

And once more, he thought in disgust, Big Jack was under the radar and on the move.

He wouldn't go far, Max mused. Not with Willy's quarter share at stake.

He'd be holed up somewhere, working on the angles. That was good. It would give Max the time and the opportunity to run him to ground and collect another quarter share.

166

He'd keep his word to Laine. He wasn't interested in turning Big Jack over to the cops. But he was interested, in fact he was deeply invested, in tearing a strip off the man for putting Laine in jeopardy.

Which brought him back to Crew.

He wouldn't go far either. Now that he knew the investigation was centered right here in Angel's Gap – and Max could only lay that on his own head – he'd be more careful. But he wouldn't want too much distance between himself and the prize.

He'd killed for another quarter of the take. He sure as hell wouldn't hesitate to kill for another half.

In Crew's place, Max would set his sights on O'Hara. There was only one thing standing between O'Hara and twenty-eight million. That was Laine.

He'd hand the diamonds in his possession over to his client, dust his hands and say that's the best I can do and scoop Laine up, tuck her away in Savannah. Of course, he'd have to sedate her, hogtie her and keep her in a locked room, but he'd do it if he believed it would take her out of the mix and keep her safe.

But since he didn't think either of them would be very happy with her drugged, tied up and locked away for the next several years, it didn't seem like the way to go.

Crew would just wait, bide his time and come after her when he chose.

Best if Crew made the move while he was on their ground, with them both on full alert.

Because she had to know. Two things Laine wasn't, were slow and stupid. So she knew a man didn't steal millions, kill for it, then count his losses cheerfully and walk away from half that pie.

It wasn't just a case with the fun and challenge of the investigation, and a fat fee at the end of it, any longer. It was their lives now. To secure their future, he'd do whatever it took.

He scanned his notes again, stopped and nearly kicked back in the delicate chair before he remembered it wasn't suited to the move. He hunched forward instead, tapping his fingers along his own printout.

Alex Crew married Judith P. Fines on May 20, 1994. Marriage license registered New York City. One child, male, Westley Fines Crew, born Mount Sinai Hospital, September 13, 1996.

Subject filed for divorce; divorce granted by New York courts, January 28, 1999.

Judith Fines Crew relocated, with son, to Connecticut in November 1998. Subsequently left that location. Current whereabouts unknown.

'Well, we can fix that,' Max muttered.

He hadn't pursued that avenue very far. His initial canvass of Judith's neighbors, associates, family had netted him little, and nothing to indicate she'd continued contact with Crew.

He flipped through more notes, found his write-up on Judith Crew née Fines. She was twenty-seven when they married. Employed as manager of a Soho art gallery. No criminal record. Upper-middle-class upbringing, solid education and very attractive, Max noted as he looked over the newspaper photo he'd copied during his run of her.

She had a sister, two years younger, and neither she nor the parents had been very forthcoming, nor very interested in passing on information. Judith had cut herself off from her family, her friends. And vanished sometime in the summer of 2000 with her young son.

Wouldn't Crew keep tabs on them? Max wondered. Wouldn't a man who took such pride, had such an ego, want to see some reflection of self, some hint of his own immortality in a son? Maybe he wasn't particularly interested in maintaining a relationship with the ex, or with a small boy who'd make demands. But he'd keep tabs, you bet your ass. Because one day that boy would grow up, and a man wanted to pass on his legacy to his blood.

'All right, Judy and little Wes.' Max wiggled his fingers like a pianist about to arpeggiate. 'Let's see where you got to.' He played those fingers over the keyboard and started the search.

Walking voluntarily into a police station went against the grain. Jack didn't have anything against cops. They were only doing what

168

they were paid to do, but since they were paid to round up people just like him and put them in small, barred rooms, they were a species he preferred to avoid.

Still, there were times even the criminal needed a cop.

Besides, if he couldn't outwit the locals and wheedle what he needed to know out of some hayseed badge in a little backwater town, he might as well give it up and get a straight job.

He'd waited until the evening shift. Logically, anyone left in charge after seven was bound to be closer to the bottom of the police feeding chain.

He'd shoplifted his wardrobe from the mall outside of town with an eye to the personality he wanted to convey. Jack was a firm believer in the clothes making the man whatever the man might elect to be.

The pin-striped suit was off the rack, and he'd had to run up the hem of the pants himself, but it wasn't a bad fit. The clown-red bow tie added just the right touch, hinting at harmless.

He'd lifted the rimless glasses from a Wal-Mart, and wasn't quite ready to admit they actually sharpened his vision. In his opinion, he was entirely too young and viral to need glasses.

But the look of them finished off the intellectual-heading-toward-nerd image he wanted to project.

He had a brown leather briefcase, which he'd taken the time to bang up so it wouldn't look new, and he'd filled it as meticulously as a man might when traveling to an out-of-town meeting.

A smart player became the part.

He'd browsed through Office Depot, helping himself to the pens, notepads, sticky notes and other paraphernalia the administrative assistant of an important man might carry. As usual, such office toys both fascinated and bemused him.

He'd actually spent an entertaining hour playing with a personal data assistant. He did love technology.

As he walked down the sidewalk toward the station house, his gait became clipped, and his big shoulders hunched into a slump that looked habitual. He tapped the glasses back up his nose in an absent gesture he'd practiced in the mirror.

His hair was brutally slicked back, and – courtesy of the dye he'd purloined from a CVS drugstore that afternoon – was a glossy and obviously false shoe-polish black.

He thought Peter P. Pinkerton, his temporary alter ego, would be vain enough to dye his hair, and oblivious enough to believe it looked natural.

Though there was no one around to notice, he was already in character. He pulled out his pocketwatch, just the sort of affectation Peter would enjoy, and checked the time with a worried little frown.

Peter would always be worried about something.

He climbed the short flight of stairs and walked into the small-town cop shop. As he expected, it boasted a smallish, open waiting area, with a uniformed deputy manning the counter toward the rear.

There were black plastic chairs, a couple of cheap tables and a few magazines – *Field and Stream, Sports Illustrated, People* – all months out of date.

The air smelled like coffee and Lysol.

Jack, now Peter, tapped his fingers nervously at his tie and nudged up his glasses as he approached the counter.

'Can I help you?'

Jack blinked myopically at the deputy, cleared his throat. 'I'm not entirely sure, Officer . . . ah, Russ. You see, I was supposed to meet an associate this afternoon. One p.m., at the Wayfarer Hotel dining room. A lunch meeting, you see. But my appointment never arrived and I've been unable to reach him. When I inquired at the hotel desk, I was informed he never checked in. I'm quite concerned, really. He was very specific about the time and place, and I've come here all the way from Boston for this appointment.'

'You looking to file a missing persons report on a guy who's only been gone, what, eight hours?'

'Yes, but you see, I've been unable to reach him, and this was an important appointment. I'm concerned something may have happened to him on his trip from New York.'

'Name?'

'Pinkerton. Peter P.' Jack reached inside his suit jacket as if to produce a card.

170

'The name of the man you're looking for.'

'Oh yes, of course. Peterson, Jasper R. Peterson. He's a rare-book dealer, and was to acquire a particular volume my employer is most interested in.'

'Jasper Peterson?' For the first time, the deputy's eyes sharpened.

'Yes, that's right. He was traveling from New York, into Baltimore, I believe, and through D.C. before taking some appointments in this area. I realize I may seem to be overreacting, but in all my dealings with Mr. Peterson, he's always been prompt and reliable.'

'Going to ask you to wait a minute, Mr. Pinkerton.'

Russ pushed back from the counter and disappeared into the warren of rooms in the back.

So far, so good, Jack thought. Now he'd express shock and upset at the news that the man he sought had recently met with an accident. Willy would forgive him for it. In fact, he thought his long-time friend would appreciate the layers of the ruse.

He'd probe and pick at the deputy and work his way around to learning exactly what effects the police had impounded.

Once he knew for certain they had the pooch, he'd take the next step and nip it from the property room.

He'd have the diamonds, and he'd take them – and himself – as far away from Laine as possible. Leaving a trail for Crew that a blind man on a galloping horse could follow.

After that . . . well, a man couldn't always plan so far ahead.

He turned back toward the counter, a distracted look on his face. And felt a quick lurch in the belly when instead of the bored deputy, a big, blond cop stepped out of the side door.

He didn't look nearly slow enough to suit Jack.

'Mr. Pinkerton?' Vince gave Jack one long, quiet study. 'I'm Chief Burger. Why don't you step back into my office?'

Chapter Thirteen

A thin worm of sweat dribbled down Jack's spine as he stepped into the office of Angel Gap's chief of police. In matters of law and order, he much preferred working with underlings.

Still, he sat, fussily hitching his trousers, then setting his brief-case tidily beside his chair, just as Peter would have done. The smell of coffee was stronger here, and the novelty mug boasting a cartoon cow with bright red Mick Jagger lips told Jack the chief was having some java with his after-hours paperwork.

'You're from Boston, Mr. Pinkerton?'

'That's right.' The Boston accent was one of Jack's favorites for its subtle snoot factor. He'd perfected it watching reruns of 'MASH' and emulating the character of Charles Winchester. 'I'm only here overnight. I'm scheduled to leave in the morning, but as I've yet to complete my purpose I may need to reschedule. I apologize for bothering you with my problems, Chief Burger, but I'm really quite concerned about Mr. Peterson.'

'You know him well?'

'Yes. That is, fairly well. I've done business with him for the last three years – for my employer. Mr. Peterson is a rare-book dealer, and my employer, Cyrus Mantz, the Third – perhaps you've heard of him?'

'Can't say.'

'Ah, well, Mr. Mantz is a businessman of some note in the Boston and Cambridge areas. And an avid collector of rare books. He has one of the most extensive libraries on the East Coast.' Jack fiddled with his tie. 'In any case, I've come down specifically, at

Mr. Peterson's request, to see, and hopefully purchase, a first-edition copy of William Faulkner's *The Sound and the Fury* – with dust jacket. I was to meet Mr. Peterson for lunch—'

'Have you ever met him before?'

Jack blinked behind his stolen lenses, as if puzzled by both the question and the interruption. 'Of course. On numerous occasions.'

'Could you describe him?'

'Yes, certainly. He's rather a small man. Perhaps five feet six inches tall, ah . . . I'd estimate about one hundred and forty pounds. He's in the neighborhood of sixty years of age, with gray hair. I believe his eyes are brown.' He scrunched up his own. 'I believe. Is that helpful?'

'Would this be your Mr. Peterson?' Vince offered him a copy of the photo he'd pulled from the police files.

Jack pursed his lips. 'Yes. He's considerably younger here, of course, but yes, this is Jasper Peterson. I'm afraid I don't understand.'

'The man you identified as Jasper Peterson was involved in an accident a few days ago.'

'Oh dear. Oh dear, I was afraid it was something of the kind.' In a nervous gesture, Jack removed the glasses, polished the lenses briskly on a stiff white handkerchief. 'He was injured then? He's in the hospital?'

Vince waited until he'd perched the glasses back on his nose. 'He's dead.'

'Dead? *Dead*?' It was a fist slammed into the belly, hearing it again, just that way. And the genuine jolt had his voice squeaking. 'Oh, this is dreadful. I can't . . . I never imagined. How did it happen?'

'He was hit by a car. He died almost instantly.'

'This is such a shock.'

Willy. God, Willy. He knew he'd gone pale. He could feel the chill under his skin where the blood had drained. His hands trembled. He wanted to weep, even to wail, but he held back. Peter Pinkerton would never commit such a public display of emotion.

'I don't know precisely what to do next. All the time I was

waiting for him to meet me, growing impatient, even annoyed, he was . . . Terrible. I'll have to call my employer, tell him . . . Oh dear, this is just dreadful.'

'Did you know any of Mr. Peterson's other associates? Family?'

'No.' He fiddled with his tie, fussily, though he wanted to yank at it as his throat swelled. *I'm all he had*, Jack thought. *I'm the only family he had. And I got him killed.* But Peter Pinkerton continued in his snooty Harvard drawl. 'We rarely talked of anything other than books. Could you possibly tell me what arrangements have been made? I'm sure Mr. Mantz would want to send flowers, or make a donation to a charity in lieu.'

'Nothing's set, as yet.'

'Oh. Well.' Jack got to his feet, then sat again. 'Could you tell me, possibly, if Mr. Peterson was in possession of the book when he . . . I apologize for sounding ghoulish, but Mr. Mantz will ask. The Faulkner?'

Vince tipped back in his chair, swiveled gently side to side with his cop's eyes trained on Jack's face. 'He had a couple paperback novels.'

'Are you certain? I'm sorry for the trouble, but is there any way to check, a list of some sort? Mr. Mantz has his sights set on that edition – you see it's a rare find with the dust jacket. A first edition in, we were assured – mint condition – and he'll, Mr. Mantz, he'll be very . . . oh dear, insistent about my following through.'

Obligingly Vince opened a drawer, took out a file. 'Nothing like that here. Clothes, toiletries, keys, a watch, cell phone and recharger, wallet and contents. That's it. Guy was traveling light.'

'I see. Perhaps he put it in a safe-deposit box for safekeeping until we met. Of course, he wouldn't have been able to retrieve it before . . . I've taken enough of your time.'

'Where are you staying, Mr. Pinkerton?'

'Staying?'

'Tonight. Where are you staying, in case I have something further on those arrangements.'

'Ah. I'm at the Wayfarer tonight. I suppose I'll fly out as scheduled

174

tomorrow. Oh dear, oh dear, I don't know *what* I'm going to say to Mr. Mantz.'

'And if I need to reach you, in Boston?'

Jack produced a card. 'Either of those numbers will do. Please do contact me, Chief Burger, if you have any word.' He offered his hand.

'I'll be in touch.'

Vince walked him out, stood watching as he walked away.

It wouldn't take long to check the details of the story, and to run the names Pinkerton and Mantz. But since he'd looked through those cheap lenses into Laine's blue eyes, he figured he'd find they were bogus.

'Russ, call over to the Wayfarer, see if they've got this Pinkerton registered.'

He'd confirm that little detail, haul one of his men out of bed to keep tabs on the man for the night.

He'd have another look at the effects, see what O'Hara – if that was O'Hara – had been interested in finding. Since he was damn sure he didn't have a few million in diamonds sitting back in the property room, he'd just have to see if he had something that pointed to them.

Where the hell *was* it? Jack walked briskly for two blocks before he began to breathe easily again. Cop houses, cop smells, cop eyes tended to constrict his lungs. There was no ceramic dog on the list of effects. Surely even a suspicious cop – and that was a redundant phrase – would have listed something like that. So there went his tidy little plan to break into the property room and take it. Couldn't steal what wasn't there to be stolen.

The dog had been in Willy's possession when they'd split up, in the hopes that Crew would track Jack himself to give Willy time to slip away, get to Laine and give her the figurine for safekeeping.

But the vicious, double-crossing Crew had tracked Willy instead. Nervous old Willy, who'd wanted nothing more than to retire to some pretty beach somewhere and live out the rest of his days painting bad watercolors and watching birds.

Should never have left him, should never have sent him out on his own. And now his oldest friend in the world was dead. There was no one he could talk with about the old days now, no one who understood what he was thinking before the words were out of his mouth. No one who got the jokes.

He'd lost his wife and his daughter. That was the way the ball bounced and the cookie crumbled. He couldn't blame Marilyn for pulling stakes and taking little Lainie with her. She'd asked him, God knew, a thousand times to give the straight life a decent try. And he'd promised her that many times in return he would. Broken every one of those thousand promises.

You just can't fight nature, was Jack's opinion. It was his nature to play the game. As long as there were marks, well, what the hell could he do? If God hadn't intended for him to play those marks, He wouldn't have made so damn many of them.

He knew it was weak, but that was the way God had made *him*, so how could he argue the point? People who argued with God were prime suckers. And Kate O'Hara's boy, Jack, was no sucker.

He'd loved three people in his life: Marilyn, his Lainie and Willy Young. He'd let two of them go because you can't keep what didn't want to be yours. But Willy had stuck.

As long as he'd had Willy, he'd had family.

There was no bringing him back. But one day, when all was well again, he'd stand on some pretty beach and lift a glass to the best friend a man ever had.

But meanwhile, there was work to be done, thoughts to be thought and a back-stabbing killer to outwit.

Willy had gotten to Laine, and surely he'd had the dog in his possession when he had or why make contact? He could've hidden it, of course. A sensible man would've locked it away until he was sure of his ground.

But that wasn't Willy's style. If Jack knew Willy – and who better? – he'd make book he had that statue with the diamonds in its belly when he'd walked into Laine's little store.

And he hadn't had it when he walked out again.

That left two possibilities: Willy had stashed it in the shop without Laine knowing. Or Daddy's little girl was telling fibs.

Either way, he had to find out.

His first stop would be a quiet little search of his darling daughter's commercial enterprise.

Max found Laine in her home office working some sort of design onto graph paper. She had several tiny cutouts lined up on her desk. After a minute's study he recognized them as paper furniture.

'Is this like an adult version of a doll house?'

'In a way. It's my house, room by room.' She tapped a stack of graph paper. 'I'm going to have to replace some of my pieces, so I've made scale models of some of the things I have in stock that might work. Now I'm seeing if they do, and how I might arrange them if I bring them home.'

He stared another moment. 'I'm wondering how anyone that careful about picking out a sofa ended up engaged to me.'

'Who says I didn't make a scale model of you, then try it out in different scenarios?'

'Huh.'

'Besides, I don't love a sofa. I like and admire it, and am always willing to part with it for the right price. I'm keeping you.'

'Took you a minute to think that one out, but I like it.' He leaned on the corner of the desk. 'Looks like I've located Crew's ex-wife and kid. Got a line on them in Ohio, a suburb of Columbus.'

'You think she knows something?'

'I have to speculate Crew would have some interest in his son. Wouldn't a man like that see an offspring, particularly a male offspring, as a kind of possession? The wife's different, she's just a woman, and easily replaced.'

'Really?'

'From Crew's point of view. From mine, when you're lucky enough to find the right woman, she's irreplaceable.'

'Took you a minute, but I like it.'

'The other thing is, in my line when you pick loose any thread,

177

you keep tugging until it leads to something or falls out of the whole. I need to check this out. So, change of plans. I'll be heading to New York first thing in the morning, with the diamonds we have. I'll deliver them personally, then bounce over to Ohio and see if I can finesse anything from the former Mrs. Crew or Junior.'

'How old is Junior?'

'About seven.'

'Oh, Max, he's just a child.'

'You know the whole thing about little pitchers, big ears? Jesus, Laine,' he added when he saw her face. 'I'm not going to tune him up. I'm just going to talk to them.'

'If they're divorced, it could be she doesn't want any part of Crew, and doesn't want her son to know what his father is.'

'Doesn't mean the kid doesn't know or that Daddy doesn't drop in now and then. It needs to be checked, Laine. I'll be leaving first thing. If you want to come with me, I'll make the arrangements for both of us.'

She turned back to her graph, used the eraser end of a pencil to poke the cut-out sofa to a different angle. 'You'd move quicker without me.'

'Probably, but not as cheerfully.'

She glanced up. 'A quick trip to New York, a flip over to Ohio. Seems like old times, and it's appealing. But I can't. There's work, there's Henry, there's putting this house back together. And I have to practice calling your mother.' She turned the pencil around to poke him when he laughed. 'No comments on the last one, friend, it's how I do things.'

He didn't want to leave her, not even for a day. Part of that, he knew, was the obsessive insanity of new love, but part was worry. 'If you came with me, you could call her from wherever, you could leave Henry with the Burgers, close the shop for the day and deal with the house when we get back. You can take your graph paper.'

'You're worried about leaving me while you go do your job. You shouldn't. In fact, you can't. I've been taking care of myself for a very long time, Max. I'm going to keep on taking care of myself after we're married.'

'You won't have a homicidal jewel thief looking in your direction after we're married.'

'You can guarantee that? Go,' she said without waiting for his answer. 'Do what you do. I'll do what I do. And when you get back . . .' She ran her hand along his thigh. 'We'll do something together.'

'You're trying to distract me. No, wait, you did distract me.' He leaned down, kissed her. 'How about this? I go do what I do, you stay and do what you do. I'll be back tomorrow night, earlier if I can manage it. Until I'm back, you'll go over and hang with the cop and his wife. You and Henry. You're not staying here alone until this is wrapped. Now, we can fight about that or we can take the compromise.'

She continued to walk her fingers along his thigh. 'I like to fight.'

'Okay.' He pushed to his feet as if preparing for the round.

'But not when I agree with the other person's point of view. It's an unnecessary risk for me to stay out here alone. So I'll impose on Jenny and Vince.'

'Good. Well . . . good. Want to fight about something else?'

'Maybe later?'

'Sure. I'm going to go nail down my flights. Oh, any chance that sofa can be long enough for a guy to take a Sunday afternoon nap on?'

'That's a distinct possibility.'

'I'm going to like being married to you.'

'Yes, you are.'

It was after one by the time Jack finished searching Laine's shop. Torn in two directions, he locked up after himself. He was bitterly disappointed not to have found the diamonds. Life would be so much simpler if he had the little dog tucked under his arm. He could be on his way out of town, leaving enough bread crumbs for Crew to follow that would lead him and any trouble away from Laine.

Then he'd vanish down the rabbit hole. Fourteen million in

diamonds – even figuring on half of that due to a quick turnover – would provide a very plush rabbit hole.

At the same time he was struck with a kind of stupefied pride. Just look what his little girl had done, and in the *straight* world. How the hell had she learned to buy all those things? The furniture, the fancy pieces, the little fussy table sitters. It was a pretty place. His little girl had herself a very pretty business. And since he'd been curious enough to take the time to hack into her computer and check, it appeared she had herself a reasonably profitable one.

She'd made a good life. Not what he'd wanted for her, certainly, but if it was what she wanted, he'd accept that. He didn't understand it, and never would, but he'd accept.

She was never going to come back with him on the road. That fantasy had finally been put to rest after a good look at her house, her shop, her life.

A waste of considerable talent, to his way of thinking, but he understood a father couldn't push an offspring into a mold. Hadn't he rebelled against his own? It was natural enough for Laine to rebel and to seek her own path.

But it wasn't natural for her to try to scam her own blood. She had the diamonds. Had to have them. If she had some sort of twisted idea that she needed to hold out on him to protect him, he'd have to set her straight.

Time for a father-daughter chat, Jack decided.

It meant he'd have to boost a car. He really hated to steal cars, it was so common, but a man needed transportation when his daughter decided to live in the boondocks.

He'd drive out to see her, have that chat, get the diamonds and be gone by morning.

He settled on a Chevy Cavalier – a nice, steady ride – and took the precaution of switching its plates with a Ford Taurus a few miles away. All things being equal, the Chevy should get him through Virginia and into North Carolina, where he had an associate who could turn it for him. With the cash, he could spring for a new ride.

He'd leave enough footprints for Crew to follow, just enough of a scent to draw the man away from Maryland and Laine.

Then Jack had an appointment in southern California, where he'd turn those sparkly stones into hard green cash.

After that, the world was his fricking oyster.

He was humming along to the classic rock station he'd found, his mood lifted by The Beatles' cheerful claim of getting by with a little help from friends.

Jack knew all about getting by.

As a precaution, he stopped the car halfway up the lane. The dog was the friendly sort when it wasn't wetting itself in fear, he recalled, but dogs barked. No point in setting it off until he scoped things out.

With his penlight, he started the hike. The dark was pitch, making him wonder again what had possessed Laine to choose such a place. The only sound he heard other than his own feet crunching on gravel was an owl, and the occasional rustle in the brush.

Why anyone would want brush anything could rustle in was beyond him.

Then he caught the scent of lilacs and smiled. That was a nice sort of thing, he thought. To walk along in the quiet dark and smell flowers. Nice, he added, for the occasional change of pace. Maybe he'd pick a few of the blooms, take them with him to the door. A kind of peace offering.

He started to follow his nose when his light hit chrome.

And scanning the beam over the car, Jack felt his mood plummet.

The insurance cop's car was at the end of the drive with Laine's.

Eyes narrowed, he studied the house. No lights glowed in the windows. It was near two in the morning. A man's car was parked in front of his daughter's house.

His little girl was . . . he searched for a word his father's mind could handle without imploding. Dallying. His little girl was dallying with a cop. To Jack's mind a private investigator was just a cop with a higher annual income than the ones who carried badges.

His own flesh and blood, with a cop. Where had he gone wrong?

With a huge sigh, he stared down at his feet. He couldn't risk breaking in a second time with the PI in there. He needed privacy, damnit, to talk some sense into his Lainie.

Cop had to leave sometime, Jack reminded himself. He'd find a place to stash the car, and wait.

It was a testament to her love, Laine concluded, that nudged her into altering her morning routine in order to see Jack off at five forty-five a.m. She liked to think it also demonstrated she was flexible, but she knew better.

Her routine would snap right back into place once she and Max became more accustomed to each other. It might take on a slightly different form, but in the end, it would be routine.

She was looking forward to it and, thinking just that, gave him a very enthusiastic kiss at the door.

'If that's the goodbye I get when I'm only going to be gone a day, what do I have to look forward to if I have to be out of town overnight?'

'I was just realizing how nice it's going to be to get used to you, to take you for granted, to have your little habits and quirks irritate me.'

'God, you're a strange woman.' He took her face in his hands. 'Am I supposed to look forward to irritating you?'

'And the bickering. Married people tend to bicker. I'm going to call you Maxfield when we bicker.'

'Oh, hell.'

'I think that'll be fun. I really can't wait until we fight about household expenditures or the color of the bathroom towels.' And as that was perfect truth, she flung her arms around his neck and kissed him enthusiastically again. 'Travel safe.'

'I'll be home by eight, earlier if I can manage it. I'll call.' He pressed his face into the curve of her shoulder. 'I'll think of something to bicker about.'

'That's so sweet.'

He eased away, leaned down to pet Henry, who was trying to

nose between them. 'Take care of my girl.' He hefted his brief-case, gave Laine a quick wink, then walked to his car.

She waved him off, then, as promised, shut the door and locked it.

She didn't mind the early start. She'd go into town, take a closer look at her stock to see what she might want to transfer to her home. She'd take Henry for a romp in the park, then make some calls to see about repairing some of her damaged furniture, and make arrangements to have what she considered a lost cause removed.

She could indulge herself by surfing some of the bridal sites on-line, drooling over gowns and flowers and favors. Laine Tavish was getting married! Delight had her doing a quick dance that inspired Henry to race in mad circles. She wanted to buy some bridal magazines, but needed to go to the mall for that, where she could buy them without causing gossip in town. Until she was ready for town gossip.

She wanted a big, splashy wedding, and it surprised her to realize it. She wanted a gorgeous and ridiculously expensive dress. A once-in-a-lifetime dress. She wanted to spend hours agonizing over flowers and music and menus.

Laughing at herself, she started upstairs to dress for the day. Snapping back into place, she thought. Her normal life had taken a hard, unexpected stretch, but it was snapping right back into the normal. Was there anything more normal than a woman dreaming about her wedding day?

'Need to make lists, Henry. Lots and lots of lists. You know how I love that.'

She buttoned up a tailored white shirt, slipped on trim navy pants. 'Of course, we have to set a date. I'm thinking October. All those beautiful fall colors. Rusts and umbers and burnt golds. *Rich* colors. It'll be a bitch to get things organized in time, but I can do it.'

Imagining, she twisted her hair into a single French braid, tossed on a jacket with tiny blue-and-white checks.

A romp in the park first, she decided, and slipped into comfort-able canvas flats.

She was halfway downstairs when Henry gave a series of alarmed barks and raced back up again.

Laine froze where she was, then rolled to her toes as her heart slammed against her ribs. Before she could follow Henry's lead, Jack strolled out of the living room to the bottom of the steps.

'That dog go to get his gun?'

'Dad.' She shut her eyes, caught her breath. 'Why do you *do* this? Can't you just knock on the damn door?'

'This saves time. You always talk to the dog?'

'Yes, I do.'

'He ever talk back?'

'In his way. Henry! It's all right, Henry. He won't hurt you.' She continued down, letting her gaze pass over the dyed hair, the rumpled suit. 'Working, I see.'

'In my way.'

'Looks like you slept in that suit.'

'I damn well did.'

The bite in his tone had her lifting her brows. 'Well, don't snap at me, Jack. It's not my fault.'

'It *is* your fault. We need to have a talk. Elaine.'

'We certainly do.' Voice crisp, she nodded, then turned on her heel and marched into the kitchen. 'There's coffee, and some apple muffins if you're hungry. I'm not cooking.'

'What are you *doing* with your life?'

His explosion had Henry, who'd bellied in to test the waters, scramble back to the doorway.

'What am *I* doing with my life? What am I doing?' She rounded on him, coffeepot in hand. Her heated response tore through Henry's fear to find his courage. He barreled in, glued himself to Laine's side and tried out a snarl in Jack's direction.

'It's all right, Henry.' Pleased, and considerably surprised by his defense, Laine reached down to soothe the dog. 'He's not dangerous.'

'I could be,' Jack muttered, but some of his temper faded into relief that the dog had some spirit.

'I'll tell you what I'm doing with my life, Dad. I'm *living* my

184

life. I have a house, a dog, a business, a car – and payments. I have a plumber.' She gestured with the pot, and nearly sloshed coffee over the rim. 'I have friends who haven't actually done time, and I can borrow a book from the library and know I'll actually still be here when it's due back. What are you doing with your life, Dad? What have you ever done with your life?'

His lips actually trembled before he firmed them and managed to speak. 'That's a hell of a way for you to talk to me.'

'Well, it's a hell of a way for you to talk to me. I never criticized your choices, because they were yours and you were entitled to make them. So don't you criticize mine.'

His shoulders hunched; his hands retreated to his pockets. And Henry, vastly relieved that his valor wouldn't be tested, stood down. 'You're spending nights with a cop. A *cop*.'

'He's a private investigator, and that's beside the point.'

'Beside the—'

'What I'm doing is spending nights with the man I love and am going to marry.'

'Ma—' He made several incoherent sounds as the blood drained out of his face. He gripped the back of a chair, slowly sank into it. 'Legs went out. Lainie, you can't get married. You're just a baby.'

'I'm not.' She set the pot aside, went to him and put her hands gently on his cheeks. 'I'm not.'

'You were five minutes ago.'

Sighing, she slid onto his lap, rested her head on his shoulder. Henry tiptoed over to push his head through the tangle of legs and lay it sympathetically on Jack's knee.

'I love him, Daddy. Be happy for me.'

He rocked with her. 'He's not good enough for you. I hope he knows that.'

'I'm sure he does. He knows who I am. Who we are,' she said and drew back to watch Jack's face. 'And it doesn't matter because he loves me. He wants to marry me, make a life with me. We'll give you grandchildren.'

The color that had come into his cheeks faded away again. 'Oh now, let's not rush that far ahead. Let me settle into the idea that you're not six anymore. What's his name?'

'Max. Maxfield Gannon.'

'Fancy.'

'He's from Savannah, and he's wonderful.'

'He make a good living?'

'Appears to – but then, so do I.' She brushed at his dyed hair. 'Are you going to ask all the clichéd father-of-the-bride questions now?'

'I'm trying to think of them.'

'Don't worry about it. Just know he makes me happy.' She kissed his cheek, then rose to deal with the coffee.

Absently, Jack scratched Henry behind the ears, and made a friend for life. 'He left pretty early this morning.'

She glanced over her shoulder. 'I don't like you watching the house, Dad. But yes, he left early.'

'How much time do we have before he gets back?'

'He won't be back until tonight.'

'Okay. Laine, I need the diamonds.'

She took out a mug, poured his coffee. She brought it to the table, set it in front of him, then sat. Folded her hands. 'I'm sorry, you can't have them.'

'Now you listen to me.' He leaned forward, gripped the hands she'd folded on the table. 'This isn't a game.'

'Isn't it? Isn't it always?'

'Alex Crew, may he rot in everlasting, fiery hell, is looking for those stones. He's killed one man, and he's responsible for Willy's death. Has to be. He'll hurt you, Laine. He'll worse than hurt you to get them. Because it's not a game to him. To him it's cold, brutal business.'

'Why did you get mixed up with him?'

'I got blinded by the sparkle.' Setting his teeth, he eased back, picked up his coffee. Then just stared into the black. 'I figured I could handle him. He thought he had me conned. Son of a bitch. Thought I bought the high-toned game he was playing with his fancy fake name and patter. I knew who he was, what he'd been into. But there was all that shine, Lainie.'

186

'I know.' And because she did know, because she could remember how it felt to be blinded by the shine, she rubbed her hand over his.

'Had to figure he might try a double cross along the way, but I thought I could handle him. He killed Myers, the inside man. Just a greedy schmuck who wanted to grab the prize. That changed the tune, Lainie. You know I don't work that way. I never hurt anybody, not in all the years in the game. Put a hole in their wallets, sure, a sting in their pride, but I never hurt anybody.'

'And you don't understand people who do, not deep down, Dad.'

'You think you do?'

'Better than you, yeah. For you it's the rush. It's not even the score itself, but the rush of the score. The shine,' she said with some affection. 'For someone like Crew, it's the score, it's about taking it all, and if he gets to hurt somebody along the way, all the better because it only ups the stakes. He's never going to stop until he gets it all.'

'So give me the diamonds. I can lead him away from here, and he'll know you don't have them. He'll leave you alone. You're not important to him, but there's nothing in this world more important to me than you.'

It was truth. From a man skilled as a three-armed juggler with lies, it was perfect truth. He loved her, always had, always would. And she was in the exact same boat.

'I don't have them. And because I love you, I wouldn't give them to you if I did.'

'Willy had to have them when he walked into your shop. There's no point in him coming in, talking to you, if he didn't plan to give them to you. He walked out empty-handed.'

'He had them when he came in. I found them yesterday. Found the little dog. Do you want that muffin?'

'Elaine.'

She rose to get it, set it on a plate. 'Max has them. He's taking them back to New York right now.'

He literally lost his breath. 'You – you *gave* them to the cop?'

'PI, and yes, I did.'

187

'Did he hold you at gunpoint? Did you have a seizure? Or did you *just lose your mind*?'

'The stones are going back where they belong. There'll be a press release announcing the partial recovery, which will get Crew off my back.'

He lunged up, pulling at his hair as he circled the room. Thinking it was a game now that they were friends, Henry scooped up his rope and pranced behind Jack. 'For all you know he's heading to Martinique. To Belize. To Rio or Timbukfuckingtu. Sweet Baby Jesus, how could my own daughter fall for a scam so old it has mold on it?'

'He's going exactly where he said he was going, to do exactly what he said he was doing. And when he gets back, you and I are going to give him your share, so he can do exactly the same thing with them.'

'In a pig's beady eye.'

To settle the dog, Laine got up and poured kibble into a bowl. 'Henry, time to eat. You're going to give them to me, Jack, because I'm not going to have my father hunted down and killed over a sack of shiny rocks.' She slapped her hands on the table between them. 'I'm not going to lie to my own children one day when they ask what happened to their granddaddy.'

'Don't you pull that shit on me.'

'You're going to give them to me because it's the only thing in my life I've ever asked of you.'

'Damnit, Laine. Damnit to hell and back again.'

'And you're going to give them to me because when Max turns them over and collects the fee, I'm going to give you my share. Well, half my share. That's one and a quarter percent of the twenty-eight, Dad. It's not the score of a lifetime, but it's not sneezable. And we'll all live happy ever after.'

'I can't just—'

'Consider it a wedding present.' She angled her head. 'I want you to dance at my wedding, Dad. You can't do that if you go to prison, or if Crew's breathing down your neck.'

On an explosive sigh, he sat again. 'Lainie.'

'They're bad luck for you, Dad. Those diamonds are cursed for you. They took Willy away from you, and you're on the run, not from the cops but from someone who wants you dead. Give them to me, get the monkey off your back. Max will find a way to square it with New York. The insurance company just wants them back. They don't care about you.'

She came to him, touched his cheek. 'But I do.'

He stared up at her, into the only face he loved more than his own. 'What the hell was I going to do with all that money anyway?'

Chapter Fourteen

Laine drummed her fingers on the steering wheel as she sat parked on her own lane, studying the dark green Chevy.

'You know, precious, your mother used to get that look on her face when . . .' Jack trailed off when she turned her head, slowly, and stared at him. 'That one, too.'

'You stole a car.'

'I consider it more of a lend/lease situation.'

'You boosted a car and drove it to my house?'

'What was I supposed to do? Hitchhike? Be reasonable, Lainie.'

'I'm sorry. I can see how unreasonable it is for me to object to my father committing grand theft auto in my own backyard. Shame on me.'

'Don't get pissy about it,' he muttered.

'Unreasonable *and* pissy. Well, slap me silly. You're going to take that car right back where you found it.'

'But—'

'No, no.' She lowered her head into her hands, squeezed her temples. 'It's too late for that. You'll get caught, go to jail, and I'll have to explain why my father thinks it's perfectly okay to steal a car. We'll leave it on the side of the road somewhere. Not here. Somewhere. God.'

Concerned by the tone of her voice, Henry stuck his head over the front seat to lap at her ear.

'All right. It'll be all right. We'll leave the car outside of town.' She sucked in a breath, straightened. 'No harm, no foul.'

'If I don't have the car, how the hell am I supposed to get to

New Jersey. Let's just consider, Lainie. I have to get to Atlantic City, to the locker, get the diamonds and bring them back to you. That's what you want, isn't it?'

'Yes, that's what I want.'

'I'm doing this for you, sweetheart, against my better judgment, because it's what you want. What my baby girl wants comes first with me. But I can't walk to Atlantic City and back, now can I?'

She knew that tone. Using it, Jack O'Hara could sell bottled swamp water out of a tent pitched beside a sparkling mountain stream. 'There are planes, trains, there are goddamn buses.'

'Don't swear at your father,' he said mildly. 'And you don't really expect me to ride a bus.'

'Of course not. Of course not. There I go being pissy and unreasonable again. You can take my car. Borrow,' she amended swiftly. 'You can borrow my car for the day. I won't need it anyway. I'll be busy at work, beating my head against the wall to try to find my brain.'

'If that's the way you want it, honey.'

She cast her eyes to heaven. 'I still can't believe you left millions of dollars' worth of diamonds in a rental locker, then sent Willy here with several million more.'

'We had to move fast. Jesus, Laine, we'd just found out Crew killed Myers. We'd be next. Tucked my share away, took off. Bastard Crew was supposed to come after me. I all but drew him a damn map. Stash was safe. Willy gets another chunk of it here, then he'd double back for the rest while Crew's a thousand miles away tracking me. That was going to be our traveling money, our cushion.'

To live on like kings, Jack thought, on that pretty beach.

'Never figured Crew would track you down. I'd never have brought that on you, baby. Crew was supposed to be off chasing me.'

'And if he'd caught up with you?'

Jack only smiled. 'I wasn't going to let him catch up. I still got the moves, Lainie.'

'Yeah, you still got the moves.'

'Just buying Willy time. He'd get to Mexico, liquidate the first quarter of the take. We'd meet up, take off, and with that much backing, we'd hide out in comfort until the heat was off.'

'Then slip back and pick up the rest from me.'

'Two, three years down the road maybe. We were working it out as we went.'

'You and Willy both had keys to the locker in AC?'

'Nobody on the planet I trusted like Willy. Except you, Lainie,' he added, patting her knee. 'Cops got it now.' He pursed his lips in thought. 'Take them a while to trace it, if they ever do.'

'Max has it now. I took it off Willy's key ring. I gave it to him.'

'How'd you get . . . ?' The irritation in his tone faded to affection. 'You stole it.'

'In a manner of speaking. But if you're going to equate that with boosting a car, don't even start. It's entirely different.'

'Did it right under their noses, didn't you?'

Her lips twitched. 'Maybe.'

He gave her a little elbow nudge. 'You still got the moves, too.'

'Apparently. But I don't want them.'

'Don't you want to know how we pulled it off?'

'I've figured out most of it. Your inside man takes the blinds – the dog, the doll, et cetera – into his office. Innocuous things, who pays attention? They sit around in plain sight. The shipment or shipment come in, he replaces them – or some of them – with fakes. Tucks a quarter share of the score in each of the four blinds. And there they sit.'

'Myers sweated that part. He was greedy, but he didn't have good nerves.'

'Hmm. Couldn't wait long, or he'd crack. Besides, you wouldn't trust him longer. A couple of days at most. He puts out the alarm on the fakes himself, helps cover his ass. Cops swoop in, investigation starts. Blinds go out under their nose.'

'We each took one. Fact is, I posed as one of the insurance suits, walked into Myers's office while everybody's swarming around, walked out with my share in my briefcase. It was beautiful.'

He shot her a grin. 'Me and Willy had lunch a couple blocks

192

away at T.G.I. Friday's after the scoop, with fourteen million warming our pockets. I had the nachos. Not bad.'

She shifted in her seat so they were face-to-face. 'I'm not going to say it wasn't a great score. I'm not going to pretend I don't understand the rush either. But I'm trusting you, Dad. I'm trusting you to keep your promise. I need this life. I need it even more than you need that rush. Please don't mess it up for me.'

'I'm going to fix everything.' He leaned over, kissed her cheek. 'Just you wait and see.'

She watched him saunter to the stolen car. One for every minute, she thought. 'Don't make me one of them, Dad,' she murmured.

She had Jack drop her off at the park with Henry, and counted on it still being early enough no one who knew her would be around to comment on the strange man driving off in her car.

She gave Henry a half hour to romp, roll and chase the town squirrels.

Then she took out her cell phone and called Max.

'Gannon.'

'Tavish.'

'Hi, baby. What's up?'

'I . . . you're at the airport?'

'Yeah. Just set down in New York.'

'I thought I should tell you, my father came by to see me this morning.'

'That so?'

She heard the chill in his tone, and winced. No point in mentioning her father's morning mode of transportation. 'We settled some things, Max, straightened some things out. He's on his way to get his share of the diamonds. He's going to give them to me so I can give them to you, and you . . . well, et cetera.'

'Where are they, Laine?'

'Before I get to that, I want you to know he understands he screwed up.'

'Oh, which screwup does he understand?'

'Max.' She bent to take the branch Henry dumped at her feet.

She had to wing it like a javelin, but it had the dog racing off in delight. 'They panicked. When they heard about Myers's death, they just panicked. It was a bad plan, no question, but it was impulse. My father didn't realize Crew knew about me, much less that he'd come here. He just thought Willy could get me the figurine, and I'd tuck it away for a few years while they . . .' She let it go as she realized how the rest would sound.

'While they fenced the remaining share of the stolen gems and lived off the fat.'

'More or less. But the point is he's agreed to give them up. He's getting them.'

'Where?'

'A locker in Atlantic City. Mail Boxes, Etc. He's driving up now. It'll take him most of the day for the round-trip, but—'

'Driving what?'

She cleared her throat. 'I lent him my car. I had to. I know you don't trust him, Max, but he's my father. I've got to trust him.'

'Okay.'

'That's it?'

'Your father's your father, Laine. You did what you needed to do. But no, I don't have to trust him, and I'm not going to reel in shock if we find out he's living in a pretty casa in Barcelona.'

'He doesn't trust you either. He thinks you're on your way to Martinique.'

'Saint Bart's, maybe. I like Saint Bart's better.' There was a moment's pause. 'You're really stuck right smack in the middle, aren't you?'

'Just my luck to love both of you.' She heard the change in background noise and realized he'd walked outside the terminal. 'Guess you're going to catch a cab.'

'Yeah.'

'I'd better let you go. I'll see you when you get back.'

'Counting on that. I love you, Laine.'

'It's nice to hear that. I love you, too. Bye.'

On his end, Max slipped the phone back into his pocket and checked his watch as he strode over to the cab stand. Depending on traffic, he could have the New York leg of the day knocked in a couple hours. By his calculation he could make the detour to Atlantic City without too much trouble.

If Laine was going to be stuck in the middle, he was going to make damn sure she didn't get squeezed.

Laine walked from the park to Market Street with Henry doing his best to swivel his head a hundred and eighty degrees to chew off the hated leash.

'Rules are rules, Henry. Believe it or not, I all but had that tattooed on my butt up to a couple of weeks ago.' When his response to that was to collapse on his belly and whimper, she crouched until they were nose to snout. 'Listen up, pal. There's a leash law in this town. If you can't handle that, and comport yourself with some dignity, there'll be no more playing in the park.'

'Having a little trouble there?'

She jolted, cringed at the waves of guilt that washed hot over her as she looked up into Vince's wide, friendly face. 'He objects to the leash.'

'He'll have to take that up with the town council. Come on, Henry, I got part of a cruller here with your name on it. I'll walk with you,' he said to Laine. 'Need to talk to you anyway.'

'Sure.'

'Getting an early start today.'

'Yes. I've had a lot of things piling up. Thanks,' she added when he took the leash and dragged Henry along.

'Been an interesting space of time recently.'

'I'm looking forward to it sliding back to dull.'

'Guess you probably are.'

He waited while she got out her keys, unlocked the front door of the shop. While she deactivated the alarm, he squatted down to unclip the leash and give the grateful Henry a rub.

'Heard you were in the station a couple days ago.'

'Yes.' To keep busy, she walked over to unlock the cash register. 'I told you that I knew Willy, and I thought . . . I wanted to see about making arrangements.'

195

'Yeah, you did. You can do that. Make the arrangements. That's been cleared.'

'Good. That's good.'

'Funny thing. Somebody else came in, last night, interested in the same guy. Only thing, he said he knew him by the other name. Name that was on the card he gave you.'

'Really? I'm going to put Henry in the back.'

'I'll do it. Come on, Henry.' Bribed with half a cruller, Henry scrambled into the back room. 'This guy who came in, he said Willy – or Jasper – was a rare-book dealer.'

'It's possible he was. Or that he was posing as one. I told you, Vince, I haven't seen Willy since I was a kid. That's the truth.'

'I believe that. Just a funny thing.' He walked over to lean on the counter. 'Like it's a funny thing there were five keys in his effects, and when I looked through them last night, there were only four.' He waited a beat. 'Not going to suggest they were miscounted.'

'No. I'm not going to lie to you.'

'Appreciate that. The man who came in last night, he had your eyes.'

'It's more accurate to say I have his. If you recognized him, why didn't you arrest him?'

'That's complicated, too. Best to say you don't arrest a man because you see something in his eyes. I'm going to ask you for that key, Laine.'

'I don't have it.'

'Damn it, Laine.' He straightened.

'I gave it to Max,' she said quickly. 'I'm trying to do what's right, what should be done – and not be responsible for putting my father in prison. Or getting him killed.'

'One of those things that should be done is keeping me informed. The diamond theft might be New York's business, Laine, but one of the men suspected of stealing them died in my town. One or more of his buddies is in my town, or has been. That puts my citizenship at risk.'

'You're right. I'm having a hard time keeping my balance on

196

this very thin line. And I know you're trying to help me. I found Willy's share of the diamonds. I didn't know they were here, Vince, I swear it.'

'If you didn't know, how'd you find them?'

'They were in some stupid statue. Dog – pooch. I've been trying to piece it together and can only conclude that he stuck it on a shelf when he was here, or put it somewhere – in a cabinet or drawer – and either Jenny or Angie shelved it. Angie, most likely. Jenny would've asked me about it, and when I asked her, she didn't remember seeing it before. I gave them to Max, and he's in New York right now, turning them over. You can check. You can call Reliance and check.'

He said nothing for a moment. 'We haven't run that far out of bounds, have we, Laine, that I have to check?'

'I don't want to lose your friendship, or Jenny's.' She had to take a steadying breath. 'I don't want to lose my place in this town. I wouldn't be insulted if you checked, Vince.'

'That's why I don't have to.'

She needed a tissue after all, and yanked one out of the box behind the counter. 'Okay. Okay. I know where another share is. I found out this morning. Please don't ask me how I found out.'

'All right.'

'The key I took from Willy's things is to a locker. I called Max as soon as I could to tell him. In fact, I was talking to him about it when I was in the park with Henry. They're going to be turned in, too. That's half of them. I can't do anything about the other half. Max has leads, and he'll do what he does. But once the half of the diamonds is back where it belongs, I've done all I can.

'Am I going to have to move away?'

'Break Jenny's heart if you did. I don't want your father in the Gap, Laine.'

'I understand. This should all be taken care of by tonight, tomorrow at the latest. He'll be gone.'

'Until it's taken care of, I want you to stay close.'

'That I can promise.'

*

By the time Jack crossed over into New Jersey, he'd come up with a dozen reasons why taking the diamonds back was a mistake. Obviously, this Gannon character was stringing his little girl along so he could cop his fat fee. Wasn't it better for her to find that out sooner rather than later?

And going back to Maryland might lead Crew back to Maryland, and Laine.

Then there was the fact that turning over all those pretty stones fit him as well as a prison jumpsuit.

Besides, Willy would've wanted him to keep them. A man couldn't deny a dead friend's wish, could he?

He was feeling considerably better as he maneuvered through Atlantic City traffic. Enough to whistle cheerily between sips of his on-the-road Big Gulp. He parked in the lot of the strip mall and considered the best way out was to hop a flight at the airport and head straight to Mexico.

He'd send Laine a postcard. She'd understand. The kid knew how the game was played.

He strolled the walkway first, scanning faces, looking for marks, looking for cops. Places like this always gave him itchy fingers. Malls, shopping centers, little packs of stores where people breezed in and out with their cash and credit cards so handy.

Day after day. The straights buying their puppy chow and greeting cards, sold to them by other straights.

What was the point?

Places like this made him want to fall on his knees and give thanks for the life he led – right before he helped himself to some of that cash, some of those credit cards and made tracks to anywhere else.

He wandered into a Subway, bought a ham and cheese with hot pepper sauce to give himself more time to scope out the area. He washed it down with another big shot of cold caffeine, used the facilities.

Satisfied, he crossed to the Mail Boxes, Etc., strolled to the lockers, slid in his key.

Come to Papa, he thought, and opened the door.

He made a sound, something similar to a duck being punched in the belly, and snagged the only contents of the locker. A piece of notepaper with a on-line message.

Hi, Jack. Look behind you.

He spun around, one meaty fist already balled.

'Take a swing, I'll deck you,' Max told him conversationally. 'Think about running, consider that I'm younger and faster. You'll just embarrass yourself.'

'You son of a bitch.' He had to wheeze it, but even that had a couple of heads turning in their direction. 'Double-crossing son of a bitch.'

'Pots calling kettles only prove pots lack imagination. Keys.' He held out a hand. 'Laine's car keys.'

In disgust, Jack slapped them into Max's hand. 'You got what you came for.'

'So far. Why don't we talk in the car? Don't make me haul you out,' he said quietly. 'We'd not only cause a scene that might bring the cops in on this, but Laine wouldn't like it.'

'You don't give two damns about her.'

'You're right, I don't. I give a hell of a lot more than that, which is why I'm not turning your sorry ass over to the cops. You got one chance, O'Hara, and you've got it because of her. In the car.'

Running occurred to him. But he knew his limitations. And if he ran, there was no chance to recoup the diamonds. He walked back out with Max, then settled himself in the passenger seat. Max took the driver's seat, set his briefcase on his lap.

'Here's the way it's going to be. You're sticking to me like gum on the bottom of my shoe. We're catching a flight to Columbus.'

'What the—'

'Shut up, Jack. I've got a lead to check, and until I'm done you and me, we're Siamese twins.'

'She told you. My own flesh and blood. She told you where I had the stash.'

'Yeah, she did. She told me because she loves me, and she believes – convinced herself to believe – you'd keep your end and bring them in. Because she loves you. Me, I don't love you, Jack, and I figure you had other plans for this.'

Opening his briefcase, Max took out a ceramic piggy bank. 'I've got to give you points for the sense of the ridiculous. Me, you and the pig, we're going to Columbus, then heading back to Maryland. And I'm going to give you that chance. That one chance to deserve Laine. You're going to give her this.' He tapped the pig, then put it away. 'Just as if you'd planned to all along.'

'Who says I didn't?'

'I do. You had fucking dollar signs in your eyes when you opened that locker. Let's show a little respect for each other here. My client wants the stones returned. I want my fee. Laine wants you safe. We're going to make all that happen.' He started the car. 'You finish this out, I'll see that your slate's wiped clean on this. You ditch me, you hurt Laine, and I'll hunt you down like I would a rabid dog. You'll be my goddamn life's work. That's a promise, Jack.'

'You're not bullshitting. I know when a man's bullshitting. Son of a gun.' Jack's grin spread wide and bright as he leaned over to embrace Jack. 'Welcome to the family.'

'Briefcase is locked, Jack.' Max pulled back, then set the brief-case out of reach in the back.

'Can't blame a guy for trying,' Jack said cheerfully, and settled back for the ride.

In his cabin, Crew selected a shirt the color of eggplant. He'd ditched the mustache, replacing it with a soul patch he thought suited the sleek, chestnut-hued ponytail. He wanted an arty look for this trip. He selected a pair of round-lensed sunglasses from his supply and studied the effect.

It was probably unnecessary to go to such trouble, but he did enjoy a good costume.

Everything was ready for company. He smiled as he looked around the cabin. Rustic, certainly, but he doubted Ms. Tavish would complain about the accommodations. He didn't plan on her staying for long.

He hooked the little .22 on the back of his belt, covered it with a hip-length black jacket. Anything else he might need was in the bag he slung on his shoulder before he strode out of the cabin.

He thought he might have a bite to eat before he had his date with the attractive Ms. Tavish. He might be too busy to dine that evening.

'I did the legwork,' Jack said as he and Max had a beer in the airport bar. 'Courted Myers for months. Now, I'll admit, I never dreamed of a score that big. Was thinking small, taking a couple of briefkes, clearing a couple hundred thousand each. Then Crew came into it.'

Jack shook his head, sipped through the foam. 'For all his faults, that's a man who thinks big.'

'Faults being he's a cold-blooded killer.'

Frowning, Jack dug his big hand into a bowl of nuts. 'Biggest mistake of my life, and I'm not ashamed to admit I've made a few, was hooking up with a man like Crew. He suckered me in, no question. I got dazzled by the idea of all those rocks. All those pretty, shiny rocks. He had the know-it-all for something like that, the vision. I had the connections. Poor Myers. I'm the one who brought him in, played him. He had a gambling problem, you know.'

'Yeah.'

'Far as I can see, any gambling's a problem. House is always going to win, so it's better to be the house. Gamblers are either rich people who don't give a shit if they lose, or suckers who actually think they can win. Myers was a sucker, word go. Had himself in deep, and with some nudging from me he was in deeper. He saw this as his way out.'

Jack drank more beer. 'Guess it was. Anyway, the deal went down smooth enough. Quick, clean. Had to figure they'd cop to Myers, but he was supposed to go straight under. Nobody was to know where anybody else was heading. Willy and me drove right out of the city, I dumped the pig in AC, and we dumped Willy's in a locker in Delaware. Got ourselves a nice hotel room in Virginia, had a fine meal, a couple bottles of champagne. Good time,' he said and toasted with his glass.

'Heard about Myers on CNN. Willy loved CNN. Tried to tell ourselves it was because of the gambling, but we knew. Switched cars, drove to North Carolina. Willy was spooked. Hell, we were both spooked, but he was nervous as a whore in church. Wanted to light out, just forget it all and head for the hills. I talked him down from that. Goddamnit.'

He studied his beer, then lifted it and drank deep. 'I'd lead Crew off, and he'd double back, get his share, take it to Laine. She could put him up for a little while. I thought he'd be safe. Thought they both would.'

'But he knew about her. Crew.'

'I got pictures of her in my wallet.'

He drew it out and flipped it open.

Max saw photos of a newborn with a bright thatch of red hair and skin as white as cream, and an expression on her little face that seemed to say, 'What the *hell* am I doing here?'

There were several of Laine as a child, all bright hair and eyes, who from the grin had obviously figured out what she was doing here. Then of the nubile teenager, pretty and dignified in her graduation shot. Of Laine wearing cutoffs and a skinny top, laughing as she stood in the blue surf of what Max deduced was Barbados.

'Always been a looker, hasn't she?'

'Prettiest baby you ever saw, and she just got prettier every day. I get sentimental, especially after a beer or two.' Jack shrugged. It was just another God-given weakness, after all. Closing the wallet, he tucked it away again.

'I must've shown her off to Crew sometime. Or he just dug down and looked for something he could use against me, should the need arise. There's no honor among thieves, Max, and anybody who thinks different is a sucker. But to kill over money? That's a sickness. I knew he had it in him, but I thought I could beat him at the game.'

'I'll find him. And I'll put him down, one way or the other. That's our flight.'

Laine fought not to pace, to just look busy. She checked the time again. Her father should be on his way back by now. She should've told him to call when he was on his way back. She should've insisted.

She could call Max again, but what was the point? He'd be on his way to Columbus. Maybe he was already there.

She just had to get through the day, that was all. Just this one day. Tomorrow, the news would hit that a large portion of the stolen diamonds had been recovered. She'd be in the clear, her father would be in the clear, and life would get back some semblance of normality.

Maybe Jack would pick up Crew's trail from this Ohio connection. They'd track him down, put him away. She'd never have to worry about him again.

'You keep going away.' Jenny gave her a little nudge as she carried a George Jones cheese dish to the counter for a customer.

'Sorry. I'm sorry. Wandering mind. I'll take the next one who comes in.'

'You could take Henry for another walk.'

'No, he's had enough walks today. He gets sprung from the back-room in another hour anyway.'

She heard the bells ring. 'I'll take this one.'

'All yours.' Jenny lifted her brows as she glanced at the new customer. 'Little old for that look,' she said under her breath, and moved on.

Laine fixed on her welcome face and crossed over to greet Crew. 'Good afternoon. Can I help you?'

'I'm sure you can.' From his previous visits to her store, he knew the arrangements and exactly where he wanted her. 'I'm interested in kitchen equipment. Butter crocks, specifically. My sister collects.'

'Then she's in luck. We have some very nice ones just now. Why don't I show you?'

'Please.'

He followed her through the main room, into the area she'd set up for kitchen equipment, furnishings and novelties. As they passed the door to the back room, Henry began to growl.

'You have a dog in here?'

'Yes.' Puzzled, Laine looked toward the door. She'd never known

203

Henry to growl at store sounds and voices. 'He's harmless and he's secured in the back room. I needed to bring him in with me today.' Because she sensed her customer's annoyance, she took his arm and led him to the crocks.

'The Caledonian's especially nice, I think, for a collector.'

'Mmm.' There were two customers and the pregnant clerk. As the customers were at the counter, he assumed they were paying for purchases. 'I don't know anything about it, really. What in the world is this?'

'It's a Victorian coal box, brass. If she enjoys antique and unique kitchen items, this is a winner.'

'Could be.' He slipped the .22 out of his belt and jammed the barrel into her side. 'Be very, very quiet. If you scream, if you make any move at all, I'll kill everyone in this shop, beginning with you. Understand?'

The heat of panic washed over her, then chilled to ice as she heard Jenny laugh. 'Yes.'

'Do you know who I am, Ms. Tavish?'

'Yes.'

'Good, that spares us introductions. You're going to make an excuse to walk out with me.' He'd planned to take her out the back, but the damned dog made that impossible. 'To give me directions, we'll say, to walk me to the corner. If you alert or alarm anyone, I'll kill you.'

'If you kill me, you won't get the diamonds back.'

'How fond are you of your very pregnant employee?'

Nausea rolled up her throat. 'Very fond. I'll go with you. I won't give you any trouble.'

'Sensible.' He slipped the gun in his pocket, kept his hand on it. 'I need to get to the post office,' he said, lifting his voice to a normal tone. 'Can you tell me where it is?'

'Of course. Actually, I need some stamps. Why don't I take you over?'

'I'd appreciate that.'

She turned, ordered her legs to move. She couldn't feel them, but she saw Jenny, saw her glance up, smile.

'I'm just going to run to the post office. Just be a minute.'

'Okay. Hey, why don't you take Henry?' Jenny motioned toward the back where the growls grew louder and were punctuated by desperate barks.

'No.' She reached out blindly for the doorknob, snatched her hand back when it bumped Crew's. 'He'll just fight the leash.'

'Yeah, but . . .' She frowned as Laine walked out without another word. 'Funny, she . . . oh, she forgot her purse. Excuse me just a minute.'

Jenny grabbed it from under the counter and was halfway to the door when she stopped, glanced back at her customers. 'Did she say she was going to buy stamps? The post office closed at four.'

'So, she forgot. Miss?' The woman gestured toward her purchases.

'She never forgets.' Gripping the purse, Jenny bolted for the door, pressing a hand to her belly as she dashed onto the sidewalk. She saw Laine's arm gripped in the man's hand as they turned the corner away from the post office.

'Oh God, oh my God.' She rushed back in, all but knocking her customers aside as she snatched up the phone and speed-dialed Vince's direct line.

Chapter Fifteen

It was a quiet suburban neighborhood, a middle-class bull's-eye with well-kept lawns and big leafy trees so old their roots had heaved up through portions of the sidewalks. Most driveways boasted SUVs, the suburbanites' transportation of choice. Many had car seats, and there were enough bikes and clunky second-handers to tell Max the age of kids in the neighborhood ranged from babies to teens.

The house was an attractive two-story English Tudor with a pretty blanket of lawn decorated with sedate flower bed and neatly trimmed shrubs. And a sold sign.

Max didn't need the realtors sign to tell him the place was empty. There were no curtains at the windows, no cars in the drive, no debris a young boy might leave in his wake.

'Skipped,' Jack said.

'Gee, Jack, thanks for the bulletin.'

'Guess it's irksome to come all this way and hit a dead end.'

'There are no dead ends, just detours.'

'Nice philosophy, son.'

Max stuck his hands in his pockets, rocked on his heels. 'Irksome?' he repeated, and Jack just grinned. 'Neighborhood like this has to have at least one nosy neighbor. Let's knock on doors, Jack.'

'What's the line?'

'I don't need a line. I've got an investigator's license.'

Jack nodded as they started toward the house on the left. 'People in this kind of place like talking to PIs. Adds excitement to the day. But I don't think you're going to tell Nosy Alice you're looking for a lead on twenty-eight mill in stolen diamonds.'

'I'm trying to locate Laura Gregory – that's the name she's using here – and verify if she is the Laura Gregory who's a beneficiary in a will. Details are confidential.'

'Good one. Simple and clean. People like wills, too. Free money.' Jack fussed with the knot of his tie. 'How do I look?'

'You're a fine-looking man, Jack, but I still don't want to date you.'

'Ha!' He gave Max a slap on the back. 'I like you, Max, damned if I don't.'

'Thanks. Now just keep quiet and let me handle this.'

They were still several paces from the door of a modified split-level when it opened. The woman who stepped out was in her middle thirties and wearing a faded sweatshirt over faded jeans. The anthem-like theme music from *Star Wars* poured out the door behind her.

'Can I help you with something?'

'Yes, ma'am.' Max reached for his ID. 'I'm Max Gannon, a private investigator. I'm looking for Laura Gregory.'

She looked hard at the identification, with a glimmer of excitement in her eyes. 'Oh?'

'It's nothing untoward, Mrs . . . .'

'Gates. Hayley Gates.'

'Mrs. Gates. I've been hired to locate Ms. Gregory and verify that she's the Laura Gregory named as a beneficiary in a will.'

'Oh,' she repeated as the glimmer spread to a sparkle.

'My associate and I . . . I'm Bill Sullivan, by the way.' To Max's annoyance, Jack stepped forward, took Mrs. Gates's hand and pumped it heartily. 'We were hoping to speak to Mrs. Gregory personally to verify that she is indeed the grand-niece of the late Spiro Hanroe. There was a bit of a family schism in the previous generation, and several of the family members, including Mrs. Gregory's parents, broke contact.' He lifted his hands in a shrug. 'Families. What can you do?'

'I know just what you mean. Excuse me just a minute.' She

207

stuck her head back in the door. 'Matthew? I'm right outside. My oldest is home sick,' she explained as she eased the door closed but for a crack. 'I'd ask you in, but it's a madhouse in there. You can see Laura sold the house.' She gestured toward the house next door. 'Put it on the market about a month ago – rock-bottom price, too. My sister's the realtor who listed it. Laura wanted to sell it fast, and the fact is, she moved even before it sold. She was planting her summer annuals one day and packing dishes the next.'

'That's odd, isn't it?' Max commented. 'She mention why?'

'Well, she *said* her mother in Florida was ill, seriously ill, and she was moving down there to take care of her. She lived next door for three years, and I don't remember her ever mentioning her mother. Her son and my oldest played together. He's a sweet boy, her Nate. Quiet. They were both quiet. It was nice for my Matt to have a friend next door, and Laura was easy to get along with. I always thought she came from money though.'

'Did you?'

'Just a feeling. And she worked part-time at an upscale gift shop at the mall. She couldn't have afforded the house, the car, the lifestyle, if you know what I mean, on her salary. She told me she came into an inheritance. It's funny she came into two, isn't it?'

'Did she tell you where in Florida?'

'No. Just Florida, and she was in a tearing hurry to get going. Sold or gave away a lot of her things, and Nate's, too. Packed up her car and zipped. She left . . . I guess it's three weeks ago. Little better than that. She said she'd call when she was settled, but she hasn't. It was almost like she was running away.'

'From?'

'I always—' She cut herself off, eyed them both a bit more cautiously. 'Are you sure she's not in trouble?'

'Not with us.' Max sent out a brilliant smile before Jack could speak. 'We're just paid by the Hanroe estate to find the beneficiaries and confirm identification. Do you think she's in trouble?'

'I can't imagine how, really. But I always figured a man –

ex-husband – somewhere in the background, you know? She never dated. Not once since she's been here. And Laura never talked about Nate's father. Neither did Nate. *But*, the night before she listed the house, I saw a guy come by. Drove up in a Lexus, and he was carrying a box. All wrapped up with a bow, like a birthday present, but it wasn't Nate's birthday, or Laura's either, for that matter. He only stayed about twenty minutes. Next morning, she called my sister and put the house on the market, quit her job, and now that I think about it, she kept Nate home from school for the next week.'

'Did she tell you who her visitor was?' Jack made the question conversational, as if they were all out here enjoying the spring weather and shooting the breeze. 'You must've asked. Anybody'd be curious.'

'Not really. I mean, yes, I mentioned I'd seen the car. She just said it was someone she used to know and clammed up. But *I* think it was the ex, and she totally freaked. You don't just sell your house and your furniture and drive off that way because your mother's sick. Hey, maybe he heard about this inheritance and was trying to wheedle his way back so he could cash in. People can be so low, you know?'

'They certainly can. Thanks, Mrs. Gates.' Max offered a hand. 'You've been very helpful.'

'If you find her, tell her I'd really like her to call. Matt misses Nate something fierce.'

'We'll do that.'

'He got to her,' Jack said as they started back to the rental car.

'Oh yeah, and I don't think there was a birthday present in the pretty box. She's running.' He glanced back at the empty house. 'Running from him, running with the diamonds, or both?'

'Woman runs like that's scared,' was Jack's opinion. 'Odds are even if he dumped the diamonds on her for safekeeping, she doesn't even know she's got them. Crew's not a man to trust anybody, especially an ex-wife. That's my take on it. So . . . are we going to Florida to work on our tans?'

209

'She's not in Florida, and we're going back to Maryland. I'll pick up her trail, but I've got a date with a beautiful redhead.'

'You'll drive.' Crew shifted the gun from Laine's kidney to the base of her spine. 'I'm afraid you'll have to climb over. Do it quickly, Ms. Tavish.'

She could scream, she could run. She could die. Would die, she corrected as she lowered herself into the passenger seat, maneuvered over the center console. Since she wasn't willing to die, she'd have to wait for a reasonable chance of escape.

'Seat belt,' Crew reminded her.

As she drew it around to secure, she felt the lump of her cell phone in her left pocket. 'I'll need the keys.'

'Of course. Now, I'm going to warn you once, only once. You'll drive normally and carefully, you'll obey the traffic laws. If you make any attempt to draw attention, I'll shoot you.' He handed her the keys. 'Trust me on that.'

'I do.'

'Then let's get started. Head out of town and take Sixty-eight, east.' He shifted his body so she could see the gun. 'I don't like to be driven, but we'll make an exception. You should be grateful to your dog. If he hadn't been in the back, we'd have gone out that way and you'd be taking this ride in the trunk.'

God bless you, Henry. 'I prefer this position.' As she drove she considered, and rejected, the idea of flooring the gas or trying to whip the wheel. Maybe, just maybe, that kind of heroic action worked in the movies, but movie bullets were blanks.

What she needed to do was somehow leave a trail. And stay alive long enough for someone to follow it. 'Were you what scared Willy into running into the street?'

'One of those twists of fate or timing or just bad luck. Where are the diamonds?'

'This conversation, and my existence, would both be over very quickly if I told you.'

'At least you're bright enough not to pretend you don't know what I'm talking about.'

'What would be the point?' She flicked a glance at the rearview mirror, let her eyes widen, then slid her eyes toward it again. It was enough to have him turning his head, looking behind. And when he did, she dipped her hand in her pocket, played her fingers over the buttons, praying she was counting correctly, and hit what she hoped was Redial.

'Eyes on the road,' he snapped.

She gripped the wheel with both hands, squeezed once and thought, *Answer the phone, Max, answer the phone and listen.* 'Where are we going, Mr. Crew?'

'Just drive.'

'Sixty-eight East is a long road. Are you adding interstate abduction to your list?'

'It would hardly make the top of it.'

'I guess you're right. I'd drive better if you weren't pointing that gun at me.'

'The better you drive, the less chance there is it will go off and put an ugly hole in your very pretty skin. True redheads – as I assume you are, given your father – have such delicate skin.'

She didn't want him thinking about her skin or putting holes in it. 'Jenny's going to send out an alarm when I don't come back.'

'It'll be too late to make any difference. Stay at the speed limit.'

She sped up until she hit sixty-five. 'Nice pickup. I've never driven a Mercedes. It's heavy.' She ran a hand over her throat as if nervous and babbling. 'Smooth though. Looks like a diplomat's car or something. You know, black Mercedes sedan.'

'You won't distract me with small talk.'

'I'm trying to distract myself, if you don't mind. It's the first time I've been kidnapped at gunpoint. You broke into my house.'

'And if I'd found my property, we wouldn't be taking this little trip together.'

'You made a hell of a mess.'

'I didn't have the luxury of time.'

'I don't suppose it would do any good to point out that you already have half the take when the deal was a quarter? And to say that once you get past, oh, say, ten million, the rest is superfluous.'

'No, it wouldn't. You'll take the next exit.'

'Three twenty-six?'

'South, to One forty-four East.'

'All right. All right. Three twenty-six South to One forty-four East.' She glanced over. 'You don't look like the sort of man to spend much time in state forests. We're not going camping, are we?'

'You and your father have inconvenienced me considerably, and added to my expenses. He'll pay for that.'

She followed his directions, carefully repeating them. She had to believe the call to Max had gone through. That her phone's batteries were still up, that she hadn't dropped out of range.

'Alleghany Recreation Park,' she said as she turned off the macadam and onto gravel at Crew's instructions. 'Really doesn't fit the Mercedes.'

'Take the left fork.'

'Cabins. Rustic, private.'

'Bear right.'

'A lot of trees. Deerwalk Lane. Cute. I'm being abducted to a cabin on Deerwalk Lane. It just doesn't sound menacing enough.'

'The last, on the left.'

'Good choice. Completely sheltered by the trees, barely within sight of the next cabin.'

She had to turn off the phone. He'd find it, she thought. He was bound to find it, and if it was on when he did, she'd lose even that slim advantage.

'Turn off the car.' He slapped it into Park himself. 'Give me the keys.'

She obeyed, turning her head, meeting his eyes, holding them. 'I don't intend to do anything that gets me shot. I'm not going to be brave or stupid.' As she spoke, she slipped her hand into her pocket, ran her thumb over the buttons and pushed End.

'You can start by climbing out this way.' He opened the door at his back, slid out. The gun remained pointed at her heart as she hefted her hips over the console.

'Now, let's go inside.' He nudged her forward. 'And chat.'

*

He'd made good time, Max thought as he strode across the terminal toward the exit. He'd be able to pick up Laine from Jenny's after he tucked Jack away. He didn't think it the best idea to take his future father-in-law to a cop's house.

The problem was trusting him.

He glanced back, noted Jack was still wearing a sickly tinge of green. They'd caught a prop plane out of Columbus to the local municipal, and Jack had been varying shades of green since takeoff.

'Hate those tin cans – tin cans with wings, that's all they are.' His skin was still gleaming with sweat as he leaned against the hood of Max's car. 'Need to get my legs under me.'

'Get them under you in the car.' Because he felt some sympathy, he opened the door, helped Jack settle his bulk inside. 'You puke in my ride, I'm going to kick your ass. Just FYI.'

He rounded the hood, got behind the wheel. He figured Big Jack could fake all manner of illnesses, but it took more talent than he could possess to change color. 'Here's what else is going to happen. I'm taking you to Laine's, and you're staying there until I get back with her. You take off, I'll find you, haul you back and beat you senseless with a stick. Clear on that?'

'I want a bed. All I want's a bed.'

Amused, Jack backed out of his parking slot. Remembering his phone, he dug it out of his pocket. He'd had to turn it off during the flight. Switching it back on, he ignored the beep that told him he had voice mail and called Laine, cell to cell. He heard her recorded voice tell him to leave a message.

'Hey, baby, I'm back, heading out of the airport. Gotta make one stop, then I'll be by to pick you up. Fill you in when I see you. Oh, got a few things for you. Later.'

Jack spoke with his head back, his eyes closed. 'It's dangerous to drive talking on one of those things.'

'Shut up, Jack.' But because he agreed, Max started to put it aside, when it beeped for an incoming. Certain it was Laine, he answered. 'You're quick. I was just . . . Vince?'

When fear bounced like an ice ball into his belly, he whipped the car to the side of the road. 'When? For Christ's sake, that's more than an hour ago. I'm on my way.'

He tossed the phone on the console, punched the gas. 'He's got her.'

'No, no, that's not true.' Even the sickly green had died away, leaving Jack's face bone white. 'He can't have her, not my baby girl.'

'He got her out of the shop just after five o'clock. He thinks they're in a dark sedan. A couple of people saw her get into a car with a man, but he doesn't have a good description of the vehicle.' He had the Porsche up to ninety. 'Jenny's got a good description of the guy. Long brown hair, ponytail, soul patch, sunglasses. White male, forty-five to fifty, six-foot, average build.'

'The hair's a blind, but it'd be him. He's got to get to me to get the diamonds. He'll hurt her.'

'We're not going to think about that. We're going to think of how to find them and get her back.' His hands were ice cold on the wheel. 'He needs a place. If he thinks the stones are here, he won't go far. He needs a private place, not a hotel. He'll contact you, or me. He'll – *shit*!'

He fumbled for the phone.

'Give it to me. You kill us, we can't help her.' Jack snatched it away, punched for the voice mail.

'You have two new messages. First new message received May eighteenth, at five-fifteen p.m.

They heard Laine's voice, dead calm. 'Sixty-eight East is a long road. Are you adding interstate abduction to your list?'

'Smart,' Max breathed. 'She's very smart.' He shot the Porsche like a bullet onto an off-ramp, spun it like a top and rocketed to backtrack toward the interstate.

He listened to every word, blocked the fear. When the call ended, he had to order himself not to tell Jack to replay it just so he could hear her voice. 'Get Vince back, give him the vehicle description and the destination. Alleghany Recreational Park. Tell him we're en route and that Crew is armed.'

'But we're not waiting for the cops?'

214

'No, we're not waiting for them.'

He flew toward the forest.

Laine stepped into the cabin, looked around the spacious living area with its stone fireplace and dark, heavy wood. It was time, she concluded, for a change of tack.

Stalling was fine, it was good. Anything that kept her from getting shot or beaten was fine and good. But it never paid to depend on a last-minute cavalry charge. Smart money depended on yourself.

So she turned, offered Crew an easy smile. 'First, let me say I'm not going to give you any reason to hurt me. I'm not into pain. You could, of course, hurt me anyway, but I'm hoping you've more style than that. We're both civilized people. I have something, you want something.' She strolled over to an overstuffed checked sofa, sat, crossed her legs. 'Let's negotiate.'

'This' – he gestured with the gun – 'speaks for itself.'

'Use it, get nothing. Why don't you offer me a glass of wine instead?'

He angled his head in consideration and, she thought, reevaluation. 'You're a cool one.'

'I've had time to settle down. I won't deny you scared me. You certainly did, and still could, but I'm hoping you're open to a reasonable dialogue here.'

She flipped quickly through her mental file of what she knew of him and what she could observe.

Towering ego, vanity, greed, sociopathic and homicidal tendencies.

'We're alone, I've got no way out. You're in the driver's seat, but still . . . I have something you want.'

She threw back her head and laughed, and could see she'd surprised him. Good. Keep him off balance, keep him thinking. 'Oh God, who would have believed the old man had it in him? He's been second-rate all his life, and a serious pain in my ass. Now he comes along with the score of a lifetime. Hell, the score of ten lifetimes. And he drops it right into my lap. I'm sorry about Willy though, he had a sweet nature. But, spilled milk.'

She caught of flicker of interest on Crew's face before he opened a drawer, took out a pair of handcuffs.

'Why, Alex, if there's going to be bondage fun, I'd really appreciate that wine first.'

'You think I'm buying this?'

'I'm not selling anything.' And maybe he wasn't buying, but he was listening to the pitch. She sighed as the cuffs landed in her lap. 'All right, your way. Where do you want them?'

'Arm of the couch, to your right hand.'

Though the idea of locking herself up had her throat going dry, she did what he said, then sent him a sultry look. 'How about that drink?'

With a nod, he walked over to the kitchen, took a bottle out of a cupboard. 'Cabernet?'

'Perfect. Do you mind if I ask why a man with your skills and tastes hooked up with Jack?'

'He was useful. And why are you trying to play the hard-edged opportunist?'

She pretended to pout. 'I don't like to think I'm hard, just realistic.'

'What you are is a small-town shopkeeper who has the bad luck to have my property.'

'I think it's remarkably good luck.' She took the wine he offered, sipped. 'The shop's a nice, steady game. Selling old, often useless items at a nice profit. Also gives me entry into a lot of places that have more old, often useless and very valuable items. I keep my hand in.'

'Well.' And she could see that while he hadn't considered that angle before, he was now.

'Look, you've got a beef with the old man, fine. He's nothing to me but an albatross. And if he ever taught me anything, it was to look out for number one.'

Crew shook his head slowly. 'You walked out of that shop with me without a sound, primarily to protect the clerk.'

'I wasn't going to argue with the gun you were shoving into my side. And you're right, I didn't want you to hurt her. She's a friend, and for God's sake, she's nearly seven months pregnant. I've got some lines, Alex. I steer clear of violence.'

'This is entertaining.' He sat, gestured. 'How do you explain the fact you're having an affair with Gannon, the insurance investigator?'

'He's terrific in bed, but even if he was a wash in that area, I'd have gotten him there. Keep your friends close, Alex, and your enemies closer. I know every move he makes before he makes it. And here's one for free, show of good faith: he's in New York today.' She leaned forward. 'They're cooking up a scam to smoke you out. There should be a press release by tomorrow, claiming Max recovered a portion of the diamonds. Max's bright idea is that will set you off, push you into doing something rash. He's smart, I'll give him that, but so far, he can't get a handle on you.'

'I guess that makes me smarter.'

'I guess it does,' she agreed. 'He's closing in on Jack, and God knows dear old Dad won't shake him for long. But he hasn't got a clue how to run you down.' Ego, ego, ego. Pump his ego. 'He's trying this Hail Mary pass.'

'Interesting, but an insurance investigator hardly concerns me.'

'Why should he? You took him out once already. I had to kiss his hurts.' She chuckled. 'And doing that, I've kept him busy enough to give you room.'

'You want me to thank you. Consider the fact you're not currently in any pain my thanks. Where are the diamonds, Ms. Tavish?'

'Let's make it Laine. I think we're beyond formalities. I've got them. Jack's and Willy's.' She shifted on the seat, put a purr in her voice. 'What are you going to do with all that money, Alex? Travel? Buy a small country? Sip mimosas on a beach somewhere? Don't you think all of those things, all of the lovely, lovely things people can do with big, fat piles of money is more fun with a like-thinking companion?'

His gaze drifted to her mouth, back up to her eyes. 'Is this how you seduced Gannon?'

'No, actually, in that case, I pretended to let him seduce me.

He's the type that needs to chase and conquer. I bring a lot to the table. You can have the diamonds, and you can have me.'

'I could have them both anyway.'

She sat back, sipped. 'You could. I find men who enjoy rape the lowest form. If you're one of them, I've misjudged you. You could rape me, beat me, shoot me. I'd certainly tell you where the diamonds are. But then . . .' She sipped again, and put a wicked gleam in her eye. 'You wouldn't know if I was telling the truth. You could waste a great deal of time, and I could suffer considerable discomfort. Not very practical when I'm willing to make a deal that gives us both exactly what we want, with a little extra.'

He rose. 'You're an intriguing woman, Laine.' Absently, he pulled off the wig.

'Mmm, better.' She pursed her lips as she studied his pewter hair. 'Much better. Could I have a refill?' She held out her glass, waggled it gently from side to side. 'I'd like to ask you something,' she continued when he went back for the bottle. 'If you have the rest of the diamonds—'

'If?'

'I've only got your word you do. I don't consider my father a reliable source.'

'Oh, I've got them.'

'If you do, why not take the bird in the hand and fly rather than beating the bush for the rest?'

His face was stone, the smile carved onto it, and the eyes dead. 'I don't settle for half of anything.'

'I respect that. Still, I could make sharing very pleasant for you.'

He filled her glass, set the bottle on the table. 'Sex is overrated.'

She gave a low, throaty laugh. 'Wanna bet?'

'As attractive as you are, you're just not worth twenty-eight million.'

'Now you've hurt my feelings.' Get him closer, she thought, get him closer and distract him. It'll hurt, but it'll only hurt for a minute. Bracing herself for it, she leaned forward for the wine, then shifted so the phone in her pocket slapped against the arm of the couch.

218

He was on her like fury, yanking her hair to drag her down, tearing at her pocket. There were floating black dots of pain and fear whirling in front of her eyes, but she pushed herself up shakily and stared in what she hoped passed as disgust at the wine stains on her pants.

'Oh, for God's sake. I hope you've got some club soda.'

He backhanded her so that the black dots exploded into red.

Chapter Sixteen

Max angled his car across the gravel road, just out of sight of the last cabin on the left. If Crew tried to run, he'd have to go through the Porsche first.

It was quiet and near dusk. He'd seen little activity in the woods, or in the cabins he'd passed. Hikers would be back by this time of day, vacationers settling in for dinner or a drink.

He shut off the engine, then leaned across Jack to unlock the glove box.

'We can't just sit here.'

'We're not going to just sit here.' Max removed his gun, a second clip, then tossed a pair of binoculars in Jack's lap. 'Keep an eye on the place.'

'You go in there with that, somebody's going to get hurt. Guns are trouble,' Jack added when Max merely looked at him.

'Right on both counts.' He checked the clip, slapped it back into place, shoved the spare into his pocket. 'Cops are on their way. It'll take them some time to secure the area, set up for a hostage situation. They know he's armed, they know he has Laine. They'll try to negotiate.'

'How do you negotiate with a fucking lunatic? My girl's in there, Max. That's my baby girl in there.'

'She's my girl, too. And I don't negotiate.'

Jack swiped the back of his hand over his mouth. 'We're not waiting for the cops here either.'

'We're not waiting.' Since Jack had yet to use the field glasses, Max took them, focused in on the cabin. 'Closed up tight. Curtains are pulled over the windows. From this angle, I see one door, four windows. Probably a rear door, couple more windows on the other side, couple in the back. He can't get out this way, but if he gets past me, he could swing around the other side, take one of the side roads and loop to the main. I don't think we're going to let that happen.'

Once again, he reached into the glove box. This time he pulled out a sheathed knife. When he drew the leather off, the blade was a sheen of bright silver with a vicious jagged edge.

'Jesus Christ.'

'You take care of the tires on that Mercedes with this?'

'Tires.' Jack breathed deep, in, out. 'Yeah. I can do that.'

'All right. Here's the way we play it.'

Inside, Laine pushed herself up. Her ears rang from the blow, and under the pounding, she cursed herself for not moving quickly enough, not anticipating his reaction so she'd taken a swipe rather than a direct hit.

She knew her eyes were bright with tears, but she wouldn't shed them. Instead she burned them away with a hot stare as she laid a hand on her throbbing cheekbone. 'You bastard. You son of a bitch.'

He gripped her by the shirt, hauled her an inch off the couch. She stretched out her free arm as she stared back at him, but she was still short of her goal. 'Who were you going to call, Laine? Dear old Dad?'

'You idiot.' Her response, and the furious shove surprised him enough to have him dropping her back onto the couch. 'Did you tell me to empty my pockets? Did you ask if I had a phone? It's off, isn't it? I always carry it around with me in the shop. You've been with me the whole time, Einstein. Did I make any calls?'

He seemed to consider, then turned the phone over and studied it. 'It appears to be off.' He powered it up. After it searched for and found service, the phone gave a little trill. 'It seems you have a message. Why don't we see who's been trying to reach you?'

'Kiss my ass.' She gave an annoyed shrug, scooted closer to the table, reached for the wine bottle and refilled her glass. Her hand remained perfectly steady when she heard Max's voice announce he was back.

'There, does that sound like I've contacted him by phone or the power of my mind? Jesus.' He was a good four feet away now. Too far. Setting the bottle down, she cupped her injured cheek. 'Get me some goddamn ice for this.'

'I don't like orders.'

'Yeah, well, I don't like getting clocked by some guy with an impulse-control problem. How the hell am I going to explain this bruise, and believe me, it'll be a beaut. You just complicated everything. And you know what else, hotshot? My previous offer is now off the table. I don't sleep with men who hit me. Not ever, not for anything.' She eased forward a bit, as if comforting herself, and continued to rub her cheek.

'Straight business deal now. No side bennies.'

'You seem to forget, this isn't a negotiation.'

'Everything's negotiable. You've got half, I've got half. You want all. I, on the other hand, am more realistic, and a lot less greedy. Take these damn things off,' she demanded, rattling the cuffs. 'Where the hell am I going?'

She saw his hand move, very slightly, toward his left pants pocket. Then drop away again. 'I don't think so. Now . . .' He started toward her. 'The diamonds.'

'You hit me again, you lay a hand on me, and I swear, I'll see the cops get them before you get one more stone.'

'You have a delicate build, Laine. Delicate bones break easily. I think you have a strong mind; it might take a great deal to break that. I could start with your hand. Do you know how many bones there are in the human hand? I can't quite remember, but I believe there are quite a few.'

His eyes came alive as he said it, and nothing in the whole of her life had ever frightened her more than that amused gleam. 'Some will snap, some will shatter. It would be very painful. You'll tell me where they are, and you'll tell me the truth, because even a strong mind can tolerate only so much pain.'

Her pulse was pounding in her temples, in her throat, in her fingertips, drums of terror, all but deafening. 'And only a sick one gets juiced at the thought of causing it. You know, without that little flaw, I would've enjoyed spending some time with you.'

She had to keep her eyes on his, steady on his. Survival depended on it. 'I like stealing,' she continued. 'I like taking what belongs to someone else and making it mine. It's such a rush. But the rush isn't worth pain. It's never worth my life. That's a little something I picked up from my father. I think we've reached a point where you want the diamonds more than I do. You want to know where they are? That's easier than you think. But getting to them, well . . .'

Her heart was thumping like a jackhammer as she curved her lips, curled her finger. 'Come here, and I'll give you a little hint.'

'You'll do better than that.'

'Oh, come on. At least let me have some fun with it.' She toyed with the pendant around her neck, held it up. 'What does this look like to you?' She let out a soft laugh. 'Come on, Alex, take a closer look.'

She knew she had him when he stepped to her, when his gaze fastened on the pendant. She let it drop again, to free her hand, then leaned forward again as if to pick up her wineglass. 'It's all about misdirection, really. Another little thing I picked up from my father.'

She tilted her face up so his attention would lock on it. There would only be one chance. He reached down for the necklace, bending, angling his head so he could get a closer look.

And she came off the couch, swinging the wine bottle in a furious roundhouse. There was the hideous crack of glass on bone, the splatter of red wine like a gush of blood. The momentum had him spilling over backward as she stood in her half crouch, panting, the bottle still clutched in her hand.

She dropped to her knees, fighting off a wave of nausea as she stretched out to try to reach him. She had to get the key out of his pocket, get the gun, get the phone. Get away.

'No! Goddamnit.' Tears of frustration burned in her eyes as she strained her muscles and found he'd fallen just out of her reach. She scrambled up again, climbed over the couch, ramming it with her shoulder to nudge it across the floor. Just a little closer. Just a little.

The blood roared in her ears, and her own voice, high and desperate, sounded miles away as she ordered herself to *Come on, come on, come* on!

She dived back on the floor, snatching at his pant leg, tugging his body toward her. 'The key, the key, oh God, please, let him have the key.'

She glanced over. The gun was on the kitchen counter eight feet away. Until she'd unlocked the cuffs, it might as well have been eight hundred. Bearing down, she stretched out until the metal cut into her wrist, but her free hand reached his pocket and her trembling fingers dipped in.

Those stinging tears spilled over when her fingers met the small piece of metal. Breath wheezing, she fumbled it into the lock, cursed herself again and gritted her teeth. The tiny click was like a gunshot. She offered incoherent prayers of thanks as she shoved the cuff off her wrist.

'Think. Just think. Breathe and think.' She sat on the floor, taking a few precious seconds to cut through the panic.

Maybe she'd killed him. Maybe she'd stunned him. She was damned if she was going to check. But if he wasn't dead, he'd come after her. She could run, but he'd come after her.

She scrambled up again and, grunting, panting, began to drag him toward the couch. Toward the cuffs. She'd lock him down, that's what she'd do. She'd lock him down. Get the phone, get the gun, call for help.

Relief flooded in when she snapped the cuff on his wrist. Blood trickled down his face, dripped on her hand as she pushed his jacket aside, reached into the inside pocket for her phone.

The sudden blare of a car alarm ripped a short scream out of her throat. She jolted, looked toward the door. Someone was out there. Someone could help.

'Help.' The word came out in a whisper, and she pushed herself to her feet. As she sprang forward, a hand grabbed her ankle and sent her slamming facedown onto the floor.

224

She didn't scream. The sounds she made were feral growls as she kicked back, crawled forward. He yanked, hooking an arm around her legs so she was forced to swivel, shoving herself up from the waist to use her fists, her nails.

The horn continued to sound, like a two-tone scream, over and over while she tore at him, while he pulled her closer. Blood matted his hair, streaked his face, gushed out of fresh wounds where her nails ripped.

She heard a crash, and one of her flailing arms landed on broken glass. The new jolt of pain had her rolling over, digging in with elbows to gain a few precious inches. Once again her hand closed over the wine bottle.

This time when her body jerked around she had it gripped in both hands like a batter at the plate. And she swung hard for the fences.

There was a pounding – in her head? In the room? Outside? Somewhere a pounding. But his grip on her released, his eyes rolled back and his body went still.

Whimpering, she scuttled back like a crab.

That's how Max saw her when he rushed into the room. Crouched on the floor, blood on her hands, her pants and shirt torn and splotched with red.

'Laine. Jesus God almighty.' He lunged to her, the cold control he'd snapped on to get inside, to get to her, shattered like glass. He was on his knees beside her, running his hands over her face, her hair, her body. 'How bad are you hurt? Where are you hurt? Are you shot?'

'What? Shot?' Her vision skipped, like a scratched film. 'No. I'm . . . it's wine.' A giddy bubble exploded in her throat and came out as a crazed laugh. 'Red wine, and, oh, some of this is blood. His. Mostly his. Is he dead?' She said it almost conversationally. 'Did I kill him?'

He brushed the hair back from her face, skimmed his thumb gently over her bruised cheekbone. 'Can you hold on?'

'Sure. No problem. I just want to sit here.'

Max walked over, crouched by Crew. 'Alive,' he said after he checked for a pulse. Then he studied the torn, battered and bloodied face. 'Did a number on him, didn't you?'

'I hit him with the wine bottle.' The room was moving, she realized, ever so slightly. And there seemed to be little waves in the air, like water. 'Twice. You came. You got my message.'

'Yeah. I got your message.' He patted Crew down for weapons, then went back to Laine. 'You sure you're not hurt?'

'I just feel numb right now.'

'Okay then.' He set his gun on the floor beside them and wrapped his arms around her. All the fear, the fury, the desperation he'd fought off for the last hour rolled into him, rolled out again. 'I gotta hold on,' he murmured against her throat. 'I don't want to hurt you, but I've gotta hold on.'

'Me too.' She burrowed into him. 'Me too. I knew you'd come. I knew you'd be here. Doesn't mean I can't take care of myself.' She eased back a little. 'I told you I can take care of myself.'

'Hard to argue with that. Let's see if we can stand up.'

When they gained their feet, she leaned into him, looked down at Crew. 'I really laid him out. I feel . . . empowered and satisfied and . . .' She swallowed, pressed a hand to her stomach. 'And a little bit sick.'

'Let's get you outside, get you some air. I'll take care of things in here. Cops are on their way.'

'Okay. Am I shaking or is that you?'

'Little of both. You've got a little shock going on, Laine. We'll get you out, and I want you to just sit down on the ground, lie down if it makes you feel better. We'll call for an ambulance.'

'I don't need an ambulance.'

'That's debatable, but he sure as hell does. Here we go.'

He led her out. Jack sprang from the corner of the house, the knife in one hand, a rock in the other. Laine's first muddled thought was how silly he looked.

Then he lowered both arms, and the knife and rock fell from his limp fingers to the ground. He stumbled forward, swept her in.

'Lainie. Lainie.' Pressing his face to her shoulder, he burst into tears.

'It's all right. I'm all right. Shh.' She cupped his face, drawing back to kiss his cheeks. 'We're all right, Dad.'

'I couldn't've lived. I couldn't—'

'You came. You came when I needed you. Aren't I lucky to love two men who are there when I need them?'

'I didn't know if I was coming back,' he began.

On a wave of tenderness, she brushed tears from his cheeks. 'But you did, didn't you? Now you've got to go.'

'Lainie.'

'The police will be here any minute. I haven't gone through all this to see you arrested. Go. Before they come.'

'There are things I need to say to you.'

'Later. You can say them later. You know where I live. Please, Daddy, go.'

Max stepped back out with the phone to his ear. 'Crew's secured. Laine's banged up but she's okay. Crew's going to need some medical attention. Laine and I'll wait here. What's your ETA? Good. We'll wait.' He clicked off. 'Vince and the rest of them will be rolling in. You've got about five minutes,' he said to Jack. 'Better get moving.'

'Thanks.' Jack offered his hand. 'Maybe you are – almost – good enough for her. I'll be seeing you. Soon,' he added as he turned to Laine. 'Soon, baby girl.'

'They're coming.' She heard the sirens. 'Hurry.'

'Take more than some hick cops to catch Big Jack O'Hara.' He winked at her. 'Keep a light burning for me.' He jogged toward the woods, turned for a quick salute, then disappeared into them.

'Well.' Laine let out a long breath. 'There he goes. Thanks.'

'For what?' Max asked as she kissed him.

'For letting my father go.'

'I don't know what you're talking about. I've never met your father.'

On a muffled laugh, she rubbed her eyes. 'I think I'm going to do that sitting-on-the-ground thing now.'

It wasn't difficult to win a debate about a visit to the ER with a man who was so relieved you were alive and whole he'd have given you anything you asked for. Laine took advantage of it, and of Vince's friendship, to go straight home.

She'd be required to give a more complete statement to the chief of police the next morning. But he'd accepted her abbreviated account of events.

She'd given it while she sat on the ground outside the cabin, with a blanket around her shoulders. Though she'd come through her ordeal with Crew with nothing more serious than cuts and bruises, she didn't object when Max cut off the police questioning, scooped her off the ground and carried her to his car.

It gave her a lot of satisfaction to watch Crew hauled out on a stretcher.

A lot of satisfaction.

Jack O'Hara's daughter still had the moves.

Grateful, was all Laine could think as she spent a full twenty minutes under the hot pulsing spray of the shower. She was so grateful to Max, to Vince, to fate. Hell, she was grateful for digital communication. So much so she was going to retire her cell phone, have it mounted and hung in a place of honor.

And she would never drink cabernet again as long as she lived.

She stepped out of the shower, dried herself gingerly. The numbness was long gone, and every bump, scrape and bruise ached like fury. She swallowed four aspirin, then gathered her courage and took a look at herself in the full-length mirror.

'Oh. Ouch.' She hissed out a breath as she turned for the rear view. She was a colorful mess of bruises. Hips, shins, knees, arms. And the beaut she'd predicted on her right cheek.

But they'd fade, she thought. They'd fade and be forgotten as she went back to living her life. And Alex Crew would spend the rest of his behind bars. She hoped he cursed her name every day of that life. And she hoped he spent every night dreaming of diamonds.

As a concession to the bruises, she dressed in loose sweats, tied her damp hair back loosely. As a concession to vanity, she spent some time with makeup to downplay the mark of violence on her face.

Then she turned, spread her arms and addressed Henry, who'd

shadowed her – even in the bathroom – since she'd retrieved him from Jenny's. 'Not too bad, right?'

She found Max in the kitchen, heating the contents of a can of soup on the stove. 'Thought you might be hungry.'

'You thought right.'

He stepped to her, played his fingers over the bruise. 'I'm sorry I wasn't faster.'

'If you're sorry, you're diminishing my own courage and cleverness and I've been congratulating myself on them.'

'Wouldn't want to do that, but I've got to say, I feel cheated. You robbed me of a chance to beat that son of a bitch into pulp.'

'Next time we deal with a homicidal sociopath, you can take him down.'

'Next time.' He turned back to stir the soup. Laine linked her hands.

'We've rushed into all this, Max.'

'Sure have.'

'People . . . I imagine people who come together in intense or dangerous situations often rush into things. All those emotions spiking. When things level off, they probably regret following those impulses.'

'Logical.'

'We could regret it if we move ahead the way we talked about before. We could regret rushing into a relationship, much less marriage.'

'We could.' He tapped the spoon on the edge of the pot, then set it down and turned to her. 'Do you care?'

She pressed her lips together before they could tremble. There he was, at her stove, all tall and rangy, with those dangerous eyes and that easy stance. 'No. No, I don't care. Not even a little.' She flew into him, rising up on her toes when his arms clamped around her. 'Oh God, I don't care. I love you so much.'

'Whew. That's good.' His mouth crushed to hers, then softened, then lingered. 'I don't care either. Besides, I just picked this up for you in New York. It'd be wasted if you wanted to start getting sensible on me now.'

He tugged the box out of his pocket. 'Pretty sure I remember what you said you liked.'

'You took time to buy me a ring in all of this?'

He blinked. 'Oh. You wanted a ring?'

'Smart-ass.' She opened the box, and her heart turned slowly, beautifully, over in her breast as she stared at the square-cut diamond in the simple platinum setting. 'It's perfect. You know it's perfect.'

'Not yet.' He took it out, slipped it on her finger. 'Now it is.' He kissed her scraped knuckles just beneath it. 'I'm going to spend my life with you, Laine. We'll start tonight with you sitting down there and me making you soup. Nothing intense about that.'

'Sounds nice. Nice and normal.'

'We can even bicker if you want.'

'That doesn't sound so bad either. Maybe before we do, we should get the rest of it out of the way. Can I see them?'

He turned the soup down, opened the briefcase he'd set on the table. The sight of him taking out the piggy bank made her laugh and lower to a chair.

'It's horrible really, to think I might've been killed over what's in the belly of a piggy bank. But somehow it's not. It's just so Jack.'

'A rep of the insurance company will be picking them up tomorrow.' He spread a newspaper, picked up the little hammer he'd found in the mudroom. 'Want the honors?'

'No. Be my guest.'

It took a couple of good whacks before he could slide the padding out, then the pouch. He poured the sparkling waterfall in it into Laine's hand.

'They don't get less dazzling, do they?'

'I like the one on your finger better.'

She smiled. 'So do I.'

While he dumped the shards and newspaper, she sprinkled the diamonds onto velvet. 'They'll have half of them back now. And since Crew's been identified and captured, they might find the rest of them where he lived, or in a safe-deposit box under his name.'

'Maybe. Might have a portion of them stashed that way. But he didn't go to Columbus, he didn't take something to that kid out of the goodness of his heart or a parental obligation. The ex and the son have something, or know something.'

'Max, don't go after them.' She reached out for his hand. 'Let it go. They're only trying to get away from him. Everything you told me says she's just trying to protect her child, give him a normal life. If you go after them, she'll feel hunted, she'll run again. I know what that's like. I know what it was like for my mother until she found some peace, until she found Rob. And my father, well, he's a thief and a con, and a liar, but he's not crazy, he's not a killer.'

She nudged the diamonds toward him. 'No amount of these is worth making that innocent boy live with the fact that his father's a killer. They're just stones. They're just things.'

'Let me think about it.'

'Okay.' She got up, kissed the top of his head. 'Okay. Tell you what. I'll put a couple of sandwiches together to go with this soup. You can cross-check the diamonds with your list. Then we'll put them away and eat like boring, normal people.'

She got up to get the bread. 'So when do you suppose I can get my car back from New Jersey?'

'I know a guy who'll transport it down. Couple of days.' He set to work. 'I'll run you around meanwhile, or you can use my car.'

'See, boring and normal. Mustard or mayo on the ham?'

'Mustard,' he said absently, then fell into silence with the dog snoring at his feet.

'Son of a bitch.'

She glanced back. 'Hmm?'

He shook his head. 'Let me do this again.'

Laine cut the sandwiches she'd built in two. 'Doesn't add up, does it?' She set the plates on the table as Max tapped his fingers and studied her. 'I was afraid of that. Or not afraid, really, just resigned. A little short of the quarter share?'

'About twenty-five carats short.'

'Uh-huh. Well, your client would accept, I'm sure, that the shares might not have been evenly divided. That the portions that are left might be just a little heavy.'

'But that wouldn't be the case, would it?'

'No. No, I doubt very much that was the case.'

'He pocketed them. Your father.'

'He'd have taken his share out, selected a few of the stones, just as a kind of insurance, then he'd have put them into another container – the pig – and kept the insurance on him. In a money belt or a bag around his neck, even in his pocket. `Put all your eggs in one basket, Lainie, the handle's going to break. Then all you've got is scrambled eggs.' You want coffee with this?'

'I want a damn beer. I let him walk.'

'You'd have let him walk anyway.' She got the beer, popped the top for him, then slid into his lap. 'You'd have taken the diamonds back if you'd known he had them, but you'd have let him walk. Really, nothing's changed. It's just a measly twenty-five carats.' She kissed his cheek, then the other, then his mouth. 'We're okay, right?'

When she settled her head on his shoulder, he stroked her hair. 'Yeah, we're okay. I might put a boot in your father's ass if I ever see him again, but we're okay.'

'Good.'

He sat, stroking her hair. There were ham sandwiches on the table, soup on the stove. A dog snoozed on the floor. A few million – give or take – in diamonds sparkled in the kitchen light.

They were okay, Max thought. In fact, they were terrific.

But they were never going to be boring and normal.

Part Two

All things change;
nothing perishes

OVID

Commit the oldest sins
the newest kind of ways.

WILLIAM SHAKESPEARE

Chapter Seventeen

New York, 2059

She was dying to get home. Knowing her own house, her own bed, her own *things* were waiting for her made even the filthy afternoon traffic from the airport a pleasure.

There were small skirmishes, petty betrayals, outright treachery and bitter combat among the cabs, commuters and tank-like maxibuses. Overhead, the air-trams, blimps and mini-shuttles strafed the sky. But watching the traffic wars wage made her antsy enough to imagine herself leaping into the front seat to grab the wheel and plunge into the fray, with a great deal more viciousness and enthusiasm than her driver.

God, she *loved* New York.

While her driver crept along the FDR as one of the army of vehicles battling their way into the city, she entertained herself by watching the animated billboards. Some were little stories, and as a writer herself, and the lover of a good tale, Samantha Gannon appreciated that.

Observe, she thought, the pretty woman lounging poolside at a resort, obviously alone and lonely while couples splash or stroll. She orders a drink, and with the first sip her eyes meet those of a gorgeous man just emerging from the water. Wet muscles, killer grin. An electric moment that dissolves into a moonlight scene where the now happy couple walk hand in hand along the beach.

Moral? Drink Silby's Rum and open your world to adventure, romance and really good sex.

It should be so easy.

But then, for some, it was. For her grandparents there'd been an electric moment. Rum hadn't played a part, at least not in any of the versions she'd heard. But their eyes had met, and something had snapped and sizzled through the bloodstream of fate.

Since they'd be married for fifty-six years this coming fall, whatever that something had been had done a solid job.

And because of it, because fate had brought them together, she was sitting in the back of a big, black sedan, heading uptown, heading toward home, home, home, after two weeks traveling on bumpy, endless roads of a national book tour.

Without her grandparents, what they'd done, what they'd chosen, there would have been no book. No tour. No homecoming. She owed them all of it – well, not the tour, she amended. She could hardly blame them for that.

She only hoped they were half as proud of her as she was of them.

Samantha E. Gannon, national best-selling author of *Hot Rocks.* Was that iced or what?

Hyping the book in fourteen cities – coast to coast – over fifteen days, the interviews, the appearances, the hotels and transport stations had been exhausting.

And, let's be honest, she told herself, *fabulous in its insane way.*

Every morning she'd dragged herself from a strange bed, propped open her bleary eyes and stared at the mirror just to be sure she'd see herself staring back. It was really happening, to her, Sam Gannon.

She'd been writing it all of her life, she thought, every time she'd heard the family story, every time she'd begged her grandparents to tell it, wheedled for more details. She'd been honing her craft in every hour she'd spent lying in bed as a child, imagining the adventure.

It had seemed so romantic to her, so exciting. And the best part was that it was her family, her blood.

Her current project was coming along well. She was calling it just *Big Jack,* and she thought her great-grandfather would have gotten a very large charge out of it.

236

She wanted to get back to it, to dive headlong into Jack O'Hara's world of cons and scams and life on the lam. Between the tour and the pre-tour rounds, she hadn't had a full hour to write. And she was due.

But she wasn't going straight to work. She wasn't going to think about work for at least forty-eight blissful hours. She was going to dump her bags, and she might just burn everything in them. She was going to lock herself in her own wonderful, quiet house. She was going to run a bubble bath, open a bottle of champagne.

She'd soak and she'd drink, then she'd soak and drink some more. If she was hungry, she'd buzz something up in the AutoChef. She didn't care what it was because it would be her food, in her kitchen.

Then she was going to sleep for ten hours.

She wasn't going to answer the tele-link. She'd contacted her parents, her brother, her sister, her grandparents from the air, and told them all she was going under for a couple of days. Her friends and business associates could wait a day or two. Since she'd ended what had passed for a relationship over a month before, there wasn't any man waiting for her.

That was probably just as well.

She sat up when the car veered toward the curb. Home! She'd been drifting, she realized, lost in her own thoughts, as usual, and hadn't realized she was home.

She gathered her notebook, her travel bag. Riding on delight, she overtipped the driver when he hauled her suitcase and carry-on to the door for her. She was so happy to see him go, so thrilled that he'd be the last person she'd have to speak to until she decided to surface again, she nearly kissed him on the mouth.

Instead, she resisted, waved him off, then dragged her things into the tiny foyer of what her grandmother liked to call Sam's Urban Doll House.

'I'm back!' She leaned against the door, breathed deep, then did a hip-shaking, shoulder-rolling dance across the floor. 'Mine, mine, mine. It's all mine. Baby, I'm back!'

She stopped short, arms still flung out in her dance of delight, and gaped at her living area. Tables and chairs were overturned, and her lovely little settee was lying on its back like a turtle on its shell. Her screen was off the wall and lay smashed in the middle of the floor, along with her collection of framed family photos and holograms. The walls had been stripped of paintings and prints.

Sam slapped both hands to her head, fisted her fingers in her short red hair and let out a bellow. 'For God's *sake*, Andrea! House-sitting doesn't mean you actually sit on the goddamn house.'

Having a party was one thing, but this was . . . just beyond. She was going to kick some serious ass.

She yanked her pocket 'link out of her jacket and snapped out the name. 'Andrea Jacobs. Former friend,' she added on a mutter as the transmission went through. Gritting her teeth, she spun on her heel and headed out of the room, started up the stairs as she listened to Andrea's recorded message.

'What the hell did you do?' she barked into the 'link, 'set off a bomb? How could you do this, Andrea? How could you destroy my things and leave this mess for me to come home to? Where the hell are you? You'd better be running for your life, because when I get my hands . . . Jesus Christ, what is that smell! I'm going to kill you for this, Andrea.'

The stench was so strong, she was forced to cover her mouth with her hand as she booted open the bedroom door. 'It *reeks* in here, and, oh God, oh God, my bedroom. I'm never going to forgive you. I swear to God, Andrea, you're dead. Lights!' she snapped out.

And when they flashed on, when she blinked her eyes clear, she saw Andrea sprawled on the floor on a heap of stained bedclothes.

She saw she was right. Andrea was dead.

She'd nearly been out the door. Five more minutes and she'd have been off-shift and heading home. Odds were someone else would have caught the case. Someone else would be spending a steaming summer night dealing with a bloater.

She'd barely closed the last case and that had been a horror.

But Andrea Jacobs was hers now. For better, for worse.

238

Lieutenant Eve Dallas breathed through a filtered mask. They didn't really work and looked, in her opinion, ridiculous, but it helped cut down on the worst of the smell when you were dealing with the very ripe dead.

Though the temperature controls of the room were set at a pleasant seventy-three degrees, the body had, essentially, cooked for five days. It was bloated with gases, had voided its wastes. Whoever had slit Andrea Jacobs's throat hadn't just killed her. He'd left her to rot.

'Victim's identification verified. Jacobs, Andrea. Twenty-nine year old mixed-race female. The throat's been slashed in what appears to be a left-to-right downward motion. Indications are the killer attacked from behind. The deterioration of the body makes it difficult to ascertain if there are other injuries, defensive wounds, through visual exam on scene. Victim is dressed in street clothes.'

Party clothes, Eve thought, noting the soiled sparkle on the hem of the dress, the ice-pick heels kicked across the room.

'She came in, after a date, maybe trolling the clubs. Could've brought somebody back with her, but it doesn't look like that.'

She gazed around the room while she put the pictures in her head. She wished, briefly, for Peabody. But she'd sent her former aide and very new partner home early. There wasn't any point in dragging her back and spoiling what Eve knew was a celebration dinner with Peabody's main squeeze.

'She came back alone. If she'd come back with someone, even if he was going to kill her, he'd have gone for the sex first. Why waste it? And this isn't struggle. This isn't a fight. One clean swipe. No other stab wounds.'

She looked back at the body and brought Andrea Jacobs to life in her mind. 'She comes back from her date, her night out. Had a few drinks. Starts upstairs. Does she hear something? Probably not. Maybe she's stupid and she comes upstairs after she hears somebody up here. We'll find out if she was stupid, but I bet he heard her. Hears her come in.'

Eve walked out into the hall, stood there a moment, picturing it, and ignoring the movements of the crime-scene team working in the house.

She walked back, imagined kicking off those sky-high heels. Your arches would just weep with relief. Maybe she lifted one foot, bent over a little, rubbed it.

And when she straightened, he was on her.

Came from behind the door, Eve thought, or out of the closet on the wall beside the door. Stepped right up behind her, yanked her head back by the hair, then sliced.

Lips pursed, she studied the pattern of blood spatter.

Spurted out of the jugular, she thought, onto the bed. She's facing the bed, he's behind. He doesn't get messy. Just slices down quick, gives her a little shove forward. She's still spurting as she falls.

She glanced toward the windows. Drapes were drawn. Moving over, she eased them back, noted the privacy screen was engaged as well. He'd have done that. Wouldn't want anyone to notice the light, or movement.

She stepped out again, tossed the mask into her field kit.

Crime scene and the sweepers were already crawling around the place in their safe suits. She nodded toward a uniform. 'Tell the ME's team she's cleared to be bagged, tagged and transported. Where's the witness?'

'Got her down in the kitchen, Lieutenant.'

She checked her wrist unit. 'Take your partner, start a neighborhood canvass. You're first on scene, right?'

He straightened a little. 'Yes, sir.'

She waited a beat. 'And?'

She had a rep. You didn't want to screw up with Dallas. She was tall, lean and dressed now in summer-weight pants, T-shirt and jacket. He'd seen her seal up before she went into the bedroom, and her right hand had a smear of blood on the thumb.

He wasn't sure if he should mention it.

Her hair was brown and chopped short. Her eyes were the same color and all cop.

He'd heard it said she chewed up lazy cops for breakfast and spit them out at lunch.

He wanted to make it through the day.

'Dispatch came through at sixteen-forty, report of a break-in and possible death at this address.'

Eve looked back toward the bedroom. 'Yeah, extremely possible.'

'My partner and I responded, arrived on scene at sixteen-fifty-two. The witness, identified as Samantha Gannon, resident, met us at the door. She was in extreme distress.'

'Cut through it. Lopkre,' she added, reading his name tag.

'She was hysterical, Lieutenant. She'd already vomited, just outside the front door.'

'Yeah, I noticed that.'

He relaxed a little, since she didn't seem inclined to take a bite out of it. 'Tossed it again, same spot, right after she opened the door for us. Sort of folded in on herself there in the foyer, crying. She kept saying, "Andrea's dead, upstairs." My partner stayed with her while I went up to check it out. Didn't have to get far.'

He grimaced, nodded toward the bedroom. 'The smell. Looked into the bedroom, saw the body. Ah, as I could verify death from the visual from the doorway, I did not enter the scene and risk contaminating same. I conducted a brief search of the second floor to confirm no one else, alive or dead, was on the premises, then called it in.'

'And your partner?'

'My partner's stayed with the witness throughout. She – Officer Ricky – she's got a soothing way with victims and witnesses. She's calmed her down considerably.'

'All right. I'll send Ricky out. Start the canvass.'

She started downstairs. She noted the suitcase just inside the door, the notebook case, the big-ass purse some women couldn't seem to make a move without.

The living area looked as if it had been hit by a high wind, as did the small media room off the central hallway. In the kitchen, it looked more like a crew of mad cooks – a redundancy in Eve's mind – had been hard at work.

The uniform sat at a small eating nook in the corner, across a dark blue table from a redhead Eve pegged as middle twenties. She was so pale the freckles that sprinkled over her nose and cheekbones stood out like cinnamon dashed over milk. Her eyes were a strong and bright blue, glassy from shock and tears and rimmed in red.

Her hair was clipped short, even shorter than Eve wore her own, and followed the shape of her head with a little fringe over the brow. She wore enormous silver hoops in her ears, and New York black in pants, shirt, jacket.

Traveling clothes, Eve assumed, thinking of the cases in the foyer.

The uniform – Ricky, Eve remembered – had been speaking in a low, soothing voice. She broke off now, looked toward Eve. The look they exchanged was brief: cop to cop. 'You call that number I gave you, Samantha.'

'I will. Thank you. Thanks for staying with me.'

'It's okay.' Ricky slid out from the table, walked to where Eve waited just inside the doorway. 'Sir. She's pretty shaky, but she'll hold a bit longer. She's going to break again though, 'cause she's holding by her fingernails.'

'What number did you give her?'

'Victim's Aid.'

'Good. You record your conversation with her?'

'With her permission, yes, sir.'

'See it lands on my desk.' Eve hesitated a moment. Peabody also had a soothing way, and Peabody wasn't here. 'I told your partner to take you and do the knock-on-doors. Find him, tell him I've requested you remain on scene for now, and to take another uniform for the canvass. If she breaks, it might be better if we have somebody she relates to nearby.'

'Yes, sir.'

'Give me some space with her now.' Eve moved into the kitchen, stopped by the table. 'Ms. Gannon? I'm Lieutenant Dallas. I need to ask you some questions.'

'Yes, Beth, Officer Ricky, explained that someone would . . . I'm sorry, what was your name?'

'Dallas. Lieutenant Dallas.' Eve sat. 'I understand this is difficult for you. I'd like to record this, if that's all right? Why don't you just tell me what happened.'

'I don't know what happened.' Her eyes glimmered, her voice thickened dangerously. But she stared down at her hands, breathed in and out several times. It was a struggle for control Eve appreciated. 'I came home. I came home from the airport. I've been out of town. I've been away for two weeks.'

'Where were you?'

'Um. Boston, Cleveland, East Washington, Lexington, Dallas, Denver, New LA, Portland, Seattle. I think I forgot one. Or two.' She smiled weakly. 'I was on a book tour. I wrote a book. They published it – e, audio and paper forms. I'm really lucky.'

Her lips trembled, and she sucked in a sob. 'It's doing very well, and they sent – the publisher – they send me on a tour to promote it. I've been bouncing around for a couple weeks. I just got home. I just got here.'

Eve could see by the way Samantha's gaze flickered around the room that she was moving toward another breakdown. 'Do you live here alone? Ms. Gannon?'

'What? Alone? Yes, I live by myself. Andrea doesn't – didn't – Oh God . . .'

Her breath began to hitch, and from the way her knuckles whitened as she gripped her hands together, Eve knew this time the struggle was a full-out war. 'I want to help Andrea. I need you to help me understand so I can start helping her. So I need you to try to hold on until I do.'

'I'm not a weak woman.' She rubbed the heels of her hands over her face, violently. 'I'm not. I'm good in a crisis. I don't fall apart like this. I just don't.'

Bet you don't, Eve thought. 'Everybody has a threshold. You came home. Tell me what happened. Was the door locked?'

'Yes. I uncoded the locks, the alarm. I stepped in, dumped my stuff. I was so happy to be in my own space again. I was tired, so happy. I wanted a glass of wine and a bubble bath. Then I saw the living room. I couldn't believe it. I was so angry. Just furious and

243

outraged. I grabbed my 'link from my pocket and called Andrea.'

'Because?'

'Oh. Oh. Andrea, she was house-sitting. I didn't want to leave the house empty for two weeks, and she wanted to have her apartment painted, so it worked out. She could stay here, water my plants, feed the fish . . . Oh Jesus, my fish!' She started to slide out, but Eve grabbed her arm.

'Hold on.'

'My fish. I have two goldfish. Live fish, in my office. I didn't even look in there.'

'Sit.' Eve held up a finger to hold Samantha in place, then got up, stepped to the door and signaled to one of the sweepers. 'Check out the home office, get me the status on a couple of goldfish.'

'Huh?'

'Just do it.' She went back to the table. A tear was tracking down Samantha's cheek, and the delicate redhead's skin was blotchy. But she hadn't broken yet. 'Andrea was staying here while you were gone. Just Andrea?'

'Yes. She probably had someone over now and again. She's sociable. She likes to party. That's what I thought when I saw the living area. That she'd had some insane party and trashed my place. I was yelling at her machine through the 'link when I started upstairs. I said terrible things.' She dropped her head into her hands.

'Terrible things,' she murmured. 'Then there was that horrible smell. I was even more furious. I slammed into the bedroom, and . . . she was there. She was there, lying on the floor by the bed. All the blood, that didn't even look like blood anymore, but, you know, somehow, you know. I think I screamed. Maybe I blacked out. I don't know.'

She looked up again, and her eyes were shattered. 'I don't remember. I just remember seeing her, then running down the stairs again. I called nine-one-one. And I was sick. I ran outside and got sick. And then I was stupid.'

'How were you stupid?'

'I went back in the house. I know better. I should've stayed outside, waited for the police outside or gone to a neighbor's. But

I wasn't thinking straight, and I came back in and just stood in the foyer, shaking.'

'You weren't stupid, you were in shock. There's a difference. When's the last time you talked to Andrea?'

'I'm not sure. Early in the tour. From East Washington, I think. Just a quick check.' She dashed a second tear away as if irritated to find it there. 'I was awfully busy, and I didn't have a lot of free time. I called once or twice, left messages. Just to remind her when I was heading home.'

'Did she ever say anything to you about being concerned? About anyone giving her trouble, making threats?'

'No. Nothing like that.'

'What about you? Anyone making threats?'

'Me? No. No.' She shook her head.

'Who knew you were out of town?'

'Ah . . . well, everyone. My family, my friends, my agent, publisher, publicist, editor, neighbors. It wasn't a secret, that's for sure. I was so juiced about the book, about the opportunity, I pretty much told anyone who'd listen. So . . . It was a burglary, don't you think? God, I'm sorry, I can't keep your name in my head.'

'Dallas.'

'Don't you think it was some sort of burglary, Lieutenant Dallas? Somebody who heard I was gone and figured the house was empty, and . . .'

'Possibly. We'll need you to check your belongings, see if anything's missing.' But she'd noted the electronics, the artwork any self-respecting burglar would have taken. And Andrea Jacobs had been wearing a very nice wrist unit, and considerable jewelry. Real or knockoff, it hardly mattered. A B&E man wouldn't have left them behind.

'Have you had any calls, mail, any contact of an unusual nature recently?'

'Well, since the book was published, I've gotten some communications. Mostly through my publisher. People who want to meet me, or who want me to help them get their book published, or

245

want me to write their story. Some of them are pretty strange, I guess. Not threatening, though. And there's some who want to tell me their theory about the diamonds.'

'What diamonds?'

'From the book. My book's about a major diamond heist in the early part of the century. Here in New York. My grandparents were involved. They didn't steal anything,' she said quickly. 'My grandfather was the insurance investigator who took the case, and my grandmother – it's complicated. But a quarter of the diamonds were never recovered.'

'Is that so.'

'Pretty frosty, really. Some of the people who've contacted me are just playing detective. It's one of the reasons for the book's success. Millions of dollars in diamonds – where are they? It's been more than half a century, and as far as anyone knows, they've never surfaced.'

'You publish under your own name?'

'Yes. See the diamonds are how my grandparents met. It's part of Gannon family history. That's the heart of the book, really. The diamonds are the punch, but the love story is the heart.'

Heart or no heart, Eve thought cynically, a few million in diamonds was a hell of a punch. And a hell of a motive.

'Okay. Have you or Andrea broken off any relationships recently?'

'Andrea didn't have relationships – per se. She just liked men.' Her white skin turned flaming red. 'That didn't sound right. I mean she dated a lot. She liked to go out, she enjoyed going out with men. She didn't have a serious monogamous relationship.'

'Any of the men she liked to go out with want something more serious?'

'She never mentioned it. And she would have. She'd have told me if some guy got pushy. She generally went out with men who wanted what she wanted. A good time, no strings.'

'How about you?'

'I'm not seeing anyone right now. Between the writing and the tour, juggling in the day-to-day, I haven't had the time or inclination.

I broke a relationship off about a month ago, but there weren't any hard feelings.'

'His name?'

'But he'd never – Chad would *never* hurt anyone. He's a little bit of an asshole – well, potentially a major asshole – but he's not . . .'

'It's just routine. It helps to eliminate. Chad?'

'Oh Jesus. Chad Dix. He lives on East Seventy-first.'

'Does he have your codes and access to the house?'

'No. I mean, he did but I changed them after we broke up. I'm not stupid – and my grandfather was a cop before he went private. He'd have skinned me if I hadn't taken basic security precautions.'

'He'd have been right to. Who else had the new codes?'

Samantha scrubbed her hands over her hair until it stood up in short, flaming spikes. 'The only one who had them besides me is Andrea, and my cleaning service. They're bonded. That's Maid In New York. Oh, and my parents. They live in Maryland. I give them all my codes. Just in case.'

Her eyes widened. 'The security cam. I have a security cam on the front door.'

'Yes. It's been shut down, and your disks are missing.'

'Oh.' Her color was coming back, a kind of healthy-girl roses and cream. 'That sounds very professional. Why would they be so professional, then trash the house?'

'That's a good question. I'm going to need to talk to you again at some point, but for now, is there someone you'd like to call?'

'I just don't think I could talk to anyone. I'm talked out. My parents are on vacation. They're sailing the Med.' She bit her lip as if chewing on a thought. 'I don't want them to know about this. They've been planning this trip for nearly a year and only left a week ago. They'd head straight back.'

'Up to you.'

'My brother's off planet on business.' She tapped her fingers against her teeth as she thought it through. 'He'll be gone a few more days at least, and my sister's in Europe. She'll be hooking up with my parents in about ten days, so I can just keep them all

247

out of this for now. Yeah, I can keep them out of it. I'll have to contact my grandparents, but that can wait until tomorrow.'

Eve had been thinking more of Samantha contacting someone to stay with her, someone to lean on. But it seemed the woman's initial self-estimate was on the mark. She wasn't a weak woman.

'Do I have to stay here?' Samantha asked her. 'As much as I hate the idea, I think I want to go to a hotel for the night – for a while, actually. I don't want to stay here alone. I don't want to be here tonight.'

'I'll arrange for you to be taken anywhere you want to go. I'll need to know how to reach you.'

'Okay.' She closed her eyes a moment, drew in a breath as Eve got to her feet. 'Lieutenant, she's dead, Andrea's dead because she was here. She's dead, isn't she, because she was here while I was away.'

'She's dead because someone killed her. Whoever did is the only one responsible for what happened. You're not. She's not. It's my job to find whoever's responsible.'

'You're good at your job, aren't you?'

'Yeah. I am. I'm going to have Officer Ricky take you to a hotel. If you think of anything else, you can contact me through Cop Central. Oh, these diamonds you wrote about. When were they stolen?'

'Two thousand and three. March 2003. Appraised at over twenty-eight million at that time. About three-quarters of them were recovered and returned.'

'That leaves a lot of loose rocks. Thanks for your cooperation, Ms. Gannon. I'm sorry about your friend.'

She stepped out, working various theories in her mind. One of the sweepers tapped her shoulder as she passed.

'Hey, Lieutenant? The fish? They didn't make it.'

'Shit.' Eve jammed her hands in her pockets and headed out.

Chapter Eighteen

She was closer to home than to Central, and it was late enough to justify avoiding the trip downtown. Her equipment at home was superior to anything the cops could offer – outside of the lauded Electronic Detective Division.

The fact was, she had access to equipment superior than the Pentagon's, in all likelihood. One of her marital side bennies, she thought. Marry one of the world's wealthiest and most powerful men – one who loved his e-toys – and you got to play with them whenever you liked.

More to the point, Roarke would talk her into letting him help her use that equipment. Since Peabody wasn't around to do any drone work, Eve was planning to let him, without too much of an argument.

She liked the diamond angle, and wanted to dig up some data on that. Who better to assist in gathering data regarding a heist than a former thief? Roarke's murky past could be a definite plus on that end.

Marriage, for all its scary pockets and weird corners, was turning out to be a pretty good deal on the whole.

It would do him good to play research assistant. Take his mind off the revelations that had reared up out of that murky past and sucker punched him. When a grown man discovered his mother wasn't the stone bitch who'd slapped him around through childhood then deserted him, but a young woman who'd loved him, who'd been murdered while he was still a baby – and by his own father – it sent him reeling. Even a man as firmly balanced as Roarke.

So having him help her would help him.

It would make up, a little, for having her plans for the evening ditched. She'd had something a little more personal, and a lot more energetic, in mind. Summerset, her personal bane and Roarke's majordomo, was off on vacation. Every minute counted. She and Roarke would be alone in the house, and there'd been no mention, that she remembered, of social or business engagements.

She'd hoped to spend the evening screwing her husband's brains out, then letting him return the favor.

Still, working together had its points.

She drove through the big iron gates that guarded the world that Roarke built.

It was spectacular, with a roll of lawn as green as the grass she'd seen in Ireland, with huge leafy trees and lovely flowering shrubs. A sanctuary of elegance and peace in the heart of the city they'd both adopted as their own. The house itself was part fortress, part castle, and somehow had come to epitomize home to her. It rose and spread, jutted and spiked with its stones dignified against the deepening sky, and its countless windows flaming from the setting sun.

As she'd come to understand him, the desperation of his childhood and his single-minded determination never to go back, she'd come to understand, even appreciate, Roarke's need to create a home base so sumptuous – so uniquely his own.

She'd needed her badge, and the home base of the law for exactly the same reasons.

She left her ugly police-issue vehicle in front of the dignified entrance, jogged up the stairs through the filthy summer heat and into the glorious cool of the foyer.

She was already itching to get to work, to put her field notes into some sort of order, to do her first runs, but she turned to the house scanner.

'Where is Roarke?'

Welcome home, darling Eve.

As usual the recorded voice using that particular endearment had slivers of embarrassment pricking at her spine.

'Yeah, yeah. Answer the question.'

'He's right behind you.'

'Jesus!' She whirled, biting back another curse as she saw Roarke leaning casually in the archway to the parlor. 'Why don't you just pull a blaster and fire away?'

'That wasn't the welcome home I'd planned. You've blood on your pants.'

She glanced down. 'It's not mine.' Rubbing at it absently, she studied him.

It wasn't just his greeting that spiked her heart rate. That could happen, did happen, just by looking at him. It wasn't the face. Or not just the face, with its blinding blue eyes, with that incredible mouth curved now in an easy smile, or the miracle of planes and angles that combined into a stunning specimen of male beauty framed by a mane of silky black hair. It wasn't just that long, rangy build, one she knew was hard with muscle under the business elegance of the dark suit he wore.

It was all she knew of him, all she had yet to discover, that combined and blew love through her like a storm.

It was senseless and impossible. And the most true and genuine thing she knew.

'How did you plan to welcome me home?'

He held out a hand, linking his fingers with hers when she crossed the marble floor to take it. Then he leaned in, leaned down, watching her as he brushed his lips over hers, watching her still as he deepened the kiss.

'Something like that,' he murmured, with Ireland drifting through his voice. 'To start.'

'Good start. What's next?'

He laughed. 'I thought a glass of wine in the parlor.'

'All by ourselves, you and me, drinking wine in the parlor.'

The glee in her voice had him lifting a brow. 'Yes, I'm sure Summerset's enjoying his holiday. How sweet of you to ask.'

'Blah blah.' She strolled into the parlor, dropped down on one of the antique sofas and deliberately planted her boots on a priceless coffee table. 'See what I'm doing? Think he just felt a sharp pain in his ass?'

'That's very childish, Lieutenant.'

'What's your point?'

He had to laugh, and poured wine from a bottle he'd already opened. 'Well then.' He gave her a glass, sat and propped his feet on the table as well. 'How was your day?'

'Uh-uh, you first.'

'You want to hear about my various meetings, and the progress of plans for the acquisition of the Eton Group, the rehab of the residential complex in Frankfort and the restructuring of the nano-tech division in Chicago?'

'Okay, enough about you.' She lifted her arm to make room when Galahad, their enormous cat, landed on the cushion beside her with a thump.

'I thought so.' Roarke toyed with Eve's hair as she stroked the cat. 'How is our new detective?'

'She's fine. She's loaded down with paperwork yet. Clearing up old business so she can start on the new. I wanted to give her a few days as a desk jockey before she takes her shiny new detective's badge out on the street.'

He glanced down at the bloodstain on Eve's pants. 'But you've caught a case.'

'Mmm.' She sipped the wine, let it smooth out the edges of the day. 'I handled the on-scene solo.'

'Having a little trouble adjusting to having a partner rather than an aide, Lieutenant?'

'No. Maybe. I don't know.' She gave an irritable shrug. 'I couldn't just cut her loose, could I?'

He flicked a finger down the shallow dent in her chin. 'You didn't want to cut her loose.'

'Why should I? We work well together. We've got a rhythm. I might as well keep her around. She's a good cop. Anyway, I didn't tag her for this because she had this whole big night planned, and she was already gone. You get enough plans fucked in this job without me pulling her in and botching her big celebration.'

He gave her a kiss on the cheek. 'Very sweet of you.'

'It was not.' Her shoulders wanted to hunch. 'It was easier than hearing her bitch and moan about losing reservations and wasting some fancy dress or something. I'll fill her in tomorrow anyway.'

'Why don't you fill me in tonight?'

'Planned on it.' She slid her gaze in his direction, smirked. 'I think you could be useful.'

'And we know I love being useful.' His fingers skimmed up her thigh.

She set down her glass, then lifted the tonnage of Galahad who'd sprawled his girth over her lap. 'Come along with me then, pal. I got a use for you.'

'That sounds . . . interesting.'

He started out with her, then cocked his head when she stopped halfway up the stairs. 'Problem?'

'I had this thought. You know how Summerset took that header down the steps?'

'I could hardly forget.'

'Yeah, well, I'm sorry he busted his pin and so on, even over and above the fact that it delayed his getting the hell out of the house for several days.'

'You're entirely too sensitive, darling Eve. It can't be good for you to take on the weight of the world this way.'

'Ha ha. So it's like bad luck. The stairs, I mean. We need to fix that or one of us could be next.'

'How do you propose to—'

It was impossible to finish the question, and difficult to remember what that question was when her mouth was hot on his, and her hands already busy tugging at his belt.

He all but felt his eyes roll up in his skull and out the back of his head.

'Can't have enough good luck, to my mind,' he managed, and spun her around so her back hit the wall and he could yank off her jacket.

'If we don't fall and kill ourselves, then we've broken the curse. This is a really good suit, right?'

'I have others.'

She laughed, pulled at his jacket, bit his throat. He hit the release on the weapon harness, shoved at the straps so it and the weapon thudded down the steps.

Restraints followed, and pocket "links, a raw silk tie, a single boot. He had her pinned to the wall, not quite naked, when she came. Her nails bit into his back, then slid down so she could squeeze his butt. 'I think it's working.'

With a breathless laugh, he pulled her down to the steps. They bumped and rolled. Thumped down, climbed up. In self-defense, she flung out a hand and gripped one of the spindles of the banister, hooked her legs around him like a vise to keep them both from tumbling down in a heap to the bottom.

He ravaged her breasts while her arching hips drove him toward delirium. When she shuddered, when she choked out his name, he pressed his hand between them and watched her crest again.

For all that he'd wanted the whole of his life, he'd never wanted anything as he did her. The more he had of her, the more he craved in an endless cycle of love and lust and longing. He could live with whatever had come before, whatever would come after, as long as there was Eve.

'Don't let go.' He cupped her hips, lifted them. 'Don't let go.' And drove himself into her.

There was a moment of blind, blasting pleasure, and her fingers trembled on the wood. The force of his need for her, and hers for him, rammed together, all but stopped her heart. Dazed, she opened her eyes, looked into his. She could see him lose himself, as linked with her now as if there'd been steel forging them.

So she wrapped herself around him and didn't let go.

They sprawled together on the stairs like two survivors of an earth-quake. She wasn't entirely sure the ground didn't tremble still.

She had on one boot, and her pants were inside out and stuck on that leg at the ankle. She had no doubt it looked ridiculous, but couldn't drum up the energy to care.

'I'm pretty sure it's safe now,' she commented.

'I hope to Christ, as I don't fancy having a go at it on these stairs a second time right at the moment.'

'I'm the one with a tread in my back.'

'So you are. Sorry.' He rolled off her, sat up, skimmed back his hair. 'That was . . . I'm not entirely sure. Memorable. I'd say memorable.'

She wouldn't forget it anytime soon. 'Most of our stuff's at the bottom, or nearly.'

He looked down, as she did. For a moment, while they pondered, there was no sound except their ragged breathing. 'There, you see, this is where having someone come along picking up after you comes in handy.'

'If a certain someone – who shall remain nameless for the next wonderful three weeks – was here to pick up after us, you wouldn't have gotten your rocks off on the steps.'

'Point taken. I suppose I'll go gather things up then. You're still wearing a boot,' he pointed out.

She debated for a moment, then decided working the boot off would be simpler than untangling the trousers. Once she had, she picked up whatever was reasonably in reach.

Then she sat where she was, chin on fist, and watched him tidy up the mess they'd made. It was never a hardship to look at him naked. 'I've got to dump this stuff, throw something on.'

'Why don't we eat while you tell me how else I might be useful?'

'Deal.'

Since they'd eat in her home office for her convenience, she let him pick the menu. She even manned the AutoChef herself for the lobster salad he had a yen for. She decided the sex had burned the alcohol out of her system and allowed herself a second glass of wine as they ate.

'Okay, woman who owns the residence – private town house, Upper East – was out of town for two weeks. A female friend was house-sitting. Owner comes home this afternoon, late this afternoon, sees her living area trashed. Her statement is that the doors were locked, the security alarm set. She goes upstairs. There's a strong odor, which pisses her off as much as the mess downstairs. She walks into her bedroom, finds her house sitter dead. Dead for

255

five days, according to my on-site. Throat slit. No other visible injuries. Indications are the attack came from behind. The security camera at the entrance was deactivated, disks removed. There's no sign of forced entry. The victim was wearing a lot of baubles. Possibly – even probable – they're fake, but her wrist unit was a good brand.'

'Sexual assault?'

'My prelim on scene indicates no. I'll wait and see what the ME says on that one. She was still dressed in club clothes. When the owner settles down some, we'll have her check to see if anything was taken. I saw what appeared to be antiques, original artworks, upscale electronics. My initial search of the crime scene turned up some jewelry in a drawer. It looked like good stuff, but I'm no judge. Possibly, it was a standard B and E that went wrong, but—'

'And here you are a judge.'

'It didn't look like it. It doesn't feel like it. It looks like, and feels like, somebody breaking in looking for something, or someone specific. It looked like this woman came home before he was finished.'

'Bad timing, all around.'

'Absolutely. It was known that the owner was out of town. Could be he wasn't expecting anyone to be there. She walked into the bedroom, he stepped in behind her, slit her throat from ear to ear, and either continued his search or left.'

'No, not your average B-and-E man. They want in and out quickly, no mess, no fuss. No weapons. You get an extra boot on your time if you get tagged carrying.'

'You'd know.'

He merely smiled. 'As I was never tagged, or booted, I find that dry sarcasm inappropriate. He didn't burgle in the traditional sense,' Roarke continued, 'so traditional burglary wasn't the purpose.'

'My thought. So we run Gannon and Jacobs – owner, victim – and see if anything pops that would make someone want them dead.'

'Ex-spouses, lovers?'

'According to the witness, Jacobs liked to play. No specific play-mate. Gannon has a recent ex. Claims they parted ways amicably, and no hard feelings, about a month back. But people can be really stupid about that sort of thing, hold grudges, or torches.'

'You'd know.'

She went blank for a moment, then had an image of Roarke pounding the crap out of one of her colleagues and a former one-nighter. 'Webster wasn't an ex. You have to be naked with some-body for more than two hours for them to qualify as an ex. It's a law.'

'I stand corrected.'

'You can stop looking smug anytime. I'll run the ex. Chad Dix. Upper East addy.' It wasn't pizza, she mused, but the lobster salad wasn't bad. She scooped up more as she flipped through her mental files. 'The victim was a travel agent, worked for Work or Play Travel, midtown. Know them?'

'No. Don't use them.'

'Some people travel for reasons other than work or play. Smuggling, for instance.'

He lifted his glass, contemplated his wine. 'To some points of view, smuggling might fall into the categories of either work or play.'

'It'll get boring to keep saying "you should know." We'll look into the travel agency, but I don't think Jacobs was a target. It was Gannon's house, Gannon's things. She was out of town, known to be out of town.'

'Work or play?'

'Work. She was on some sort of a tour deal for a book. It's the book that interests me.'

'Really? Now you have my attention.'

'Look, I read.' She scooped up more lobster. 'Stuff.'

'Case files don't count.' He gestured with his fork. 'But go on. What interests you about this book?'

'Do too count,' she retorted. 'It's some sort of family story, but the big hook is a diamond heist, early twenty-first, here in New York. It—'

'The Forty-seventh Street job. *Hot Rocks.* I know this book.'

'You read it?'

'As a matter of fact. The property was auctioned last year. Starline acquired.'

'Starline? Publishing? That's yours.'

'It is. I caught the pitch from the acquiring editor in one of the monthly reports. It interested me. Everyone – well, everyone with certain interests – knows about the Forty-seventh Street job.'

'You'd have those certain interests.'

'I would, yes. Close to thirty million in diamonds walk out of the Exchange. About three-quarters of them are scooped back up. But that leaves a lot of sparkling stones out there. Gannon. Sylvia . . . Susan . . . no, Samantha Gannon. Of course.'

Yeah, Roarke was a guy who came in handy. 'Okay, so you know what you know. Her grandfather recovered or helped recover the stones they got back.'

'Yes. And her great-grandfather – mother's side – was one of the team who stole them.'

'Is that so?' She leaned back, considered. 'We didn't get into that end.'

'It's in the book. She doesn't hide the connection. In fact, the connections, the ins and outs, are strong selling points.'

'Give me the highlights.'

'There were four known members of the heist team. One was an inside man, who handled the switch. The others posed as clients or part of the investigative team after the diamonds were discovered missing. Each scheduled a meeting with one of the designers or wholesalers upstairs. Each picked up a novelty item planted by the inside man. A ceramic dog, a rag doll, and so on.'

'Back up. A doll?'

'Hide in plain sight,' he explained. 'Innocuously. In each blind was a quarter share of the take. They walked in, walked out in broad daylight. Legend has it – and Samantha Gannon perpetuates this in her book – that two of them had lunch a block or so away with their share on their person.'

'They just walked out.'

'Brilliant in its simplicity, really. There's a retail section, street level. Almost a bazaar. And in those days – still in these from time to time – some of the jewelers walk from store to store, from shop to shop, carrying a fortune in gems tucked into paper cups they call briefkes. With enough balls, data and some inside assistance, it's easier than you might think to walk off with sparkles in the daylight. Easier by far than an after-hours job. Do you want coffee?'

'Are you getting it?'

'I will.' He rose to go into the kitchen. 'They'd never have gotten away with it,' he called out. 'There are careful records kept for stones of that sort. It would take a great deal of patience and willpower to wait until enough time had passed to turn them, and careful research and a strong sense of character to select the right source for that liquidation. Human nature being human nature, they were bound to get nipped.'

'They got away with a chunk.'

'Not exactly.' He came back in with a pot and two cups. 'Things went wrong almost immediately, starting with dishonor among thieves – as there invariably is. One of the lot, who went by the name of Crew, decided why take a quarter when you can take all. He was a different sort than O'Hara – that's the grandfather – and the others, and they should've known better than to throw in with him. He lured the inside man – probably promising a sweeter deal. He gave him two bullets in the brain. They used bullets with alarming regularity back then. He took his dead partner's share, and so had half.'

'And went after the others.'

'He did. News traveled, and they rabbited before he got to them. And that's how they ended up bringing O'Hara's daughter into it. It got messy, as you'll see when you read the book yourself. Another of them was killed. Both Crew and the insurance cop sniffed out the trail. The cop and the thief's daughter fell in love, happily enough, and she helped him with the recovery of the half O'Hara had access to. Though they rounded up Crew as well, with some drama and heroics, he was killed in prison less than three years after his term began. They found his original share tucked away

259

in a safe-deposit box here in the city, tracked from a key he had on his person at the time of arrest. But he never revealed where the other portion of the diamonds were.'

'More than fifty years ago. They could be long gone by now. Right back in some jewelry case in the form of rings, bracelets, whatever.'

'Certainly. But it's more fun to imagine them hidden inside some ceramic cat getting dusty on a shelf in a thrift store, isn't it?'

The fun didn't equate with her, but the motive did. 'She talks about the family connection in her book, missing diamonds. Sexy stuff. Somebody's going to decide she must have them, or know where they are.'

'There's a disclaimer in the book, of course. But yes, some are bound to wonder if she or someone in her family has them. If they're still out there, and unset, they'd be worth a great deal more today than they were at the beginning of the century. The legend alone bumps the value.'

'How much?'

'Conservatively, fifteen million.'

'There's nothing conservative about fifteen million. That kind of number could push a lot of people to go on a treasure hunt. Which, if pursuing that angle, narrows the field to, what, a couple million people?'

'More, I'd think, as she's been on a media tour. Even those who haven't bought or read the book could have heard the basic story in one of her interviews.'

'Well, what's life without a challenge? Did you ever look for them? The Forty-seventh Street diamonds?'

'No. But it was always entertaining to speculate about them with friends over a pint in the pub. I recall, in my youth, there was some pride that Jack O'Hara, the one who got away, was an Irishman. Some liked to imagine he'd nicked the rest of them after all and lived out his days hog high on the proceeds.'

'You don't think so.'

'I don't know. Had he managed it, Crew would have rolled on him quick as a dog rolls on a flea that bites his back. It's Crew

260

who had that ice, and took the location to hell with him. Out of spite, perhaps, but more – I think, more because it made them his. Kept them his.'

'Obsessed, was he?'

'He's painted that way in the book, and from what I've gleaned, Samantha Gannon made it a mission to be as truthful and accurate as possible in the telling.'

'All right, let's take a look at our cast of characters.' She moved over to the computer on her desk. 'I won't have the ME's or forensic reports until tomorrow earliest. But Gannon stated the place was locked and security was on when she returned. I took a good look, and entry wasn't forced. He either came in with Jacobs or got in himself. I'm leaning toward the latter, which would require some security experience, or knowledge of the codes.'

'The ex?'

'Gannon states she changed the codes after the breakup. Doesn't mean he didn't cop to the changes. While I'm looking at him, you could get me whatever you can on the diamonds, and the people involved.'

'Much more entertaining.' He topped off his coffee, took it with him to his adjoining office.

She set up a standard run on Chad Dix, and brooded into her coffee while her computer pooled the data. Cold, wasteful, pointless. That was how Andrea Jacobs's murder struck her. It wasn't a panic kill. The wound was too clean, the method itself too deliberate for panic. Coming up from behind, it would've been just as easy, just as effective, to knock her unconscious. Her death had added nothing.

She discounted any real possibility of a professional hit. The state of the house put that in the low percentile. A botched burglary was a decent enough cover for a target murder, but no pro would so completely botch the botch by leaving so many portable valuables behind.

Dix, Chad, her computer began. *Resides number five, 41 East Seventy-ninth Street, New York, New York. DOB, 28, March, 2027. Parents Mitchell Dix, Gracia Long Dix Unger. Divorced. One sibling, brother Wheaton. One half-sibling, sister Maylee Unger Brooks.*

She skimmed over his education, highlighted his employment record. Financial planner for Tarbo, Chassie and Dix. A money guy, then. It seemed to her that guys who fiddled with other people's money really enjoyed having bunches of their own.

She studied his ID photo. Square-jawed, high-browed, clean-shaven. Studiously handsome, she supposed, with the well-trimmed brown hair and heavy brown eyes.

'Computer, does subject have any criminal record? Include any arrest with charges dropped or suspended.

Working . . . Drunk and disorderly, fine paid, November 12, 2049. Possession of illegals, fine paid, April 3, 2050. Destruction of public property, public drunkenness, restitution made, fine paid, July 4, 2050. Drunk and disorderly, fine paid, June 15, 2053.

'Got a little pattern working here, don't we, Chad? Computer, records of alcohol and/or chemical rehabilitation?'

Working . . . Voluntary rehabilitation program, Stokley Clinic, Chicago, Illinois. Four-week program July 13–August 10, 2050, completed. Voluntary rehabilitation program, Stokley Clinic, Chicago, Illinois. Two-week program June 16–30, 2053, completed.

'Still clean and sober, Chad?' she wondered. Regardless, his record showed no predilection for violence.

She'd interview him the next day, dig deeper if it was warranted. For now, she brought up the data on the victim.

Andrea Jacobs had been twenty-nine. Born in Brooklyn, only child, parents still living, still married to each other. They resided in Florida now, and she'd shattered their lives a few hours before when she'd notified them that their only child was dead.

Andrea's ID picture showed an attractive blonde with a wide, brilliant smile. There was no criminal record. She'd worked for the same employer for eight years, lived in the same apartment for the same amount of time.

Moved over from Brooklyn, Eve thought. Got yourself a job and a place of your own. New York girl, beginning to end. Since she had next of kin's permission to go into the victim's financials, she coded in, brought up the data.

She'd lived close, Eve noted, but no closer than any young, single woman who liked fancy shoes and nights at the club might live. Rent was paid. Saks bill was overdue, as was someplace called Clones. A quick check informed her Clones was a designer knockoff shop downtown.

With the data still up, she switched to her notes and began to order them into a report. It helped her think to take the facts, observations and statements and link them together into a whole.

She glanced over as Roarke came to the doorway.

'There's quite a bit of information about the diamonds, including detailed descriptions, photographs. A great deal more on each of the men allegedly responsible for the theft. It's still compiling. I'm having it sent to your unit simultaneously.'

'Thanks. You need to oversee the run?'

'Not really, no.'

'Want to go for a ride?'

'With you, Lieutenant? Always.'

Chapter Nineteen

She went back to the scene. It was dark, she thought. Not as late as it had been on the night of the murder, but near enough. She uncoded the police seal.

'How long would it take to deactivate the alarm, uncode the locks? Average?'

'But, darling, I'm not average in such matters.'

She rolled her eyes. 'Is it a good system? Would you need experience to get through, or just the right tools?'

'First, it's a good neighborhood. Safe and upscale. There's considerable foot and street traffic. You wouldn't want to bungle about, have anyone wondering, Now what's that guy doing over there? Even in the middle of the night. What time was the murder, by the way?'

'Time of death's estimated due to the condition of the body. But between twelve and one a.m.'

'Not so very late then, particularly if we believe he was inside already. Shank of the evening, really. So you'd want to get in without too much time. If it were me – and it hasn't been for many the year – I'd have studied the system before the event. Either gotten a good firsthand look at it or done my research and found what sort was installed and studied it at the supplier's, or on-line. I'd've known what I had to do before I got here.'

Sensible, she thought, in a larcenous way. 'And if you'd done all that?'

He made a low, considering sound and studied the locks. 'With any sort of skill, you'd have the locks lifted inside four minutes. Three if you had good hands.'

'Three to four minutes,' she repeated.

'A longer space of time than you'd think when you're standing somewhere you shouldn't be, doing something you've got no business doing.'

'Yeah, I get that.'

'If you're an amateur, it would take considerably longer. The alarm, well, you see our resident has graciously put this little warning plaque here, telling those with an interest that she's protected by First Alarm Group.'

Eve hissed out a breath in disgust. 'Hey, Mr. Burglar Man, let me give you a hand with this break-in. Her grandfather was a cop, then went private,' Eve added. 'Wouldn't he have told her how stupid it is to advertise your security system?'

'Likely. So it could be a blind. For argument's sake, we'll assume, or assume our killer assumed, she's giving the honest data. Their best-selling residential package is wired into the lock itself. You'd need to take it out while you were at the lock, and that takes steady fingers. Then you'd need to reset it on the panel she's likely to have just inside the door. So that might take your man another minute, even two, providing he knew what he was about. He'd have done better if he'd purchased the system himself, then practiced on it. Did you bring me here so I could have a go at it?'

'I wanted to see—' She broke off as a man hailed them from the sidewalk.

'What're you doing there?'

He was mid-thirties, with the look of a regular health-club goer. Solid muscle over a lean frame. Behind him, across the street, a woman stood in the light spilling from an open front door. She had a pocket 'link in her hand.

'Problem?' Eve asked.

'That's what I'm asking you.' The man rolled his shoulders, rocked up on the balls of his feet. Combative stance. 'Nobody's home there. If you're a friend of the person who lives there, you should know that.'

'You a friend of hers?'

'I live across the street.' He gestured with his thumb. 'We look out for each other around here.'

'Glad to hear it.' Eve pulled out her badge. 'You know what happened here?'

'Yeah. Wait a sec.' He held up a hand, turned and called out to the woman in the doorway, 'It's okay, honey. They're cops. Sort of figured you were,' he said when he turned back to them. 'But I wanted to make sure. Couple of cops came by and talked to us already. Sorry about jumping on you. We're all a little edgy right now.'

'No problem. Were you around last Thursday night?'

'We were home. We were right there across the street while . . .' He stared hard at the Gannon house. 'Jesus, it's tough to think about. We knew Andrea, too. We've been to parties at Sam's, and she and my wife did the girls'-night-out thing a couple times with friends. We were right across the street when this happened.'

'You knew Andrea Jacobs was staying here while Ms. Gannon was out of town?'

'My wife came over here the night before Sam left for her book tour deal – just to say goodbye, wish her luck, ask if she wanted us to feed the fish or anything. Sam told her Andrea would be around to take care of stuff.'

'Did you see or speak to her, to Andrea Jacobs, during the time Samantha Gannon was out of town?'

'Don't think I saw her more than once. A quick wave across the street kind of thing. I leave the house about six-thirty most mornings. Hit the gym before the office. Wife's out by eight. Andrea kept different hours, so I didn't expect to see much of her. Never thought anything when I didn't.'

'But you noticed us at the door tonight. Is that because of what happened, or do you usually keep an eye out?'

'I keep an eye. Not like an eagle,' he said with a half smile. 'Just try to stay aware, you know. And you guys were sort of loitering there, you know?'

'Yeah.' Like someone might who was trying to lift the locks and bypass the alarm. 'Have you noticed anyone who doesn't belong?

266

Did you see anyone at the door, or just hanging around the area in the last couple weeks?'

'Cops asked me the same thing before. I've thought and thought about it. I just didn't. My wife either, because we've talked about it since we found out what happened. Haven't talked about much else.'

He let out a long breath. 'And last Thursday, my wife and I went to bed about ten. Watched some screen in the sack. I locked up right before we headed up. I'd've looked out. I always look out, just habit. But I didn't see anything. Anyone. It's terrible what happened. You're not supposed to know people this happens to,' he said as he looked at the house. 'Somebody else is supposed to know them.'

She knew them, Eve thought as she walked back to Roarke. She knew countless dead.

'See how long it takes,' she said to Roarke, and gestured toward the door.

'All right then.' He drew a small leather case out of his pocket, selected a tool. 'You'll take into consideration that I've not researched nor practiced on this particular system.' He crouched.

'Yeah, yeah. You get a handicap. I just want to reconstruct a possible scenario. I don't think anybody casing this house would've gotten past Joe Gym across the street. Not if they spent any time in the neighborhood.'

'While you were talking to him, half a dozen people came to doors or windows and watched.'

'Yeah, I made that.'

'Still, if you were casing, you might walk by, take photos.' He straightened, opened the door. 'And you might invest in a remote clone, if you could afford one.' While he spoke, he opened the security panel inside the door, interfaced a mini-pocket unit to it and manually keyed in a command. 'Dress differently, take another walk. You'd just need some patience. There, that's done.'

'You said three or four minutes. That was under two.'

'I said someone with some skill. I didn't say me. It's a decent system, but Roarke Industries makes better.'

267

'I'll give you a plug next time I talk to her. He went upstairs first.'

'Did he?'

'He went up first because if he wasn't expecting anyone to come in, he'd have left the lights on after he hit the privacy screens. She'd have noticed that when she came in. She'd have noticed the lights, and the mess in the living area. But she didn't. Assuming she had a working brain, if she'd walked in on that, she'd have run right out again, called the cops. But she went upstairs.'

She opened the front door again, let it slam shut. 'He heard her. She checks the locks, the alarms. Maybe she checks the 'link down here for messages.' Eve walked through the living area, skirting around the mess, ignoring the chemical smell left behind by the sweepers. 'She's been clubbing, probably had a few drinks. She doesn't spend much time down here. She's wearing arch-killing shoes, but she doesn't take them off until she's in the bedroom. Can't see why she'd walk around down here in them for long with nobody around to admire her legs. She starts upstairs.'

She moved up the steps. 'I bet she likes the house. She's lived in an apartment for nearly a decade. I bet she likes having all this room. She turns into the bedroom, kicks off the fuck-me shoes.'

'Minor point, but how do you know she didn't take off the shoes downstairs, walk up barefoot, carrying them?'

'Hmm? Oh, their position – and hers. If they'd been in her hand when she got sliced, they'd have dropped closer to her body. If she'd carried them up, she'd have turned toward, or at least have tossed them closer to, the closet. Seems to me. See where I'm standing?'

He saw where she was standing, just as he saw the splotches and splatters of blood on the bed, the floor, the lamp, the wall. The stench of it all was barely hidden under the chemicals. And he wondered how, how in God's name, anyone could come back and sleep in this room again. Live with the nightmare of this room.

Then he looked at his wife, saw she was waiting. Saw her cop's eyes were cool and flat. She lived with nightmares, waking and sleeping.

'Yes, I see.'

'Closet doors were open. I'm betting the closet. He didn't start in here. I think he started in the office down the hall. I think that was his first stop, and he didn't get very far.'

'Why?'

'If he'd tossed this room, she'd have seen the mess as soon as she opened the door. No defensive wounds, no sign she tried to run or fight. Second, there's a workstation in the office, and it's still neat as a pin. I figure that was his starting point, and he'd planned to be careful, to be tidy. Jacobs comes in, screws that plan for him.'

'And Plan B is murder.'

'Yeah. No way he missed her work station, but he didn't mess it up. He went through everything else, and wasn't worried about being neat, but he'd already searched the workstation. Why mess with it again?'

Roarke looked at the horror of blood and fluids staining the floor and walls. 'And slicing a woman's throat is more time-efficient.'

'That could factor. I think he heard her come in, and instead of waiting until she went to sleep and getting the hell out, instead of knocking her senseless, he slipped right in here, slid back into the closet and watched her come in and kick off her fancy shoes. Push that stuff out of the way, will you? We've already been through here, scene's on record. Stand in the closet.'

'Christ.' He pushed the heaps of clothes and pillows aside, stepped back inside the open closet.

'See the angle? This had to be the angle from the way she landed. She's standing like this, facing away. He came up behind, yanked her head back by the hair – she had long hair, and the angle of the wound – had to be. Slice down, left to right. Do that. Just fake the hair.'

He reached her in two strides, gave her short hair a tug, feigned the swipe with a knife.

She imagined herself jerking once. The shock the system experienced, the alarm screaming in the brain even as the body died. And looked down at the floor, brought the position of the body back into her mind.

'Had to be. Had to be just like that. He couldn't have hesitated, not for a second. Even a second warning, she'd have turned, changed the angle some. Had to be fast and smooth. See, she hit the side of the bed when she fell. Spatter indicates. Hits the side of the bed, bounced, rolled, landed. Then he went back to work. He had to do most of this after he'd killed her. He must've spent another hour, maybe two, in the house with her, some of that right in this room with her while she was bleeding out. He's got steady hands. And he's got cold blood.'

'Have you got a watch on Samantha Gannon?'

'Yeah. And it's going to stay on her until I take him down. Let's get out of here.'

He waited until they were outside again, in the hot, summer air. Until she'd resealed the door. Then he ran his hands down her arms, drew her against him and kissed her lightly.

'What was that for?' she asked.

'We needed it.'

'Guess you're right.' She took his hand, walked down the steps. 'We did.'

The media had already caught the scent. Eve's office 'link at Cop Central was clogged with requests, pleas, demands for information. She dumped them all, with some pleasure, shooting them to the media liaison. They could sniff for blood all they wanted, but they weren't getting any from her until she was ready.

She expected to get a personal visit from Nadine Furst before much longer. She'd deal with that when the time came. The fact was there was probably a way for her to use Channel 75's hotshot on-air reporter.

She programmed coffee and decided it was never too early to nag the ME or the lab.

She was arguing with the ME assigned to her case, disgusted to be informed Chief Medical Examiner Morris was on leave, when she heard hoots and whistles erupt from the bull pen outside her office.

'I don't care if it is the summer crunch in your line of work,'

270

Eve snapped. 'Sending in bodies doesn't happen to be my little hobby. I need results, not excuses.'

She broke transmission, decided her first ass-kicking of the day put her in the perfect mood to bitch at the lab. Then scowled at the clicking sound approaching her office.

'Morning, Dallas.'

The stalwart Peabody, newly promoted to detective, no longer wore her spit-and-polish uniform. And Eve was discovering that was a damn pity. Her sturdy body, which showed a lot more curves out of her blues, was decked out in a pair of pegged lavender pants, a snug purple top and a floaty sort of jacket that picked up both colors in thin stripes. Instead of her clunky and perfectly respectable cop shoes she had on pointy-toed purple shoes with short skinny heels.

Which explained the clicking.

'What the hell have you got on?'

'Clothes. They're my clothes. I'm trying out different looks so I can settle on my particular work style. I'm thinking about new hair, too.'

'Why do you have to have new hair?' She was *used* to Peabody's dark bowl of hair, damnit. 'Why do people always have to have new hair? If you didn't like the old hair, why did you have the old hair? Then you won't like the new hair, and you'll have to have new new hair. It makes me crazy.'

'So much does.'

'And what the hell are those?' She jabbed a finger at the shoes.

'Aren't they great?' She turned her ankle to show them off. 'Surprisingly comfortable, too.'

'Those are girl shoes.'

'Dallas, I don't know how to tell you this, but I am a girl.'

'My partner's not a girl. I don't have girl partners. I have cops. My partner is a cop, and those are not the shoes of a cop. You click.'

'Thanks, Lieutenant.' Peabody smiled down at herself. 'I do think it all works well together.'

'No, Jesus Christ in spandex. You click when you walk.'

'They just need to be broken in.' She started to sulk, then saw the case file, the crime-scene stills, on Eve's desk. 'What're you doing? Are you working on a cold case?'

'It's hot. I caught it yesterday, right before end of shift.'

'You caught a case and you didn't tag me?'

'Don't whine. I didn't call you in because you had The Big Night. Remember how you kept saying it, like it was a vid title? I know how to work a scene, Peabody. There was no reason to screw up your plans.'

'Despite your opinion of my shoes, I'm a cop. I expect to have my plans screwed.'

'This time they weren't. Shit, I wanted you to have it. If you're going to make a big deal here, you're just going to piss me off.'

Peabody folded in her lips. Shifted her stance as the shoes weren't quite as comfortable as she'd claimed. Then she smiled. 'I'm not. I appreciate it. It was important to me, and McNab went to a lot of trouble. So thanks. We had a great time. I drank a little more than I should, so I'm a little fuzzy this morning. But a hit of real coffee should help that.'

She looked hopefully toward Eve's AutoChef, where there was real as opposed to the sludge disguised as coffee in the bull pen.

'Go ahead. Then sit down. I'll bring you up to speed.'

'Missing diamonds. It's like a treasure hunt,' Peabody decided. 'Like booty. It could be fun.'

Saying nothing, Eve passed her one of the on-scene stills of Andrea Jacobs's body. Peabody let out a hiss between her teeth. 'Okay, not so much. No sign of forced entry? Sexual assault?'

'None apparent from the on-scene.'

'She could've brought someone home with her. Bad choice. People make them.'

'We'll check that out. I ran her debit card. Her last transaction, which looks like clearing the evening's tab, was at Club Six-Oh. Sixtieth and Second, at eleven forty-five on Thursday night. Estimated time of death was between midnight and one.'

'So she'd have gone straight to the Gannon residence from the club. If she had company, she found it there.'

'We're in the field,' Eve said, gathering the file. 'We talk to Gannon's ex, Jacobs's employer and co-workers, hit the club and swing by the morgue to harass people.'

'I always like that part. I get to flash my new badge,' she added as they walked out. She flipped her jacket open to reveal the detective's badge hooked to her waistband.

'Very nice.'

'My new favorite accessory.'

The powers-that-be at Tarbo, Chassie and Dix obviously subscribed to the theory that a display of excess drew in clients whose finances needed planning. The midtown offices were spread over four floors with a main information center the size of the Yankees' outfield. Eight young men and women, certainly hired as much for their perky good looks as their communication skills, manned an alarm-red island counter that could have housed a small suburb. Each wore a personal communicator and manned slick mini data and communication centers.

Each obviously practiced superior dental hygiene if their dazzling, identical smiles were any gauge.

Around them were smaller counters with more perky, toothy men and women in snappy suits, three waiting areas with cushy-looking chairs, equipped with screens for passing the time with magazines or short vids, and a little, tastefully planted garden with its own tiny blue pool.

Bouncy, repetitive music danced through the air at a discreet volume.

Eve decided she'd be in a padded room for mental defectives in under a week if she worked under similar conditions.

She walked to the main counter over a springy silver carpet. 'Chad Dix.'

'Mr. Dix is on forty-two.' The beaming brunette tapped her screen. 'I'll be happy to have one of his assistants escort you. If I might have your name, and the time of your appointment?'

Eve laid her badge on the glossy red counter. 'Lieutenant Dallas, NYPSD. And I'd say my appointment is now. We can get up to

273

forty-two ourselves, thanks, but you might want to tell Mr. Dix we're on our way.'

'But you have to be cleared for the elevator.'

Eve picked up her badge, wiggled it back and forth. 'Then you'd better take care of that.' She pocketed the badge and strode to the bank of elevators with Peabody.

'Can I be bitch cop next time?' Peabody whispered as they waited for the doors to open. 'I really need to practice.'

'Seems to me if you need to practice, it's not a true calling, but you can take a shot.' She stepped onto the elevator. 'Forty-two,' she demanded. And leaned back on the side wall as the car whisked them up. 'Take the assistant they're going to toss in our way.'

'Hot dog.' Peabody rubbed her hands together. Then rolled her shoulders, circled her neck.

'Definitely not a true calling,' Eve muttered, but let Peabody lead when the doors opened on forty-two.

This floor was no less opulent than the other, though the color scheme was electric blue and silver rather than red. The waiting areas were bigger, with the addition of wall screens tuned to various financial programs. This information station was the size and shape of a small wading pool, but there was no need to bother with it as the assistant clipped hurriedly through the double glass doors that slid soundlessly open at her approach.

This one was blond with the sunshine hair done in a mass of corkscrew curls that spilled and spun around her head like a halo. She had pink lips and cheeks, and a body of impressive curves tucked snugly into a narrow skirt and jacket the color of cotton candy.

Not wanting to miss her chance, Peabody stepped forward, flipped her jacket open. 'Detective Peabody, NYPSD. My partner, Lieutenant Dallas. We need to speak to Chad Dix regarding an investigation.'

'Mr. Dix is meeting with a client, but I'd be happy to review his schedule and clear some time for you later today. If you could give me some idea of the nature of your business, and how much time you'll require.'

'The nature of our business is murder, and the time we require will depend entirely on Mr. Dix.' Peabody dipped her head, lowered her eyebrows in a stern look she enjoyed practicing in the bathroom mirror. 'If he feels unable to meet with us here and now, we'll be happy to take him downtown and hold our meeting there. You can come with him,' Peabody added.

'I . . . If you'll give me just a moment.'

When she scurried off, Peabody elbowed Eve. '"Our business is murder." I thought that was good.'

'It didn't suck.' She nodded as the blonde came bustling back. 'Let's check the scores.'

'If you'll come with me, Mr. Dix will see you now.'

'I thought he would.' Peabody started to saunter after her.

'Don't rub their noses in it,' Eve muttered. 'It's tacky.'

'Check.'

They moved through a fan-shaped hallway to the wide end and another set of double doors. These were opaque and opened when the assistant tapped.

'Detective Peabody and Lieutenant Dallas, Mr. Dix.'

'Thank you, Juna.'

He was behind a U-shaped workstation with the requisite window-wall at his back. His office suite had a luxurious sitting area with several wide chairs and a display shelf holding a number of antique games and toys.

He wore a stone-gray suit with muted chalk stripes, and a braided silver chain under the collar of his snowy white shirt.

'Officers.' His expression sober, he gestured toward chairs. 'I assume this has something to do with the tragedy at Samantha Gannon's. I heard about it last night on a media report. I haven't been able to reach Samantha. Are you able to tell me if she's all right?'

'As much as can be expected,' Eve answered. 'You also knew Andrea Jacobs?'

'Yes.' He shook his head and sat behind his desk. 'I can't believe this happened. I met her through Samantha. We socialized quite a bit while Samantha and I were seeing each other. She was . . . It

275

probably sounds clichéd, but she was one of those people who are just full of life. The reports are vague, even this morning. There was a burglary?'

'We're in the process of verifying that. You and Ms. Gannon are no longer seeing each other?'

'No, not romantically.'

'Why is that?'

'It wasn't working out.'

'For whom?'

'Either of us. Sam's a beautiful, interesting woman, but we weren't enjoying ourselves together any longer. We decided to break it off.'

'You had the codes to her residence.'

'I . . .' He missed a beat, quietly cleared his throat. 'Yes. I did. As she had mine. I assume she changed them after we broke up – as I changed mine.'

'Can you tell us where you were on the night in question?'

'Yes, of course. I was here, in the office until just after seven. I had a dinner meeting with a client at Bistro, just down on Fifty-first. Juna can give you the client's information, if you need it. I left the restaurant about ten-thirty and went home. I caught up on some paperwork for an hour or so, watched the media reports, as I do every night before I turn in. That must have been nearly midnight. Then I went to bed.'

'Can anyone verify this?'

'No, not after I left the restaurant, in any case. I took a cab home, but I couldn't tell you the number of the cab. I wouldn't have any reason to break into Sam's house and steal anything, or for God's sake kill Andrea.'

'You've had some substance-abuse problems over the years, Mr. Dix.'

A muscle twitched in his jaw. 'I'm clean, and have been for a number of years. I've been through rehabilitation programs and continue to go to regular meetings. If necessary, I'll submit to a screening, but I'll want legal representation.'

'We'll let you know. When's the last time you had contact with Andrea Jacobs?'

276

'A couple of months, six weeks ago, at least. It seems to me we all went to a jazz club downtown this summer. Sam and I, Andrea and whoever she was seeing at the time, a couple of other people. It was a few weeks before Sam and I called things off.'

'Did you and Ms. Jacobs ever see each other separately?'

'No.' His tone took on an edge. 'I didn't cheat on Sam, certainly not with one of her friends. And Andrea, as much as she enjoyed men, wouldn't have poached. That's insulting on every level.'

'I insult a lot of people, on every level, in my work. Murder doesn't make for nice manners. Thanks for your cooperation, Mr. Dix.' Eve rose. 'We'll be in touch if there's anything else.'

She started for the door, then turned. 'By the way, have your read Ms. Gannon's book?'

'Of course. She gave me an advance copy several weeks ago. And I bought one on the day of its release.'

'Any theories on the diamonds?'

'Fascinating stuff, isn't it? I think Crew's ex-wife skipped with them and made a really nice life for herself somewhere.'

'Could be. Thanks again.'

Eve waited until they were riding down to street level. 'Impressions, Detective?'

'I just love when you call me that. He's sharp, he's smooth, and he wasn't in a meeting. He had his assistant say so to flip us off, if possible.'

'Yeah. People just don't like talking to cops. Why is that? He was prepared,' she added, as they stepped out and started across the lobby. 'Had his night in question all laid out, didn't even have to remind him of the date. Six days ago, and he doesn't even have to think about it. Rattled it off like a student reciting a school report.'

'He still isn't clear for the time of the murder.'

'Nope, which is probably why he wanted to flip us off awhile. Let's hit the travel agency next.'

Eve supposed under most circumstances Work or Play would've been a cheerful place. The walls were covered with screens where impossibly pretty people romped in exotic locales that probably convinced potential travelers they'd look just as impossibly pretty frolicking half-naked on some tropical beach.

There were half a dozen agents at workstations rather than cubes, and each station was decorated with personal memorabilia: photos, little dolls or amusing paperweights, posters.

All of the agents were female, and the office smelled of girls. Sort of candy-coated sex, to Eve's mind. They were all dressed in fashionable casualwear – or she assumed it was fashionable – even the woman who appeared to be pregnant enough to be carting around three healthy toddlers in her womb.

Just looking at her made Eve jittery.

Even worse were the six pairs of swollen, teary eyes, the occasional broken sob or sniffle.

The room pulsed with estrogen and emotion.

'It's the most horrible thing. The most horrible.' The pregnant woman somehow levered herself up from her chair. She had her streaky brown hair pulled back, and her face was wide as the moon and the color of milk chocolate. She laid her hand on the shoulder of one of the other women as she began to cry.

'It might be easier if we go back to my office. This is actually Andrea's station. I've been manning it this morning. I'm Cecily Newberry. I'm, well, the boss.'

She led the way to a tiny, tidy adjoining office and shut the door. 'The girls are – well, we're a mess. We're just a mess. I honestly didn't believe Nara when she called me this morning, crying and babbling about Andrea. Then I switched on the news channel and got the report. I'm sorry.' She braced a hand at the small of her back and lowered herself into a chair. 'I have to sit. It feels like a maxibus is parked on my bladder.'

'When are you due, Ms. Newberry?' Peabody asked.

'Ten more days.' She patted her belly. 'It's my second. I don't know what I was thinking, timing this baby so I'd carry it through the summer heat. I came in today – I'd intended to take the next several weeks off. But I came in because . . . I didn't know what else I could do. Should do. Andrea worked here almost since I opened the place. She manages it with me, and was going to take over while I was on maternity.'

'She hasn't been in to work for several days. Weren't you concerned?'

'She was taking some leave now. She was actually due back today, when I'd planned to start mine. Oh God.' She rubbed at her face. 'Usually she'd take advantage of our benefits and go somewhere, but she decided to house-sit for her friend and get her apartment painted, do some shopping, she said, hit a few of the spas and salons around town. I expected to hear from her yesterday or the day before, just to check in with me before we switched over. But I really didn't think anything of it when I didn't. I didn't think at all, to be frank. Between this baby, my little girl at home, the business, my husband's mother deciding now's a dandy time to come stay with us, I've been distracted.'

'When's the last time you did talk to her?'

'A couple of weeks. I'm . . . I was very fond of Andrea, and she was wonderful to work with. But we had very different lifestyles. She was single and loved to go out. I'm incredibly married and raising a three-year-old, having another child and running a business. So we didn't see each other often outside of work, or talk often unless it was work related.'

'Has anyone come in asking about her or for her specifically?'

'She has a regular customer base. Most of my girls do. Customers who ask for them specifically when they're planning a trip.'

'She'd have a customer list.'

'Absolutely. There's probably some legal thing I'm supposed to do before I agree to give that to you, but I'm not going to waste my time or yours. I have all my employees' passcodes. I'll give it to you. You can copy anything you feel might help off her work unit.'

'I appreciate your cooperation.'

'She was a delightful woman.' She made me laugh, and she did a good job for me. I never knew her to hurt anyone. I'll do whatever I can to help you find who did this to her. She was one of my girls, you know. She was one of mine.'

It took an hour to copy the files, search through and document the contents of the workstation and interview the other employees.

Every one of Andrea's co-workers had gone out with her to clubs, bars, parties, with dates, without dates. There was a great deal of weeping but little new to be learned.

Eve could barely wait to get away from the scent of grief and lipdye.

'Start doing a standard run on the names on her customer base. I'm going to check in with Samantha Gannon and verbally smack this asshole ME around.'

'Morris?'

'No, Morris is tanning his fine self on some tropical beach. We caught Duluc. She's slower than a one-legged snail. I'm going to warm up with her, then, if there's time, drop-kick Dickhead,' she added, referring to the chief lab tech.

'Boy, that should round out the morning. Then maybe we can have lunch.'

'We're dealing with the cleaning service before the morgue and lab. Didn't you have breakfast a couple hours ago?'

'Yeah, but if I start nagging you about lunch now, you'll cave before I get faint from hunger.'

'Detectives eat less often than aides.'

'I never heard that. You're just saying that to scare me.' She trotted on her increasingly uncomfortable shoes after Eve. 'Right?'

Chapter Twenty

Maid In New York was a pared-down, storefront operation that put all its focus and frills into the services. This was explained to Eve with some snippiness by the personnel manager, who reigned in an office even smaller and stingier than Eve's at Central.

'We keep the overhead to a minimum,' Ms. Tesky of the sensible bun and shoes informed Eve. 'Our clients aren't interested in our offices – and rarely come here in any case – but are concerned about their own offices and homes.'

'I can see why,' Eve observed, and Tesky's nostrils pinched. It was sort of interesting to watch.

'Our employees are the product, and all are strictly and comprehensively interviewed, tested, screened, trained and must meet the highest of standards in personal appearance, demeanor and skill. Our clients are also screened, to ensure our employees' safety.'

'I just bet they are.'

'We provide residential and business housekeeping services, in teams, pairs or individually. We use human and droid personnel. We service all of greater New York and New Jersey and will, upon request, arrange for maids to travel with a client who requires or desires approved out-of-town, out-of-country and even off-planet services.'

'Right.' She wondered how many of the maids were also licensed companions, but it didn't really apply. 'I'm interested in the employee or employees who handled Samantha Gannon's residence.'

'I see. Do you have a warrant? I consider our personnel and client files confidential.'

'I bet you do. I could get a warrant. A little time, a little trouble, but I could get a warrant. But because you made me take that time and that trouble when I'm investigating a murder – a really nasty, messy murder, by the way, that's going to take a whole slew of your mighty maids to tidy up – I'm going to wonder why you slowed me down. I'm going to ask myself, Hey, I wonder what Ms. Testy—'

'Tes-*ky.*'

'Right. What she has to hide. I have a suspicious mind, that's why I got to be a lieutenant. So when I get that warrant, and I start wondering those things, I'm going to dig, and I'm going to keep digging, getting my suspicious little finger smears all over your nice tidy files. We'll just have to give INS a heads up so they can breeze in here and make another big mess, making sure you didn't miss any illegals in all that testing and screening.'

The nostrils pinched again, even as a thin breath hooted up them. 'Your implication is insulting.'

'People keep saying that to me. The fact that I'm innately suspicious and insulting means I'll probably make a bigger mess then those anal-retentives in INS. Won't I, Detective Peabody?'

'As someone who's cleaned up after you before, sir, I can verify that you will, absolutely, make a bigger mess than anyone. You'll also find something – you always do – that will certainly inconvenience Ms. Tesky and her employer.'

'What do they call that? Tit for tat?'

Throughout Eve's recital, Ms. Tesky had turned several interesting colors. She appeared to have settled on fuchsia. 'You can't threaten me.'

'Threaten? Golly, Peabody, insult, sure, but did I threaten anyone?'

'No, Lieutenant. You're just making conversation, in your own unique style.'

'That's what I thought. Just making conversation. So, let's arrange for that warrant, shall we? And since we're taking the time and trouble, let's make it for the financials, and civil and criminal cases or suits brought, as well as those personnel files.'

'I find you very disagreeable.'

'There you go,' Eve said with an easy smile. 'Tit for tat one more time.'

Tesky spun her chair around to her desk unit, coded in.

'Ms. Gannon's residence is on a twice-monthly schedule, with quarterly extended services, and priority for emergency calls and entertainment requests. She was due for her regular service yesterday.'

Several more frown lines dug into Tesky's forehead. 'Her maid failed to confirm completed service. That's simply unacceptable.'

'Who's the maid?'

'Tina Cobb. She's seen to the Gannon residence for the last eight months.'

'Can you check on there if she's missed any other jobs recently?'

'One moment.' She called up another program. 'All Cobb's jobs were completed and confirmed through Saturday. She had Sunday off. No confirmation of the Gannon residence yesterday. There's a flag by her name today, which means the client notified us she didn't report for work. Scheduling had to replace her.'

Ms. Tesky did what Eve assumed anyone named Tesky would. She tsked.

'Give me her home address.'

Tina Cobb lived in one of the post-Urban War boxes that edged the Bowery. They'd been a temporary fix when buildings had been burned or bombed. The temporary fix had lasted more than a generation. Lewd, creative and often ungrammatical graffiti swirled over the pitted, reconstituted concrete. The windows were riot-barred, and the loiterers on the stoops looked as though they'd be more than happy to burn or bomb the place again, just to break the monotony.

Eve climbed out of her car, scanned the faces, ignored the unmistakable aroma of Zoner. She took out her badge, held it up.

'You can probably guess that's mine,' she said, pointing at her vehicle. 'What you might not be able to guess is that if anybody messes with it, I'll hunt you down and pop your eyes out with my thumbs.'

'Hey.' A guy wearing a dingy muscle shirt and a gleaming silver earring flipped her the bird. 'Fuck you.'

'No, thanks, but it's sweet of you to ask. I'm looking for Tina Cobb.'

There were whistles, catcalls, kissy noises. 'That's one fiiine piece of ass.'

'I'm sure she's delighted you think so. Is she around?'

Muscle Shirt stood up. He poked out his chest and jabbed a finger at Eve's. Fortunately for him, he stopped short of actual contact. 'What you want to hassle Tina for? She don't do nothing. Girl works hard, minds her own.'

'Who said I was going to hassle her? She might be in trouble. If you're a friend of hers, you'll want to help.'

'Didn't say I was a friend. Just said she minds her own. So do I. Whyn't you?'

'Because I get paid to mind other people's own, and you're starting to make me wonder why you can't answer a simple question. In a minute, I'm going to start minding yours instead of Tina Cobb's.'

'Cops is all shit.'

She bared her teeth in a glittering grin. 'Want to test that theory?'

He snorted, shot a glance over his shoulder at his companions as if to let them see he wasn't worried about it. 'Too hot to bother,' he said, and shrugged his skinny shoulders. 'Ain't seen Tina for a couple of days anyway. Don't run a tab on her, do I? Her sister works across the street at the bodega. Whyn't you ask her?'

'I'll do that. Mitts off the car, boys. Pitiful as it is, it's mine.'

They walked across the street. Eve assumed the kissing noises and invitations for sexual adventure that came from the stoop were now aimed at her and Peabody. But she let it go. The skinny asshole was right about one thing. It was too hot to bother.

Inside, she noted the girl manning the checkout counter. Short, thin, olive complexion, an odd updo of hair with purple fringes over the ink black.

'I could get us something,' Peabody offered. 'Something to do with food.'

'Go ahead.' Eve walked to the counter, waited while the customer in front of her paid for a pack of milk powder and a minuscule box of sugar substitute.

'Help you?' the woman said, without much interest.

'I'm looking for Tina Cobb. You're her sister?'

The dark eyes widened. 'What do you want with Tina?'

'I want to talk to her.' Eve slipped out her badge.

'I don't know where she is, okay? She wants to take off for a couple days, it's nobody's sweat, is it?'

'Shouldn't be.' Eve had run Tina Cobb in the car and knew the sister's name was Essie. 'Essie, why don't you take a break?'

'I can't, okay. I can't. I'm working alone today.'

'And nobody's in here right now. Did she tell you where she was going?'

'No. Shit.' Essie sat down on a high stool. 'Oh shit. She's never been in trouble in her life. She spends all the time cleaning up after rich people. Maybe she just wanted some time off.' There was fear lurking behind the eyes now. 'She maybe went on a trip.'

'Was she planning a trip?'

'She's always planning. When she had enough saved she was going to do this, and that, and six million other things. Only she never saved enough for any of it. I don't know where she is. I don't know what to do.'

'How long's she been gone?'

'Since Saturday. Saturday night she goes out, doesn't come back since. Sometimes she doesn't come home at night. Sometimes I don't. You get a guy, you want to stay out, you stay, right?'

'Sure. So she's been gone since Saturday?'

'Yeah. She's got Sundays off, so what the hell, you know? But she's never been gone like this without letting me know. I called her work today and asked for her, and they said she didn't show. I probably got her in trouble. I shouldn'ta called her work.'

'You haven't reported her missing?'

'Shit, you don't report somebody missing 'cause they don't come home a couple nights. You don't go to the cops for every damn thing. Around here, you don't go to them for nothing.'

'She take any of her things?'

'I dunno. Her maid suit's still there, but her red shirt and her black jeans aren't. Her new air sandals neither.'

'I want to go inside the apartment, look around.'

'She's gonna be pissed at me.' Essie scooped up the soft tacos and Pepsis Peabody laid on the counter, did the transaction. 'What the hell. She shouldn'ta gone off without saying. I wouldn't do it to her. I gotta close up. I can't take more than fifteen, or I'll get in real trouble.'

'That's fine.'

It was two tiny rooms with a bump on the living area that served as the kitchen. The sink was about the width and depth of a man's cupped palm. In lieu of the pricier privacy screens, there were manual shades at the windows that did absolutely nothing to cut the street or sky noise.

Eve thought it was like living in a transpo station.

There was a two-seater couch Eve imagined converted to a bed, an ancient and clunky entertainment screen and a single lamp in the shape of a cartoon mouse she suspected one of them had saved from childhood.

Despite its size and sparseness, the apartment was pin neat. And, oddly enough to her mind, smelled as female as the girl-powered travel agency had.

'Bedroom's through there.' Essie pointed at the doorway. 'Tina won the toss when we moved in, so she has the bedroom and I sleep out here. But it's still pretty tight, you know? So that's why if one of us has a guy, we usually go to his place.'

'She have a guy?' Eve asked as Peabody walked toward the bedroom.

'She's been seeing somebody a couple of weeks. His name's Bobby.'

'Bobby got a last name?'

'Probably.' Essie shrugged. 'I don't know it. She's with him, probably. Tina's got this real romantic heart. She falls for a guy, she falls hard.'

Eve scanned the bedroom. One narrow bed, neatly made, one child-sized dresser, likely brought from home. There was a pretty little decorative box on it and a cheap vase with fake roses. Eve lifted the top of the box, heard the tinkling tune it played and saw a few pieces of inexpensive jewelry inside.

'We share the closet,' Essie said as Peabody poked inside the tiny closet.

'Where'd she meet this Bobby?' Peabody asked her, and moved from the closet into the bathroom.

'I don't know. We live in this box together, but we try to stay out of each other's faces, you know? She just says she met this guy, and he's really cute and sweet and smart. Said he knew all about books and art and shit. She goes for that. She went out to meet him like at an art gallery or something one night.'

'You never met him?' Eve asked.

'No. She was always meeting him somewhere. We don't bring guys here much. Jeez, look at this place.' She looked around it with the forlorn and resigned expression of a woman who knew it was the best she was going to do. 'She was going out to meet him Saturday night, after work and shit. To a play or something. When she didn't come home, I figured she'd stayed at his place. No big. But she doesn't miss work, and she hasn't even stayed out of touch this long, so I'm starting to worry, you know?'

'Why don't we file a report?' Peabody stepped back out of the bath. 'A missing person's report.'

'Oh man, you think?' Essie scratched at her bicolored hair. 'She comes waltzing in here and finds out I did that, she'll be on my case for a month. We don't have to tell my parents, do we? They'll get all twisted inside out and come running over here hysterical and whatever.'

'Have you checked with them? Maybe she went home for a couple days.'

'Nah. I mean yeah, I checked. I buzzed my mom and did the hey, how're things, la la la. She said to have Tina call 'cause she likes to hear from her girls. So I know she hasn't seen her. My mom would flip sideways if she thought Tina's shacked up with some guy.'

'We'll take care of it. Why don't you give the information to Detective Peabody?' Eve looked at the tidily made bed.

'She's not off with some guy for extended nooky,' Eve said when they were back in the car. 'Girls like that don't take off without a change of clothes, without taking earrings and their toothbrush. She doesn't miss a day of work in eight months, but she just happens to miss the Gannon job?'

'You think she was in on it?'

Eve thought of the tiny, tidy apartment. The little music box of trinkets. 'Not on purpose. I doubt the same can be said for Bobby.'

'It's going to be tough to track down some guy named Bobby. No full name, no description.'

'He left footprints somewhere. Do a check on Jane Does, any that came in since Saturday night. We're heading down to the morgue anyway. Let's just hope we don't find her there.'

'Want your taco?'

Eve unwrapped it on her lap, then decided eating it while she drove was just asking to go through the rest of the day with taco juice on her shirt. She switched to auto, clicked back a couple inches and chowed down.

When the in-dash 'link signaled, she shook her head. 'Screen it,' she said with a mouthful of mystery meat by-product and sinus-clearing sauce.

'Nadine Furst,' Peabody announced.

'Too bad I'm on lunch break.' She slurped up Pepsi and ignored the call. 'So, a maid from the projects somehow hooks up with some guy named Bobby, who takes her to art galleries and the theater, but he never comes to her place and meets her sister. She's out of touch, missing work, among the missing for three days, but her new boyfriend doesn't call, leave a message, scoot by to see what's up. Nothing.'

'He wouldn't if she was with him.'

'Point for that. But this girl, who makes her bed like a Youth Scout, doesn't call in to work sick, doesn't tell her sister she's cozied down in a love nest, doesn't want extra clothes or all the equipment females take on sex safaris. She risks her paycheck, ignores her family, stays in the same outfit? I don't think so.'

'You think she's dead.'

'I think she had the access code to Gannon's place, and somebody wanted that code. I think if she was alive and well or able, she'd have seen or heard the media reports bombarding the screen about best-selling author Samantha Gannon's recent problem and she'd have gotten to her sister if no one else.'

'Three Jane Does last seventy-two,' Peabody reported. 'Two elderly indigents, no official ID on record. Third's a crispy critter, status pending.'

'Where'd they find her?'

'Abandoned lot,' Peabody read off her ppc. 'Alphabet City. About three hundred Sunday morning. Somebody doused her with gasoline – Jesus, they had some credit to tap on – lit her up. By the time somebody called it in, she was toasted. That's all I've got.'

'Who's primary?'

'Hold on. Aha! It's our good pal Baxter, ably assisted by the adorable Officer Trueheart.'

'Simplifies. Tag him. See if they can meet us at the morgue.'

Eve had to pace her cooling heels in the white-tiled corridor outside the exam room where Duluc completed an autopsy. Morris never made her jump through hoops, she thought. She wouldn't be jumping through them now if Duluc hadn't taken the precaution of locking the exam room doors.

When the buzzer sounded, indicating she was cleared, Eve slammed the doors open, strode through. The stench under the smear of disinfectant made her eyes water, but she fought back the gag reflex and glowered at Duluc.

Unlike Morris, who had both wit and style, Duluc was a stern-minded, by-the-book woman. She wore the clear protective suit over a spotless white lab coat and pale green scrubs. Her hair was completely hidden under a skull cap. Goggles hung around her neck.

She was barely five feet in height, with a chunky build and a face of wide planes. Her skin was the color of roasted chestnuts, and her one good feature – in Eve's opinion – was her hands. They looked as though they could play a mean piano, and were, in fact, greatly skilled at carving cadavers.

Eve jerked her chin at the draped form on an exam table. 'That one mine?'

'If you mean is that the remains of the victim of your current investigation, yes, it is.'

Duluc's voice always sounded to Eve's ear as if she had a bubble of thick liquid stuck in her throat. As she spoke she washed her hands in a sink. 'I told you I'd send through my findings as soon as possible. I don't like being hounded, Lieutenant.'

'You get the tox screen?'

Duluc stared at her. 'Do you have a particular problem understanding me?'

'No, I understand you just fine. You're stringing me because you're pissed I jumped on you this morning. You're going to have to get over it because she doesn't care we're irritated with each other.' She moved toward Andrea. 'She just wants us to deal, so we're going to deal.'

'Your on-scene was accurate, as far as cause of death. The single throat wound. A keen, smooth-edged blade. Stiletto perhaps. There are no defensive wounds, no other indications of violence. There was no sexual assault or recent sexual activity. Her blood-alcohol was a bit high. I'd estimate she had four vodka martinis with olives. No illegals on the tox. Her last meal was a salad, leafy greens with a lemon dressing, consumed approximately five hours pre-mortem.'

'Do you concur that the attacker was behind the victim?'

'From the angle of the wound, yes. Given her height, I'd say he or she is about six feet tall. Average enough for a man, tall for a woman. All of which will be in my official report, delivered to you in the proper fashion. This is not a priority case, Lieutenant, and we are extremely busy.'

'They're all priorities. You've got a Jane Doe. Crispy critter, brought in from Alphabet City.'

Duluc sighed heavily. 'I have no burn victim on my schedule.'

'It's on someone's. I need to see the body, and the data.'

'Then give your case number to one of the attendants. I have other things to do.'

'It's not my case.'

'Then you have no need to see the body or the data.'

She started to walk by, but Eve grabbed her arm. 'Maybe you don't know how this works, Duluc, but I'm a lieutenant in Homicide and can damn well see any body that strikes my fancy. As it happens, Detective Baxter, who's primary, is meeting me here as I believe our respective cases may converge. Just keep pissing on me and I promise you, you'll end up drowning in it.'

'I don't like your attitude.'

'Wow. Media alert. I need the Jane Doe.'

Duluc wrenched away and stalked over to a workstation. She keyed in, brought up data. 'The unidentified female burn victim is in Section C, room three, assigned to Foster. She hasn't been examined yet. Backlog.'

'You going to clear me?'

'I've done so. Now if you'll excuse me?'

'No problem.' She swung back out the doors. How do all these people walk around with sticks up their asses? Eve wondered.

She turned into Section C, gave the door of room three a push and found it secured. 'Shit!' She whirled, pointed to an attendant who was sitting in one of the plastic chairs in the corridor, dozing. 'You. I'm cleared for this room. Why's it locked?'

'Duluc. She locks every damn thing. Surprised the vendings aren't wired with explosives.' He yawned and stretched. 'Dallas, right?'

'That's right.'

'Getcha in. I was just catching a break. Pulling a double today. Who you coming to see?'

'Jane Doe.'

'Little Jane. She's mine.'

'You Foster?'

'Yeah. I just finished an unattended. Natural causes. Guy was a hundred and six, and his second ticker conked on him in his sleep. Good way to go if you gotta.'

He unlocked the door, led them in. 'This is not a good way,' he added, gesturing to the charred bones on a table. 'I thought this was Bax's case.'

'It is. We may have a connected. He's on his way in.'

'Okay by me. I haven't gotten to her yet.'

He brought up the file, scanned it as he pulled out his protective gear. 'Didn't come in until Sunday, and I had the day off – fond, fond memory. You guys get Sundays off?'

'Now and again.'

'Something about sleeping in on a Sunday morning, or sleeping off Saturday night until Sunday afternoon. But Monday always comes.' He snapped on his cap. 'Been backed up since I clocked in Monday morning. Got no flag on here from Bax saying she matches a missing persons. Still little Jane Doe,' he said and glanced back toward the body on the table. 'No way to print her, obviously. We'll send the dental off for a search.'

'What do we know?'

He called up more data on the screen. 'Female between twenty-three and twenty-five. Five feet three inches tall, a hundred and twenty pounds. That's approximate from the virtual reconstruct, which is as far as we've got. That's just prelim check-in data.'

'You got time to take a look at her now?'

'Sure. Let me set up.'

'Want some coffee?'

He looked at her with love. 'Oh, Mommy.'

Appreciating him, she waved Peabody back and went out to Vending herself.

She ordered three, black.

'Love of my life, we can't keep meeting like this.'

She didn't even turn. 'Bite me, Baxter.'

'I do, nightly, in my dreams. I'll take one of those.'

Reminding herself he'd come in at her request, she programmed for a fourth, then glanced back. 'Trueheart?'

'I'll have a lemon fizz if it's all the same to you, Lieutenant. Thank you.'

He looked like the lemon-fizz type with his clean-cut, boyish face. Adorable, Peabody had called him, and it wasn't possible to deny it. An all-American boy, cute as a button – whatever the hell that meant – in his summer blues.

Beside him, Baxter was slick and smooth and cagey. Good-looking, but with an edge to him. He had a fondness for a well-cut suit and a well-endowed female.

They were good cops, both of them, Eve thought. And tucking the earnest Trueheart in as the smart-ass Baxter's aide had been one of her better ideas.

'To the dead,' Baxter said, and tapped his coffee cup lightly to Eve's. 'What do you want with our Jane?'

'She might connect to one of mine. Foster's doing her workup right now.'

'Let me help you with those, Lieutenant.' Trueheart took his fizz and one of the coffees.

Eve briefed them on the way back to the exam room.

'Whether she's your maid or not, somebody wanted her dead real bad,' Baxter commented. 'Skull cracked, broken bones. Had to be dead, or at least blessedly unconscious, when he lit her up. He didn't kill her where he lit her. It was dump and fry. We co-ordinated with Missing Persons on the prelim data and came up goose egg. Been canvassing the area all day. Nobody saw anything, heard anything, knew anything. Guy who made the nine-one-one saw the fire from his window but not the source. Statement goes it was too hot to sleep, and he was going to go sit out on the fire escape. Saw the flames, called it in. Call came through at oh-three-sixteen. Fire department responded, arrived on scene at oh-three-twenty – gotta give those guys points for speed. She was still burning.'

'Couldn't've lit her up too much earlier.'

Foster glanced up as they came in. 'Thanks, Lieutenant, just set it down over there. Hey, Bax, hanging low?'

'Low and long, baby, low and long.'

Foster continued to run the scanner over the body. 'Broken right index finger. That's an old break. Early childhood. Between five and seven. Scanned the teeth already. Running them in the national bank for a match. This one? The skull injury?'

Eve nodded, stepped closer.

'You got severe trauma here. Ubiquitous blunt instrument, most likely. Bat maybe, or a pipe. Skull's fractured. She's got three broken ribs, a fractured tibia, jawbone. Somebody wailed on this girl. She was dead before he poured the gas on her. That's a blessing.'

'He didn't kill her where he dumped her,' Baxter commented. 'We find a blood trail from the street. Not a lot of blood. She must've bled a hell of a lot more where he beat her.'

'From the angle of the breaks – see on screen here?' Foster nodded toward it, and the enhanced images in blues and reds. 'It looks like he hit the leg first. Did that while she was standing. When she went down, he went for the ribs, the face. The skull was the coup de grâce. She was probably unconscious when he bashed her head in.'

Did she try to crawl? Eve wondered. Did she cry out in shock and pain and try to crawl away? 'To keep her from running,' she murmured. 'Take the leg out first so she can't run. He doesn't care how much noise she makes. Otherwise, he'd have gone for the head first. It's calculated, calculated to look like rage. But it's not rage. It's cold-blooded. He had to have a place where it wouldn't matter if she screamed. Sound-proofed, private. He had to have private transpo to get her to the lot.'

The data center beeped, had them all turning.

'Hit the match,' Baxter murmured, and he and Eve stepped to the data screen together. 'That who you're looking for?'

'Yeah.' Eve set her coffee aside and stared into Tina Cobb's smiling face.

Chapter Twenty-One

'Book us a conference room. I want to coordinate with Baxter and Trueheart when they get back from Essie Cobb's.' Eve stepped into the garage-level elevator at Central.

'Has to be the same killer,' Peabody said.

'Nothing has to be. We'll run probabilities. Let's get all current data together into a report and send it to Mira for a profile.'

'You want a meet with her?'

When the doors opened, Eve shifted back as cops and civilians piled on. Dr. Charlotte Mira was the best profiler in the city, possibly on the East Coast. But it was early days for a consult. 'Not yet.'

The car stopped again, and this time rather than deal with the press of bodies and personal aromas, she elbowed her way off to take the glide. 'We'll put what we've got together first, run some standards, conference with Baxter and Trueheart. We need a follow-up with Samantha Gannon and a swing by the club.'

'A lot of on-the-ass work.' Peabody could only be grateful. Her shoes were killing her.

'Get us the room,' Eve began as she stepped off the glide. And stopped when she saw Samantha Gannon sitting on a wait bench outside the Homicide division. Beside her, looking camera-ready, and very chatty, was Nadine Furst.

Eve muttered *shit* under her breath, but there wasn't much heat in it.

Nadine fluffed back her streaky blond hair and aimed one of her feline smiles in Eve's direction. 'Dallas. Hey, Peabody, look at you! Mag shoes.'

'Thanks.' She was going to burn them, first chance.

'Shouldn't you be in front of a camera somewhere?' Eve asked.

'There's more to the job than looking pretty on screen. I've just about wrapped an interview with Samantha. A few comments from the primary on the investigation would put a nice cap on the segment.'

'Turn off the recorder, Nadine.'

For form, Nadine sighed before she deactivated her lapel recorder. 'She's so strict,' she said to Samantha. 'I really appreciate the time, and I'm very sorry about your friend.'

'Thank you.'

'Dallas, if I could just have one word?'

'Peabody, why don't you show Ms. Gannon into the lounge. I'll be right with you.'

Eve waited until they'd moved off, then turned a cool stare toward Nadine.

'Just doing my job.' Nadine lifted her hands, palms out for peace.

'Me too.'

'Gannon's a hot ticket, Dallas. Her book is this month's cocktail party game. Everybody's playing Where Are the Diamonds? You toss murder in and it's top story, every market. I had vacation plans. Three fun-filled days at the Vineyard, starting tomorrow. I canceled them.'

'You were going to make wine?'

'No. Though I'd planned to drink quite a bit. Martha's Vineyard, Dallas. I want out of the city, out of this heat. I want a beach and a long cold adult beverage and a parade of tanned and buff male bodies. So I'm hoping you're going to tell me you're wrapping this one up in a hurry.'

'I can't tell you any more than the media liaison would've told you. Pursuing all leads, et cetera and so on. That's it, Nadine. That's really it.'

'Yeah, I was afraid of that. Well, there's always a hologram program. I can set it for the Vineyard and spend an hour in fantasyland. I'll be around,' she added as she walked away.

Gave up too easy, Eve decided.

She thought about that as she headed off to what the cops called the lounge. It was a room set up for breaks and informal meetings. A scatter of tables, even a skinny, sagging sofa, and several vending machines.

She plugged in a couple of credits and ordered a large bottle of water.

You have selected Aquafree, the natural refreshment, in a twelve-ounce bottle. Aquafree is distilled and bottled in the peaceful and pristine mountains of –

'Jesus, cut the commercial and give me the damn water.' She thumped a fist against the machine.

You are in violation of City Code 20613-A. Any tampering with, any vandalism of this vending unit can result in fine and/or imprisonment.

Even as Eve reared back to kick, Peabody was popping up. 'Dallas! Don't! I'll get it. I'll get the water. Go sit down.'

'A person ought to be able to get a damn drink of water without the lecture.' She flopped down at the table beside Samantha. 'Sorry.'

'No, that's okay. It's really irritating, isn't it, to get the whole list of ingredients, by-products, caloric intake, whatever. Especially when you're ordering a candy bar or a cupcake.'

'*Yes!*' Finally, Eve thought, someone who got it.

'She has issues with machines all over the city,' Peabody commented. 'Your water, Lieutenant.'

'You pander to them.' Eve opened the bottle, drank long and deep. 'I appreciate your coming in, Ms. Gannon. We were going to contact you and arrange to speak with you. You've saved us some time.'

'Call me Samantha, or Sam, if that's okay. I hoped you'd have something to tell me. Shouldn't I have been talking to the reporter?'

'Free country. Free press.' Eve shrugged. 'She's okay. Are you planning on staying at the hotel for the time being?'

'I – yes. I thought, as soon as you tell me I can – I'd have my house cleaned. There are specialists, I'm told, who deal with . . . with crime scenes. Cleaning up crime scenes. I don't want to go back until it's dealt with. That's cowardly.'

'It's not. It's sensible.' That's what she looked like today, Eve thought. A very tired, sensible woman. 'I can offer you continued police protection for the short term. You may want to consider hiring private security.'

'You don't think it was just a burglary. You think whoever killed Andrea will come after me.'

'I don't think there's any point in taking risks. Beyond that, reporters who aren't as polite as Nadine are going to scent you out and hassle you.'

'I guess you're right about that. All right, I'll look into it. My grandparents are very upset about all this. I played it down as much as I could, but . . . Hell, you don't pull anything over on them. If I can tell them I've hired a bodyguard and have the police looking out for me, too, it'll go a long way to keeping everyone settled. I'm letting them think it was about Andrea.'

Her eyes, very bright, very blue, settled levelly on Eve's. 'But I've had time to play this all out in my head. A long night's worth of time, and I don't think that. You don't think that.'

'I don't. Ms. Gannon – Samantha – the woman who was assigned to clean your house has been murdered.'

'I don't understand. I haven't hired anyone to clean my house yet.'

'Your regular cleaning service. Maid In New York assigned Tina Cobb over the last several months to your house.'

'She's dead? Murdered? Like Andrea?'

'Did you know her? Personally?'

Without thinking, Samantha picked up Eve's bottle of water, drank. 'I don't know what to think. I was just talking about her ten minutes ago, just talking about her with Nadine.'

'You told Nadine about Tina Cobb?'

'I mentioned her. Not by name. Just the cleaning service and how I remembered – just when we were talking, I remembered – that I hadn't canceled the service for this week.'

No wonder Nadine had given up so easily. She'd already had another line to tug. 'Did you know her?'

'Not really. Oh God, I'm sorry,' she said, staring at the bottle of water in her hand. She passed it back to Eve.

298

'No problem. You didn't know Tina Cobb?'

'I met her. I mean, she was in my house, *cleaning* my house,' she added as she rubbed her forehead. 'Can I have a minute?'

'Sure.'

Samantha got up, walked around the room once, started around it again.

'Pulling it together,' Peabody murmured. 'Calming herself down.'

'Yeah. She's got spine. Makes it easier from our end.'

After the second circuit, Samantha ordered her own bottle of water, stood patiently until the machine had finished its recital and spat the selection into the slot.

She walked back, opening the bottle as she sat. After one long pull, she nodded at Eve. 'Okay. I had to settle down.'

'You need more time, it's not a problem.'

'No. She always seemed like such a little thing to me. Tina. Young and little, though I guess she wasn't that much younger or smaller than me. I always wondered how she handled all that heavy cleaning. Usually, I'd hole up in my office when she was there, or schedule outside meetings or errands.'

She stopped, cleared her throat. 'I sort of come from money. Not big mountains of it, but nice comfortable hills. We always had household help. But my place here? It's my first place all my own, and it felt weird having somebody around, even a couple times a month, picking up after me.'

She brushed her hands over her hair. 'And that is completely beside the point.'

'Not completely.' Peabody nudged the bottle of water toward Samantha because it seemed she'd forgotten it was there. 'It gives us an idea of the dynamics between you.'

'We didn't have much of one.' She drank again. 'I just stayed out of her way. She was very pleasant, very efficient. We might have a brief conversation, but both of us would usually just get to work. Is it because she was in my house? Is she dead because she was in my house?'

'We're looking into that,' Eve said. 'You told us in your earlier statement that the cleaning service had your access and security codes.'

'Yes. They're bonded. They have a top-level reputation. Their employees all go through intense screening. Actually, it's a little scary and nothing I'd want to go through. But for someone like me, who can't always be at home to let a cleaning service into the house, it was ideal. She knew how to get in,' Samantha stated. 'Someone killed her because she knew how to get in.'

'I believe that's true. Did she ever mention a friend – a boyfriend?'

'No. We didn't talk about personal matters. We were polite and easy with each other but not personal.'

'Did she ever bring anyone with her? To help her with her work?'

'No. I have a team every three months. The company sets that up. Otherwise, it was just one maid, twice a month. I live alone, and I have what my mother says is my grandmother's obsession with order. I don't need more help than that, domestically.'

'You never noticed, when she came or went, if anyone dropped her off, picked her up?'

'No. I think she took the bus. Once she was late, and she apologized and said her bus got caught in a jam. You haven't told me how she was killed. Was it like Andrea?'

'No.'

'But you still think it's a connection. It's too much of a coincidence not to be.'

'We're looking carefully at the connection.'

'I always wanted to write this book. Always. I'd beg my grandparents to tell me the story, again and again. Until I could play it backwards in my mind. I loved picturing how my grandparents met, seeing them sitting at her kitchen table with a pool of diamonds. And how they'd won. It was so satisfying for me to know they'd beaten the odds and won. Lived their lives as they chose to live. That's a real victory, don't you think, living as you choose to live?'

'Yeah.' She thought of her badge. She thought of Roarke's empire. 'It is.'

300

'The villain of the piece, I suppose you could call him, Alex Crew, he killed. He killed for those shiny stones and, I think, because he could. As much because he could as for the diamonds. He would have killed my grandmother if she hadn't been strong enough, smart enough to best him. That's always been a matter of pride for me, and I wanted to tell that story. Now I have, and two people I know are dead.'

'You're not responsible for that.'

'I'm telling myself that. Intellectually, I know that. And still, there's a part of me that's separating, and observing. That part that wants very much to tell *this* story. To write down what's happening now. I wonder what that makes me.'

'A writer, I'd say,' Peabody answered.

Samantha let out a half laugh. 'Well, I guess so. I've made a list, everyone I could think of. People I've talked with about the book. Odd communications I've had from readers or people claiming to have known my great-grandfather.' She drew a disk out of her bag. The enormous one Eve had noted the day before. 'I don't know if it'll help.'

'Everything helps. Did Tina Cobb know you'd be out of town?'

'I let the service know, yes. In fact, I remember telling Tina I'd be away and asking her to check the houseplants and my fish. I wasn't sure Andrea would be able to stay, not until just a couple days before I left.'

'Did you let the service know you'd have a house-sitter?'

'No. That slipped by me. The last few days in New York were insane. I was doing media and appearances here, packing, doing holographic interviews. And it didn't seem important.'

Eve rose, extended a hand. 'Thanks for coming in. Detective Peabody will arrange for you to be taken back to your hotel.'

'Lieutenant. You didn't tell me how Tina Cobb was killed.'

'No, I didn't. We'll be in touch.'

Samantha watched her walk out, drew a long breath. 'I bet she wins, doesn't she? I bet she almost always wins.'

'She won't give up. That comes to the same thing.'

*

301

Eve sat at her desk, input the data from the Cobb case into a sub file, then updated her files on the Jacobs homicide.

'Computer, analyze data on two current case files and run probability. What is the probability that Andrea Jacobs and Tina Cobb were killed by the same person?'

Beginning analysis . . .

She pushed away from the desk as the computer worked and walked to her skinny window. Sky traffic was relatively light. Tourists looked for cooler spots than stewing Manhattan, she imagined, this time of year. Office drones were busy in their hives. She saw a sky-tram stream by with more than half its seats empty.

Tina Cobb had taken the bus. The sky-tram would've been faster, but that convenience cost. Tina'd been careful with her money then. Saving for a life she'd never have.

Analysis and probability run complete. Probability that Andrea Jacobs and Tina Cobb were murdered by the same person or persons is seventy-eight point eight.

High enough, Eve thought, given the computer's limitations. It would factor in the difference in victim types, the different methodology, geographic location of the murders.

A computer couldn't see what she saw, or feel what she felt.

She turned back as a beep signaled an incoming transmission. The sweepers had been quick, she noted, and sat to read the report.

Fingerprints were Gannon's, Jacobs's, Cobb's. There were no other prints found anywhere in the house. Hair samples found matched Gannon's and the victim's. Eve imagined they'd find some that matched Cobb's.

He'd sealed up, and that wasn't a surprise to her. He'd sealed his hands, his hair. Whether or not he'd planned to kill, he'd planned to leave no trace of himself behind.

If Jacobs hadn't come in, he might have gone through the entire house without leaving a thing out of place. And Samantha would've been none the wiser.

She contacted Maid In New York to check a few details and was adding them to her notes when Peabody came in.

'Gannon had her quarterly clean about four weeks ago,' Eve

said. 'Do you know, the crew's required to wear gloves and hair protectors? Safety goggles, protective jumpsuit. The works. Like a damn sweeper's team. They all but sterilize the damn place, top to bottom.'

'I think, maybe, McNab and I could afford something like that. Once we're in the new apartment, it'd be worth it to have somebody sterilize the place three or four times a year. We can get pretty messy when we're both pumping it on the job – and you know, doing each other.'

'Shut up. Just shut up. You're trying to make me twitch.'

'I haven't mentioned sex and McNab all day. It was time.'

'The point I was making before you stuck the image of you and McNab doing each other in my head, is Gannon's place was polished up bright a few weeks ago and maintained thereafter. There are no prints other than hers, the maid's, Jacobs's. He sealed up before he went in. He's very careful. Meticulous even. But, unless this was a direct hit on Jacobs, he still missed the house-sitter angle. What does that tell you?'

'He probably doesn't know either the vic or Gannon, not personally. Not enough to be privy to personal arrangements like that. He knew Gannon would be out of town. Could've gotten that from the maid, or from following her media schedule. But he couldn't have gotten the house-sitter angle from the maid or the service because they didn't know.'

'He's not inner circle. So we start going outside that circle. And we look for where else Cobb and Gannon and Jacobs connect.'

'Baxter and Trueheart are back. We've got conference room three.'

'Round them up.'

She set up a board in the conference room, pinning up crime-scene photos, victim photos, copies of scene reports and the time line for the Jacobs murder she'd worked up.

She waited while Baxter did the same for his case, and considered, as she programmed a cup of lousy station house coffee, how to handle the meeting.

Tact might not be her middle name, but she didn't like to step on another cop's toes. Cobb was Baxter's case. Outranking him didn't, in her mind, give her the right to tug it away from him.

She leaned a hip on the conference table as a compromise between standing – taking over – and sitting. 'You get anything more out of your vic's sister?'

Baxter shook his head. 'Took some time to talk her out of going down to the morgue. No point in her seeing that. She didn't have anything to add to what she told you. She's going to her parents'. Trueheart and I offered to go inform them, or at least go with her. She said she wanted to do it herself. That it would be easier on them if she did. She never met this Bobby character. None of the stoop sitters or neighbors remember seeing the vic with a guy either. They've got a cheap d and c unit. Trueheart checked it for transmissions.'

'She – Tina Cobb,' Trueheart began, 'sent and received transmissions from an account registered to a Bobby Smith. A quick check indicates the account was opened five weeks ago and closed two days ago. The address listed is bogus. The unit doesn't store transmission over twenty-four hours. If there were 'link trans, to and from, we'd need EDD to dig them out.'

'Yippee,' Peabody said under her breath and earned a stony stare from Eve.

'You tagging EDD?' Eve asked Baxter.

'Worth a shot. It's probable he used public "links, but if they can dig out a transmission or two, we might be able to get some sort of geographic. Get a voice print. Get a sense of him.'

'Agreed.'

'We're going to talk to her co-workers. See if she gabbed about the guy. But from what her sister says, she was keeping him pretty close. Like a big secret. She was only twenty-two, and her record's shiny. Not a smudge.'

'She wanted to get married, be a professional mother.' Trueheart flushed as all eyes turned to him. 'I talked to the sister about her. It, um, I think you can learn about the killer if you know the victim.'

'He's my pride and joy,' Baxter said with a big grin.

Eve remembered that Trueheart was barely older than the victim they were discussing. And that he'd nearly become a victim himself only a short time before.

The quick glance she exchanged with Baxter told her he was thinking the same thing. Both let it go.

'The theory is the killer used a romantic involvement to lure her.' She waited until Baxter nodded. 'Your case and ours come together through her. She was Samantha Gannon's maid, and as such had knowledge of the security codes to her residence and knew, intimately, the contents and setup of that residence. She was aware that the owner would be out of town for a two-week period. But she was unaware that there would be a house-sitter. Those arrangements were last minute and, as far as we can know, between Jacobs and Gannon.'

'Lieutenant.' Trueheart raised a hand like a student in the classroom. 'It's hard for me to see someone like Tina Cobb betraying security. She worked hard, her employment record's as clean as the rest of it. There isn't a single complaint filed against her on the job. She doesn't seem the type to give out a security code.'

'I gotta go with the kid on this one,' Baxter confirmed. 'I don't see her giving it out willingly.'

'You've never been a girl in love,' Peabody said to Baxter. 'It can make you stupid. You look at the time line, you see that the break-in and Jacobs's murder were prior to Cobb's murder. And, when you calculate the time between her last being seen and time of death, there isn't a lot. He'd been working her for weeks, right? Smoothing her up. It seems to me he'd be more sure she was giving him the straight scoop if it was willing pillow talk or something than if he tried to beat it out of her.'

'My pride and joy,' Eve said to Baxter and earned a chuckle. 'He beats or threatens or tortures, she might lie or just get mixed up. He eases it out of her, it's more secure. But . . .'

She paused while her pride and joy wrinkled her forehead. 'He seduces it out, she might talk, or get the guilts and report the lapse to her superior. That's a risk. Either way, if we're right about this connection, he got it out of her. Then after he broke in, killed Jacobs, he had to cover tracks. So he killed Cobb, dumped her.

Killed and dumped her in such a way that identification would be delayed long enough for him to tidy up any connection between himself and Cobb.'

'What's Gannon got that he wants?' Baxter asked.

'It's more what he thinks she has or has access to. And that's several million in stolen diamonds.'

She filled them in and gave them each a disk copy of her file. Without realizing it, she'd straightened and was standing. 'The more we find out about this old case, and the stolen gems, the more we know about our current cases. We'd learn more, faster, if we coordinate our time and effort.'

'I got no problem with that.' Baxter nodded in agreement. 'We'll shoot you both copies of our file on Cobb. What angle do you want us to work?'

'Track Bobby. He didn't leave us much, but there's always something. We'll see what EDD can dig out of the vics' 'links.'

'Somebody should go through her personal items,' Peabody added. 'She might've kept mementos. Girls do that. Something from a restaurant where they ate.'

'Good one.' Baxter winked at her. 'The sister said he took Tina to an art gallery and a play. We'll work on that. After all, how many art galleries and theaters are there in New York?' He slapped a hand on Trueheart's shoulder. 'Shouldn't take my earnest side-kick more than a couple hundred man-hours to find out.'

'Somebody saw them together somewhere,' Eve agreed. 'Peabody and I will continue to work Jacobs. We pool all information. For homework assignment, read Gannon's book. Let's know all we can know about these diamonds and the people who stole them. Class dismissed. Peabody, you're with me in ten. Baxter? Can I have a minute?'

'Teacher's pet,' Baxter said, tapping his heart and winking at Trueheart.

To stall until they were alone, Eve wandered to the board, studied the faces.

'Are you giving him that drone work to keep his ass in the chair?'

'As much as I can,' Baxter confirmed. 'He's bounced back – Christ, to be that young again. But he's not a hundred percent. I'm keeping him on light duty for now.'

'Good. Any problems combining these investigations under me?'

'Look at that face.' Baxter lifted his chin toward the ID photo of Tina Cobb. Even the cheap, official image radiated youth and innocence.

'Yeah.'

'I play pretty well with others, Dallas. And I want, I really want to find out who turned that into that.' He tapped a finger on the crime-scene still of Tina Cobb. 'So I got no problem.'

'Does it sit right with you if Peabody and I go through your vic's things? Peabody's got an eye for that kind of thing.'

'All right.'

'You want to take the club where my vic was last seen?'

'Can do.'

'Then we'll have a briefing in the morning. Nine hundred.'

'Make my world complete and tell me we're having it at your home office. Where the AutoChef has real pig meat and eggs from chickens that cluck.'

'Here – unless I let you know different.'

'Spoilsport.'

Eve headed back uptown in irritable traffic. A breakdown on Eighth clogged the road for blocks and had what seemed like half of New York breaking the noise pollution codes in order to blast their horns in pitiful and useless protest.

Her own solution was a bit more direct. She hit the sirens, punched into vertical and skimmed the corner to take the crosstown to Tenth.

They were fifteen blocks away when her climate control sputtered and died.

'I hate technology. I hate Maintenance. I hate the goddamn stupid NYPSD budget that sticks me with these pieces-of-shit vehicles.'

'There, there, sir,' Peabody crooned as she hunkered down to work on the controls manually. 'There, there.'

After the sweat began to run into her eyes, Peabody gave up. 'You know, I could call Maintenance. Yes, we hate them like poison, like rat poison on a cracker,' she said quickly. 'So I was thinking, I could ask McNab to take a whack at it. He's good with this kind of thing.'

'Great, good, fine.' Eve rolled down the windows before they suffocated. The stinking, steamy air outside wasn't much of an improvement. 'When we finish at Cobb's, you drop me home, take this rolling disaster with you. You can pick me up in the morning.'

When she reached the apartment building she considered, actively, the rewards of giving one of the stoop sitters twenty to steal the damn car. Instead, she decided to hope somebody boosted it while they were inside.

As they started inside, she heard Peabody's quiet whimper. 'What?'

'Nothing. I didn't say anything.'

'It's those shoes, isn't it? You're limping. Goddamn it, what if we have to pursue some asshole on foot?'

'Maybe they weren't the best choice, but I'm still finding my personal look. There may be some miscues along the way.'

'Tomorrow you'd better be in something normal. Something you can walk in.'

'Yeah, yeah, yeah.' Peabody hunched her shoulders at Eve's glare. 'I don't have to say "sir" all the time because, hey, look, *detective* now. And we're partners and all.'

'Not when you're wearing those shoes.'

'I was going to burn them when I got home. But now I'm thinking of getting a hatchet and chopping them into tiny, tiny pieces.'

Eve knocked on the apartment door. Essie answered. Her eyes were red and swollen, her face splotchy from tears. She simply stared at Eve, saying nothing.

'We appreciate your coming back from your parents to let us go through your sister's things,' Eve began. 'We're very sorry for your loss and regret having to intrude at this time.'

'I'm going to go back and stay with them tonight. I needed to come and get some of my things anyway. I don't want to stay here tonight. I don't know if I'll ever stay here again. I should've called the police right away. As soon as she didn't come home, I should've called.'

'It wouldn't have mattered.'

'The other cops, the ones who came to tell me? They said I shouldn't go down to see her.'

'They're right.'

'Why don't you sit down, Essie.' Peabody moved in, took her arm and led her to a chair. 'You know why we need to go through her things?'

'In case you find something that tells you who did this to her. I don't care what you have to do, as long as you find who did this to her. She never hurt anybody in her whole life. Sometimes she used to piss me off, but your sister's supposed to, right?'

Peabody left her hand on Essie's shoulder another moment. 'Mine sure does.'

'She never hurt anybody.'

'Do you want to stay here while we do this? Or maybe you have a friend in the building. You could go there until we're done.'

'I don't want to talk to anybody. Just do what you have to do. I'll be right here.'

Eve took the closet, Peabody the dresser. In various pockets, Eve found a tiny bottle of breath freshener, a sample-size tube of lipdye and a mini pocket organizer that turned out to belong to Essie.

'I got something.'

'What?'

'They give these little buttons out at the Met.' Peabody held up a little red tab. 'It's a tradition. You put it on your collar or lapel, and they know you paid for the exhibit. He probably took her there. It's the kind of thing you keep if it's a date.'

'The odds of anybody remembering her at the Metropolitan Museum are slim to none, but it's a start.'

'She's got a little memento box here. Bus token, candle stub.'

'Bag the candle stub. We'll run for prints. Maybe it's from his place.'

'Here's a pocket guide for the Guggenheim, and a theater directory. Looks like she printed it out from on-line. She's circled the Chelsea Playhouse in a little heart. It's from last month,' she said as she turned to Eve. 'A limited run of *Chips Are Down*. He took her there, Dallas. This is her "I love Bobby" box.'

'Take it in. Take it all in.' She moved over to the dented metal stand by the bed, yanked on the single drawer. Inside she found a stash of gummy candy, a small emergency flashlight, sample tubes and packs of hand cream, lotion, perfume, all tucked into a box. And sealed in a protective bag was a carefully folded napkin. On the cheap recycled material, written in sentimental red, was:

Bobby
First Date
July 26, 2059
Ciprioni's

Peabody came over to read over Eve's shoulder. 'She must've taken it out to look at every night,' she murmured. 'Sealed it up so it didn't get dirty or torn.'

'Do a run on Ciprioni's.'

'I don't have to. It's a restaurant. Italian place down in Little Italy. Inexpensive, good food. Noisy, usually crowded, slow service, terrific pasta.'

'He didn't know she was keeping tabs, little tabs like this. He didn't understand her. He didn't get her. He thought he was safe. None of the places we're finding are anywhere near here. Get her away from where she lives, where people she knows might see them. See him. Take her to places where there are lots of people. Who's going to notice them? But she's picking up souvenirs to mark their dates. She left us a nice trail, Peabody.'

Chapter Twenty-Two

After dropping Eve at home, Peabody drove off in the sauna on wheels. And Eve let herself into the blessed cool. The cat thumped down the steps, greeting her with a series of irritated feline growls.

'What, are you standing in for Summerset? Bitch, bitch, bitch.' But she squatted down to scrub a hand over his fur. 'What the hell do the two of you do around here all day anyway? Never mind. I don't think I want to know.'

She checked with the in-house and was told Roarke was not on the premises.

'Jeez.' She looked back down at the cat, who was doing his best to claw up her leg. 'Kinda weird. Nobody home but you and me. Well . . . I got stuff. You should come.' She scooped him up and carted him up the stairs.

It wasn't that she minded being home alone. She just wasn't used to it. And it was pretty damn quiet, if you bothered to listen.

But she'd fix that. She'd download an audio of Samantha Gannon's book. She could get in a solid workout while she listened to it. Take a swim, loosen up. Grab a shower, take care of some details.

'There's a lot you can get done when nobody's around to distract you,' she told Galahad. 'I spent most of my life with nobody around anyway, so, you know, no problem.'

No problem, she thought. Before Roarke she'd come home to an empty apartment every night. Maybe she'd connect with her pal Mavis, but even if she'd had time to blow off a little steam after the job with the woman who was the blowing-off-steam expert, she'd still come home alone.

She liked alone.

When had she stopped liking alone?

God, it was irritating.

She dumped the cat on her desk, but he complained and bumped his head against her arm. 'Okay, okay, give me a minute, will you?' Brushing the bulk of him aside, she picked up the memo cube.

'Hello, Lieutenant.' Roarke's voice drifted out. 'I thought this would be your first stop. I downloaded an audio of Gannon's book as I couldn't visualize you curling up with the paper version. See you when I get home. I believe there are fresh peaches around. Why don't you have one instead of the candy bar you're thinking about?'

'Think you know me inside out, don't you, smart guy? Thinks he knows me back and forth,' she said to the cat. 'The annoying part is he does.' She put the memo down, picked up the headset. Even as she started to slip it into place, she noted the message light blinking on her desk unit.

She nudged the cat aside again. 'Just wait, for God's sake.' She ordered up the message and listened once again to Roarke's voice.

'Eve, I'm running late. A few problems that need to be dealt with.'

She cocked her head, studied his face on the screen. A little annoyed, she noted. A little rushed. He wasn't the only one who knew his partner.

'If I get through them I'll be home before you get to this in any case. If not, well, soon as possible. You can reach me if you need to. Don't work too hard.'

She touched the screen as his image faded. 'You either.'

She put on the headset, engaged, then much to the cat's relief, headed into the kitchen. The minute she filled his bowl with tuna and set it down for him, he pounced.

Listening to the narrative of the diamond heist, she grabbed a bottle of water, took a peach as an afterthought, then walked through the quiet, empty house and down to the gym.

She stripped down, hanging her weapon harness on a hook, then pulled on a short skinsuit.

She started with stretches, concentrating on the audio and her form. Then she moved to the machine, programming in an obstacle course that pushed her to run, climb, row, cycle on and over various objects and surfaces.

By the time she started on free weights, she'd been introduced to the main players in the book and had a sense of New York and small-town America in the dawn of the century.

Gossip, crime, bad guys, good guys, sex and murder.

The more things changed, she thought, the more they didn't.

She activated the sparring droid for a ten-minute bout and felt limber, energized and virtuous by the time she'd kicked his ass.

She snagged a second bottle of water out of the mini-fridge and, to give herself more time with the book, added a session for flexibility and balance.

She peeled off the skinsuit, tossed it in the laundry chute, then walked naked into the pool house. With the audio still playing in her ear, she dove into the cool blue water. After some lazy laps, she floated her way over to the corner and called for jets.

Her long, blissful sigh echoed off the ceiling.

There was home alone, she thought, and there was home alone.

When her eyes started to droop, she boosted herself out. She pulled on a robe, gathered up her street clothes, her weapon, and took the elevator up to the bedroom before she thought of missed opportunity.

She could have run naked through the house. She could have *danced* naked through the house.

She'd have to hold that little pleasure in reserve.

After a shower and fresh clothes, she went back to her office. She turned off the audio long enough to handle some details, to make new notes.

Top of her list were: Jack O'Hara, Alex Crew, William Young and Jerome Myers. Young and Myers had been dead for more than half a century, with their lives ending before the first act of the drama.

Crew had died in prison, and O'Hara had been in and out of the wind until his death fifteen years ago. So the four men who'd stolen the diamonds were dead. But people rarely got through life without connections. Family, associates, enemies.

A connection to a thief might consider himself entitled to the booty. A kind of reward, an inheritance, a payback. A connection to a thief might know how to gain access to a secured residence.

Blood tells, she thought. People often said that. She, for one, had reason to hope it wasn't true. If it was true, what did that make her, the daughter of a monster and a junkie whore? If it was all a matter of genes, DNA, inherited traits, what chance was there for a child created by two people for the purpose of using her for profit? For whoring her. For raising her like an animal. Worse than an animal.

Locking her in the dark. Alone, nameless. Beating her. Raping her. Twisting her until at the age of eight she would kill to escape.

Blood on her hands. So much blood on her hands.

'Damnit. Damnit, damnit.' Eve squeezed her eyes shut and willed the images away before their ghosts could solidify into another waking nightmare.

Blood didn't tell. DNA didn't make us. We made ourselves, if we had any guts we made ourselves.

She pulled her badge out of her pocket, held it like a talisman, like an anchor. We made ourselves, she thought again. And that was that.

She laid her badge on the desk where she could see it if she needed to, then, reengaging the audio, she listened as she ordered runs on the names of her four thieves.

Thinking about coffee, she rose to wander into the kitchen. She toyed with programming a pot, then cut it back to a single cup. One of the candy bars she'd stashed began to call her name. And after all, she'd eaten the damn peach.

She dug it out from under the ice in the freezer bin. With coffee in one hand, frozen chocolate in the other, she walked back into the office. And nearly into Roarke.

He took one look, raised an eyebrow. 'Dinner?'

314

'Not exactly.' He made her feel like a kid stealing treats. And she'd never *been* a kid with treats to steal. 'I was just . . . shit.' She pulled off the headset. 'Working. Taking a little break. What's it to you?'

He laughed, pulled her in for a kiss. 'Hello, Lieutenant.'

'Hello back. Ignore him,' she said when Galahad slithered up to meow and beg. 'I fed him already.'

'Better, no doubt, than you fed yourself.'

'Did you eat?'

'Not yet.' He slid a hand around her throat, squeezed lightly. 'Give me half that candy.'

'It's frozen. You gotta wait it out.'

'This then.' He took her coffee, smirked at her scowl. 'You smell . . . delicious.'

When the hand at her throat slid around to cup the nape of her neck, she realized he meant her, not the coffee. 'Back up, pal.' She jabbed a finger into his chest. 'I've got agendas here. Since you haven't eaten, why don't we go try this Italian place I heard about downtown.'

When he said nothing, just sipped her coffee, studied her over the rim, she frowned. 'What?'

'Nothing. Just making certain you really are my wife. You want to go out to dinner, sit in a restaurant where there are other people.'

'We've been out to dinner before. Millions of times. What's the bfd?'

'Mmm-hmm. What does an Italian restaurant downtown have to do with your case?'

'Smarty-pants. Maybe I just heard they have really good lasagna. And maybe I'll tell you the rest on the way because I sort of made reservations. I made them before I realized you'd be this late and might not want to go out. I can check it out tomorrow.'

'Is there time for me to have a shower and change out of this bloody suit? It feels as though I were born in it.'

'Sure. But I can cancel if you just want to kick back.'

'I could use some lasagna, as long as it comes with a great deal of wine.'

315

'Long one, huh?'

'More annoying than long, actually,' he told her as she walked with him to the bedroom. 'A couple of systemic problems. One in Baltimore, one in Chicago, and both required my personal attention.'

She pursed her lips as he undressed for the shower. 'You've been to Baltimore and Chicago today?'

'With a quick stop in Philadelphia, since it was handy.'

'Did you get a cheese steak?'

'I didn't, no. Time didn't allow for such indulgences. Jets full,' he ordered when he stepped into the shower. 'Seventy-two degrees.'

Even the thought of a shower at that temperature made her shiver. But, somehow, she could still enjoy standing there watching him drench himself in the cold water. 'Did you get them fixed? The systemic problems?'

'Bet your gorgeous ass. An engineer, an office manager and two VPs will be seeking other employment. An overworked admin just copped herself a corner office and a new title – along with a nice salary boost – and a young man out of R and D is out celebrating his promotion to project head about now.'

'Wow, you've been pretty busy out there, changing lives.'

He slicked back that wonderful and wet mane of black hair. 'A little padding of the expense account, that's a time-honored tradition, corporately speaking. I don't mind it. But you don't want to get greedy, and sloppy, and fucking arrogant about it. Or next you know, you're out on your ear and wondering how the hell you're going to afford that condo on Maui and the side dish who likes trinkets that come in Tiffany's little blue boxes.'

'Hold it.' She stepped back as he walked out of the shower. 'Embezzlement? Are you talking embezzlement?'

'That would be Chicago. Baltimore was just ineptitude, which is, somehow, even more annoying.'

'Did you have them charged? Chicago?'

He flipped a towel, began to dry off. 'I handled it. My way, Lieutenant,' he said before she could speak. 'I don't call the cops at every bump in the road.'

'I keep hearing that lately. Embezzlement's a crime, Roarke.'

'Is it now? Well, fancy that.' With the towel hooked over his hips, he brushed by her and went to his closet. 'They'll pay, you can be sure of that. I imagine they're even now drinking themselves into a sweaty stupor and weeping bitter tears over their respective career suicides. Be lucky to cop a job sweeping up around a desk now much less sitting behind one. Buggering sods.'

She thought it over. 'The cops would've been easier on them.'

He glanced back, his grin fierce and cold. 'Undoubtedly.'

'I've said it before, I'll say it again. You're a very scary guy.'

'So . . .' He pulled on a shirt, buttoned it. 'And how was your day, darling Eve?'

'Fill you in on the way.'

She told him so that by the time they arrived at the restaurant he was thoroughly briefed.

Peabody, Eve noted, had given an accurate description. The place was packed, and noisy, and the air smelled amazing. Wait staff, with white bib aprons over their street clothes, moved at a turtle pace as they carried trays loaded with food to tables or hauled away empty plates.

When wait staff didn't have to bust ass for tips, Eve had to figure it all came down to the food or the snob factor. From the looks of the process here, and the simplicity of decor, the food must be superior.

Someone crooned over the speakers in what she assumed was Italian, just as she assumed the almost childlike murals that decorated the walls were of Italian locales.

And she noted the stubby candles on each table. Just like the one Tina Cobb had kept among her mementos.

'I booked in your name.' She had to raise her voice, aim it toward Roarke's ear to be heard over the din.

'Oh?'

'They were booked solid. Roarke clears a table quicker than Dallas.'

'Ah.'

'Oh. Ah. Blah Blah.'

He laughed, pinched her, then turned to the apparently disinterested maître d'. 'You've a table for two, under Roarke.'

The man was squat, with his ample bulk squeezed into an old-fashioned tuxedo like a soy sausage pumped into a casing. His bored eyes popped wide, and he lurched from his stool station to his feet. When he bowed, Eve expected him to pop out of the tuxedo.

'Yes, yes! Mr. Roarke. Your table is waiting. Best table in the house.' His Italian accent had a definite New York edge. Rome via the Bronx. 'Please, come with me. Shoo, shoo.' He waved at and jostled waiters and customers alike to clear a path. 'I am Gino. Please to tell me if you wish for anything. Anything. Tonight's pasta is spaghetti con polpettone, and the special is rollatini di pollo. You will have wine, yes? A complimentary bottle of our Barolo. It's very fine. Handsome and bold, but not overpowering.'

'Sounds perfect. Thank you very much.'

'It's nothing. Nothing at all.' He snapped his fingers toward a waiter who'd obviously been put on alert. In short order, the wine was displayed, opened, poured and approved. Menus were offered with a flourish, and the staff retreated to hover and largely ignore diners who hoped to be served sometime in the next decade.

'Do you ever get tired of being fawned over?' Eve asked him.

'Let me think.' Roarke sipped his wine, leaned back. Smiled. 'No.'

'Figured.' She glanced at the menu. 'What's that spaghetti polepot stuff he was talking about.

'*Polpettone*. Spaghetti and meatballs.'

'Really?' She perked up. 'Okay, that sets me up.' She laid the menu aside. 'What are you having?'

'I think I'll try the two-sauce lasagna. You put it in my head, and I can't get it out. We'll have some antipasto to start, or we'll disappoint our hosts.'

'Let's keep them happy.'

The instant Roarke set down his menu, both the maître d' and the waiter materialized at the table. She let Roarke order, and drew

318

the ID photo of Tina Cobb out of her bag. 'Do you recognize this woman?' she asked Gino.

'I'm sorry?'

'She was in here on a date in July. Do you remember seeing her?'

'I'm sorry,' he repeated. He looked apologetic, then apoplectic as he glanced at Roarke. 'We have so many customers.' His brow pearled with sweat; he wrung his hands and stood like a nervous student failing a vital test.

'Just take a look. Maybe you'll remember her coming in. Young, probably spruced up for a date. About five feet three inches, a hundred and twenty pounds. First-date glow on her.'

'Ah . . .'

'You could do me a favor,' Eve said before the guy dripped into a nerve puddle at her feet. 'You could show that to the wait staff, see if she rings any bells.'

'I'd be happy to. *Honored* to, of course. Right away.'

'I like it better when they're annoyed or pissed off,' Eve decided as he scurried away. 'Well, either way, it's a long shot.'

'We'll get a good meal out of it. And . . .' He lifted her hand, kissed her knuckles. 'I get a date with my wife.'

'Place does a hell of a business. How come you don't own it?'

He kept her hand as he sipped his wine. There was no sign of a man who'd bounced from city to city all day, firing embezzlers and incompetents. 'Would you like to?'

She only shook her head. 'Two dead women. One a means to an end, the other just in the right place at the wrong time. He's not a killer by design. He kills because it's expedient. Wants to reach the goal. To reach it, you have to utilize tools, dispose of obstacles. Sort of like what you did today, only with real blood.'

'Hmm,' was Roarke's comment.

'What I mean is you're going to get from point A to point B, and if you have to take a side trip and mow over somebody, you do. I mean, he's directed.'

'Understood.'

'If Jacobs hadn't been there, he wouldn't have had to kill her.

319

If he hadn't had to kill Jacobs, he probably wouldn't have killed Cobb. At least not right away, though I'd lay odds he'd worked out how he'd do it when and if. If he'd found the diamonds – fat chance – or more likely found something that led him to them, he'd have followed the trail.'

She grabbed a bread stick, broke it in half, then crunched down. 'He doesn't quibble at murder, and must have – because he thinks ahead – he must have considered the possibility of disposing of Samantha Gannon once he had his prize in hand. But he didn't go into her house with murder on the agenda.'

'He adjusts. Understands the value of being flexible and of keeping his eye on the ball, so to speak. What you have so far doesn't indicate a man who panics when something alters his game plan. He works with it, and moves on accordingly.'

'That's a pretty flattering description.'

'Not at all,' Roarke disagreed. 'As his flexibility and focus are completely amoral and self-serving. As you pointed out, I've had – and have – game plans of my own, and I know, very well, the seductive pull of glittering stones. Cash, however sexy it might be, doesn't hook into you the same way. The light of them, the dazzle and the colors and shapes. There's something primitive about the attraction, something visceral. Despite that, to kill over a handful of sparkles demeans the whole business. To my mind, in any case.'

'Stealing them's okay though.'

He grinned now, and took the second half of her bread stick. 'If you do it right. Once – in another life, of course – I . . . relieved a London bird of a number of her sparkling feathers. She kept them locked away in a vault – in the dark – such a pity. What's the point in locking all those beauties away, after all, where they only wait to shine again? She kept a house in Mayfair, guarded like Buckingham bloody Palace. I did the job solo, just to see if I could.'

She knew she shouldn't be amused, but she couldn't help it. 'Bet you could.'

'You win. Christ, what a rush. I think I was twenty, and still I remember – remember exactly – what it was to take those stones out of the dark and watch them come alive in my hands. They need the light to come alive.'

'What did you do with them?'

'Well now, that's another story, Lieutenant.' He topped off their wineglasses. 'Another story entirely.'

The waiter served their antipasto. On his heels the maître d' came hurrying back, pulling a waitress by the arm.

'Tell the signora,' he ordered.

'Okay. I think that maybe I waited on her.'

'She thinks maybe,' Gino echoed. He almost sang it.

'She with a guy?'

'Yeah. Listen, I'm not a hundred percent.'

'Is it okay if she sits down a minute?' Eve asked Gino.

'Whatever you like. Anything you like. The antipasto, it's good?'

'It's great.'

'And the wine?'

Noting the flicker in Eve's eyes, Roarke shifted. 'It's very nice wine. A wonderful choice. I wonder, could we have a chair for . . .'

'I'm Carmen,' the waitress told him.

Fortunately there was a chair available as Eve had no doubt Gino would have personally dumped another diner out of one to accommodate Roarke's request.

Though he continued to hover, Eve ignored him and turned to Carmen. 'What do you remember?'

'Well.' Carmen looked hard at the photo she'd given back to Eve. 'Gino said it was a first-date thing. And I think I remember waiting on her – them. She was all nervous and giddy like she didn't get out much, and she looked young enough that I had to card her. I sort of hated to do it because she got all flustered, but it was okay because she was legal. Barely. That's why I sort of remember.'

'What about him. What do you remember about him?'

'Um . . . He wasn't as young as her, and he was a lot smoother. Like he'd been around some. He ordered in Italian, casual like. I remember that because some guys do and it's a real show-off deal, and others pull it off. He pulled it off. And he didn't stint on the tip.'

321

'How'd he pay?'

'Cash. I always remember when they pay cash, especially when they don't stiff me.'

'Can you describe him?'

'Oh, I don't know. I didn't pay that close. I think he had dark hair. Not too dark. I mean not . . .' She shifted her gaze to Roarke and her eyes skimmed over his hair and would have sighed if they could. 'Not black.'

'Uh-huh. Carmen.' Eve tapped her on the hand to regain her attention. 'What about skin color?'

'Oh, well, he was white. But he had a tan. I remember that now. Like he'd had a really good flash or a nice vacation. No, he had light hair! That's right. He had blondish hair because it was a real contrast with the tan. I think. Anyway. He was really attentive to her, too. Now that I'm thinking, I remember most times I went by he was listening to her, or asking her questions. A lot of guys – hell, most guys – don't listen.'

'You said he was older than she was. How much older?'

'Jeez, it's hard to say. To remember. I don't think it was one of those daddy-type things.'

'How about build?'

'I don't really know. He was sitting, you know. He wasn't a porker. He just looked normal.'

'Piercings, tattoos?'

'Oh wow. Not that I remember. He had a really good wrist unit. I noticed it. She was in the ladies' when I brought out their coffee, and he checked the time. It was really sharp-looking, thin and silvery with a pearly face. What do they call that?'

'Mother of pearl?' Roarke suggested.

'Yeah. Yeah, mother of pearl. It was one sharp-looking piece. Expensive-looking.'

'Would you be willing to work with a police artist?'

'This is a cop thing? Wow. What did they do?'

'It's him I'm interested in. I'd like to arrange for you to come down to Central tomorrow. I can have you transported.'

'I guess. Sure. It'd be kind of a kick.'

'If you'd give me your information, someone will contact you.'

Eve plucked an olive from the plate as Carmen carried her chair away. 'I love when long shots pay off.' She saw the plates of pasta heading in their direction and struggled not to salivate. 'Just give me one minute to set this up.'

She pulled out her 'link to call Central and arrange for an artist session. While she listened to the desk sergeant, asked a couple of pithy questions, she twirled pasta on her fork.

She ended the call, stuffed the pasta in her mouth. 'Nadine broadcast the connection.'

'What?'

'Sorry.' She swallowed and repeated the statement more coherently. 'Figured she'd make it after talking to Gannon, and that she'd go on air.'

'Problem?'

'If it was dicey I'd've stopped her. And to give her credit, she'd have let me. No, it's no problem. He'll catch a broadcast and he'll know we've got lines to tug. Make him think, make him wonder.'

She stabbed a meatball, broke off a forkful, wrapped pasta around it. 'Bobby Smith, whoever the hell he is, should be doing a lot of thinking tonight.'

And he was. He'd come home early from a cocktail party that had bored him to death. The same people, the same conversations, the same ennui. There was never anything new.

Of course, he had a great deal new to talk about. But he hardly thought his recent activities were cocktail conversation.

He'd switched on the screen. Before he'd gone out he'd programmed his entertainment unit to record any mention of various key words: Gannon, Jacobs – as that had turned out to be her name – Cobb. Sweet little Tina. And sure enough, there'd been an extended report by the delicious Nadine Furst on 75 that had combined all of those key words.

So, they'd made the connection. He hadn't expected the police to make it quite that quickly. Not that it mattered.

He changed into lounging pants, a silk robe. He poured himself a brandy and fixed a small plate of fruit and cheese, so that he could be comfortable while he viewed the report again.

Settled on the sofa in the media room of his two-level apartment on Park Avenue, he nibbled on Brie and tart green grapes while Nadine relayed the story again.

Nothing to link him to the naive little maid, he concluded. He'd been careful. There'd been a few transmissions, true, but all to the account he'd created for that purpose, and sent or received from a public unit. He'd always taken her places where they were absorbed by a crowd. And when he'd decided he needed to kill her, he'd taken her to the building on Avenue B.

His father's company was renovating that property. It was untenanted, and though there had been some blood – actually considerable blood – he'd tidied up. Even if he'd missed a spot or two, crews of carpenters and plumbers would hardly notice a new stain or two among the old.

No, there was nothing to connect a silly maid from the projects to the well-educated, socially advanced and cultured son of one of the city's top businessmen.

Nothing to connect him to the earnest and struggling young artist Bobby Smith.

The artist angle had been brilliant – naturally. He could draw competently enough, and he'd charmed the naive and foolish Tina with a little sketch of her face.

Of course he'd had to ride a *bus* to create the 'chance' meeting. Hideous ordeal. He had no idea how people tolerated such experiences, but imagined those who did neither knew nor deserved any better.

After that, it was all so simple. She'd fallen in love with him. He'd hardly had to expend any effort there. A few cheap dates, a few kisses and soulful looks, and he'd had his entrée into Gannon's house.

He'd had only to moon around her, to go with her one morning – claiming as he met her at the bus stop near the town house that he hadn't been able to sleep thinking of her.

Oh, how she'd blushed and fluttered and strolled with him right to Gannon's front door.

He'd watched her code in – memorized the sequence, then, ignoring her halfhearted and whispered protests, had nipped in behind her, stealing another kiss.

Oh Bobby, you can't. *If Miz Gannon comes down, I could get in trouble. I could get fired. You have to go.*

But she'd giggled, as if they were children pulling a prank, as she shooed at him.

So simple then to watch her quickly code into the alarm. So simple.

Not as simple, he admitted now, not nearly as simple for him to walk out again and leave her waving after him. For a moment, just one hot moment, he'd considered killing her then. Just bashing in that smiling, *ordinary* face and being done with it. Imagined going upstairs, rooting Gannon out and beating the location of the diamonds out of her.

Beating her until she told him everything, *everything* she hadn't put in her ridiculous book.

But that hadn't been the plan. The very careful plan.

Then again, he thought with a shrug, plans changed. And so he'd gotten away with murder. Twice.

After toasting himself, he sipped brandy.

The police could speculate all they liked, they'd never connect him, a man like him, with someone as common as Tina Cobb. And Bobby Smith? A figment, a ghost, a puff of smoke.

He wasn't any closer to the diamonds, but he would be. Oh, he would be. And at least he wasn't, by God, *bored.*

Samantha Gannon was the key. He'd read her book countless times after the first shocked reading, when he'd found so many of his own family secrets spread out on the page. It amazed him, astounded him, infuriated him.

Why hadn't he been told there were millions of dollars – *millions* – tucked away somewhere? Diamonds that belonged, by right, to him.

Dear old Dad had left that little detail out of the telling.

He wanted them. He would have them. It really was that simple.

With them he could, he would, break away from his father and his tedious work ethic. Away from the boredom, the sameness of his circle of friends.

He would be, as his grandfather had been, unique.

Stretching out, he called up another program and watched the series of interviews he'd recorded. In each, Samantha was articulate, bright, attractive. For that precise reason he hadn't attempted to contact her directly.

No, the dim-witted, stars-in-her-eyes Tina had been a much safer, much smarter move.

Still, he was really looking forward to getting to know Samantha better. Much more intimately.

Chapter Twenty-Three

Eve woke, as usual, to find Roarke up before her, already dressed and settled into the sitting area of the bedroom with coffee, the cat and the morning stock reports on-screen.

He was, she saw through one bleary eye, eating what looked like fresh melon and manually keying in codes, figures or state secrets for all she knew on a 'link pad.

She gave a grunt as way of good morning and stumbled off to the bathroom.

As she closed the door, she heard Roarke address the cat. 'Not at her best before coffee, is she?'

By the time she came out, he'd switched the screen to news, added the audio and was doctoring up a bagel. She nipped it out of his hand, stole his coffee and carried them both to her closet.

'You're as bad as the cat,' he complained.

'But faster. I've got a morning briefing. Did you catch a weather report?'

'Hot.'

'Bitching hot or just regular hot?'

'It's August in New York, Eve. Guess.'

Resigned, she pulled out whatever looked less likely to plaster itself against her skin after five minutes outside.

'Oh, I've a bit of information on the diamonds for you. I did some poking around yesterday.'

'You did?' She glanced around, half expecting him to tell her the shirt didn't go with the pants, or the jacket didn't suit the shirt. But it seemed she'd lucked out and grabbed pieces that met his standards. 'I didn't think you'd have time with all that ass-kicking.'

'That did eat up considerable time and effort. But I carved out a little time between bloodbaths. I've just put it together for you this morning, while you were getting a little more beauty sleep.'

'Is that a dig?'

'Darling, how is telling you you're beautiful a dig?'

Her answer was a snort as she strapped on her weapon.

'That jacket looks well on you.'

She eyed him warily as she adjusted her weapon harness under the shoulder. 'But?'

'No buts.'

It was tan, though she imagined he'd call it something else. Like pumpernickel. She never understood why people had to assign strange names to colors.

'My lovely urban warrior.'

'Cut it out. What did you get?'

'Precious little, really.' He tapped the disk he'd set on the table. 'The insurance company paid out for the quarter of them and the investigator's fee of five percent on the rest. So it was a heavy loss. Could've been considerably worse, but insurance companies tend to take a dim view on multimillion-dollar payouts.'

'It's their gamble,' she said with a shrug. 'Don't play if you don't wanna pay.'

'Indeed. They did a hard press on O'Hara's daughter, but couldn't squeeze anything out. Added to that, she was the one to find or help the investigator find what there was to recover, and she was instrumental in nailing Crew for the police.'

'Yeah, I got that far. Tell me what I don't know.'

'They pushed at the inside man's family, associates, at his co-workers. Came up empty there, but watched them for years. Any one of them had upped their lifestyle without having, say, won the lottery, they'd have been hauled in. But they could never find Crew's ex-wife or his son.'

'He had a kid?' And she kicked herself for not going back in and checking the runs after they'd returned home the night before.

'He did, apparently. Though it's not in Gannon's book. He was married, divorced and had a son who'd have been just shy of seven when the heist went down. I couldn't find anything on her with a standard starting six months after the divorce.'

Interest piqued, she walked back to the sitting area. 'She went under?'

'She went under, the way it looks, and stayed there.'

He'd gotten another bagel while he spoke, and more coffee. Now he sat again. 'I could track her, if you like. It'd take a bit more than a standard, and some time as we're going back half a century. I wouldn't mind it. It's the sort of thing I find entertaining.'

'Why isn't it in the book?'

'I imagine you'll ask Samantha just that.'

'Damn right. It's a thread.' She considered it as she disbursed her equipment in various pockets. Communicator, memo book, 'link, restraints. 'If you've got time, great. I'll pass it to Feeney. EDD ought to be able to sniff out a woman and a kid. We've got better toys for that than they did fifty years ago.'

She thought of the Electronic Detective Division's captain, her former partner. 'I bet it's the sort of thing that gets him off, too. Peabody's picking me up.' She checked her wrist unit. 'Pretty much now. I'll tag Feeney, see if he's got some time.'

She scooped up the disk. 'The ex Mrs. Crew's data on here?'

'Naturally.' He heard the signal from the gate and, after a quick check, cleared Peabody through. 'I'll walk you down.'

'You going to be in the city today?'

'That's my plan.' He skimmed a hand over her hair as they started down the steps, then stopped when she turned her head and smiled at him. 'What's that about?'

'Maybe I just think you're pretty. Or it could be I'm remembering other uses for stairs. Or maybe, just maybe, it's because I know there's no bony-assed, droid-brained puss face waiting down there to curl his lip at me on my way out.'

'You miss him.'

The sound she made was the vocal equivalent of a sneer. 'Please. You must need a pill.'

'You do. You miss the little routine, the dance of it.'

'Oh ick. Now you've got this picture in my head of Summerset dancing. It's horrible. He's wearing one of those . . .' She made brushing motions at her hips.

'Tutus?'

'Yeah, that's it.'

'Thanks very much for putting that in *my* head.'

'Love to share. Know what? You really are pretty.' She stopped at the bottom of the steps, grabbed two handfuls of his hair and jerked his head toward hers for a long, smoldering kiss.

'Well, that put other images entirely in my head,' he managed when she released him.

'Me too. Good for us.' Satisfied, she strode to the door, pulled it open.

Her brow knit when she saw Peabody along with the young EDD ace McNab climbing out of opposite sides of her pea-green police unit. They looked like . . . She didn't know what the hell they looked like.

She was used to seeing McNab, Central's top fashion plate, in something eye-searing and strange, so the shiny chili-pepper pants with their dozen pockets and the electric-blue tank shirt covered with – ha ha – pictures of chili peppers didn't give her more than a moment's pause. Neither did the hip-length vest in hot red, or the blue air boots that climbed up to his knobby knees.

That was just McNab, with his shiny gold hair slicked back in a long, sleek tail, his narrow and oddly attractive face half covered by red sunshades with mirrored blue lenses and a dozen or so silver spikes glinting at his ears.

But her aide – no, partner now, she had to remember that – was a different story. She wore skinpants that stopped abruptly mid-calf and were the color of . . . mold, Eve decided. The mold that grew on cheese you'd forgotten you stuck in the back of the fridge. She wore some sort of drapey, blousy number of the same color that looked like it had been slept in for a couple of weeks, and a shit-colored jacket that hung to her knees. Rather than the fancy shoes she'd suffered through the day before, she'd opted for some sort of sandal deal that seemed to be made of rope tied into knots by a crazed Youth Scout. There were a lot of chains and pendants and strange-colored stones hanging around her neck and from her ears.

'What are you supposed to be, some upscale street peddler from a Third World country and her pet monkey?'

'This is a nod to my Free-Ager upbringing. And it's comfortable. All natural fabrics.' Peabody adjusted her sunshades with their tiny round lenses. 'Mostly.'

'I think she looks hot,' McNab said, giving Peabody a quick squeeze. 'Sort of medieval.'

'You think tree bark looks hot,' Eve tossed back.

'Yeah. Makes me think of the forest. She-body running naked through the forest.'

Peabody elbowed him, but she chuckled. 'I'm searching for my detective look,' she told Roarke. 'It's a work in progress.'

'I think you look charming.'

'Oh shut *up,*' was Eve's response as Peabody's cheeks pinked in pleasure. 'You fix that heap?' she asked McNab.

'There's good news and bad news. Bad news is that's a piece of crap with a faulty comp system, which makes it about the same as every other police-issue on the streets. Good news is I'm a fricking genius and got her up and running with some spare parts I keep around. She'll hold until you get lucky and wreck it or some asshole who doesn't know better boosts it.'

'Thanks. Backseat,' she ordered. 'Behind the driver. I'm afraid if I keep catching sight of you in the rearview I'll go blind.' She turned to Roarke. 'Later.'

'I'll look forward to it. Hey.' He caught her chin in his hand before she could walk away, then, ignoring her wince, brushed his lips lightly over hers. 'Be careful with my cop.'

Peabody sighed as she slid into the car. 'I just love the way he says that. "My cop."' She scooted around to face McNab. 'You never call me that.'

'It doesn't work when you're a cop, too.'

'Yeah, and you don't have the accent anyway. But you're cute.' She pursed her lips at him.

'And you're my absolutely female She-body.'

'Stop it, stop it, stop it! The neurons in my head are popping.' Eve slapped her safety harness in place. 'There will be no gooey talk in this vehicle. There will be no gooey talk within ten yards of my person. This is my official ban on gooey talk, and violators will be beaten unconscious with a lead pipe.'

'You don't have a lead pipe,' Peabody pointed out.

'I'll get one.' She slid her eyes over as she drove toward the gates. 'Why do you wear something that's wrinkled all to shit?'

'It's the natural state of the natural fabric. My sister wove this material.'

'Well, why didn't she smooth it out or something while she was at it? And I can't believe how much time I waste these days discussing your wardrobe.'

'Yeah. It's kind of frosty.' Her smile turned to a frown as she looked down at her legs. 'Do you think these pants make my calves look fat?'

'I can't hear you because something just burst in my brain and my ears are filled with blood.'

'In that case, McNab and I will return to our rudely interrupted gooey talk.' She yipped when Eve snaked out a hand and twisted her earlobe. 'Jeez. Just checking.'

Eve considered it a testament to her astounding self-control that she didn't kill either one of them on the way to Central. To keep her record clean, she strode away from them in the garage, nabbing the elevator alone. She had no doubt they'd have to exchange sloppy words or kisses before each separated to check in with their squad.

And judging by the sleepy, satisfied look in Peabody's eye when she strolled in, Eve assumed there'd been some groping added to the lip locks.

It didn't bear thinking about.

'Briefing in fifteen,' Eve said briskly. 'I have some new data and need to skim over it. I want to bring Feeney in, if he can manage it. To pursue one angle, we're going to need a person search that goes back over fifty years.'

Peabody sobered. 'The diamonds. We're looking for one of the thieves? Aren't they all dead?'

'Records would indicate. We're looking for the ex-wife and son of Alex Crew. They went into the wind shortly after the divorce and weren't mentioned in Gannon's book. I want to know why.'

'Do you want me to contact Feeney?'

'I'll do that. You contact Gannon, schedule a meeting with her.'

'Yes, sir.'

After loading the disk Roarke had given her and getting coffee, Eve called Feeney's office in EDD.

His familiar, droopy face came on-screen. 'Seventy-two,' he said before she could speak, 'and I'm outta here.'

She'd forgotten he had vacation coming up and juggled the time factor in with her other internal data. 'Got time for a person search before you clock out with your sunscreen and party hat?'

'Didn't say I wasn't on the job until. Besides, you need a person search, I can put one of my boys on it.' All his department were boys to Feeney, regardless of chromosomes.

'I'm looking for brilliance on this one, so I'm asking you to see to it personally.'

'How much butter you got to slather on me to grease me up for it? I've got a lot of *i*'s to dot before I take off.'

'It involves multiple homicides, a shitload of diamonds and a vanishing act going back over half a century. But if you're too busy packing your hula skirt, I can order up a couple of drones.'

'Hula skirt's the wife's.' He drew air in and out his nose. 'Fifty years?'

'Plus a few. I've got a briefing down here in about ten.'

'The one you hooked McNab for?'

'That's the one.'

He pulled on his lips, scratched his chin. 'I'll be there.'

'Thanks.' She cut off, then opened Roarke's file to familiarize herself with the data. While it played, she made copies, added them to the packs she'd already put together for the team, made up another for Feeney.

And thought fondly of the days when Peabody would've done all the grunt work.

As a result, she was the last one in the conference room.

'Detective Peabody, brief Captain Feeney on the investigation to date.'

Peabody blinked. 'Huh?'

'All those things in your ears clogging your hearing? Summarize the case, Detective, and bring Captain Feeney up to speed.'

'Yes, sir.'

Her voice squeaked a bit, and she stumbled over the initial data, but Eve was pleased Peabody found her rhythm. It would be a while yet before she had the stones to lead a team, but she had a good, agile mind and, once she got past the nerves, a straightforward and cohesive method of relaying data.

'Thank you, Detective.' Eve waited while Feeney finished up making notes. 'Baxter, anything from the club on Jacobs?'

'No leads. She was a regular. Came in solo or with a date, with a group. Night in question it was solo, and that's how she left. Hit the dance floor, had some drinks, chatted up a couple guys. Bartender knows she left alone because she talked to him over the last drink. Told him she was in a dry spell. Nobody she met lately did it for her. We got some names, and we'll check them out today, but it looks like a bust.'

'Well, tie it up. Pursuant to the information gathered re Cobb, I flashed her picture around the restaurant Ciprioni's, where it's believed she had a date with the man we know as Bobby Smith.'

'You went to Ciprioni's?' Peabody exclaimed.

'I needed to eat, I needed to follow up the lead. Two birds.'

'Other people like Italian food,' Peabody whined.

Eve ignored her. 'I found the waitress who had their table in July. She remembers Cobb, and I've set her up with a police artist to try to jog her memory a little more on her description of Cobb's date. We can check the museums, galleries, theaters we believe they visited. Somebody might remember them.'

'We'll take it,' Baxter told her. 'We've knocked down a few already.'

'Good. Now that the media's announced the possible connection between these murders, our quarry is aware, almost certainly aware, we've made the link and are investigating concurrently. I don't see this as a deterrent to the investigation.'

She waited a beat. 'In your packs you'll find data relating to Alex Crew, one of the diamond thieves, and the only one of the four who demonstrated violent behavior. My source related that Crew had an ex-wife and a son. Both of these individuals vanished between the divorce and the heist. I want to find them.'

'Crew might have killed them,' Peabody suggested.

'Yes, I've considered that. He didn't have any problem killing one of his partners, or attempting murder on another partner's daughter. He'd done some time previously and was suspected of other crimes. He was into the life. Killing an ex wouldn't have been beyond his pathology. Neither would harming or killing a child. His child.'

Fathers did, she thought. Fathers could be monsters as easily as anyone else.

'Dead or alive, I want to find them. We have their birth names, and their locations prior to their disappearance. Peabody and I will talk to Gannon this morning.' She cocked a brow at Peabody.

'Eleven hundred at the Rembrandt.'

'It's possible she has more information on them gathered through her family or her research for her book. I also want her reasoning for leaving them out of that book when others are named. Feeney, you're on the search?'

'On it.'

'Ah . . . Roarke has offered to assist, if necessary, as civilian consultant. As he gathered the current data for me, he has an interest in following through.'

'Never a problem for me to use the boy. I'll tag him.'

'McNab, I want anything you can get me off Cobb's d and c, her 'links. Gannon's and Jacobs's communications equipment are already in-house. Check with the officer assigned to clearing those units.'

'You got it.'

'I've urged Gannon to consider private security, and she appears to be amenable. We'll keep a man on her as long as the budget allows. This perpetrator is very specific in his goal. Very specific in his targets. Both victims connected to Gannon. If he feels she's in his way, or has information he wants, he won't hesitate to try for her. At this point, we have nothing that leads to him but a fifty-year-old crime. Let's get more.'

On the way back to the division, Eve watched idly as two plain-clothes muscled along a restrained woman who weighed in at about three hundred pounds and was flinging out an impressive array of obscenities. Since both cops had facial cuts and bruises, Eve assumed the prisoner had flung more than curses before they'd cuffed her.

God, she loved the job.

'Peabody, my office.'

She led the way in, closed the door, which had Peabody sending it a puzzled look. Then she programmed two cups of coffee, gestured to a chair.

'Am I in trouble?'

'No.'

'I know I didn't handle the briefing very well. It threw me a minute, that's all, to do the stand-up. I—'

'You did fine. You want to work on focusing on the data instead of yourself. Self-conscious cops don't lead teams. Neither do cops who second-guess themselves every two minutes. You earned the shield, Peabody, now you have to use it. But that's not what this is about.'

'The clothes are . . .' She trailed off at Eve's stony stare. 'Self-conscious again. Putting it away. What is this about, then?'

'I work after shift a lot. Regularly. Go back out into the field to tug on a lead, work up various scenarios or do 'link or comp work in my home office. Bounce the case off Roarke. It's how I work. Are you going to have a problem with me not hooking you in every time I do?'

'Well, no. Well . . . I guess I'm trying to find the partner rhythm. Maybe you are, too.'

'Maybe I am. It's not because I'm flipping you off. Let's get that clear. I live the job, Peabody. I breathe it and I eat it and I sleep with it. I don't recommend it.'

'It works for you.'

'Yeah, it works for me. There are reasons it works for me. My reasons. They're not yours.'

She looked down into her coffee and thought of the long line of victims, and they all led back to herself, a child, bleeding and broken in a freezing hotel room in Dallas.

'I can't do this any other way. I won't do this any other way. I need what this gives me. You don't need the same thing. That doesn't make you less of a cop. And when I go out on my own on something, I'm not thinking you're less of a cop.'

'I can't always put it away either.'

'None of us can. And those who can't find a way to deal with that burnout, get mean, get drunk or off themselves. You've got ways to deal. You've got family and outside interests. And shit, I'll say it this once, you've got McNab.'

Peabody's lips curved. 'That must've hurt.'

'Some.'

'I love him. It's weird, but I love him.'

Eve met her eyes, a brief but steady acknowledgment. 'Yeah, I get that.'

'And it does make a difference. And I get what you're saying, too. I can't always put it away, but sometimes I have to. So I do. I probably won't ever be able to spin it around in my head the way you do, but that's okay. I'm probably still going to bitch some when I find out you went out without me.'

'Understood. We're all right then?'

'We're all right.'

'Then get out of my office so I can get some work done before we see Gannon.'

She wrangled for a consult with Mira and after some heated negotiations with the doctor's admin, was given a thirty-minute during lunch break at Central's infamous Eatery. Eve couldn't figure out

337

why anyone with Mira's class would suffer the Eatery's indignities, but she didn't argue.

She managed, with considerable footwork, to delay her report to Commander Whitney until late that afternoon.

Another call included threats of doubtful anatomical possibility and a bribe of box seats at a Mets game. The combination netted her the promise from the chief lab tech of a full report on both cases by fourteen hundred.

Considered her 'link work a job well done, she grabbed her files, signaled Peabody and went into the field.

Peabody fisted her hands on her hips. 'This is returning to the scene of the crime way, way after the fact.'

'We didn't commit a crime, so technically we're not returning.' Eve ignored the people who trooped or stalked around her as she stood at the corner of Fifth and Forty-seventh. 'I just wanted a look at the place.'

'Got hit pretty hard in the Urban Wars,' Peabody commented. 'Easy target, I guess. Conspicuous consumption. The haves and have-nots. All that fancy jewelry showcased while the economy took a nosedive, illegals were sold on the street like soy dogs and guns were strapped on like fashion accessories.'

She edged closer to one of the displays. 'Shiny.'

'So three guys walk in, do a little switch-and-grab with the fourth, and walk out with pockets full of diamonds. Nobody's prepared for it as the inside guy's long-term, trusted, considered above reproach.'

Eve studied the window displays as she spoke, and the people who stopped to huddle at them, dreaming over that shine. Gold and silver – metals; rubies and emeralds, and diamonds bright as the sun – stones. Since they couldn't be consumed for fuel, didn't keep you warm in the winter, it was tough for her to relate to the pull.

Yet she wore a circle of gold on her finger and a bright, glittering diamond on a chain under her shirt. Symbols, she thought. Just symbols. But she'd fight for them, wouldn't she?

'Inside man has to walk out, too,' she went on, 'practically on their heels, and go straight under. Finger's going to point at him, he knows that going in. But he wants what he wants and he tosses everything else away for it. And gets taken out before he can pat himself on the back. Crew did him, so Crew had to know how to get to him. Not only his location, but how to lure him out.'

She looked up, as a tourist might, to the upper floors. No people glides on a building like this. There wouldn't have been any early century either, she mused. It had been rehabbed and rebuilt after the wars but was, essentially, the same as the history image she'd studied.

And leading down from the corner it dominated were shop after shop, display after display of body adornments. This single cross-town block held millions in merchandise. It was a wonder it wasn't hit on a daily basis.

'They didn't even bother to take out the security cams,' she commented. 'In and out and no sweat. But the cops would've ID'd them eventually. Every one of them had a sheet but the inside guy, and his gambling problem would've flagged him. So they were just going to stay under, keep the stones tucked away, wait for the air to cool. Then poof. You know why it might've worked?'

'The investigation would have focused, at least initially, on the inside man. They'd figure he cracked up, planned and executed. He's gone, diamonds are gone. They move on him.'

'Yeah, while the rest of them scatter and wait it out. Crew was smart to eliminate him, but he went off when he didn't dispose of the body. Smarter, much smarter to dump the guy in the river so the cops waste time and resources looking for a dead man. Didn't think it through all the way, because he wanted what he wanted, too. Once he had it, he just wanted more. That's why he ended up dying in prison. This guy, our guy, he's a little smarter.'

She studied a group of three women who stopped by a display window to make ooohing noises and exclamations. Yeah, the stuff was shiny and sparkly. She wasn't entirely sure why people wanted to shine and sparkle, but they did – and had since the dawn.

'But he's just as obsessed,' Peabody commented. 'Crew was

339

obsessed with the diamonds, I think. That's what I get from the book. He had to have all of them. He couldn't settle for his cut, no matter what it took. I think this guy's the same in that area. Obsessed. Even possessed, in a way. Like they were – the diamonds – cursed.'

'They're carbon-based stones, Peabody. Inanimate objects.' Unconsciously she rubbed a finger over the tear-shaped diamond she wore on a chain under her shirt. 'They don't do anything but sit there.'

Peabody looked back in the window. 'Shiny,' she said again with her eyes unfocused and her jaw slack.

Despite herself, Eve laughed. 'Let's get out of this heat and go see Gannon.'

Chapter Twenty-Four

The Rembrandt, Eve discovered, was one of those small, exclusive, European-style hotels snuggled into New York almost like a secret. No sky-reaching towers or mile-wide lobby, no gilt-encased entrance. Instead it was a lovely old building she assumed had once been a high-dollar residence in a style that murmured elegant discretion.

Rather than her usual snarling match with a doorman, this one trotted over in his sedate navy blue uniform and cap to greet her with a respectful nod.

'Welcome to the Rembrandt. Will you be checking in, madam?'

'No.' She flashed her badge, but his polite manner took some of the fun out of it. 'I'm here to see a guest.'

'Shall I arrange parking for you during your visit?'

'No, you should leave this vehicle exactly where I've put it.'

'Of course,' he said without a wince or a gasp, and sucked the rest of the wind from her sails. 'Enjoy your visit at the Rembrandt, Lieutenant. My name's Malcolm if you need any assistance while you're here.'

'Yeah. Well. Thanks.' His manner took her off-guard enough to have her break her own firm policy. She pulled out ten credits and handed it to him.

'Thank you very much.' He was at the door before her, sweeping it open.

The lobby was small and furnished like someone's very tasteful parlor with deeply cushioned chairs and gleaming wood, glossy marble, paintings that might have been original work. There were flowers, but rather than the twenty-foot arrangements Eve often found a little scary, there were small, attractive bouquets arranged on various tables.

Instead of a check-in counter with a platoon of uniformed, toothy clerks, there was a woman at an antique desk.

With security in mind, Eve scanned the area and spotted four discreetly placed cameras. So that was something.

'Welcome to the Rembrandt.' The woman, slender, dressed in pale peach, with her short shock of hair streaked blond and black, rose. 'How may I assist you?'

'I'm here to see Samantha Gannon. What room is she in?'

'One moment.' The woman sat back down, scanned the screen on her desk unit. She looked up at Eve with an apologetic smile. 'I'm sorry. We have no guest by that name.'

The words were hardly out of her mouth when two men stepped out of a side door. Eve tagged them as security, and noted by stance that they were armed.

'Good. I'm on the job.' She directed this to the men as she held up her right hand. 'Dallas, Lieutenant, Homicide. My partner. Peabody, Detective. IDs coming.'

She reached for her badge with two fingers and kept her eyes on the security team. 'Your security's better than it looks at first glance.'

'We're very protective of our guests,' the woman answered, and took Eve's badge to scan it, then Peabody's. 'These are in order,' she said, and nodded to the two men. 'Ms. Gannon is expecting you. I'll just ring her room and let her know you're here.'

'Fine. What do they load you with?' Eve nodded toward security, and one of them flipped aside his jacket to reveal a multi-action, mid-range hand stunner in a quick-release side holster. 'That oughta do it.'

'Ms. Gannon's ready for you, Lieutenant. She's on four. Your officer is in the alcove by the elevator. He'll show you her room.'

'Appreciate it.' She walked to the two bank elevator with Peabody. 'She showed sense picking a place like this. Solid security, probably the kind of service that gives you everything you want five minutes before you ask for it.'

They stepped on, and Peabody ordered the fourth floor. 'How much you think it costs for a night here?'

'I don't know that stuff. I don't know why people don't just stay home in the first place. No matter how snazzy the joint, there's always some stranger next door when you're in a hotel. Probably another one over your head, the other under your feet. Then there's bell service and housekeeping and other people coming in and out all the damn time.'

'You sure know how to take the romance out of it.'

The uniform was waiting when they stepped off. 'Lieutenant.' He hesitated, looked pained.

'You've got a problem asking me for an ID check, Officer? How do you know I didn't get on at two, blast Dallas and Peabody between the eyes, dump their lifeless bodies and ride the rest of the way up intending to blast you, then get to the subject?'

'Yes, sir.' He took their IDs, used his hand scanner. 'She's in four-oh-four, Lieutenant.'

'Anyone attempt entrance since your shift began?'

'Both housekeeping and room service, both ordered by subject, both checked before given access. And Roarke, who was cleared at lobby level, by subject and by myself.'

'Roarke.'

'Yes, sir. He's been with subject for the past fifteen minutes.'

'Hmm. Stand down, Officer. Take ten.'

'Yes, sir. Thank you, sir.'

'Are you going to be pissed at him?' Peabody asked. 'Roarke, I mean.'

'I don't know yet.' Eve rang the bell and was satisfied by the slight wait that told her Samantha made use of the security peep.

There were circles under Samantha's eyes, and a pallor that spoke of sleepless nights. She appeared to have dressed carefully though, in dark pants and a white tailored shirt. There were tiny square hoops at her ears and a thin matching bracelet on her wrist.

'Lieutenant. Detective. I think you know each other,' she added, gesturing to where Roarke sat, sipping what smelled like excellent coffee. 'I didn't put it together. You, my publisher. I knew the connection, of course, but with everything . . . with everything, it just didn't input.'

'You get around,' Eve said to Roarke.

'As much as possible. I wanted to check on one of our valued authors, and convince her to accept security. I believe you recommended private security in this matter, Lieutenant.'

'I did.' Eve nodded. 'It's a good idea. If he's providing it,' she told Samantha, 'you'll have the best.'

'I didn't take any convincing. I want to live a long and happy life, and I'll take whatever help I can get to make sure of it. Do you want coffee? Anything?'

'It's real coffee?'

'She has a weakness.' Roarke smiled. 'She married me for the coffee.'

Some of the bloom came back into Samantha's cheeks. 'I could write a hell of a book about the two of you. Glamour, sex, murder, the cop and the gazillionaire.'

'No,' they said together, and Roarke laughed.

'I don't think so. I'll deal with the coffee, Samantha. Why don't you sit down? You're tired.'

'And it shows.' Samantha sat, sighed and let Roarke go into the kitchen area for more coffee and cups. 'I can't sleep. I can work. I can put my head into the work, but when I stop, I can't sleep. I want to be home, and I can't stand the thought of being home. I'm tired of myself. I'm alive, I'm well and whole, and others aren't, and I keep spiraling into self-pity anyway.'

'You should give yourself a break.'

'Dallas is right,' Peabody put in. 'You were up and running a couple of weeks, come home to something that would put a lot of people under. You've been hit with everything all at once. A little self-pity doesn't hurt. You should take a tranq and check out for eight or ten hours.'

'I hate tranqs.'

'There you take hands with the lieutenant.' Roarke came in with a tray. 'She won't take them voluntarily either.' He set the coffee down. 'Do you want me out of your way?'

Eve studied him. 'You're not in it yet. I'll let you know when you are.'

'You never fail.'

'Samantha, why did you leave out Alex Crew's family connections in your book?'

'Connections?' Samantha leaned forward for her coffee and, Eve noted, avoided eye contact.

'Specifically Crew's ex-wife and son. You give considerable details regarding Myers's family and what they dealt with after his death. You speak at great length of William Young and your own family. And though you feature Crew prominently, there's no mention of a wife or a child.'

'How do you know he had a wife and child?'

'I'm asking the questions. You didn't miss those details in your research. Why aren't they in the book?'

'You put me in a difficult position.' Samantha held the coffee, stirring, stirring, long after the minute sprinkle of sugar she'd added would have dissolved. 'I made a promise. I couldn't and wouldn't have written the book without my family's blessing. Most specifically without my grandparents' permission. And I promised them I'd leave Crew's son out of it.'

As if realizing what her hand was doing, she tapped the spoon on the rim of her cup, then set it aside. 'He was only a little boy when this happened. My grandmother felt – still feels – that his mother was trying to protect him from Crew. Hide him from Crew.'

'Why did she think that?'

After setting her untasted coffee down, Samantha dragged her fingers through her hair. 'I'm not free to talk about it. I swore I wouldn't write about it, or talk about it in interviews. No.' She held up her hands before Eve could speak. 'I know what you're going to say, and you're absolutely right. These are not ordinary circumstances. This is murder.'

'Then answer the question.'

'I need to make a call. I need to speak with my grandmother, which is going to start another round of demands, debates and worry with her and my grandfather. Another reason I'm not sleeping.'

She pressed her fingers to her eyes before dropping them into her lap. 'They want me to come to Maryland, stay with them, or they threaten to descend on me here. It's tough going to keep them from calling my parents and sibs. I'm holding them off, and I'm gratefully accepting Roarke's offer for security on them until this is resolved. Until it is, I'm staying here. I think it's important that I see this through, that I deal in my way with what's happening now just as they did in theirs with what happened then.'

'Part of dealing is giving the primary any and all data that may pertain to this investigation.'

'Yes, you're right again. Just let me call, speak to her first. We don't break promises in my family. It's like a religion to my grandmother. I'll go in the bedroom, call her now, if you can just wait a few minutes.'

'Go ahead.'

'Admirable,' Roarke said when she'd gone. 'To set such store by your word, particularly to family when for some reason the more intimate you are, the easier a promise is to break. Or at least bend to circumstance.'

'Her great-grandfather broke a lot of promises,' Eve reflected. 'Jack O'Hara broke a lot of promises, to Laine and Laine's mother. So Samantha's grandmother wanted to end the cycle. You don't intend to keep your word, even when it's hard, you don't give it. You have to respect that.'

She glanced toward the bedroom, back at him. 'Offering to take care of her security, and the Maryland Gannons', is classy. But you could've sent a lackey to handle it.'

'I wanted to meet her. She struck a chord with you, and I wanted to see why. I do.'

When Samantha came out of the bedroom a few minutes later, she was teary-eyed. 'I'm sorry. I hate worrying her. Worrying them. I'm going to have to go down to Maryland and put their minds at ease very soon.'

She sat, took a bracing sip of coffee. 'Judith and Westley Crew,' she began. She gave them the foundation data she had, and at one point went to get some of her own notes to refresh her memory.

'So you see, when my grandfather tracked her and found Crew had been there, he believed he might've given the child something that held the diamonds. A portion of them, in any case. It was a safe place to keep them while he went about his work.'

'He would've had half of them, or access to half of them, at that time?' Eve made her own notes.

'Yes. With what was recovered in the safe-deposit box, that left a quarter of the diamonds among the missing. Crew's ex-wife and son were gone. Everything indicated, to my grandmother at least, that she'd been hiding from Crew. The change of names, the quiet job, the middle-class neighborhood. Then the way she packed up and left – sold everything she could or gave it away and just got out. It seemed she was running again because he'd found her. Or more, to my grandmother's mind, the boy. Just a little boy, you see, and his mother was trying to protect him from a man she'd come to know was dangerous and obsessive. If you look at Crew's background and criminal record, his pattern of behavior, she was right to be afraid.'

'She might have taken off because she had a few million in diamonds in her possession,' Eve pointed out.

'Yes. But my grandparents didn't believe, and I don't believe, that a man like Crew would have given them to her, would have told her. Used her, yes, and the boy, but not given her that kind of power. *He* needed to be in charge. He would've found them again when he wanted to. I've no doubt he threatened the woman and would have discarded or disposed of her when his son was older. Old enough to be of more interest and use to Crew. My grandfather let it go, let the remaining diamonds go, let them go. Because my grandmother asked it of him.'

'She'd once been a young child,' Roarke said with a nod, 'who'd had to be uprooted or moved about, who'd never had a settled home or the security that comes with it. And like Crew's ex, her mother had made a choice – to separate herself from the man and shield her child.'

'Yes. Yes. The bulk of the diamonds were back where they belonged. And they were, as my grandmother is fond of saying, only things, after all. The boy and his mother were finally safe. If they'd pursued it, and I have no doubt my grandfather could have tracked them down, they'd have been pulled into the mess. The young boy would have had everything his father had done pushed in his face, would very likely have ended up a national news story himself. His life might have been damaged or severely changed by this one thing. So they told no one.'

She leaned forward. 'Lieutenant, they withheld information. It was probably illegal for them to withhold it. But they did it for the best possible reason. They would have gained more. Five percent more of over seven million, if they'd tracked her down. They didn't, and the world's managed to sputter along without those particular stones.'

Samantha wasn't just defending herself and her grandparents, Eve noted. She was defending a woman and child she'd never met. 'I'm not interested in dragging your grandparents into this. But I am interested in finding Judith and Westley Crew. The diamonds don't mean squat to me, Samantha. I'm not Robbery, I'm Homicide. Two women are dead, you may very well be a target. The motive for this comes from the diamonds, and that's my interest in them. Someone else can do the research and dig up the fact that Crew had a wife and child. This could make them targets.'

'Well, my God.' As it struck home, Samantha squeezed her eyes shut. 'I never thought of it. Never considered it.'

'Or the person who killed Andrea Jacobs and Tina Cobb may be connected to Crew. It may be his son, who's decided he wants to get back what he feels belonged to his father.'

'We always assumed . . . Everything my grandparents found out about Judith showed, clearly showed, she was doing everything she could to give her son a normal life. We assumed she succeeded. Just because his father was a murderer, a thief, a son of a bitch, doesn't mean the child took on his image. I don't believe we work that way, Lieutenant. That we're genetically fated. Do you?'

'No.' She glanced at Roarke. 'No, I don't. But I do believe, whatever their parentage, some people are just born bad.'

'What a happy thought,' Roarke murmured.

'Not finished. However we're born, we end up making choices. Right ones, wrong ones. I need to find Westley Crew and determine what choices he made. This needs to be closed out, Samantha. It needs to end.'

'They'll never forgive themselves. If somehow this has come full circle and struck out at me, my grandparents will never forgive themselves for making the choice they made all those years ago.'

'I hope they're smarter than that,' Roarke said. 'They made a choice, for a child they didn't even know. If that child made choices as a man, it's on him. What we do with our lives always is.'

They left together, with Eve bouncing the new information in her head until she formed patterns. 'I need you to find them,' she said to Roarke.

'Understood.'

'Coincidence happens, but mostly it's bullshit. I'm not buying that some guy read Gannon's book and got a hard-on for missing diamonds and decided to kill a couple of women in order to find them. He's got an investment in them, a connection to them. The book set it off, but the connection goes further back. How long before the book came out did the hype for it start?'

'I'll find out. There will also be a list of some sort of people, reviewers, accounts and so forth, that were sent advanced copies. You have to add word of mouth to that, I'm afraid. People the editorial staff, publicity and others might have spoken to.'

'We've got this great book coming out,' Peabody began. 'It's about this diamond heist right here in New York.'

'Exactly so. The man you're looking for might have heard of it over drinks somewhere. Might have an acquaintance or attended a party with one of the editors, a reviewer, someone in sales who spoke about it.'

'Won't that be fun to wade through? Get me the list,' she repeated as they stepped out into the lobby. 'And let me know who you put on her, security-wise. I want my people to know your people. Oh, and I need two box seats, Mets game.'

'Personal use or bribe?'

'Bribe. Please, you know I'm a Yankees fan.'

'What was I thinking. How do you want them?'

'Just send the authorization to Dickhead at the lab. Berenski. Thanks. I gotta book.'

'Kiss me goodbye.'

'I already kissed you goodbye this morning. Twice.'

'Third time lucky.' He planted his lips firmly on hers. 'I'll be in touch, Lieutenant.' He strolled out. Even before he hit the sidewalk a sleek black car pulled up to the curb, and a driver hopped out to open the door.

Like magic, Eve thought.

'I'd like to be in touch with him. Anytime. Anywhere. Any way.'

Eve turned her head slowly. 'Did you say something, Peabody?'

'Who, sir, me, sir? Nope. Absolutely not.'

'Good.'

She took the meeting with Mira next while Peabody ate lunch at her desk and updated the file. As far as food went, Eve figured Peabody had the better end of the stick.

The Eatery was always crowded, always noisy, no matter what the time of day. It made Eve think of a public school cafeteria, except the food was even worse and most of the people chowing down were armed.

Mira was there ahead of her and had a booth. She'd either gotten very lucky, Eve thought, or had used some clout to order one up earlier. Either way, a booth was a big step up from one of the tiny four-tops crammed together, or the counter service, where cop asses hung over the stingy stools.

Mira wasn't a cop – technically – and sure as hell didn't look like one. She didn't, to Eve's mind, look like a criminologist, a doctor or a psychiatrist either. Though she was all of those.

What she looked like was a pretty, well-dressed woman who might be seen browsing the high-end shops along Madison.

She might've bought the suit in one of them. Surely only the very brave or very stylish would wear that lemon-foam shade in a city like New York, where grime just sprang up off the asphalt and clung to any available surface like a leach to flesh.

But the suit was spotless and looked cool and fresh. It set off the highlights in Mira's soft brown hair and made her eyes seem bluer. She wore a trio of long, thin, gold ropes with it where stones of a deeper yellow glinted like little pieces of sunlight.

She was drinking something out of a tall glass that looked as frosty as her suit, and smiled over the rim as Eve slid into the booth across from her.

'You look hot and harried. You should have one of these.'

'What is it?'

'Delicious.' Without waiting for Eve's assent, Mira ordered one from the comp menu bolted to the side of the booth. 'How are you otherwise?'

'Okay.' It always took Eve a moment to adjust when small talk was involved. And with Mira it wasn't exactly small talk. People made that when they didn't give a damn one way or the other, and mostly, she assumed, to hear their own voices. Mira cared. 'Good. Summerset's vacationing far, far away. Cheers me right up.'

'He made a quick recovery from his injuries.'

'He was still a little wobbly on the one pin, but yeah.'

'And how is our newest detective?'

'She likes to sneak her badge out and grin at it a lot yet. And she manages to work the word "detective" into a sentence several times a day. She's dressing really weird. Throws me off. Otherwise, she's jetting along with it.'

Eve glanced at the drink that slid out of the serving slot. It did look pretty good. She took one cautious sip. 'It tastes like your suit. Cool and summery and a little tart.' She thought it over. 'That probably sounded wrong.'

'No.' With a laugh, Mira sat back. 'Thank you. A color like this? Completely impractical. That's why I couldn't resist it. I was just admiring your jacket, and how that wonderful shade of toast looks on you. It would turn my complexion muddy. And I just can't wear separates with the same panache as you.'

'Separates?'

It took Mira a moment to realize such a basic fashion word

351

baffled her favorite cop. 'Jacket, pants, whatever, sold individually rather than as part of a unit, as a suit would be.'

'Hah. Separates. How about that. And I always thought they were, you know, jacket, pants, whatever.'

'My God, I would *love* to go shopping with you.' This time Mira's laugh flowed over the cranky noises of the Eatery. 'And you look as if I've just stabbed you with my fork under the table. One day I'll rope you into it, but for now rather than ruin your appetite, why don't I ask you how Mavis is doing?'

'Good.' Though Eve wasn't sure talking about pregnancy was any less of an appetite blower than shopping. 'You wouldn't know she was, ah, cooking anything in there if she didn't advertise it. She and Leonardo might rent blimp space. He's designing her all kinds of pregnant-chick clothes, but I can't really tell the difference.'

'Give them all my best. I know you want to get to business. Why don't we order first? I'm having a Greek salad. You can usually trust those here.'

'Yeah, that's fine.'

Mira ordered two from the menu. 'Do you know I remember bits and pieces about the robbery at the Exchange? It was very big news at the time.'

'How? You're too young.'

'Now *that* has set me up for the day. Actually, I was only, what . . . oh, how depressing. I'd've been about four, I suppose. But my uncle happened to be dating a woman who had a booth in the Exchange. She was a jewelry designer and was there, on the main floor, when the robbery happened. I remember hearing my parents talk about it, and when I was a bit older I developed such an interest in crime that I looked up the details. The family connection, however distant, added to the excitement for me.'

'Is she still around? The designer?'

'I have no idea. It didn't work out between her and my uncle. I do know that she didn't know a thing until security shut the place down. She didn't know the inside man. At least that's what I got from my uncle when I asked him about it later. I could get you her name, I'm sure, if you want to try to track her down.'

'I might, but it's probably the wrong direction. At least at this point. Tell me about the killer.'

'Well. The act, the murders themselves aren't his priority. They're a by-product. His victims and his methods are different, each suiting his needs at the time. He would be most interested in his own needs. The fact that they were both women, even attractive, isn't important. I doubt he has a spouse or serious relationship as either would interfere with his self-absorption. There was nothing sexual, despite his romancing of Tina Cobb, and that romancing was not only a means to an end but on his own terms.'

'Taking her places he preferred in order to show off his superior intellect and taste.'

'Yes. There was nothing personal in either murder. He sees the big picture, from his own narrow view. Cobb could be utilized and exploited, and so she was. He plans and considers, so it follows that he knew he could kill her when her use to him ended. He knew her, set out to know her. He knew her face, the touch of her hand, the sound of her voice, may have been intimate with her physically if it moved him toward his goal, but there would be no personal connection for him.'

'He destroyed her face.'

'Yes, but not out of rage, not out of personal emotion. Out of self-preservation. Both murders were a result of his need to protect himself. He will remove, destroy, eliminate anything or anyone who gets in the way of his goal or his own personal safety.'

'There was violence in his elimination of Cobb.'

'Yes.'

'He hurt her. To extract information?'

'Possibly, yes. More likely to attempt to mislead the police, to make them think it was a crime of passion. It may have been both. He would have considered. He has time to consider. He took Cobb to crowded places, away from her own aegis. But his choices reflect a certain style. Art, theater, a trendy restaurant.'

'Reflecting his aegis.'

'He would want to be comfortable, yes.' The first salad plate slid out, and Mira set it in front of Eve. 'He entered Gannon's home when he knew she was out. He was careful to shut down the security, to take the disks. To protect himself. He brought a weapon – though he believed the house empty, he brought the knife. He prepares for eventualities, takes detours when necessary. He didn't attempt to make the break-in and murder appear to be a burglary gone wrong by taking away valuables.'

'Because it had already been done? Because Alex Crew used that method with Laine Tavish?'

Mira took the second plate, smiled. 'It reflects a powerful ego, doesn't it? "I won't repeat, I'll create." And a respect for art and antiques. He didn't vandalize, didn't destroy the artwork, the valuable furniture. He'd consider such a thing beneath him. He has knowledge of such things, likely owns such things himself. Certainly he aspires to. But if it was only aspiration, he would have taken what appealed to his sense of aesthetic or avarice. He's very focused.'

'He's educated? Cultured?'

'Art galleries, museums, West Village theater?' Mira shrugged a shoulder. 'He could have taken the girl to Coney Island, to Times Square, to a dozen places a young man of her same sphere might take a girl on a date. But he didn't.'

'Because, like stealing art pieces or electronics, it would be beneath him to munch on a soy dog in Coney Island.'

'Mmm.' Mira nibbled on salad. 'He isn't looking for glory, fame or attention. He isn't looking for sex or even wealth in the traditional sense. He's looking for something very specific.'

'Alex Crew had a son.'

Mira's brows winged up. 'Did he?'

'A kid at the time this all went down.'

She filled Mira in, then let the doctor absorb the new data while they ate.

'I see what you're considering. The son hears of the book, or reads it, and learns one of his father's former partners' ancestors is right here in New York. That she has enough information for a book, and very likely has more. That she may very well have access to the diamonds. But why, if he's known of them

354

all this time, hasn't he tried to find them, or get to the Gannons before?'

'Maybe he didn't know the whole story until the book. Maybe he didn't know the connection.' Eve waved with her fork. 'Anyway, that's for me to figure out. What I want is your opinion. Does it follow pattern, profile, that the person I'm after is Crew's son?'

'It could give him what he'd consider a proprietary right to them. They were his father's property, so to speak. But if his father brought them to him when he was a child—'

'It wasn't in the book,' Eve reminded her. 'And we can't know what Crew did or didn't do or say or take when he paid that last visit.'

'All right. From what we know of Crew, he felt entitled to the entire booty, and killed for it. They were an obsession for him, one he pursued even though he had enough to ensure he'd live well for the rest of his life. It's possible the son is working with the same obsession, the same view.'

'My gut tells me it comes from Crew.'

'And your gut is usually right. Does it trouble you to take that line, Eve? To play the sins of the father in your head?'

'Yeah.' She could say it here, to Mira. 'Some.'

'Heredity can be a strong pull. Heredity and early environment together, an almost irresistible pull. Those who break it, who make their own despite it, are very strong.'

'Maybe.' Eve leaned forward. No one around them would listen, but she leaned closer, lowered her voice. 'You know, you can just sink down, you can sink and say it's somebody else's fault you're down there in the piss and the shit of the world. But it's just an excuse. The lawyers, the shrinks, the doctors and social reformers can say, "Oh, it's not her fault, she's not responsible. Look where she came from. Look what he did to her. She's traumatized. She's damaged."'

Mira laid a hand over Eve's. She knew she was thinking of herself, the child, and what the woman might have become. 'But?'

'The cops, we know that the victims, the ones who are broken or shattered or dead . . . or dead, they need somebody to stand up for them, to say, Goddamnit, it *is* your fault. You did this, and you have to pay for it, no matter if your mother beat you or your father . . . No matter what, you don't have the right to damage the next guy."

Mira gave Eve's hand a squeeze. 'And that's why you are.'

'Yeah. That's why I am.'

Chapter Twenty-Five

Eve viewed a session in the lab with Dickie Berenski as she did a dental checkup. You had to do it, and if you were lucky it wouldn't be as bad as you imagined. But it was usually worse.

And like the dental techs in her experience, Dickhead exhibited a smarmy, self-righteous satisfaction when it got worse.

She swung into the lab with Peabody and pretended not to notice several techs slide looks in her direction, then get busy elsewhere.

When she didn't see a sign of Dickie, she cornered the first tech who couldn't skitter away fast enough. 'Where's Berenski?'

'Um. Office?'

She didn't think she deserved the quaking voice or the frozen rictus of a smile. It had been months since she'd threatened a lab tech. Besides, they should know it was physically impossible for her to put a man's internal organs on display by turning him inside out.

She crossed the main lab, over the white floors, around the white stations manned by people in white coats. Only the machines and the vials and tubes filled with substances best not considered had color.

All in all, she thought she'd rather work in the morgue.

She walked into Dickie's office without knocking. He was kicked back at his desk, feet propped up as he sucked on a grape-colored ice pop.

'You got the box seats?' he asked.

'You'll get them when I get my results.'

'I got something for you.' He pushed away from the desk, started

357

out, then stopped to study Peabody. 'That you in there, Peabody? Where's the uniform?'

Delighted with the opportunity, she pulled out her badge. 'I made detective.'

'No shit? Nice going. Liked the way you filled out a uniform though.'

He hopped onto his stool and began to ride it up and down his long white counter as he ordered up files, keyed in codes with his spider-quick fingers. 'You got some of this already. No illegals in either vic. Vic one – that's Jacobs – had a blood-alcohol level of point oh-eight. She was feeling pretty happy. Got her last meal. No recent nooky. Fibers on her shoes match the crime-scene carpet. Couple others here she probably picked up in the cab on the way home.'

His fingers danced; the screens revolved with color and shapes. 'Got a couple hair samples, but says here she was clubbing prior to getting dead. Coulda picked those up in the club. If any of them are from the killer, we'll match 'em when you nab 'im.

'Now we've reconstructed the wound – used her ID photo and some others to create an image of her at time of death.'

He brought it up so Eve could look at Andrea Jacobs as she had been, on screen. A pretty woman in a fancy dress, with a gash at her throat.

'Using our techno-magic, we can pretty well determine the size and shape of your murder weapon.'

Eve studied the split-screen image of a long, smooth blade, and the specs beneath it that gave her width and length.

'Good. That's good, Dickie.'

'You're working with the best. We concur with the investigator and the ME re the positioning of vic at time of the death blow. Came from behind. Yanked her by the hair. We got some of her hair from the scene that substantiates the scenario. Unless one of those stray hairs came from the perp, and I'm not putting money on that, we got nothing from him. Nada. He was sealed up tight.

'Now vic two – Cobb – different ball game. You sure you're looking at the same guy?'

'I'm sure.'

'Your call. Smashed her up. Pipe, bat, metal, wood. Can't tell you 'cause we got nothing to work with there but the shape of the breaks in the bones. Look for something long, smooth and about two inches in diameter. Probably weighted. Leg shot took her down, rib shot kept her down. But then it gets interesting.'

Shifting to another screen, he brought up the picture of Cobb's charred skull. 'You see the busted cheekbone, and . . .' He revolved the image. 'Your classic busted-in skull. Setting her on fire took care of most of the trace, but we got some that adhered to the bone fragments – face and head.'

'What kind of trace?'

'It's a sealer.' He split the screen. A series of jagged shapes in cool blues came on. 'A fire-retardant. Smart guy missed that step. Professional-grade. Brand name's Flame Guard. Harry Homemaker can get it, but mostly it's used by contractors. You seal subflooring or walls with it.'

'Subflooring. Before the finished deal goes down?'

'Yep. She had trace in the facial and head wounds. He lit her up, but this shit didn't burn. Truth in advertising for once. Didn't seal the bone, though, so it wasn't wet when she made contact. Little tacky maybe in spots but not wet.'

Eve bent down closer, caught a whiff of grape from Dickhead. 'She picked up the trace, cheekbone hitting the floor or the wall. Then again with the skull. No trace in the leg or rib wounds because of her clothes. There was blood when she hit, when she crawled. Might've helped pick up the trace. Splinters maybe, splinters from the boards she hit, adhere to the broken bones.'

'You're the detective. But a girl that size, hit like that, she'd go down hard. So yeah, it could happen. We got our trace, so it did happen. It left a mess behind, too.'

'Yeah.' And that was a factor. 'Shoot all of this to my office. Not half bad, Dickie.'

'Hey, Dallas!' He called after her as she started out. 'Take me out to the ball game.'

'They're on their way. Peabody.' She scooped at her hair as she lined up new data. 'Let's do a run on the sealant. See what else we can find out. He could've used his own place for it. Could have. But he doesn't seem like the type to soil his own nest. Professional-grade,' she mumbled. 'He could have a place being rehabbed. Or access to a building under construction or being remodeled. Let's start on construction sites near the dump site. He didn't pick that empty lot out of a hat. He doesn't pick anything out of a hat.'

Following that line, she called Roarke. By the time he came on, she was already in her car and headed back to Central. 'Lieutenant. You have a gleam in your eye.'

'Might've caught a break. Do you have anything going up or getting a face-lift in Alphabet City?'

'Rehabbing a mid-sized apartment complex. And . . . There are a couple of small businesses being changed over. I'd have to check to get you specifics.'

'Do that. Shoot them to my office. Know of anything else? A competitor, associate, whatever?'

'Why don't I find out?'

'Appreciate it.'

'Wait, wait.' He held up a hand, well aware she'd have cut him off without another word. 'There's a bit of progress on the search. Not enough to dance about, and Feeney and I are both tied up with other matters for the next part of the day. We've agreed to put in some time this evening, at our place.'

'Good.' She turned into Central's underground garage. 'See you.'

'I gotta ask.' Peabody braced as Eve shot into her narrow parking slot, then let out a breath when there was no impact. 'When you see his face come on screen, all sexy and gorgeous with that, you know, *mouth,* do you ever just want to pant like a dog?'

'Jesus, Peabody.'

'Just wondering.'

'Stomp out the hormones and keep your mind in the game. I've got Whitney.' She looked at the time. 'Shit. Now. I wanted to see if we've had any luck with the artist rendering.'

'I can do that. If there's anything, I'll bring it up.'

'That works.'

'See how handy it is to have a detective for a partner?'

'I should've known you'd find a way to work it in.'

They separated, and Eve rode the miserably crowded elevator another three floors before she bailed and switched to the glide for the rest of the trip to Commander Whitney's office.

Whitney suited his rank. He was a commanding man with a powerful build and a steely mind. The lines dug around his eyes and mouth only added to the image of leadership, and the toll it took on the man.

His skin was dark, and his hair had sprinkles of gray, like dashes of salt. He sat at his desk, surrounded by his com unit, his data center, disk files and the framed holos of his wife and family.

Eve respected the man, the rank and what he'd accomplished. And secretly marveled he'd kept his sanity between the job and a wife who lived to socialize.

'Commander, I apologize for being late. I was detained at the lab.'

He brushed that away with one of his huge hands. 'Progress?'

'Sir. My case and Detective Baxter's connect through Samantha Gannon.'

'So I see from the files.'

'Further information has come to light after a follow-up interview with Gannon this morning. We're pursuing the possibility that Alex Crew's son or another connection or descendant may be involved in the current cases.'

She sat only because he pointed to a chair. She preferred giving her orals standing. She relayed the details of the morning interview.

'Captain Feeney is handling the search personally,' she continued. 'I haven't yet spoken with him this afternoon, but have word there's been some progress in that area.'

'The son would be in his sixties. A bit old to have interested a girl of Cobb's age.'

'Some are attracted to older men for their experience, their stability. And he may have passed as younger.' Though she doubted it. 'More likely, he has a partner he used to get to Cobb. If this link holds, Commander, there are numerous possibilities. Judith Crew may have remarried, had another child, and that child may have learned of the diamonds and Gannon. Westley Crew may have children, and have passed his father's story to them, much as Gannon was passed the family legend. But it's someone with a proprietary interest. I feel certain of it, and Mira's profile concurs. I hope to have an artist rendering shortly.

'We got a break through the lab. There was trace of a fire-retardant substance on Cobb. A sealant, professional-grade. We'll run it down and concentrate on buildings near the dump site. He's been very careful, Commander, and this was a big mistake. One I don't believe he would have made if he had applied the sealant himself. Why kill her on or around flame-retardant material when you plan to light her up? It's too basic a mistake for this guy. Once we find the crime scene, we're a big step closer to finding him.'

'Then find it.' He shifted when his interoffice 'link signaled. 'Yes.'

'Commander, Detectives Peabody and Yancy.'

'Send them in.'

'Commander, Lieutenant.' Peabody angled over so Yancy, the Ident artist, could precede her. 'We thought it would be more expedient if Detective Yancy reported to both of you at once.'

'Wish I had more.' He handed out printouts and a disk. 'I worked with the witness for three hours. I think I got her close, but I'm not passing out cigars. You can only lead them so far,' he explained, and studied the printout image Eve held. 'And you can tell when they're just making things up, or mixing them up, or just going along so you'll finish and let them go.'

Eve stared at the rendering and tried to see a resemblance to Alex Crew. Maybe, maybe around the eyes. Or maybe she just wanted to see it.

But this was no sixty-year-old man.

'She tried,' Yancy continued. 'Really gave it her best shot. If we'd gotten to her closer to the time she saw the guy, I think we could've nailed it down. But a lot of time's passed, and she sees dozens of men at her tables every day. Once we got to a certain point, she was just tossing in features at random.'

'Hypnosis could juggle her memory.'

'I tried that,' he said to Eve. 'Mentioned it to her, and she freaked. No way, no how. Added to that, she caught a media report on the murder, and she's freaked about that. This is going to be the best we get.'

'But is it him?' Eve demanded.

Yancy puffed out his cheeks, then deflated them. 'I'd say we're on, as far as the skin tone, the hair, the basic shape of the face. Eyes, the shape's close, but I wouldn't bank on color. She thought age-wise, late-twenties, early thirties, then admitted that was because of the age of the girl. She bounced to thirties, back to twenties, then maybe older, maybe younger. She figures rich because he had an expensive wrist unit, paid in cash and added a substantial tip. And some of that played into her description.' He jerked a shoulder. 'Smooth complexion, smooth manner.'

'Is it close enough to give it to the media, get some play?'

'Sorta stings the pride, but I wouldn't. You gotta call it, Lieutenant, but my sense is we're off. I think a cop, a trained observer, might be able to make him from this, but not a civilian. Sorry I couldn't dunk it for you.'

'That's okay. You probably got us closer than anybody else could. We'll run this through an ID program, see if we get any hits.'

'You're going to want to set for at least a thirty-percent adjustment.' Yancy shook his head at his own work. 'With that, you're going to get a few thousand hits, city-wide alone.'

'It's a start. Thanks, Yancy. Commander, I'd like to get moving on this.'

'Keep me in the loop.'

Back in her office, she pinned a copy of the artist rendering to her board. At her desk she cobbled her notes together into a report, then read it over to see the steps and stages.

She would leave the person search to Feeney, the electronic

363

excavation to McNab. She sent a memo to Baxter detailing the new data and included a copy of Yancy's sketch.

While Peabody worked to nail down the sealant, Eve looked at construction sites. Her 'link signaled an incoming through the data port, and switching over, she brought up a list of all properties with current construction or rehab licenses in a ten-block radius of the dump site.

Roarke was not only quick, she thought, but he got the gist without anyone having to spell it out.

She separated them into tenanted and untenanted.

Empty, she thought. Privacy. Hadn't he waited until he believed the Gannon house was empty? There was little enough pattern, so she'd try this one on for size.

Empty buildings first.

Taking them, she broke them down a second time into construction and rehab.

Had to lure her in. Smarter to lure her rather than force or debilitate. She's young and foolish, but she's a girly girl, too. Would that type want to tromp around a construction site, even to make a date happy?

She rose, paced. Probably. What did she know about that kind of thing? Young girls in love, or who believed they were in love, probably did all sorts of things that went against type.

She'd never been a young girl in love. A few lust bouts along the way, but that was a different thing. She knew that much seeing as love had sucker punched her and dumped her right into Roarke's lap. And didn't she slick herself up from time to time, fiddling with enhancements and hair, draping on fancy duds, because he liked it?

Yeah, love could easily make you go against type.

But what about the killer? No reason for him to go against type. He wasn't in love. He hadn't been in lust, either. And his type liked to impress, show off. He liked to be comfortable and in charge. He liked to plan things out with an eye toward his own goals, his own ego, his self-preservation.

A rehab with some fancy touches. A place he knew he wouldn't be disturbed. Where he wouldn't be questioned if caught on the premises. Where he could, again, deal with any security features.

She sent the data to her home unit, printed out her lists, then went into the bull pen to get Peabody. 'With me.'

'I'm running down the sealant.'

'Run it down in transit.'

'Where are we going?' Peabody demanded as she scrambled to gather her work disk, files, jacket.

'To look at buildings. To talk to guys with power tools.'

'Hot damn!'

The first stop was a small theater originally constructed in the early twentieth century. Her badge got them through to the foreman. Though he bitched about workload and schedule, he took them through. The lobby floors were the original marble, and apparently a point of pride for the foreman. The theater section was bare particle-board on the floor and as yet unsealed. The walls were old plaster.

Still, she went through the entire building, using her scope to look for blood traces.

They suffered through late-afternoon traffic en route to the next stop.

'The sealant, professional-grade, can be purchased wholesale or retail in five-, ten- and twenty-five-gallon tubs.' Peabody read the data off her ppc. 'Or you can, with a contractor's license, purchase it in powder form and mix it yourself. Residential-grade comes in one- or five-gallon tubs. No powder available. I've got the suppliers.'

'You'll need to hit those. We'll want a list of individuals and companies who've bought the sealant so we can cross-check them with the construction crews on these sites.'

'Going to take a while.'

'He's not going anywhere. He's right here.' She scanned the street. 'Thinking of his next move.'

He let himself into his condo and immediately ordered the house droid to bring him a gin and tonic. It was so annoying to have to spend half the damn day in an office doing absolutely nothing that could possibly interest him.

But the old man was tying up the purse strings, demanding he show more interest in the company.

Your legacy, son. What bullshit! His legacy was several million in Russian whites.

He couldn't care less about the company. As soon as he was able, as soon as he had what was his, by right, he'd tell the old man to fuck himself.

It would be a fine day.

But meanwhile he had to placate and coddle and pretend to be the good son.

He stripped down, letting his clothes fall as he went, and lowered himself into the one-man lap pool built into the penthouse's recreation area.

The fact that the company he despised and deplored paid for the penthouse, the clothes, the droid, never made a scratch on the surface of his ego.

He reached up a hand for the g and t, then simply sprawled in the cool water.

He had to get to Gannon now. He'd considered and rejected the idea of going to Maryland and just beating the information he needed out of the old couple. It could come back on him in too many ways.

As it stood now, they could have no clue. He could be an obsessed fan, or a lover of the maid's who'd been in league with her to burgle the Gannon residence. He could be anyone at all.

But if he went to Maryland he might be seen, or traced. He would hardly blend well in some silly small town. If he killed Samantha Gannon's grandparents, even the most dim-witted of cops might work their way back to the diamonds as the cause.

If he could get to Gannon herself . . . It was so damn *frustrating* to discover she'd vanished. None of the careful probes he'd sent out had netted him a single clue to her whereabouts.

But she had to surface sometime. She had to come home sooner or later.

If he had all the time in the world, he could wait her out. But he couldn't tolerate dragging himself into that stupid office much longer, dealing with the idiotic working class or paying lip service to his pathetic parents. All the while knowing everything he wanted, everything he deserved, was just beyond his reach.

He sipped the drink with one arm braced on the pool's edge to anchor him. 'Screen on,' he said idly, then scanned the news channels for any updates.

Nothing new, he saw with satisfaction. He couldn't understand the mind-set of those who fed on media, on what they perceived as the glory. A true criminal gained all the satisfaction necessary by succeeding at his work, in secret.

He liked being a true criminal, and liked – very much – raising the bar on his own exploits.

He smiled to himself as he looked around the room at the shelves and displays of antique toys and games. The cars, the trucks, the figures. He'd stolen some of them, simply for the buzz. The same way he sometimes stole a tie or a shirt.

Just to see if he could.

He'd stolen from friends and relatives for the same reason, and long before he'd known he came by the habit . . . honestly. That thievery was in his blood. Who'd have believed it looking at his parents?

But then, he'd gotten his interest in the toy collection from his father, and it had served him well. If his fellow collector and acquaintance Chad Dix hadn't bitched to him about his girlfriend, about the book she was writing that was taking all her time and attention, he wouldn't have known about the diamonds, the connection, as soon as he had.

He might never have read the book. It wasn't the sort of thing he did with his time, after all. But it had been a simple matter to pry Dix for more details, then to wheedle the advance copy from him.

He finished off the drink, and though he wanted another, denied himself. A clear head was important.

He set the glass aside, did a few laps. When he pulled himself

367

out of the pool, the empty glass was gone and a towel and robe were laid out. He had a party to attend that evening. He had a party of some sort to attend every evening. And he found it ironic that he'd actually met Samantha Gannon a few times at various affairs. How odd he'd had no interest in her, had assumed they had nothing in common.

He'd never had more in common with a woman.

He might have to take the time and the trouble to pursue her romantically, which would certainly be considerably less *lowering* than his brief association with Tina Cobb. No more his type, when it came to that. Not from what he'd observed of her, in any case.

Full of herself, he thought as he began to dress. Attractive enough, certainly, but one of those brainy, single-minded females who either irritated or bored him so quickly.

From what he'd been told of her by Chad, she was good in bed, but entirely too absorbed with her own needs and wants outside the sheets.

Still, unless he could figure out a more efficient, more direct way to the diamonds, he would have to spend some quality time with Jack O'Hara's great-granddaughter.

In the meantime, he thought as he flicked a finger over the scoop of a clever scale model backhoe, he thought it might be time for a heart-to-heart with dear old dad.

Chapter Twenty-Six

There was a headache simmering like a hot stew behind her eyes by the time Eve got home. She'd only managed to hit three sites. Construction workers, she learned, called it a day long before cops did. She'd gotten nothing from the ones she'd managed to survey but the headache from the clatter of tools, the blasts of music, the calls of workers all echoing in empty or near-empty buildings.

Added to that was the hassle of cajoling, browbeating or begging suppliers for their customer lists. If she never visited another building-supply warehouse or outlet in this lifetime, she would die a happy woman.

She wanted a shower, a ten-minute nap and a gallon of ice water.

Since she'd pulled up behind Feeney's vehicle, she didn't bother to check the in-house. Roarke would be upstairs with him, in the office or the computer lab, playing their e-geek games. Since he didn't come out to greet her, she assumed the cat was with them.

She scotched the idea of ten minutes with her eyes shut. She couldn't quite bring herself to get horizontal with another cop in the house, especially if the cop was on the clock. It would be too embarrassing if she got caught. She compromised with an extra ten minutes in the shower and felt justified when the headache backed off to threatening.

She traded in the day's separates – she was going to remember that one – for a T-shirt and jeans. She thought about going bare-foot, but there was that cop-in-the-house factor, and bare feet always made her feel partially naked.

She went for tennis shoes.

Since she felt nearly human again, she stopped by the computer lab on her way to her office.

Roarke and Feeney were manning individual stations. Roarke had his sleeves rolled up and his hair tied back, as was his habit when he settled into serious work. Feeney's short sleeved shirt looked as if he'd mashed it into a ball and bounced it a few times before putting it on that morning. It also showed off his bony elbows. She wondered why she found them endearing.

She must be seriously tired.

There were screens up with data zipping across them too quickly for her eye to read. The men tossed comments or questions at each other in the geek language she'd never been able to decipher.

'You guys got anything for me in regular English?'

They both looked over their shoulders in her direction, and she was struck how two men who couldn't have been more different in appearance could have identical looks in their eyes.

A kind of nerdy distraction.

'Making some headway.' Feeney reached into the bag of sugared nuts on his work counter. 'Going back a ways.'

'You look . . . fresh, Lieutenant,' Roarke commented.

'I didn't a few minutes ago. Grabbed a shower.' She moved into the room as she studied the screens. 'What's running?'

Roarke's smile spread slowly. 'If we tried to explain, your eyes would glaze over. This one here might be a little more straight-forward.' He gestured her closer so she could see the split screen working with a photo of Judith Crew on one side and a blur of images running on the other.

'Trying for a face match?'

'We dug up her driver's license from before the divorce,' Feeney explained. 'Got another run going over there from the license she used when the insurance guy located her. Different name, and she'd changed her hair, lost weight. Computer's kicking out possible matches. We're moving from those dates forward.'

'Then we're using a morph program on yet another unit,' Roarke continued. 'Searching for a match on what the computer thinks she looks like now.'

370

'The civilian thinks if the image was close, we'd have matched by now.'

'I do, yes.'

Feeney shrugged, nibbled nuts. 'Lot of people in the world. Lots of women in that age group. And she could be living off-planet.'

'She could be dead,' Eve added. 'Or she could have evaded standard IDing. She could be, shit, living in a grass shack on some uncharted island, weaving mats.'

'Or had facial restructuring.'

'Kids today.' Feeney blew out an aggrieved breath. 'No faith.'

'What about the son?'

'Working a morph on that, too. We've hit some possibles. Doing a secondary on them. And our boy here's looking for the money.'

Eve looked away from the screens. The rapid movements were bringing back the headache. 'What money?'

'She sold the house in Ohio,' Roarke reminded her. 'It takes a bit of time for the settlement, the payoff. The bank or the realtor would have had to send the check to her, or make an e-transfer per instructions. In the name she was using at the time, unless she authorized it to be paid to another party.'

'You can find out stuff like that? From that long ago?'

'If you're persistent. She was a careful woman. She authorized the settlement check to be transferred electronically to her lawyer, at that time, then sent to another law firm in Tucson.'

'Tucson?'

'Arizona, darling.'

'I know where Tucson is.' More or less. 'How do you know this?'

'I have my ways.'

She narrowed her eyes when Feeney looked up at the ceiling. 'You lied, you bribed and you broke any number of privacy laws.'

'And this is the thanks I get. She was in Tucson, from what I can find, less than a month in early 2003. Long enough to pick up the check, deposit it in a local bank. My educated guess would be, she used that point and those funds to change identities once again, then moved to another location.'

'We're narrowing it down. Once the matches are complete, we'll take a hard look at the hits.' Feeney rubbed his temple. 'I need a break.'

'Why don't you go down, have a swim, a beer?' Roarke suggested. 'We'll see what we've got in another half hour.'

'That's a plan I can get behind. You got anything for us, kid?'

Nobody but Feeney ever called her 'kid.' 'I'll bring you up to date after you take a thirty,' Eve told him. 'I need to set a few things up in my office.'

'Meet you there then.'

'I could use a beer myself,' Eve commented when Feeney walked out.

'A break seems to be in order.' Roarke ran a finger down the back of her hand, then tugged it closer to nibble.

She knew that move.

'Don't even start sniffing at me.'

'Too late. What is this scent? All over your skin?'

'I don't know.' Warily, she lifted her shoulder, sniffed at it herself. Smelled like soap to her. 'Whatever was in the shower.' She gave her hand a little yank, but made the mistake of glancing around in case Feeney was still nearby. The instant of distraction gave him the opening to hook a foot around hers, tip her off balance and into his lap.

'Jesus, cut it *out*!' Her voice was a fierce and frantic whisper. On the mortification scale, getting caught snuggled in Roarke's lap hit the top three, even above getting caught napping or barefoot by another cop. 'I'm on the clock. Feeney's right here.'

'I don't see Feeney.' He was already nuzzling his way along her neck toward her ear. 'And as an expert consultant, civilian, I'm entitled to a recreational break. I've decided I prefer adult activity to adult beverage.'

Little demons of lust began to dance along her skin. 'You can't even think I'm going to mess around with you in the computer lab. Feeney could come back in here.'

'Adds to the excitement. Yes, yes.' He chuckled as he nipped at a spot – his personal favorite – just under her jaw. 'Sick and perverted. And though I'd wager Feeney suspects we have occasional sex, we'll take our recreational break elsewhere.'

'I've got work to do, Roarke, and . . . Hey! Hands!'

'Why, yes, those are indeed my hands.' Laughing now, he cupped them under her and levered out of the chair. 'I want my thirty,' he said and carted her toward the elevator.

'The way you're going, you'll be done in five.'

'Bet.'

She struggled against a laugh of her own and put up a token struggle by clamping a hand on the opening of the elevator. 'I can't just go off and get naked with Feeney in the house. It's too weird. And if he comes back and—'

'You know, I suspect Feeney gets naked with Mrs. Feeney, and this is probably how they had their little Feeneys.'

'Oh my God!' Her hand trembled, went limp, and her face paled considerably. 'That's just despicable, the dirtiest of dirty fighting to shove that one into my head.'

Because he wanted to keep her unbalanced, he reached behind her and keyed in the bedroom rather than using audio command. 'Whatever works. Now you're too weak to hold me off.'

'Don't count on it.'

'Do you remember the first time we made love?' He touched his lips to hers as he said it, changing tactics with a gentle brush.

'I have a vague recollection.'

'We rode up in the elevator like this and couldn't keep our hands off each other, couldn't get to each other quick enough. I was mad for you. I wanted you more than I wanted to keep breathing. I still do.' He deepened the kiss as the elevator doors opened. 'It's never going to change.'

'I don't want it to change.' She combed her fingers through his hair, shoving the band away so all that thick, soft black slid through her fingers. 'You're so damn good at this.' She pressed her lips to his throat. 'But not quite good enough to have me doing this with the door open. Feeney could, you know, wander in. I can't focus.'

'We'll fix that.' With her legs hooked around his waist, her arms

373

around his neck and her lips beginning to lay a hot line over his skin, he went to the door. He closed it. Locked it. 'Better?'

'I'm not sure. Maybe you should remind me how we did this the first time again.'

'I believe, if memory serves, it went something like this.' He spun her around, trapping her between the wall and his body. And his mouth was fever hot on hers.

She felt the need, instant and primal, slice through her. It was like being cleaved in two – the woman she'd been before him, the woman she'd discovered with him.

She could be what she was, and he understood her. She could be what she'd become, and he cherished her. And the wanting each other, through all the changes, all the discoveries, never abated.

She let him ravish her, and felt the power in surrender. It pumped and swelled inside her as she slid down his body. Her hands were as busy as his, her mouth as impatient as they dragged each other toward the bed.

They stumbled up the platform, and remembering, she laughed. 'We were in a hurry then, too.'

They fell on the bed in a tangle of limbs, then rolled as they struggled to strip away clothes, to take and devour. Before, that first time, it had been in the dark. Groping and grasping and desperation in the dark. Now they were in the light that spilled through the windows, through the sky window over the bed, but the desperation was the same.

It ached in her like a wound that would never quite heal.

She'd been a mass and a maze of demands then, too, he remembered. All heat and motion, driving him toward frenzy so that he'd burned to ram himself into her and batter them both toward release.

But he'd wanted more. Even then, he'd wanted more of her. And for her. He gripped her hands, drawing her arms over her head, and she arched, pressing center to center until his pulse was a pounding of jungle drums.

'Inside me.' Her eyes were blurred and dark. 'I want you inside me. Hard. Fast.'

'Wait.' He knew what it would be now, where they would take

each other, and control was a thin and slippery wire. He cuffed her wrists with one hand. If she touched him now, that wire would snap.

But he could touch her. God, he needed to touch her, to watch her, to feel her body gather and quake from the assault of pleasure. Her skin was damp when he ran his free hand down her. The moan trembled from her lips, then broke with a hoarse cry as he used those clever fingers on her.

He watched those blurry eyes go blind, felt the scramble of her pulse in the wrists he held and heard her release a sob in the air before she went pliant. Wax melted in the heat.

Again, was all he could think as his mouth came down on hers, fierce and frantic. Again and again and again.

Then her arms were free and banded around him, and her hips pistoned up. He was inside her as she'd demanded. Hard and fast.

She knew, with the part of her brain that could still reason, that he'd gone over, gone where he could so often send her. Somewhere beyond the civilized and sensible, where there were only sensations fueled by needs. She wanted him there with her, where control was impossible and pleasure saturated both mind and body.

As her own system quivered toward that last leap, she heard his breath catch, as if on a pain. Wrapping around him, she gave herself over. 'Now,' she said, and pulled him with her.

She stretched under him, curled and uncurled her toes. She felt, Eve discovered, pretty damn good. 'Okay.' She gave Roarke a noisy slap on the ass. 'Recreational break's over.'

'Christ. Christ Jesus.'

'Come on, you've had your thirty.'

'I'm sure you're wrong. I'm sure I have five or six minutes left. And if I don't, I'm having them anyway.'

'Off.' She gave his butt another slap, then a pinch. When neither budged him, she shifted her knee over, and up.

'Son of a bitch.' That moved him. 'Mind the merchandise.'

'You mind it. I've already used it.' She was smart enough to roll over and away before he could retaliate. She landed on her feet, rolled up to the balls, back to the heels. 'Man, I'm revved.'

He stayed where he was, flat on his back, and eyed her. Long, lean, naked, with her skin glowing from the energetic recreational break.

'You look it.' Then he smiled, slyly. 'I wonder if Feeney's finished his swim.'

The color drained out of her cheeks. 'Oh jeez, oh, *shit*!' She made a dive for her clothes. 'He'll know. He'll just know, and then we'll have to avoid looking at each other while we pretend he doesn't know. Damnit.'

Roarke was laughing as she dashed with her bundle of clothes into the bath.

Feeney beat her into her office, and that made her wince. But she strode in briskly and moved straight to her desk to set up files.

'Where were you?'

'Just, ah, you know . . . dealing with a couple things.'

'I thought you were gonna . . .' He trailed off with a sound she recognized as embarrassed horror not quite suppressed. She could feel her skin heat and kept her attention trained on her computer as if it might leap off the desk and grab her by the throat.

'I think I'll – um—' His voice cracked a bit. She didn't glance over but she could *feel* him looking frantically around the room. 'Get some coffee.'

'Coffee's good. That'd be good.'

When she heard him escape to the kitchen, she rubbed her hands over her face. 'Might as well be wearing a sign,' she muttered. '"Just Got Laid."'

She set up her disks, her case board, then shot Roarke a vicious glare when he strolled in. 'I don't want that look on your face,' she hissed.

'Which look?'

'You know which look. Wipe it off.'

Relaxed, amused, he sat on the corner of her desk. When Feeney walked in, he could see the fading flush. Feeney cleared his throat, very deliberately, then set the second mug of coffee he carried on the desk. 'Didn't zap you one,' he said to Roarke.

'It's all right. I'm fine for now. How was your swim?'

'Fine. Good.' He rubbed a hand over the drying sproings of ginger and silver hair. 'Good and fine.'

He turned away to study the board.

Weren't they a pair? Roarke thought, two veteran cops who've waded through blood and madness. But put a bit of sex on the table between them, and they're fidgety as virgins at an orgy.

'I'm going to bring you both up to date,' Eve began. 'Then I'll work on my angles while you work on yours. You see the artist's sketch on the board, and on screen.'

She picked up a laser pointer, aimed it toward the wall screen. 'Detective Yancy did the Ident, but isn't confident enough in this rendering for us to pass it to the media. But I think it gives us some basics. Coloring and basic facial structure, in any case.'

'Looks, what,' Feeney asked. 'range of thirty?'

'Yeah. Even if Crew's son has spent the better part of a fortune on face work and sculpting, I don't think a guy in his sixties is going to look this young. And the witness never put him over forty. We may be looking for a family connection, or a young friend, protégé. We have to pursue the connection. It's the most logical, given pattern and profile.'

'Yeah, and it opens it up instead of narrowing it down,' Feeney commented.

'We caught a break on narrowing it.'

Eve told them about the trace evidence, and her fieldwork to date attempting to find the location of the Cobb crime scene.

'It's the first trace he's left. When we nail this down, we'll have another link toward identifying this creep. He chose the place, so he knows the place. He knew he could get in, do what he wanted to do in private and clean it up enough to have the crime unde-tected.'

'Yeah.' Feeney nodded agreement. 'Had to splash some blood around. He cleaned up, or there'd be a report. A construction crew's not going to strap on tool belts with blood all over the damn place.'

'Which means he had to spend time doing so. Again in private. Had to have transpo, had to know there was a handy dump site and access to the flammable.'

'Probably didn't seal up for that one,' Feeney commented. 'Why bother?'

'Not an efficient use of his time,' Eve agreed. 'He's going to burn the body and destroy any possible trace to him, or so he believed. Why bother to avoid any trace on the scene as long as it's reasonably cleaned? Particularly if he had some legitimate reasons for being there.'

'Could own the place, work or live in it.'

'Could be a building or construction inspector,' Roarke put in. 'Though if he is, it wouldn't have been bright of him to forget about the fire sealant.'

'You got the data I asked for, the properties being built or rehabbed in that area? Is what you sent me the whole shot?'

'It is, yes. But that doesn't take into account ones that are under the table. Small jobs,' he explained. 'A private home or apartment where the owner might decide to do some work, or hires a contractor who's willing to forgo the permits and fees and work off the books.'

Eve visualized the map of her investigation suddenly crisscrossed with hundreds of dead ends and detours. 'I'm not going to worry about side deals until we exhaust the legitimate ones. Sticking with that, don't they sometimes use gas on construction sites?'

'For some of the vehicles and machines.' Roarke nodded. 'As it's inconvenient to transport it from one of the stations outside the city, you might use a storage compartment on-site or nearby. You've a fee to pay for that as well.'

'Then we follow that down, too.'

'Bureaucrats in Permits and Licensing are going to make you jump through hoops,' Feeney reminded her.

'I'll deal with it.'

'You're going to need to put the arm on these guys, get the warrants and assorted paperwork and other bullshit. We get lucky with the matches, you'll cut back on that.' Feeney considered, pulled on his nose. 'But you got a lot to wade through one way or the other. I can put my leave off a few days, until this is closed.'

'Leave?' She frowned at him until she remembered his scheduled vacation. 'Crap. I forgot all about it. When are you going?'

'Got two more days on the clock, but I can juggle some things around.'

She was tempted to take him up on it. But she paced it off, heaved out a breath. 'Yeah, fine, you do that and your wife will eat both our livers for breakfast. Raw.'

'She's a cop's wife. She knows how it goes.' But there wasn't much conviction behind his words.

'Bet she's already packed.'

Feeney offered a hangdog smile. 'Been packed damn near a week now.'

'Well, I'm not facing her wrath. Besides, you've already juggled enough to give me this much time. We can handle the rest of it.'

He looked back at the board, as she did. 'I don't like leaving a case hanging.'

'I've got McNab and this guy.' She jerked a thumb toward Roarke. 'If we don't wrap it before you have to go, we'll keep you in the loop. Long distance. Can you give me a couple more hours tonight?'

'No problem. Look, why don't I get back to it, see if I can work some magic?'

'Do that. I'll see if I can wrangle some warrants. Okay with you if we brief here tomorrow, oh-eight hundred?'

'Not if it comes with breakfast.'

'I'll be right along,' Roarke told him, and waited until he was alone with Eve. 'I can save you time with the red tape. A little time on the unregistered, and I can have a list of permits for you.'

She jammed her hands into her pockets as she studied her murder board, as she looked at the faces of the dead. Roarke's unregistered, equipment would blind the unblinking eye of CompuGuard. No one would know he'd hacked into secured areas and nipped out data with his skilled hands.

'I can't justify it for this. I can't shortcut this just to save myself a little time and a lot of aggravation. Gannon's secure. To my knowledge she's the only one who might be in immediate jeopardy from this guy. I'll play it by the book.'

He stepped up behind her, rubbed her shoulders as they both looked at the images of Jacobs and Cobb. Before and after.

'When you don't play it by the book, when you do take that shortcut, it's always for them, Eve. It's never for yourself.'

'It's not supposed to be for me. Or about me.'

'If it wasn't for you, or about you, in some sense, you wouldn't be able to go on day after day, facing this and caring, day after day. And if you didn't, who would pick up the standard for people like Andrea Jacobs and Tina Cobb and carry it into the battle?'

'Some other cop,' she said.

'There is no other like you.' He pressed his lips to the top of her head. 'There's no other who understands them, the victims and those who victimize them, quite like you. Seeing that, knowing that, well, it's made an honest man out of me, hasn't it?'

She turned now to look him straight in the eye. 'You made yourself.'

She knew he thought of his mother, of what he'd learned only a short time before, and she knew he suffered. She couldn't stand for Roarke's dead as she did for those of strangers. She couldn't help him find justice for the woman he never knew existed, for the woman who'd loved him and died at the brutal hand of his own father.

'If I could go back,' she said slowly, 'if there was a way to twist time and go back, I'd do everything I could to bring him down and put him away for what he did. I wish I could stand for her, for you.'

'We can't change history, can we? Not for my mother, not for ourselves. If we could, you're the only one in this world I would trust with it. The only one who might make me stand back and let the law do what the law does.' He traced his finger down the dent in her chin. 'So, Lieutenant, whenever you do take one of those shortcuts, you should remember there are those of us who depend on you who don't give a rat's ass about the book.'

'Maybe not. But I do. Go help Feeney. Get me something I can use so we can make him pay for what he did to them.'

She sat alone when he'd gone, her coffee forgotten and her gaze on the murder board. She saw herself in each of the victims. In Andrea Jacobs, struck down and abandoned. In Tina Cobb, robbed of her own identity and discarded.

But she'd come back from those things. She'd been created from those things. No, you couldn't change history, she thought. But you could sure as hell use it.

Chapter Twenty-Seven

She lost track of time when she worked alone. Eve supposed, if pressed on the subject, she lost track of time when she worked with others, too.

But there was something soothing about sitting in or pacing around her office by herself, letting the data and the speculations bump around in her head with only the computer's bland voice for company.

When her 'link beeped, she jerked out of a half trance and realized the only light in the room was from her various screens.

'Dallas. What?'

'Hey, Lieutenant.' McNab's young, pretty face popped on screen. She could see the slice of pizza in his hand. Hell, since she could all but smell the pepperoni, it occurred to her she'd missed dinner. 'Were you asleep or something?'

She could feel her embarrassment scale rising just because another cop had tagged her when she'd been drifting off. 'No, I wasn't asleep. I'm working.'

'In the dark?'

'What do you want, McNab?' She knew what she wanted. She wanted his pizza.

'Okay. I put in some OT on the 'links and d and c's.' He took a bite of pizza. Eve was forced to swallow her own saliva. 'Lemme tell you, these dink units are tougher than the pricey ones. Memory's for shit, and the broadband—'

'Don't walk me down that path, McNab. Bottom line it.'

'Sure. Sorry.'

He licked – the bastard actually licked sauce from his thumb.

'I got locations on two of the transmissions we believe the killer sent Cobb. One of them matches the location of an aborted trans sent to the Gannon residence and picked up by the answering program on the night of Jacobs's murder.'

'Where?'

'The location that hit both is a public link in Grand Central. The other, generated from a cyber club downtown. Oh, and there's a second aborted to the Gannon residence, ten minutes after the first, from another public three blocks from her residence.'

Public places, public access. Phony accounts. Careful, careful, careful. 'You with Peabody?'

'Yeah. She's in the other room.'

'Why don't you check out the club? See if you can pinpoint the unit he used. Maybe you can get us a better description.'

'No problem.'

'We're going to brief at my home office, eight hundred hours.'

His mouth might've been full of pizza, but she recognized a groan when she heard one. Served him right for eating on her empty stomach.

'You get anything hot, I want to hear right away. No matter what time it is. That's good work on the 'links.'

'I am the wizard. You guys got any of that real bacon?'

She cut him off. Sitting back in the blue-shadowed dark, she thought about diamonds and pizza and murder.

'Lieutenant.'

'Hmm?'

'Lights on, twenty-five percent.' Even in the dimness, Roarke watched her blink like an owl. 'You need to eat.'

'McNab had pizza. It broke my focus.' She rubbed her tired eyes. 'Where's Feeney?'

'I sent him home, not without a struggle. His wife called. I think she's going into a low-level state of panic that he's going to do what he suggested to you earlier and postpone this family trip.'

'I won't let him. You got anything for me?'

'The first stage of matching's done on Judith Crew, nearly so on the boy. Once that's done we'll . . .' He remembered who he was talking to and edited out the techno jargon. 'Essentially, we'll cross-match and reference the two sets. If she kept her son with her until he came of age – and it certainly seems she'd do so – we should be able to locate that match, or matches.'

He cocked his head at her. 'Is it going to be pizza for you, then?'

'I would give you five hundred credits for a slice of pepperoni pizza.'

He sneered. 'Please, Lieutenant. I can't be bought.'

'I will give you the sexual favor of your choice at the next possible opportunity.'

'Done.'

'Cheap date.'

'You don't know the sexual favor I have in mind. Did you get your warrants?' he called out as he went into the kitchen.

'Yeah. Jesus, I had to tap-dance until my toes fell off, but I'm getting them. And McNab's pinned locations on transmissions. He and Peabody are going to check out a cyber club tonight where one was zipped to Cobb.'

'Tonight?'

'They're young, able and afraid of me.'

'So am I.' He brought her in a plateful of bubbling pizza and a large glass of red wine.

'Where's yours?'

'I had something with Feeney in the lab, and foolishly assumed you'd feed yourself.'

'You've already eaten and you still fixed me dinner?' She scooped up pizza, singed her fingertips. 'Wow, you're like my body slave.'

'Those roles will be reversed when I collect my payment. I think it may involve costumes.'

'Get out.' She snorted, bit into the pizza and burned her tongue. It was great. 'He made a call to both Cobb and Gannon from a port in Grand Central. Called Gannon's place the night he killed Jacobs – twice, two locations. Just covering his bases, sounds like. Gets her answering program on both aborts, confirms the all clear. Goes over.'

She washed down pizza with wine and knew God was in His heaven.

'Could've walked from there, that's how I'd've done it. Better than a cab. Safer.'

'And allows him to case the neighborhood,' Roarke added.

'Then he gets there, gets inside. Maybe he's smart enough to do a room-by-room check of the house first. Can't be too careful. Then he goes upstairs to get started, and before you know it, house-sitter comes in. All that care, all that trouble, and for what?'

'Pissed him off.'

Eve nodded, drank some more wine, considered the second slice of pizza. Why the hell not? 'I'm thinking, yeah. Had to piss him off. You know he could've gotten out. Or he could've debilitated her, restrained her. But she'd ruined his plans. She'd become the fly in his soup. So he killed her. But he wasn't in a rage when he did it. Controlled, careful. But not as smart as he thinks. What if she knows something? He didn't take that leap in logic.'

'He struck out, coldly, but didn't take the time to completely calm himself.' Roarke nodded. 'He had to improvise. We could assume he's not at his best when he hasn't been able to script the play and follow the cues.'

'Yeah, I can see inside his head, but it's not helping.' She tossed the slice of pizza down and stared at the artist's image she kept on screen. 'If I've structured this investigation right, I know what he wants. I know what he'll do to get it. I even know, if we're following the same logic, that his next step would be to go after Samantha Gannon or one of her family. To buddy up with them if he calculates it's worth the time and effort, to threaten, torture, kill, if it's not. Whatever it takes to get the diamonds or information leading to them out of her.'

'But he can't get to her, or them.'

'No, I got them covered. And maybe that's part of the problem. Why it's stalled.'

'If you use her as bait, you could lure him out.'

With the wineglass cupped in her hand, Eve tipped back, closed her eyes. 'She'd do it, too. I can see that in her. She'd do it because it's a way to end it, and because it makes a good story, and because she's gutsy. Not stupidly, but gutsy enough to go for this. Just like her grandma.'

'Gutsy enough, because she'd trust you to look out for her.'

Eve shrugged a shoulder. 'I don't like to use civilians as bait. I could put a cop in her place. We can fix one up to look enough like her to pass.'

'He'd have studied her. He might see through it.'

'Might. Hell, he might even know her. Anyway, I'm too tall. Peabody's the wrong body type.'

'A droid could be fashioned.'

'Droids only do what they're programmed to do.' And she never fully trusted machines. 'Bait needs to be able to think. There's someone else he might go for.'

'Judith Crew.'

'Yeah. If she's still alive, he might try for her. Or the son. If neither one of them is a part of this, he might push those buttons. There's nobody else left from back then, nobody with direct knowledge of what went down, and how. He can't even be sure they exist.'

'Eat.'

Distracted, she looked down at the pizza. Because it was there, she picked it up, bit in, chewed. 'It's a kind of fantasy. Now that I see he's younger than I assumed, it makes more sense to me. It's a treasure hunt. He wants them because he feels he's entitled to them, and because they're valuable, but also because they're shiny,' she added, thinking of Peabody outside the display windows at Fifth and Forty-seventh.

'You talked me into swimming around that reef off the island. Remember? You said not to wear my pendant deal. Not only because, hey, big fat diamonds can get lost in the ocean, but because, I shouldn't wear anything shiny in there. Barracudas get hyped up when something shines and gleams in the water and can take great big, nasty bites out of you.'

'So you have a barracuda on a treasure hunt.'

Yeah, she liked bouncing a case off Roarke, Eve thought. You didn't have to tell him anything twice, and half the time didn't have to tell him the first time.

'I don't know where this is taking me, but let's play it out. He wants them because he feels entitled, because they're valuable and because they're shiny. This tells me he's spoiled, greedy and childish. And mean. The way a bully's mean. He killed not only because it was expedient but because he could. Because they were weaker and he had the advantage. He hurt Cobb because there was time to, and he was probably bored by her. This is how I see him. I don't know what it gets me.'

'Recognition. Keep going.'

'I think he's used to getting what he wants. Taking it if it isn't given. Maybe he's stolen before. There was probably a safer way to get information, but he chose this way. It's more exciting to take something that isn't yours in the dark than to bargain for it in the light.'

'I certainly used to think so.'

'Then you grew up.'

'Well, in my way. There's a thrill about the dark, Eve. Once you've experienced it, it's difficult to resist.'

'Why did you? Resist.'

'I wanted something else. More.' He took her wine for a sip. 'I'd built my way toward it, with the occasional and often recreational side step. Then I wanted you. There's nothing in the dark I could want as I want you.'

'He doesn't have anyone. He doesn't love. He doesn't want anyone. It's things he craves. Shiny things that gleam in the dark. They're shinier, Roarke, because they already had blood on them. And I think, I'm damn sure, some of that blood runs in him. They're more valuable to him, more important to him, because of the blood.'

She rolled her shoulders. 'Yeah, I'll recognize him. I'll know him when I see him. But none of this gets me any closer to where he is.'

'Why don't you get some rest?'

She shook her head. 'I want to look at the matches.'

Steven Whittier sipped Earl Grey out of his favorite red mug. He claimed it added to the flavor, a statement that caused his wife, who preferred using the antique Meissen, to act annoyed. Still, she loved him as much for his everyman ways as she did for his sturdiness, dependability and humor.

The match between them – the builder and the society princess – had initially baffled and flustered her family. Patricia was vintage wine and caviar, and Steve was beer and soy dogs. But she'd dug in her fashionable heels and ignored her family's dire predictions. Thirty-two years later, everyone had forgotten those predictions except Steve and Pat.

Every year on their anniversary, they tapped glasses to the toast of 'It'll never last.' After which, they would laugh like children pulling one over on a bunch of grown-ups.

They'd built a good life, and even his early detractors had been forced to admit Steve Whittier had brains and ambition, and had managed to use both to provide Pat with a lifestyle they could accept.

From childhood he'd known what he wanted to do. To create or re-create buildings. He'd wanted to dig in his roots, as he'd never been able to do as a child, and provide places for others to do the same.

He'd structured Whittier Construction from the ground up, through his own sweat and desire, his mother's unbending belief in him – then Pat's. In the thirty-three years since he'd begun with a three-man crew and a mobile office out of his own truck, he'd cemented his foundation and added story after story onto the building of his dream.

Now, though he had managers and foremen and designers on his payroll, he still made it a habit to roll up his sleeves on every job site, to spend his day traveling from one to another or burrowing in to pick up his tools like any laborer.

There was little that made him happier than the ring and the buzz of a building being created, or improved.

His only disappointment was that Whittier had not yet become Whittier and Son. He still had hopes that it would, though Trevor had no interest in or talent for the hands-on of building.

He wanted to believe – needed to believe – that Trevor would settle down soon, would come to see the value of honest work. He worried about the boy.

They hadn't raised him to be shallow and lazy, or to expect the world handed to him on a platter. Even now, Trevor was required to report to the main offices four days a week, and to put in a day's work at his desk.

Well, half a day, Steve amended. Somehow, it was never more than half a day.

Not that he got anything done in that amount of time, Steve thought as he blew on his steaming tea. They would have to have another talk about it. The boy was paid a good salary, and a good day's work was expected. The problem, of course, or part of it, was the trust funds and glittery gifts from his mother's side of the family. The boy took the easy route no matter how often his parents had struggled to redirect him.

Given too much, too easily, Steve thought as he looked around his cozy den. But some of the fault was his own, Steve admitted. He'd expected too much, pinned too many hopes on his son. Who knew better than he how terrifying and debilitating it could be for a boy to have his father's shadow looming everywhere?

Pat was right, he thought. They should back off a bit, give Trevor more room. It might mean taking a clip out of the family strings and setting him loose. It was hard to think of doing so, of pushing Trevor out of the nest and watching him struggle to cross the wire of adulthood without the net they'd always provided. But if the business wasn't what he wanted for himself, then he should be nudged out of it. He couldn't continue to simply clock time and draw pay.

Still, he hesitated to do so. Not only out of love, for God knew, he loved his son, but out of fear the boy would simply turn to his maternal grandparents and live, all too happily, off their largess.

Sipping his tea, he studied the room his wife laughingly called

389

Steve's Cave. He had a desk there as he more often than not preferred to hunker down in that room rather than the big, airy office downtown or his own well-appointed, well-equipped office in the house. He liked the deep colors of this room, and the shelves filled with his boyhood toys – the trucks and machines and tools he'd routinely asked for at birthdays and Christmastime.

He liked his photographs, not only of Pat and Trevor, of his mother, but of himself with his crews, with his buildings, with his trucks and machines and tools he'd worked with as an adult.

And he liked the quiet. When the privacy screens were on the windows and the doors shut, it might very well be a cave instead of one of the many rooms in a three-level house.

He glanced up at the ceiling, knowing if he didn't go up to the bedroom shortly, his wife would roll over in bed, find him gone, then drag herself up to search him out.

He should go up, spare her that. But he poured a second mug of tea and lingered in the soft light and quiet. And nearly dozed off.

The buzzer on his security panel made him jolt. His first reaction was annoyance. But when he blinked his eyes clear and looked at the view screen, the image of his son brought him a quick rush of pleasure.

He rose out of his wide leather chair, a man of slightly less than average height, with the bare beginnings of a potbelly. His arms and legs were well muscled, and hard as brick. His eyes were a faded blue with webs of lines fanning out from them. Though it had gone stone gray, he still had most of his hair.

He looked his age, and eschewed any thought of face or body sculpting. He liked to say he'd earned the lines and gray hair honestly. A statement, he knew, that caused his fashionable and youth-conscious son to wince.

He supposed if he'd ever been as handsome as Trevor, he might have been a bit more vain. The boy was a picture, Steve thought. Tall and trim, tanned and golden.

And he worked at it, Steve thought with a little twinge. The boy spent a fortune on wardrobe, on salons and spas and consultants.

He shook off the thought as he reached the door. It didn't do any good to poke at the boy over things that didn't matter. And since Trevor rarely visited, he didn't want to spoil things.

He opened the door and smiled. 'Well, this is a surprise! Come on in.' He gave Trevor's back three easy pats as Trevor walked past him and into the entrance hall.

'What're you doing out this time of night?'

Deliberately, Trevor turned his wrist to check the time on the luminous mother-of-pearl face of his wrist unit. 'It's barely eleven.'

'Is it? I was dozing off in my den.' Steve shook his head. 'Your mother's already gone up to bed. I'll go get her.'

'No, don't bother.' Trevor waved him off. 'You've changed the security again.'

'Once a month. Better safe than sorry. I'll give you the new codes.' He was about to suggest they go into the den, share the pot of tea, but Trevor was already moving into the more formal living room. And helping himself from the liquor cabinet.

'It's good to see you. What're you doing out and about and all dressed up?'

The casual jacket, regardless of label and price, was hardly what Trevor considered *dressed up*. But it was certainly a step up from his father's choice of Mets T-shirt and baggy khakis.

'I've just come from a party. Dead bore.' Trevor took the snifter of brandy – at least the old man stocked decent liquor – swirling it as he sprawled into a chair. 'Cousin Marcus was there with his irritating wife. All they could do was talk and talk and talk about that baby they made. As if they were the first to procreate.'

'New parents tend to be wrapped up.' Though he'd have preferred his tea, Steven poured a brandy to be sociable. 'Your mother and I, we bored the ears off everyone who couldn't run and hide for months after you were born. You'll do the same when it's your turn.'

'I don't think there's any danger of that as I'm not the least bit interested in making something that drools and smells and demands every minute of your time.'

Steve continued to smile, though the tone, and sentiment, set his

391

teeth on edge. 'Once you meet the right woman, you'll probably change your mind.'

'There is no right woman. But there are any number of tolerable ones.'

'I hate hearing you sound so cynical and hard.'

'Honest,' Trevor corrected. 'I live in the world as it is.'

Steve let out a sigh. 'Maybe you need to begin to. It must be meant that you came by tonight. I was thinking of you before you did. About where you're going with your life, and why.'

Trevor shrugged. 'You've never understood or approved of my life because it doesn't mirror yours. Steve Whittier, man of the people, who built himself from nothing. Literally. You know, you should sell your life story. Look how well the Gannon woman has done with her family memoirs.'

Steve set his snifter down, and for the first time since Trevor had come in, there was a warning edge in his tone. 'No one is to know about any of that. I made that clear to you, Trevor. I told you because I felt you had a right to know, and that if, somehow, through that book's publication the connection was made to your grandmother, to me, to you, you'd be prepared. It's a shameful part of our family history, painful to your grandmother. And to me.'

'It hardly affects Grandma. She's out of it ninety percent of the time.' Trevor circled a finger at his ear.

Genuine anger brought a red flush to Steve's face. 'I don't ever want to hear you make light of her condition. Or to shrug off everything she did to keep me safe and whole. You wouldn't be here, swilling brandy and sneering, if it wasn't for her.'

'Or him.' Trevor inclined his head. 'He had a part in making you, after all.'

'Biology doesn't make a father. I explained to you what he was. A thief and a murderer.'

'A successful one, until the Gannons. Come on now.' Trevor shifted, leaned forward, the brandy snifter cupped between his knees. 'Don't you find him fascinating, at least? He was a man who made his own rules, lived his life on his own terms and took what he wanted.'

'Took what he wanted, no matter what it cost anyone else. Who so terrorized my mother she spent years running from him. Even after he died in prison, she kept looking over her shoulder. I know, whatever the doctors say, I *know* it was him and all those years of fear and worry that made her ill.'

'Face it, Dad, it's a mental defect, and very likely genetic. You or I could be next. Best to live it up before we end up drooling in some glorified asylum.'

'She's your grandmother, and you *will* show respect for her.'

'But not for him? Blood's blood, isn't it? Tell me about him.' He settled back again.

'I've told you all you need to know.'

'You said you kept moving from place to place. A few months, a year, and you'd be packing up again. He must've contacted her, or you. Come to see you. Otherwise why would she keep running?'

'He always found us. Until they caught him, he always found us. I didn't know he'd been caught, not till months afterward. I didn't know he'd died for more than a year. She tried to protect me, but I was curious. Curious children have a way of finding things out.'

Don't they just? Trevor thought. 'You must've wondered about the diamonds.'

'Why should I?'

'His last big job? Please, you must've wondered, and being a curious child . . .'

'I didn't think about them. I only thought of how he made her feel. How he made me feel the last time I saw him.'

'When was that?'

'He came to our house in Columbus. We had a nice house there, a nice neighborhood. I was happy. And he came, late at night. I knew when I heard my mother's voice, and his, I knew we'd have to leave. I had a friend right next door. God, I can't remember his name. I thought he was the best friend I'd ever have, and that I'd never see him again. And well, I didn't.'

Boo hoo, Trevor thought in disgust, but he kept his tone light and friendly. 'It wasn't easy for you, or Grandma. How old were you?'

'Seven, I think. About seven. It's difficult to be sure. One of the things my mother did to hide us was change my birth date. Different names, a year or two added or taken away on our ages. I was nearly eighteen when we stuck with Whittier. He'd been dead for years, and I told her I needed to stay one person now. I needed to start my life. So we kept it, and I know she worried herself sick because of that.'

Paranoid old bat, Trevor thought. 'Why do you suppose he came to see you there and then? Wouldn't that have been around the time of the heist? The diamonds?'

'Keeping tabs on me, tormenting her. I can still hear him telling her he could find her wherever she ran, that he could take me from her whenever he wanted. I can still hear her crying.'

'But to come then.' Trevor pushed. 'Of all times. It could hardly have been a coincidence. He must have wanted something. Told you something, or told her.'

'Why does this matter?'

He'd plotted it out carefully. Just because he found his father foolish didn't mean he didn't know how the man worked. 'I've given this a lot of thought since you first told me. I don't mean to argue with you, but I suppose it's upset me to realize, at this point in my life, what's in my blood.'

'He's nothing to you. Nothing to us.'

'That's just not true, Dad.' Sorrowfully, Trevor shook his head. 'Didn't you ever want to close the circle? For yourself, and for her? For your mother? There are still millions of dollars of those diamonds out there, and he had them. Your father had them.'

'They got nearly all of them back.'

'*Nearly?* A full quarter was never recovered. If we could piece things back together, if we could find them, we could close that circle. We could work a way to give them back, through this writer – this Samantha Gannon.'

'Find the diamonds, after over fifty years?' Steve would have laughed, but Trevor was so earnest, and he himself so touched that his son would think about closing that circle. 'I don't see how that's possible.'

'Aren't you the one who tells me constantly that anything's possible if you're willing to work for it? This is something I want to do. I feel strongly about it. I need you to help me put it back together. To remember exactly what happened the last time he came to see you, to remember exactly what happened next. Did he ever contact you from prison? You or my grandmother? Did he ever give you anything, send you anything, tell you anything?'

'Steve?'

Steve looked over as he heard his wife's voice. 'Let's put this away for now,' he said quietly. 'Your mother knows all about this, but I don't like dragging it out. Down here, Pat. Trevor's dropped by.'

'Trevor? Oh, I'll be right down.'

'We need to talk about this,' Trevor insisted.

'We will.' Steve gave his son a nod and an approving smile. 'We will, and I'll try to remember anything that may help. I'm proud of you, Trevor, proud of you for thinking about trying to find a way to make things right. I don't know if it can be, but knowing you want to try means the world to me. I'm ashamed I never thought of it myself. That I never thought beyond putting it all away and starting fresh instead of cleaning the slate.'

Trevor kept his annoyance behind a pleasant mask as he heard his mother hurrying downstairs. 'I haven't been able to think of much else for weeks.'

He left an hour later and strolled along in the steamy heat rather than hail a cab. He could count on his father to line up details. Steve Whittier was hell on details. But the visit had already given him his next move. He'd play concerned grandson the very next day and go see his grandmother in the loony bin.

About the time Trevor Whittier was crossing the park, Eve stifled a yawn. She wanted another hit of coffee, but knew that would mean getting through Roarke. He had a habit of knowing when her ass was dragging before she did.

'Three potentials on the woman, twice that on the kid.' She scratched her scalp, hard, to get the blood moving.

'If we discount the rest of the first-level matches.'

'I'm discounting them. The computer likes these picks, so we go with them. Let's move on the kid – man now. See if anything looks good.'

She shot those six images on screen and began to scan the attached data. 'Well, well, lookie here. Steven James Whittier, East Side address. Owns and runs his own building company. That's a nice pop for me.'

'I know him.'

She looked around sharply. 'You know this guy?'

'Mostly in that vague professional sense, though I've met his wife a number of times at various charity functions. His company has a solid rep, and so does he. Blue-collar him, meets blue-blood her. He does good work.'

'Check the lists from the job sites you got earlier. Let's see if Whittier's got anything going in or around Alphabet City.'

Roarke brought up the file, then leaned back in his chair. 'I should learn not to question your instincts.'

'Rehab on Avenue B. Five-story building, three sections.' She pursed her lips, made a popping sound. 'More than enough to take a closer look. See there, he's got a son. One son, Trevor, age twenty-nine. Let's get that image.'

Roarke did the tech, and they studied Trevor Whittier's face together. 'Not as close on the artist rendering as I'd like, but it's not a total bust. Let's see what else we can find out about Trevor.'

'You can't do anything about him tonight. It's nearly one in the morning. Unless you think you can build a case strong enough with this to go over and scoop him up and into a cage, you're going to bed. I'll set the computer to gather data while you get a few hours' sleep.'

'I could go wake him up, hassle him.' She considered. 'But that would just be for fun. And it would give him a chance to whine for a lawyer. It can wait.' She pushed to her feet.

'Until morning. We'll check out this job site, see if we can nail it to the trace from Cobb's body. I need to approach Whittier and find his mother, interview her, too. They might be in on this. This Trevor feels the best to me. Smarter to wait to move on him until I have it all lined up.'

'While it lines up, you lie down.'

She'd have argued, but her eyes were starting to throb. 'Nag, nag, nag. I'll just contact the team and tell them we're going to brief at seven hundred instead of eight.'

'You can do that in the morning. It's easier, and more humane.'

'Yeah, but it's more fun to do it now,' she protested as he took her hand and pulled her out of the room. 'This way I get to wake them up so they have to work at getting back to sleep. The other way, I just get them out of bed a little early.'

'You're a mean one, Lieutenant.'

'Yeah. So?'

Chapter Twenty-Eight

While she slept it all played in her head. Father to son, murder and greed, blood gleaming on sparkling stones. There were legacies you couldn't escape, no matter how fast or how far you ran.

She could see herself, a child, with no mother to panic or protect. No one to hide her or stand as a shield. She could see herself – she could always see herself – alone in a freezing room with the light washed red from the sign blinking, blinking, blinking from the building next door.

She could taste her fear when he came in, that bright, metallic flavor. As if there was already blood in her throat. Hot blood against the chill.

Children shouldn't fear their fathers. She knew that now, in some part of her restless brain, she knew that. But the child knew nothing but fear.

There had been no one to stop him, no one to fight for her when his hand had slashed out like a snake. No one to protect her when he'd torn at her, torn into her. There'd been no one to hear her scream, to beg him to stop.

Not again, not again. Please, please, not again.

She'd had no one to run to when the bone in her arm had snapped like a twig broken under a careless foot. She'd had only herself, and the knife.

She could feel the blood flooding over her hands, her face, and the way his body had jerked when she'd hacked that blade into his flesh. She could see herself smeared with it, coated with it, dripping with it, like an animal at the kill. And even in sleep,

398

she knew the madness of that animal, the utter lack of humanity.

The sounds she made were vile. Even after he was dead, the sounds she made were vile.

She struggled, jabbing, jabbing, jabbing.

'Come back. Oh God, baby, come back.'

Panic and protection. Someone to hear, to help. Through the madness of memory, she heard Roarke's voice, scented him and curled up tight in the arms he'd wrapped around her.

'Can't.' Couldn't shake it off. There was so much blood.

'We're here. We're both right here. I've got you.' He pressed his lips to her hair, her cheek. 'Let it go, Eve. Let it go now.'

'I'm cold. I'm so cold.'

He rubbed his hands over her back, her arms, too afraid to leave her even for the time it would take to get up for a blanket. 'Hold onto me.'

He lifted her into his lap, rocking her as he would a child. And the shudders that racked her gradually eased. Her breathing steadied.

'I'm okay.' She let her head fall limply on his shoulder. 'Sorry.' But when he didn't loosen his hold, when he continued to rock, she closed her eyes, tried to drift into the comfort he needed as much as she.

Still, she saw what she'd been, what she'd done. What she'd become in that horrible room in Dallas. Roarke could see it. He lived it with her through her nightmares.

Burrowing against him, she stared off into the dark again and wondered if she could bear the shame if anyone else caught a glimpse of how Eve Dallas had come to be.

Peabody loved briefings at Eve's home office. However serious the business, there was always an informal atmosphere when you added food. And a breakfast meeting not only meant real coffee, but real eggs, real meat and all manner of sticky, sugary pastries.

And she could justify the extra calories because it was work-related fuel. There was, in her opinion, no downside to the current situation.

They were all loaded in – Feeney, McNab, Trueheart, Baxter, Dallas, even Roarke. And boy, oh boy, a look at Roarke in the morning was as delicious a jolt to the system as the strong black coffee sweetened with honest-to-God sugar.

It was hardly a wonder the lieutenant was so slim. She had to burn up the calories just looking at him. Considering that, Peabody snatched a couple extra slices of bacon and calculated she might actually *lose* weight during the briefing.

It was a pretty good deal.

'Updates are in your packs,' Eve began, and Peabody divided her attention between her plate and her partner.

Eve leaned on the corner of her desk, coffee in one hand, laser pointer in the other. 'Feeney and our civilian made some progress last night, as did McNab. McNab, give the team your data.'

He had to swallow, fast and hard, a mouthful of Danish. 'Sir. My area deals with the 'links and d and c's from both vics.'

He ran through it, pinpointing transmission locations, with considerable comp-jock code. The jargon, and the questions and comments Feeney tossed him in the same idiom gave Eve time to finish her coffee and contemplate another cup.

'You'll scout those locations this morning,' Eve put in when there was a short lull. 'With these images. Screen One. This is Steven Whittier. Current data leads us to believe he is the son of Alex Crew. On Screen Two you see Trevor Whittier, son of Steven Whittier and likely the grandson of Crew. Given accumulated data and the profile, he fits. Steven Whittier is the founder and current owner of Whittier Construction.'

'That's a nice little pop,' Baxter commented.

'Bigger and louder one as we've determined Whittier Construction is the contractor on a major rehab job, building on Avenue B. The company is licensed for four gasoline storage facilities. None of the other potential matches have as many links as this. Steven Whittier's official data states his father is deceased. His mother . . .'

She split the screen and brought up the image of a woman known as Janine Strokes Whittier. 'Currently residing at Leisure Gardens, a retirement and care facility on Long Island, where Whittier senior has a second home. She's in the right age group, has the right racial profile and matches the computer morphs.'

'Will we bring the Whittiers in to interview, Lieutenant?' Peabody asked.

'Not at this time. We've got circumstantial and supposition. It's good circumstantial and supposition, but it's not enough to push the PA for a warrant. It's not enough to arrest much less convict. So we get more.'

'Trueheart and I can take the images, toss in a couple more and show them to the waitress. She picks out one of these guys,' Baxter said, 'we've got more.'

'Do it. McNab, find me somebody at the transmission sources who remembers seeing one or both of these men. Feeney, I need you to dig back. If Janine and Steven Whittier went by other names previous to this, I want them.'

'You'll get them,' he told her and scooped up a mouthful of eggs.

'Peabody and I will head to this job site first, match the trace and do a sweep. If Cobb was killed there, there'll be blood. I want witnesses, I want physical evidence. We lock it down, then we pull them in. Roarke, I'm counting on your security to keep Samantha Gannon and her family safe under wraps until we nail this.'

'It's done.'

'Sir.' Like any well-disciplined student, Trueheart raised his hand. 'Detective Baxter and I could go by the hotel and show Ms. Gannon the images. She might recognize one or both of these men. If so, it could give us another link.'

'That's good thinking, Trueheart. Do the legwork. Let's build this case tight.' She glanced toward the board, and the victims. 'Nobody else is going to die over a bunch of fucking rocks.'

When the team began to disperse, Roarke ran a fingertip along Eve's shoulder. 'A moment, Lieutenant?'

'Half a moment.' With her mind on dovetailing points of the investigation, she trailed after him into his office.

He closed the door, then, cupping his hands under her elbows, lifted her to the toes of her boots and took her mouth in a short and heated kiss.

'Jeez!' She dropped back to the flat of her feet with a thud. 'What is *wrong* with you?'

'Had to get that out of my system. Something about watching you take command just gets me started.'

'Watching grass grow gets you started.' She turned toward the door, but he slapped a hand on it. 'Do the words "obstruction of justice" ring a bell?'

'Several. And though a quick bout of obstruction might be entertaining, that's not what I had in mind. I have some things to deal with this morning, but some of the day can be shuffled around.'

'If Feeney wants you on board for the e-work, that's between you and him.'

'He has his teeth in it now. I don't imagine he needs me to chew through the rest. But you might want me along when you speak to Steven Whittier.'

'Why?'

'Because he knows me. And from what I know of him, he couldn't have had a part in what was done to those women. Not knowingly.'

'People can do a lot of things that are out of character when they're blinded by bright, shiny stones.'

'Agreed. Another reason you might want me along. I know a bit about that sort of thing.' He drew the chain from under her shirt so the teardrop diamond he'd once given her sparkled between them. 'I've known people who've killed for them. I'll know if he has. They're just things to you. You wear this for me. That's its only value to you.'

He smiled a little as he slid it under her shirt again. 'If I'd given you a hunk of quartz, it would mean the same.'

'He may not have done it for the diamonds, not directly, but to protect himself and his family. Samantha Gannon knows things about him that aren't in the book. Things no one outside that group formed a half century ago knows. Who he is, who he comes from. People kill for that, too.'

402

'Is this line of thinking what brought on your nightmare?'

'I don't know. Maybe this line of thinking came out of it. On the surface, Whittier's built a good, decent life. But it's often what's under the surface that drives people. He has a lot to lose if it comes out – who his father was, what he did, that Steven Whittier is a figment.'

'Is that what you think?' He touched her, a hand to her cheek, a cheek pale from a restless night. 'Because the name was given to him along the way instead of at the beginning, it isn't real?'

'It's not what I think, it's what he thinks that matters.'

Now he framed her face. 'You know who you are, Eve.'

'Most of the time.' She lifted a hand, laid it on his wrist. 'You want to come along because of the nightmare. You'd already worked it out that I was making correlations with myself on this. I won't deny I have, but it doesn't get in the way of the job.'

'I didn't think it would.'

'I'll think about it. I'll contact you and let you know.' She turned toward the door, then back. 'Thanks.'

'You're welcome.'

The building on Avenue B was a beauty. Or as she was told by the cooperative job foreman, the three buildings being turned into one multipurpose complex was a beauty. The old brick had already been blasted clean of grime and soot and graffiti so the color glowed muted rose.

She doubted that would last long.

The lines were clean and straight, with the beauty in the simplicity of form.

'Damn shame the way it was let go,' was foreman Hinkey's opinion as he walked them inside the entrance of the middle building. 'Useta be apartments and such, and the basic structures held up. But, jeemaneze, you shoulda seen the guts of the place. Torn to shit and back. Wood rotted out, floors sagging, plumbing out of the freaking Ice Age. You had your cracked drywall and your busted windows. Some people just got no respect for buildings, you know?'

403

'Guess not. You lock the place down tight when the crew's not here?'

'Damn straight. You got your vandals and your looters and your sidewalk sleepers, your assholes looking for a place to screw around or deal.' He shook his head, adorned with a dusty Whittier gimme cap. 'We got a lot of equipment in here, not to mention the supplies. Steve – Mr. Whittier – he don't stint on security. He runs a class operation.'

She didn't know about class, but she knew about noise. Inside there was plenty of it.

'Lot of space,' she commented.

'Five floors, three buildings. You got round about eighteen thousand square, not counting rooftop area. Gonna be a mix of residential and business. Keeping as much of the original structures and features we can salvage, and we'll install new where we can't, keeping the original style.'

'Yeah. This much space, three buildings, there's a lot of ways in and out. A lot to cover.'

'We got a central security system, and individual backups on each building.'

'Who's got the codes?'

'Ah, that'd be Steve, myself, head carpenter, assistant foreman and the security company.'

'You can give those names to my partner. We'd like to look around.'

'You going any farther than this, you gotta have your hard hat and goggles. That's the law.'

'No problem.' Eve took the canary-yellow construction hat and the safety glasses. 'Can you show me where you've used the flame sealant?'

'Damn near all the subflooring's been sealed.' He scratched his chin. 'You want, we can start here, work our way through. But I'm telling you, nobody coulda gotten in here after hours.'

'It's my job to check it out, Hinkey.'

'Gotta do what you gotta.' He jerked a thumb and began to wind his way around equipment. 'This here's commercial space.

Probably lease it to a restaurant. This here floor's been sealed up. Had to rip out what was left of the original. New flooring's not installed yet, just the sub and seal.'

Eve took the scanner out of her field kit and ran a standard for blood trace. Gauging the size of the building, the time it would take to scan each area of flooring, she straightened from her crouch.

'Can you do me a favor, Hinkey? How about you get somebody to take my partner through the next building while you and I go through this one? We'll hit the third after that. Save us all some time and trouble.'

'Whatever you want.' He took a two-way off his belt. 'Yo, Carmine. Need you floor one, building two.'

They divided into teams, and Eve moved from area to area on the first floor. After a while she was able, for the most part, to tune out the noise. Buzzing and whirling, the sucking of compressors and the smack of air guns.

The voices of the crew came in a variety of accents. Brooklyn and Queens, Hispanic and street jive. She filtered it out, along with the music each section selected as background tunes. Trash rock, tinny country, salsa, rap.

Because he was giving her time and no hassle, she listened to Hinkey's running commentary on the job progress and details with half an ear.

He droned on about climate controls, inspections, electrical and filter systems, walls, trims, labor, plumbing. Her brain was jammed with it by the time they hit the second floor.

He nattered on about windows, framing, stopped off to chew out a laborer and to consult with another crew member on specs. It gave Eve hope she'd shake him off, but he caught up with her before she made it to the third level.

'Apartments up here. Give people a decent place to live. Fact is, my daughter's getting married next spring. She and the guy, they've already put in for this unit right here.'

Eve glanced over in time to see him look a bit baffled and sentimental. 'Be nice for them, I guess. And I know the place is built good. Solid.' He rapped a hand on the wall. 'None of that toothpick-and-glue shit some of these places use when they slap one of these old buildings back together. Steve, he takes pride.'

'You worked for him long?'

'Seventeen years this October. He ain't no fly-by-night. Knows his building, too. Works side by side with you in a crunch.'

She found a few drops of blood, discounted it as she had in other areas. Not enough. And you put a bunch of people together with a bunch of tools, a little blood was going to spill.

'He spend much time on this job?'

'Oh yeah. Biggest we've had. Worked his ass off to get this bid, and he's by here every day.'

He walked with her out of the unit, down the hall formed by studded walls.

'How about his son?'

'What about him?'

'He put in time?'

Hinkey snorted derisively, then caught himself. 'Works in the office.'

Eve paused. 'You don't like him much.'

'Not for me to say, one way or the other.' Hinkey lifted a beefy shoulder. 'I'll just say he don't take after his old man, not that I see.'

'So he doesn't come around.'

'Been here once or twice, maybe. Doesn't take much interest. Suit-and-tie type, you know?'

'Yeah, I know.' She stepped over a stack of some sort of lumber product. 'Would he have the access codes?'

'Don't see why he would.'

'Boss's son.'

Hinkey's shrug was his response.

Her ears were ringing, her head pounding by the time they hit the fourth floor. She decided she'd have asked for ear protectors if she'd known how bad it would get. It seemed to her that the tools had gone to scream level here. She eyed, with some respect, a large, toothy saw run by a man who looked to weigh in at a hundred pounds flat.

406

She gave it a wide berth, flipped on the scanner.

And hit the mother lode.

'What the fuck is that – beg pardon.'

'It's a hell of a lot of blood, Hinkey.' She ran the scanner over the floor, revealing a bright blue pattern along the floor, splattered on the wall. 'One of your men cut off an appendage with that saw up here?'

'Jesus Christ, no. Lieutenant, I don't see how that could be blood.'

But she could. Just as she could see the smear of it running down the hall. Where Tina Cobb had tried to crawl.

He'd walked through it, she noted, squatting down for a better look. He'd left some prints, and wasn't that handy?

So had Cobb, she saw. Handprints, bloodied. Tried to pull herself up the wall, used it for support and pressed her hand there, there.

He'd taken his time with her, Eve was sure of it. He'd let her crawl, limp, stumble the entire length of the fourth-floor corridor before he delivered the death blow.

'Can't be blood.' Hinkey stared at the blue, shaking his head slowly from side to side. 'We'd've seen it. Jeezopetes, you couldn'ta missed it.'

'I need this area cleared. I've got to ask you to get your crew out of this building. This is a crime scene.' She took out her communicator. 'Peabody? I've found her. Fourth floor.'

'I've gotta . . . I gotta call the boss.'

'You do that, Hinkey. Tell him to be available, at his home, in an hour.' Eve turned to him, felt a pang of sympathy as she saw the horror in his eyes. 'Get your crew out of this building and call Whittier. I want to talk to him.'

In under an hour, the construction noise had been replaced by cop noise. Though she didn't have much hope of picking up more evidential trace, she had a team of sweepers spread throughout the building. A crime-scene unit took images of the hand- and foot-prints, and with their tech magic extracted microscopic blood traces for DNA match.

She'd already matched the index fingerprint on the wall to the prints on file for Tina Cobb.

'I know you're going to say it's just cop work, Dallas, just step-by-step investigation, but it's just short of miraculous we were able to nail this scene.'

Peabody studied the blood patterns, boldly blue under the scanners set on tripods.

'Another few weeks, maybe days, they'd have set the floor, covered the walls. He picked a good spot for this.'

'Nobody to see her, hear her,' Eve stated. 'Easy enough to get her inside, dozens of reasons he could've used. There's plenty of pipe for the murder weapon, tarps to wrap her body in to transport it. He'd get the gas first. Have that in the transfer vehicle. He got in here, he could access the gas. We'll follow up there. There'll be records of what's stored or purchased through the Whittier account.'

'I'll get on that.'

'Do it on the way. Let's go see Whittier.'

She didn't want him on scene, not yet. She wanted this first contact in his home, where a man felt most comfortable. And where a man, guilty or innocent, tended to feel most uneasy when confronted with a badge.

She didn't want him surrounded by his employees and friends.

He opened the door himself, and she saw a sleepless night on his face that was layered over now with what might have been shock and worry.

He extended a hand to her in what she took as the automatic manners of a man raised to be polite. 'Lieutenant Dallas? Steve Whittier. I don't know what to think, what to say. I'm not taking this in. Hinkey thinks there's been some mistake, and I'm inclined to agree. I'd like to get down to the site and—'

'I can't allow that, at this time. Can we come in?'

'What? Oh, yes. Sorry. Excuse me. Ah . . .' He gestured, stepped back. 'We should sit down.' He scrubbed a hand over his face. 'Somewhere. In here, I think. My wife's out, but I expect her back

408

soon. I don't want her to walk in on this. I'd rather try to tell her
. . . Well.'

He walked them into his den, held out his hands to chairs. 'Would
you like something? Something to drink?'

'No. Mr. Whittier, I'm going to record this interview. And I'm
going to give you your rights.'

'My . . .' He sank into a chair. 'Give me a minute, will you?
Am I a suspect in something? Should I . . . Do I need a lawyer?'

'You have a right to a lawyer or a representative at any time
during this process. What I want is to get a statement from you,
Mr. Whittier. To ask you some questions.' She set a recorder in
plain view on the table and recited the revised Miranda. 'Do you
understand your rights and obligations in this matter?'

'Yes, I guess I do. That's about all I do understand.'

'Can you tell me where you were on the night of August twenty-
third?'

'I don't know. Probably here at home. I need to check my book.'

He rose to go to the desk for a sleek little day calendar. 'Well,
I'm wrong about that. Pat and I had dinner out with friends. I
remember now. We met at about seven-thirty at the Mermaid. It's
a seafood place on First Avenue between Seventy-first and Second.
We had drinks first, then took the table about eight. Didn't get
home until around midnight.'

'The names of the people you were with?'

'James and Keira Sutherland.'

'And after midnight?'

'I'm sorry?'

'After midnight, Mr. Whittier, what did you do?'

'We went to bed. My wife and I went to bed.' He flushed when
he said it, and the expression reminded her of Feeney's embarrassment when he'd realized what she and Roarke had been up to
on their recreational break.

She deduced Whittier and wife had indulged in some recreation
before sleep.

'How about the night of August twenty-first?'

'I don't understand this.' He muttered it, but checked his book.

'I don't have anything down. A Thursday, a Thursday,' he said, closing his eyes. 'I think we were home, but I'd have to ask Pat. She remembers these things better than I do. We tend to stay home most evenings. It's too hot to go out.'

He was a lamb, she thought, innocent as a lamb, just as he'd been at seven. She'd have bet the bank on it. 'Do you know a Tina Cobb?'

'I don't think . . . the name's a little familiar – one of those things you think you've heard somewhere. I'm sorry. Lieutenant Dallas, if you could just tell me what's going on, exactly what's . . .' He trailed off.

Eve saw on his face the minute the name clicked for him. And seeing it, she knew she'd been right in betting the bank. This man had had no part in splattering the girl's blood.

'Oh my sweet Jesus. The girl who was burned, burned in the lot a few blocks from the site. You're here about her.'

Eve reached in her bag, just as the bell rang at the door. Roarke, she thought. She'd made the right choice in contacting him after all. Not to help her determine Whittier's involvement, but to give the man someone familiar in the room when she pushed him about his son.

'My partner will get the door,' she said, and took Tina's photo out of the bag. 'Do you recognize this woman, Mr. Whittier?'

'God, yes, oh God. From the media reports. I saw her on the reports. She was hardly more than a child. You think she was killed in my building, but I don't understand. She was found burned to death in that lot.'

'She wasn't killed there.'

'You can't expect me to believe anyone on my crew would have a part in something like this.' He glanced up, confusion running over his face as he got to his feet. 'Roarke?'

'Steve.'

'Roarke is a civilian consultant in this investigation,' Eve explained. 'Do you have any objection to his presence here at this time?'

'No. I don't—'

'Who has the security codes to your building on Avenue B?'

'Ah. God.' Steve pressed a hand to his head a moment. 'I have them, and the security company, of course. Hinkey, ah . . . can't think straight. Yule, Gainer. That should be it.'

'Your wife?'

'Pat?' He smiled weakly. 'No. No point in that.'

'Your son?'

'No.' But his eyes went blank. 'No. Trevor doesn't work on sites.'

'But he's been to that building?'

'Yes. I don't like the implication here, Lieutenant. I don't like it at all.'

'Is your son aware that his grandfather was Alex Crew?'

Every ounce of color drained from Steve's cheeks. 'I believe I'd like that lawyer now.'

'That's your choice.' Standing as shield, Eve thought. Instinct. A father protecting his son. 'More difficult to keep certain facts out of the media once the lawyers come into it, of course. Difficult to keep your connection to Alex Crew and events that transpired fifty years ago out of the public stream. I assume you'd prefer if certain details of your past remained private, Mr. Whittier.'

'What does this have to do with Alex Crew?'

'What would you do to keep your parentage private, Mr. Whittier?'

'Nearly anything. Nearly. The fact of it, the fear of it has ruined my mother's health. If this is exposed, it might kill her.'

'Samantha Gannon's book exposed quite a bit.'

'It didn't make the connection. And my mother doesn't know about the book. I can control, somewhat, what she hears about. She needs to be protected from those memories, Lieutenant. She's never hurt anyone, and she doesn't deserve to be put on display. She's not well.'

'I've no intention of doing that. I don't want to have to speak to her, to force her to speak to me about any of this.'

'You want to shield your mother,' Roarke said quietly. 'As she shielded you. But there are prices to be paid, Steve, just as she paid them in her day. You'll have to speak for her.'

'What can I tell you? For God's sake, I was a child the last time I saw him. He died in prison. He's nothing to do with me, with any of us. We *made* this life.'

'Did the diamonds pay for it?' Eve wondered, and his head snapped around, insult plain on his face.

'They did not. Even if I knew where they were, I wouldn't have touched them. I used nothing of his, want nothing of his.'

'Your son knows about them.'

'That doesn't make him a killer! That doesn't mean he'd kill some poor girl. You're talking about my *son*.'

'Could he have gotten access to the security codes?'

'I didn't give him the codes. You're asking me to implicate my son. My child.'

'I'm asking you for the truth. I'm asking you to help me close the door your father opened all those years ago.'

'Close the circle,' Steve mumbled and buried his face in his hands. 'God. God.'

'What did Alex Crew bring you that night? What did he bring to the house in Columbus?'

'What?' With a half laugh, Steve shook his head. 'A toy. Just a toy.' He gestured to the shelves, and the antique toys. 'He gave me a scale-model bulldozer. I didn't want it. I was afraid of him, but I took it because I was more afraid not to. Then he sent me upstairs. I don't know what he said to my mother in the next few minutes, other than his usual threats. I know I heard her crying for an hour after he left. Then we were packing.'

'Do you still have the toy?'

'I keep it to remind me what he was, what I overcame thanks to my mother's sacrifices. Ironic really. A bulldozer. I like to think I razed and buried the past.' He looked over to the shelves, then, frowning, rose. 'It should be here. I can't remember moving it. Odd.'

Antique toys, Eve mused while Whittier searched. Gannon's ex had antique toys in his office and an advance copy of the book.

'Does your son collect this sort of thing, too?'

'Yes, it's the one thing Trevor and I shared. He's more interested

412

in collector's values, more serious about it than I from that standpoint. It's not here.'

He turned, his face was sheet-white now and seemed to have fallen in on itself. 'It doesn't mean anything. I must have misplaced it. It's just a toy.'

Chapter Twenty-Nine

'Could it have been moved?' Eve studied the shelves. She had a vague sort of idea what a bulldozer looked like. Her knowledge of machines was more finely tuned to urban style. The maxibuses that belched up and down the avenues, the airjacks that tore up the streets in the most inconvenient places at the most inconvenient times, the droning street-cleaning units, the clanking recycler trucks.

But she recognized models of old-fashioned pickup trucks and service vans, and a shiny red tractor, not unlike the one she'd seen on Roarke's aunt's farm recently.

There were toy replicas of emergency vehicles that were boxier, clunkier to her eye than what zipped around the streets or skies of New York. And a number of bulky trucklike things with scoops or toothy blades or massive tubes attached.

She didn't see how Whittier could be sure what was missing, or what was where. To her eye, there was no rhyme or reason to the collection, but a bunch of little vehicles with wheels or wings or both cobbled together as if waiting for a traffic signal to turn green.

But he was a guy, and her experience with Roarke told her a guy knew his toys very well.

'I haven't moved it. I'd remember.' Steve was searching the shelves now, touching various vehicles or machines, scooting some along. 'I can't think why my wife would either, or the housekeeper.'

'Do you have any of this sort of thing elsewhere on the premises?' Eve asked him.

'Yes, a few pieces here and there, and the main collection upstairs in my office, but . . .'

'Why don't you take a look? Peabody, could you give Mr. Whittier a hand?'

'Sure. My brothers have a few model toys,' Peabody began as she led Steve out of the room. 'Nothing like what you've got here.'

Eve waited until their voices had faded. 'How much is this kind of deal worth?' She waved her thumb toward the shelves as she turned to Roarke.

'It's a bit out of my milieu, but antique, nostalgic, novelty collections of any kind have value.' He picked up a small, beefy truck, spun the wheels. The quick smile confirmed Eve's theory that such matters were indeed guy things. 'And the condition of the pieces add to it. These are all prime, from what I can see. You're thinking the toy's been lifted.'

'Strong possibility.'

He set the truck down but didn't release it until he'd pushed it gently back and forth. 'If Trevor Whittier stole it from his father, if the diamonds were indeed hidden inside it – and that's where you're heading?'

'Past heading. I'm there. I don't think you should be playing with those,' she added when he reached for the tractor.

He made a sound that might have been disappointment or mild embarrassment, then stuck his hands in his pockets. 'Then why kill? Why break into Samantha's house? Why not be toasting your good fortune in Belize?'

'Who says he knows they're in there?' She watched Roarke lift a brow. 'Look at his profile. He's a lazy, self-centered opportunist. I'm betting if Whittier does a check of his collection, he'll find several of the better pieces missing. Stupid bastard might just have sold them, and the diamonds along with them.'

She wandered up and down the shelves, scanning the toys. 'Samantha Gannon's ex has a collection.'

'Does he now?' Roarke nodded. 'Does he, really?'

'Yeah. Not as extensive as this, at least not the collection I saw in his office. Put Trevor Whittier together with the ex.' She put the tips of her index fingers together. 'Point of interest, antique toys and games. Gannon's ex had an advance copy of the book, and might very well have talked about it.'

'Intersections,' Roarke said with a nod. 'It really is a small little world, isn't it? The ex buys pieces from Whittier's son, or at least knows him, socializes perhaps, shares this interest. Because of that, he mentions the book, talks it up. Samantha's grandmother owned an antique store. I believe she still does. Another sort of intersection, another common thread that might've prompted a conversation.'

'Worth checking. I want an all-points out on Trevor Whittier. I want to sweep him up and into Interview, and I want a damn warrant to search his place. All of that's going to take some fast talking.' She frowned toward the doorway. 'What do you think? Will Whittier keep quiet, or will he try to warn Trevor we're looking for him?'

'I think he'll try to cooperate. That would be his first instinct. Do the right thing. He won't consider, or believe, his son's a murderer. It won't be in his scope. In trouble, yes, in need of help. But not a cold-blooded killer. If he begins to think in that direction, I don't know what he might do.'

'Then let's keep him busy as long as we can.'

She called Baxter and Trueheart in to handle Whittier. They'd accompany him to his downtown offices, where he kept a few pieces of his collection.

'I need you to wait for the wife,' Eve directed Baxter. 'Keep her with you. I don't want either of them to have the opportunity to contact the son. Let's keep him out of this mix as long as we can. We get some luck, and we pick him up before he knows we're looking for him.'

'How long do you want them wrapped up?'

'Try to get me a couple hours. I need to get a warrant for Whittier junior's place, and I want to get to Chad Dix. I'm going to send a couple uniforms out to Long Island, where Whittier's mother's living. Just to be safe.'

'We'll stall. Maybe he'll let us play with the fire truck.'

'What is it with guys and little trucks?'

416

'Come on, you had your dollies and tea parties.' A lesser man would have shrunk under her withering stare. 'Okay, maybe not.'

'Keep them wrapped,' Eve ordered as she started out. 'If it starts to unravel, I want to hear about it.'

'Yeah, yeah. I bet this sucker has a working siren.'

Eve heard the high-pitched scream of it as she passed into the foyer. 'Excuse my idiot associate, Mr. Whittier. We appreciate your cooperation.'

'It's fine. I want this straightened out.' He managed a smile. 'I'll just go and . . .' He gestured toward his den. 'I'll just make sure the detective doesn't . . .'

'Go right ahead. You're waiting for the wife,' Eve said in an undertone to Trueheart. 'If the son happens by, keep him here, contact me.'

'Yes, sir.'

'Peabody, with me.'

'No place I'd rather be.' Peabody glanced at Roarke. 'You coming with us?'

'I doubt the lieutenant has use for me at the moment.'

'I'll probably get around to you.'

'My hope eternally springs.'

She paused on the sidewalk. 'If you want to stay available, I'll let you know when we have Trevor in custody.'

'I appreciate it. Meanwhile, I could do a little search among known collectors and see if a piece fitting the description has been on the market in the last few months.'

'That'd cover some bases. Appreciate it. Let's get the commander to wheedle a warrant for us. I want to talk to Chad Dix. Proving a connection there adds a couple of bars to the cage.'

Roarke lifted Eve's chin with his hand – a gesture that had her wincing, and Peabody wandering discreetly away. 'You're very steely-minded on this one, Lieutenant.'

'No touching on the job,' she muttered and nudged his hand aside. 'And I'm always steely-minded.'

'No. There are times you run on guts and wear yourself out emotionally, physically.'

'Every case is different. This one's by the stages. Unless Trevor's figured it all out by now, he's not a particular threat to anyone. We'll have his parents under wraps, and I'm sending a couple of uniforms to keep tabs on the grandmother's place. We've got Gannon protected. Those are his most obvious targets. I'm not dealing with wondering who some psycho's going to kill next. Puts a little more air in my lungs, you know?'

'I do.' Despite her earlier warning, he touched her again, rubbing a thumb along the shadows under her eyes. 'But you could still use a good night's sleep.'

'Then I'll have to close this down so I can get one.' She hooked her thumbs in her front pockets, sighed heavily because she knew it would amuse him. 'Go ahead, get it over with. Just make it quick and no tongues allowed.'

He laughed, as she'd expected, then leaned down to give her a very chaste kiss. 'Acceptable?'

'Hardly even worth it.' And the quick gleam in his eye had her slapping a hand on his chest. 'Save it, pal. Go back to work. Buy a large metropolitan area or something.'

'I'll see what I can do.'

At Eve's signal, Peabody stepped up to the car. 'It must really set you up, having a man like that look at you the way he does every day.'

'At least it doesn't keep me off the streets.' She slid in, slammed her door. 'Let's cook this bastard and maybe we can both get home on time for a change.'

Trevor detested visiting his grandmother. The concept of age and illness disgusted him. There were ways, after all, to beat back the worst symptoms of the aging process. Face and body sculpting, youth treatments, organ transplants.

Looking old was, to his mind, a product of laziness or poverty. Either was unacceptable.

Illness was something to be avoided at all costs. Most physical ailments were temporary and easily rectified. One simply had to take proper care. Mental illness was nothing but an embarrassment to anyone associated with the patient.

He considered his grandmother a self-indulgent lunatic, overly pampered by his father. If so much time and money wasn't wasted making her comfortable in her mad little world, she'd straighten up quickly enough. He knew very well it cost enormous amounts of money – his inheritance – to keep her in the gilt-edged loony bin, to pay for her housing, her food, her care, her meds, her attendants.

Pissed away, he thought, as he drove his new two-seater Jetstream 3000 into the underground parking facility at the rest home. The crazy old bat could easily live another forty years, drooling his inheritance, what was rightfully his, away.

It was infuriating.

His father's sentimental attachment to her was equally so. She could have been seen to, decently enough, in a lesser facility, or even a state-run project. He paid taxes, didn't he, to subsidize those sort of facilities? What was the *point* of not using them since he was paying out the nose for them in any case?

She wouldn't know the damn difference. And when he was in charge of the purse strings, she damn well would be moved.

He took a white florist box out of the trunk. He'd take her the roses, play the game. It would be worth his time and the investment in the flowers she'd forget ten minutes after he gave them to her, if she knew anything. If by some miracle she remembered knowing anything.

It was worth a shot. Since the old man seemed to know nothing, maybe his crazy old mother had some lead buried in her fogged brain.

He took the elevator up to lobby level, gearing himself up for the performance. When he stepped off, he wore a pleasant, slightly concerned expression, presenting the image of a handsome young man paying an affectionate duty call on an aged and ailing relative.

He moved to the security desk, setting the box of flowers on the counter so the name of the upscale city florist could be read by the receptionist. 'I'd like to see my grandmother. Janine Whittier? I'm Trevor. I didn't call ahead as it's an impulse visit. I was passing the florist's and I thought of Grandma and how much she loves

419

pink roses. Next thing I knew I was buying a dozen and heading here. It's all right, isn't it?'

'Of course!' The woman beamed at him. 'That's so sweet. I'm sure she'll love the flowers nearly as much as she'll love seeing her grandson. Just let me bring up her schedule and make certain she's clear for visits today.'

'I know she has good days and bad days. I hope this is a good one.'

'Well, I see here she's been checked into the second-floor common room. That's a good sign. If I could just clear you through.' She gestured toward the palm plate.

'Oh, sure. Of course.' He laid his hand on it, waited while it verified his identification and his clearance. Ridiculous precautions, he thought. Who in hell would want to break into an old people's home? It was the sort of thing that added several thousand a year to the tab.

'There you are, Mr. Whittier. I'll just scan these.' She ran a handheld over the roses to verify the contents, then gestured. 'You can take the main staircase to the second floor, or the elevator if you prefer. The common area is to the left, down the hall. You can speak to one of the attendants on duty. I'm sending up your clearance now.'

'Thank you. This is a lovely place. It's such a comfort to know Grandma's being so well looked after.'

He took the stairs. He saw others, carrying flowers or gifts wrapped in colorful paper. Staff wore what he assumed were color-coded uniforms, all in calming pastels. In this unrestricted area, patients wandered, alone or with attendants. Through the wide, sunny windows he could see the extensive gardens below, with the winding paths where more patients, attendants, visitors strolled.

It amazed him, continuously, that people would work in such a place, whatever the salary. And that those who weren't paid to be here would visit, voluntarily, on any sort of regular basis.

He himself hadn't been inside the place for nearly a year and sincerely hoped this visit would be the last required of him.

As he glanced at the faces he passed he had a moment's jolt that

420

he wouldn't recognize his grandmother. He should have refreshed his memory before the trip out, taken a look at some photographs.

The old all looked the same to him. They all looked doomed. More, they all looked useless.

A woman being wheeled by reached out with a clawlike hand to snatch at the ribbon trailing from the florist's box.

'I love flowers. I love flowers.' Her voice was a pipe tooting out of a wizened face that made Trevor think of a dried apple. 'Thank you, Johnnie! I love you, Johnnie!'

'Now, Tiffany.' The attendant, a perky-looking brunette, leaned over the motorized chair, patted the ancient woman on the shoulder. 'This nice man isn't your Johnnie. Your Johnnie was just here yesterday, remember?'

'I can have the flowers.' She looked up hopefully, her bony hand like a hook in the ribbon.

Trevor had to battle back a shudder, and he shifted to prevent that hideously spotted hand from making contact with any part of him. 'They're for my grandmother.' Even as bile rose in his throat, he smiled. 'A very special lady. But . . .' Under the pleased and approving eye of the attendant, he opened the box, took out a single pink rosebud. 'I'm sure she wouldn't mind if you had one.'

'That's so kind of you,' the attendant responded. 'There you are now, Tiffany, isn't that nice? A pretty rose from a handsome man.'

'Lots of handsome men give me flowers. Lots of them.' She stroked the petals and lost herself in some blurry memory.

'You said you were here to see your grandmother?' the attendant prompted.

'Yes, that's right. Janine Whittier. They told me downstairs she was in the common room.'

'Yes, she is. Miss Janine's a lovely lady. I'm sure she'll be glad to see you. If you need any help, just let me know. I'll be back shortly. I'm Emma.'

'Thank you.' And since he couldn't be sure Emma wouldn't be useful, he braced himself and leaned down to smile in the old woman's face. 'It was nice to meet you, Miss Tiffany. I hope to see you again.'

'Pretty flowers. Cold eyes. Dead eyes. Sometimes shiny fruit's rotted at the core. You're not my Johnnie.'

'I'm sorry,' Emma whispered, and wheeled the old woman away.

Hideous old rag, Trevor thought and allowed himself that shudder before he walked the rest of the way into the common room.

It was bright, cheerful, spacious. Areas were sectioned off for specific activities. There were wall screens set to a variety of programs, tables arranged for game playing, visiting, crafts, seating areas for visiting as well, or for passing the time with books or magazines.

There were a number of people in attendance, and the noise level reminded him of a cocktail party where people broke off into groups and ignored the talk around them.

When he hesitated, another attendant, again female, came over. 'Mr. Whittier?'

'Yes, I . . .'

'She's doing really well today.' She gestured toward a table by a sunny window where two women and a man appeared to be playing cards.

He had a moment's panic as he wasn't certain which woman was his grandmother, then he saw that one of them wore a skin cast on her right leg. He'd have been told, endlessly, if his grandmother had injured herself.

'She looks wonderful. It's such a comfort to know how well she's being taken care of, and how content she is here. Ah, it's such a nice day – not as hot as it was. Do you think I could take her out into the gardens for a walk?'

'I'm sure she'd enjoy it. She'll need her medication in about an hour. If you're not back, we'll send someone out for her.'

'Thank you.' Confident now, he strolled over to the table. He smiled, crouched. 'Hi, Grandma. I brought you flowers. Pink roses.'

She didn't look at him, not even a glance, but kept her focus on the cards in her bony hands. 'I have to finish this game.'

'That's all right.' Stupid, ungrateful bitch. He straightened, holding the box of flowers as he watched her carefully select and play a card.

'Gin!' the other old woman called out in a surprisingly strong, steady voice. 'I beat the pants off you again.' She spread out her hand on the table and had their male companion swearing.

'Watch that language, you old goat.' The winner turned in her chair to study Trevor as the man carefully counted points. 'So you're Janine's grandson. First time I've seen you. Been here a month now, and haven't seen you visit. I'm only in for six weeks.' She patted the skin cast. 'Skiing accident. My granddaughter comes in every week, like clockwork. What's wrong with you?'

'I'm very busy,' he said coldly, 'and I don't believe it's any of your concern.'

'Ninety-six my last birthday, so I like to make everything my concern. Janine's son and daughter-in-law come in twice a week, sometimes more. Too bad you're so busy.'

'Come on, Grandma.' Ignoring the busybody, Trevor laid his hands on the back of Janine's chair.

'I can walk! I can walk perfectly well. I don't need to be dragged around.'

'Just until we get outside, in the gardens.' He wanted her out, and quickly, so he laid the white box across her lap and aimed her chair toward the doorway. 'It's not too hot out today, and nice and sunny. I bet you could use the fresh air.'

Despite the cleanliness of the place, the floods of money that went into maintaining it, all Trevor could smell was the decay of age and sickness. It turned his stomach.

'I haven't finished counting my points.'

'That's all right, Grandma. Why don't you open your present?'

'I'm not scheduled for a walk in the gardens now,' she said, very precisely. 'It's not on my schedule. I don't understand this change.' But her fingers worried the top off the box as he steered her into the elevator.

'Oh, they're lovely! Roses. I never had much luck with roses in the garden. I always planted at least one rosebush wherever we were. Remember, honey? I had to try. My mother had the most beautiful rose garden.'

'I bet she did,' Trevor said without interest.

'You got to see it that once.' She was animated now, and some of the beauty she'd once claimed shone through. Trevor didn't see it, but he did notice the pearl studs at her ears, the expensive shoes of soft cream-colored leather. And thought of the waste.

She continued to gently stroke the pink petals. Those who saw them pass saw a frail old woman's pleasure in the flowers, and the handsome, well-dressed young man who wheeled her.

'How old were you, baby? Four, I think.' Beaming, she took one of the long-stemmed beauties out of the box to sniff. 'You won't remember, but I do. I can remember so clearly. Why can't I remember yesterday?'

'Because yesterday's not important.'

'I had my hair done.' She fluffed at it, turning her head side to side to show off the auburn curls. 'Do you like it, baby?'

'It looks fine.' He decided, on the spot, that even millions in diamonds wouldn't induce him to touch that ancient hair. How old was the bag of bones anyway? He did the math, just to occupy his mind, and was surprised to realize she was younger than the bitch at the card table.

Seemed older, he decided. Seemed ancient because she was a lunatic.

'We went back, that one time we went back.' She nodded her head decisively. 'Just for a few hours. I missed my mother so much it nearly broke my heart. But it was winter, and the roses weren't blooming, so you didn't get to see them again.'

She laid a rosebud against her cheek. 'I always planted a garden, a flower garden wherever we went. I had to try. Oh, it's bright!' Her voice quivered as he pushed the chair outside. 'It's awfully bright out here.'

'We'll go into the shade in just a minute. Do you know who I am, Grandma?'

'I always knew who you were. It was hard, so hard for you to keep changing, but I always knew who you were, baby. We kept each other safe, didn't we?' She reached back, patted her hand on his.

'Sure.' If she wanted to think he was his father, that was fine.

424

Better, in fact. They had a link between them unlike any other. 'We kept each other safe.'

'Sometimes I can barely remember. It goes in and out, like a dream. But I can always see you, Westley. No, Matthew. No, no, *Steven*.' She let out a relieved breath as she latched onto the name. 'Steven now, for a long time now. That's who you wanted to be, so that's who you are. I'm so proud of my boy.'

'Do you remember the last time he found us? My father? Do you remember the last time you saw him?'

'I don't want to talk about that. It hurts my head.' And her head swiveled from side to side as he wheeled her down the path, away from others. 'Is it all right here? Are we safe here?'

'Perfectly safe. He's gone. He's dead, long dead.'

'They *say*,' she whispered, and it was clear she wasn't convinced.

'He can't hurt you now. But you remember that last time he came? He came at night, to the house in Ohio.'

'We'd think we were safe, but he'd come. I'd never let him hurt you. Doesn't matter what he does to me, even when he hits me, but he won't touch you. He won't hurt my baby.'

'Yes. Yes.' Jesus, he thought, get *over* it. 'But what about that last time, in Ohio? In Columbus.'

'Was that the last time? I can't remember. Sometimes I think he came but it was a dream, just a bad dream. But we had to go anyway. Couldn't take a chance. They said he was dead, but how could they know? He said he'd always find you. So we had to run. Is it time to run again?'

'No. But when we were in Columbus, he came. At night. Didn't he?'

'Oh God, he was just there. There at the door. No time to run. You were scared, you held my hand so tight.' She reached back again, squeezed Trevor's hand until the bones rubbed together. 'I wouldn't leave you with him, not even for a minute. He'd snatch you away if he could. But he didn't want you, not yet. One day, he'd tell me. One day I'd look around and you'd be gone. I'd never find you. I couldn't let him take you away, baby. I'd never, never let him hurt you.'

'He didn't.' Trevor ground his teeth with impatience. 'What happened the night he came to the house in Columbus?'

'I'd put you to bed. Frodo pajamas. My little Lord of the Rings. But I had to wake you up. I don't know what he'd have done if I'd refused. I brought you downstairs, and he gave you a present. You liked it, you were just a little boy, but still, you were frightened of him. "Not to play with," he said, "but just to keep. One day it might be worth something." And he laughed and laughed.'

'What was it?' Excitement danced up Trevor's spine. 'What did he give me?'

'He sent you away. You were too young to interest him yet. "Go back to bed, and mind what I say. Keep it with you." I can still see him standing there, smiling that horrible smile. Maybe he had a gun. He might've. He might've.'

'Keep what?'

But she was beyond him, she was back fifty years into the fear. 'Then it was just the two of us. Alone with him, and he put his hand on my throat.'

She reached up with her own as her breath stuttered. 'Maybe this would be the time he'd kill me. One day he'd kill me, if I didn't keep running. One day he'd take you away from me, if we didn't hide. I should go to the police.'

She balled a fist, thumped it on the box. 'But I'm too afraid. He'll kill us, kill us both if I go to the police. What could they do, what? He's too smart. He always said. So it's better to hide.'

'Just tell me about that night. That one night.'

'That night. That night. I don't forget. I can forget yesterday, but I never forget. I can hear him inside my head.'

She put her hands to her ears. 'Judith. My name was Judith.'

Time was running out, he thought. They'd come looking for her soon, to give her medication. Worried that they'd come sooner if anyone saw her having her little fit, or heard her sniveling, he pushed the chair farther down the path, deeper into the shade.

He forced himself to touch her, to pat her thin shoulder. 'Now, now. That doesn't matter. Just that one night matters. You'll feel better if you tell me about that one night. I'll feel better, too,' he added, inspired. 'You want me to feel better, don't you?'

'I don't want you to worry. Oh baby, I don't want you to be afraid. I'll always take care of you.'

'That's right. Tell me about the night, the night in Ohio, when he came and brought me a present.'

'He looked at me with those horrible cold eyes. Go ahead and run, run all you want, I'll just find you again. If the boy didn't have the present with him when he found us again, he'd kill both of us. No one would ever find us. No one would ever know. If I wanted to stay alive, if I wanted the boy to stay alive, I'd do exactly what he said. So I did. I ran, but I did what he said in case he found us again. Did he come back? In my dreams he kept finding us.'

'What did he bring, damnit?' He gave the chair a vicious shake, then came around to shove his face close to hers. 'Tell me what he brought.'

Her eyes went wide and glassy. 'The bulldozer, the bright yellow bulldozer. Kept it in the box, years and years in the box like a secret. You never played with it. Then you put it on your shelf. Why did you want it on the shelf? To show him you'd done what he told you?'

'Are you sure?' He gripped her shoulders now, the frail frame with its thin and brittle bones. 'Are you goddamn sure?'

'They said you were dead.' Her color went gray, her breath short and harsh. 'They said you were dead, but you're not. I knew, I knew you weren't dead. I see you. Not a dream. You came back. You found us again. It's time to run. I won't let you hurt my baby. Time to run.'

She struggled, and her color went from gray to dangerously red. Trevor let her shove him back, and watched dispassionately as she gained her feet. The roses spilled out of the box, strewn over the path. Eyes wild, she set off in a hitching run. Then she stumbled, fell like a limp doll into the colorful flowers and lay still in the streaming sun.

Chapter Thirty

Eve faced the same receptionist at Dix's offices, but the procedure moved along at a much brisker pace. The woman took one look at Eve crossing the lobby and came to attention in her chair.

'Detective Dallas.'

'Lieutenant.' Eve held up her badge to refresh the woman's memory. 'Clear me for Chad Dix's level.'

'Yes, of course. Right away.' Her gaze skimmed back and forth from Eve's face to Peabody's as she cleared security. 'Mr. Dix's office is on—'

'I know where it is,' Eve interrupted and strode to the elevator.

'Does it feel good to strike fear in the hearts of all people?' Peabody wondered. 'Or does it feel just?'

'It feels good and just. You'll get there one day, Peabody.' Eve gave Peabody's shoulder a bolstering pat. 'You'll get there.'

'It's my life's ambition, sir.' They stepped in. 'You're not figuring Dix is part of this.'

'Guy hides a fistful of diamonds in a toy truck where they've potentially sat for half a century? Nothing would surprise me. But no, Dix lacks imagination. If he has the thing, or has knowledge of its location, it's probably a fluke. If Dix knew about the diamonds and wanted more info, he'd have stuck to Samantha Gannon, played Romeo and pumped her for more data instead of twiddling his thumbs while she broke it off. No need for Tina Cobb as he had access to Gannon's place and could've conducted a dozen searches while they were still an item.'

'She wouldn't have told him about Judith and Westley Crew, even if they'd stayed an item.'

'No. Samantha's a stand-up. Gives her word, keeps it. Dix, though, he's a whiner. The book took Samantha's focus off him, so he's annoyed with the book. She gets media play and cocktail talk about it, so he's annoyed with her. The diamonds, as far as he's concerned, are nothing but a fluffy fantasy, and they inconvenienced him. But he's the direct link between Trevor Whittier and the Gannons. He's the twist of fate that brought it to a head.'

They walked off the elevator where the perky assistant was waiting. 'Lieutenant, Detective. I'm sorry, Mr. Dix isn't in the office at this time. He had an outside meeting and isn't expected back for another hour.'

'Contact him, call him in.'

'But—'

'Meanwhile, I need his office.'

'But—'

'You want me to get a warrant? One that has your name on it along with his, so you can both spend a few hours downtown on this bright, sunny day?'

'No. No, of course I don't. If you could just give me some idea of the nature of business you—'

'What was the nature of my business last time?'

The woman cleared her throat, glanced at Peabody. 'She said murder.'

'Same goes.' Without waiting for assent, Eve headed in the direction of Dix's office. The assistant scrambled at her heels.

'I'll allow you inside, but I insist on being present the entire time. I can't just give you free rein. Mr. Dix deals with a great deal of confidential material.'

'I'm just here to play with his toys. Call him in.'

The woman unlocked the doors, then marched directly to Dix's desk to use his 'link to make the call. 'He isn't answering. It's transferring to his voice mail. Mr. Dix, this is Juna. Lieutenant Dallas is in the office. She insists on speaking to you right away.

429

If you could return my call ASAP and let me know how you want to proceed. I'm calling from your office 'link. Don't touch that!'

Her voice spiked as Eve reached out for one of the mechanical trucks. Even the cool stare Eve shot over her shoulder didn't penetrate.

'I mean it, Lieutenant. Mr. Dix's collection is very valuable. And he's very particular about it. You may be able to have me taken down to the precinct or station house or whatever you call it, but he can fire me. I need this job.'

To placate the woman, Eve hooked her thumbs in her back pockets. 'Any of these things a bulldozer, Peabody?'

'That little one there.' Peabody used a jerk of her chin to point. 'But it's too small, and it's red. Doesn't fit Whittier's description.'

'What about this?' Eve reached out, stopping just an inch from touching as the assistant's breath caught on a thin scream.

'That's a – what do you call it – cougar? Mountain lion? Bobcat!' she exclaimed. 'It's called a bobcat, and don't ask me why. And there's a pumper thingee – fire truck – and, way iced, an off-planet shuttle and an air-tram. See, he's got them set up in categories. Farm machines, air transports, ground transports, construction equipment, all-terrains. Look at all the little pedals and controls. Aw, look at the little hay baler. My sister has one on her farm. And there's little farm people to ride it.'

Okay, maybe it wasn't just a guy thing. 'That's real sweet. Maybe we should just sit on the floor here and play with all the pretty toys instead of spending our time trying to catch the mean old murdering bastard.'

'Just looking,' Peabody said under her breath. 'To ascertain that the object in question is not in this location.'

Eve turned to the assistant. 'This the lot?'

'I don't know what you mean.'

'Is this the whole of Mr. Dix's collection?'

'Oh no. Mr. Dix has one of the most extensive collections in the country. He's been collecting since he was a child. This is just a sampling; he keeps the most valuable at his home. He's even

430

loaned some of the rarer pieces to museums. Several of his pieces were included in a show at the Met two years ago.'

'Where is he?'

'As I said, he has an outside meeting. He should be back—'

'Where?'

Now the assistant sighed. 'He's lunching with clients at The Red Room, on Thirty-third.'

'He calls in, you tell him to stay where he is.'

Dix had already finished his meeting and was enjoying a post-lunch martini. He'd been pleased to see Trevor's name pop on his 'link ident as the meeting had been winding down. And delighted to stretch the tedious business lunch into an entertaining personal meeting.

Enough that he'd ignored the call from his office. He deserved a break after the morning he'd put in.

'Couldn't have timed it better,' he told Trevor. 'I was stuck with a couple of stuffy old-liners with more money than imagination. I spent ninety minutes listening to them whine about taxes and brokerage fees and the state of the market.' He sampled a fat, gin-soaked olive.

Technically, his rehabilitation forbade alcohol. But hell, a martini wasn't Zoner or poppers, for God's sake. And, as Trevor had pointed out, he deserved a small indulgence. 'I'm more than ready for a break.'

They sat in the dark-paneled, red-cushioned bar of the restaurant. 'Didn't have a chance to talk to you much at the dinner party the other night. You left early.'

'Family business.' Trevor shrugged and sipped at his own martini. 'Duty call on the old man.'

'Ah. I know how that goes. Did you hear about this mess with Samantha? I wasn't able to talk about anything else all night. Everyone was pestering me for details.'

Trevor schooled his face into a puzzled blank. 'Samantha?'

'My ex. Samantha Gannon.'

'Oh. Sure, sure. Long redhead. You split?'

'Ancient history. But the cops come to my office, female storm trooper bitch. Samantha's out of town, book tour. You remember that, right? The book she wrote about that old diamond heist and her family?'

'It's all coming back to me. Fascinating really.'

'It gets more. While she's gone, somebody breaks into her place and kills her friend. Andrea Jacobs. Hot number.'

'Christ, what a world.'

'You said it. A damn shame about Andrea. You had to like her. The cops are all over me.' The faint pride in the tone had Trevor smiling into his drink.

'Over you? Don't tell me the morons thought you had anything to do with it.'

'Apparently. They call it routine, but I was this close to calling a lawyer.' He lifted his hand, putting his thumb and forefinger together. 'Later, I hear Samantha's cleaning girl got herself killed, too. You can bet I'm going to have come up with an alibi for that one, too. Idiot cops. Jesus, I didn't even know Sam's cleaning girl. Besides, do I look like some psycho? You must've heard about all this. It's all over the news.'

'I try not to watch that sort of thing. Depressing, and it has nothing to do with me. Want another?'

Dix glanced at his empty glass. He shouldn't, really. But . . . 'Why the hell not? You're behind.'

Trevor signaled for another drink for Dix, smiled as he lifted his barely touched martini. 'I'll catch up. What does Samantha have to say about all this?'

'I haven't been able to talk to her. Can you beat that? She's gone incommunicado. Nobody knows where the hell she is.'

'Somebody must,' he countered.

'Not a damn soul. Smart money says the cops got her stashed somewhere.' Scowling, he nudged his empty glass aside. 'Probably get another damn book out of it.'

'Well, she'll surface soon enough. Meanwhile, I wanted to talk to you about a piece I sold you a few months ago. The scale-model bulldozer, circa 2000.'

'Beautiful piece, prime condition. I don't know how you parted with it.' He grinned as he counted down the time to the second drink with a few cocktail nuts. 'Even for the price you scalped me for.'

'That's just the thing. I had no idea when I sold it that it was given to my father by his father. When I saw him the other night, the old man brought it up. Sentimental blah, blah, blah. He wants to come over and see it, among some of the others. I didn't have the heart to tell him I'd sold it.'

'Well . . .' Dix picked up his fresh drink. 'You did.'

'I know, I know. I'll buy it back for the full price, and add a kicker. I don't want a big, ugly family crisis over it so it's worth it to me.'

'I'd like to help you out, Trev, but I really don't want to sell it.'

'Look, I'll double what you paid me for it.'

'Double.' Dix's eyes gleamed over the rim of his glass. 'You must really want to avoid a family crisis.'

'It pays to keep the old man happy. You know about his collection.'

'And envy it,' Dix admitted.

'I can probably talk him out of a couple of pieces.'

Considering, Dix bit an olive off his swizzle stick. 'I'm looking for a well driller. Circa 1985. The article they did on him in *Scale-Model Mag* said he had one, primo.'

'I'll get it for you.'

Dix made a sound somewhere between interest and denial. Trevor curled his hand into a fist, imagined ramming it over and over into that smug face until the blood poured.

He'd wasted enough time.

'Okay, then do me a favor. Let me borrow it for a week. I'll pay you a thousand for the use of it, and I'll get the well driller, make you a good deal on it.' When Dix said nothing, just continued to sip gin, Trevor felt his control fray. 'For fuck's sake, you make a grand for nothing.'

'Don't get twisted. I didn't say no. I'm just trying to figure your angle. You don't even like your father.'

'I can't stand the stupid son of a bitch, but he's not well. He may only have a few months left.'

'No shit?'

Going with the idea, Trevor shifted on his seat, leaned in. 'He finds out I sold that piece, he's going to blow. As it stands, I inherit the collection. He finds out about this, he'll probably leave it to some museum. That happens, I won't be able to sell you any of the prime pieces, will I? I lose, you lose, friend.'

'When you put it that way . . . One week, Trev, and we're going to write this up. Business is business, especially when it's between friends.'

'No problem. Finish your drink and we'll go get it now.'

Dix checked his wrist unit. 'I'm really late getting back to the office.'

'So you'll be later *and* a thousand richer.'

Dix lifted his glass in a toast. 'Good point.'

Eve's communicator signaled as she hunted for a parking spot on Thirty-third. 'Dallas.'

'Baxter. We got a hitch here.'

'Doesn't anybody use public transportation or just stay the hell home!' Annoyed with the traffic, the jammed curb, she whipped over, flipped up her on duty light and ignored the blasts of horns. Double-parked, she jerked a thumb at Peabody to get out. 'What hitch?'

'Just got a call from the care facility where Whittier's mother's living. She fell or passed out. Took a header into a flower bed.'

'She bad?' Eve asked as she climbed over to get out curbside rather than risk life and limb getting out the driver's-side door.

'Banged up her head, from what I'm getting, maybe fractured her elbow. They got her stabilized and sedated, but Whittier and his wife both want to go see for themselves.'

'Let them go, have a couple of uniforms you pick take them and stick with them.'

'There's more. Here's the kicker. She wasn't outside strolling down the garden path alone. Her grandson paid her a visit.'

434

'Son of a bitch. Is he with her now?'

'Bastard walked off, left her lying there. Didn't tell anybody. He signed in, Dallas. Signed in, brought her flowers, talked to a couple of the attendants. He knew there was a record of him being there, but he took off. The uniforms you sent out missed him by a good half hour.'

'I want the place locked down, searched.'

'Already in progress.'

'Left himself open.' She swung into the restaurant. 'He knows what he's looking for now and where to find it. He doesn't care about leaving tracks. You'll need to take the Whittiers, handle the scene there. I've got a line on something here. I'll get back to you.'

'He left her lying there,' Peabody repeated.

'She's lucky he didn't take the time or trouble to finish her. He's got the prize in his sights. He'll move fast now. Chad Dix,' she said to the restaurant hostess. 'Where's his table?'

'I beg your pardon?'

'Don't bother, I'm in a hurry.' Eve slapped her badge on the podium. 'Chad Dix.'

'Could you be any more indiscreet?' the hostess demanded and pushed the badge back at Eve.

'Oh yeah. Want to see?'

The hostess touched a section on her reservation screen. 'He was at table fourteen. It's been turned over.'

'Get me his server. Damnit.' Stepping to the side, Eve yanked out her 'link and called Dix's office. 'Did he come back?'

'No, Lieutenant, he's running a little late. He hasn't returned my call as yet.'

'When and if, I want to hear immediately.' Eve broke the connection and turned to the young, brutally clean-cut waiter. 'Did you see Dix, table fourteen, leave?'

'Table for three, two of them left together about a half hour ago. One guy – guy who paid – took a call right as the meal was winding up. Excused himself. He walked over toward the rest rooms. I heard him say he'd meet somebody in the bar in ten. Sounded happy about it.'

'This bar?'

'Yeah. I saw him go over, get a table.'

'Thanks.'

Eve worked her way through the tables into the bar section, scanned the area. She snagged a waitress's elbow. 'There was a guy in here. Around thirty. About six feet, one-eighty, dark hair, medium complexion, poster-boy looks.'

'Sure. Gin martini, extra dry, three olives. You just missed him.'

'Was he with anyone?'

'Long, lean dream machine. Dark blond hair, great suit. Nursed half a martini to the other guy's two. Left together maybe five, ten minutes ago.'

Eve turned on her heel and charged for the door. 'Get Dix's home address.'

'Already on it,' Peabody told her. 'Do you want to pull Baxter and Trueheart back?'

'No, take too long to get them back, dump the Whittiers.' Eve dove into the car, swung her long legs over. 'This could turn into a hostage situation in a finger snap.'

'We can't be sure they're heading for Dix's home address.'

'It's best guess. Tag Feeney and McNab. We'll call for more backup if it turns ugly.' Since she was hemmed in by traffic, she jammed the vehicle into a straight vertical, smacked sirens and peeled out into a one-eighty six feet off the ground. 'Upper East, isn't it?'

'Yeah, I got it here. Goddamn sucky navi system.' Peabody cursed, rapped her fist on the dash and had the map shuddering into place across the windshield.

'You're making progress, Detective.'

'Learned from the best. Sixth is your best bet. Jeez, watch the glide cart.'

She missed it by a good two inches, and used the in-dash to contact Roarke. 'Suspect is believed to be heading to Chad Dix's residence, with Dix,' she began without preamble. 'We believe he's learned the location of the diamonds. Baxter and Trueheart are halfway to Long Island with the Whittiers. Feeney and McNab

436

are being tagged. Depending on how this shakes, I might be able to use a security expert, even a civilian. You're closer than Feeney.'

'What's the address?'

Peabody called it out and grabbed onto the chicken stick on her door. 'ETA's five minutes, unless we end up a smear on the pavement prior to that.'

'I'll be there.'

Eve punched it up Sixth, weaving around vehicles with drivers too stubborn or too stupid to make way for the sirens. She was forced to slam the brakes to avoid mowing down a mob of pedestrians who surged into an intersection at the walk sign.

They streamed by, ignoring the scream of sirens and the vicious blast of cursing she poured out her open window. Except for one grizzled old man who took the time to give her the finger.

'God love New Yorkers,' Peabody commented when her heart kicked back to beating again. 'They just don't give a shit.'

'If I had time, I'd get Traffic to haul in every last one of those *jerks.* Goddamn it!' She rammed for vertical again, but this time the car only shuddered, shook an inch off the ground and dropped again with a thump.

'We'll be clear in a minute.'

'He's going to get him inside. He's going to get him inside the apartment. Once he does . . .'

Uptown, Trevor paid off the cab in cash. It occurred to him on the way up with Dix babbling a bit drunkenly beside him that he might not be able to get out of the city, out of the country immediately and he'd already left too much of a trail.

The cops had already interviewed and dismissed good old Chad, so they were unlikely to bother with him again anytime soon. But there wasn't any point in leaving a credit trail in a cab to Dix's front door.

This was smarter. Fifteen minutes, twenty, he'd walk out with millions. He'd stroll right by the doorman and down the block, catch a cab and pick up his car from the lot on Thirty-fifth.

He needed time to get back to his own place, pick up his pass-
port and a few essentials. And he wanted a few minutes, at least
a few, to admire the diamonds in the privacy of his own home.
After that, he'd vanish. Simple enough.

He'd planned all of it already. He'd vanish, not unlike Samantha
Gannon had done the last few days, but with a great deal more
style.

A private shuttle to Europe, where he'd rent a car with a forged
ID in Paris and drive himself to Belgium and a gem dealer he'd
found through the underground. He had more than enough money
for that leg of the trip, and once he'd sold some of the diamonds,
he'd have plenty more for the rest.

Another transaction in Amsterdam, a trip to Moscow for a third.

Crisscrossing his way from point to point, using various identi-
fications, selling off the gems here and there – never too many at
a time – until, in six months perhaps, they were liquified and he
could live the life he'd always deserved to live.

He'd require some face sculpting, which was a shame as he liked
his face quite a bit. But sacrifices had to be made.

He had his eye on an island in the South Seas where he could
live like a king. Like a fucking god, for that matter. And there was
an exciting and palatial penthouse on the sumptuous off-planet
Olympus Resort that would suit him very well as a pied-à-terre.

He would never, never have to pay lip service to the rules again.
Never have to kowtow to his sniveling parents, pretend an interest
in his mother's obnoxious relatives or spend all those tedious hours
every week in some box of an office.

He'd be free, as he was meant to be free. Claiming his rightful
legacy at long, long last.

'Damn office again.'

Trevor tuned in to see Dix frowning at his beeping pocket 'link.

'Screw them.' Trevor laid a restraining hand on Dix's. 'Let them
wait.'

'Yeah, screw them.' With the gin sliding through his bloodstream,
Dix chuckled, dropped the 'link back in his pocket. 'I'm so damn
indispensable, I'll have to up my fees.'

He strolled into the building beside Trevor. 'In fact, I think I'll take the rest of the day off. Let somebody else run on the wheel for a while. You know, I haven't had a vacation in three months. Fricking nose to the fricking grindstone.'

He used his passcode to access the elevator. 'You know how it is.'

'That's right.' As Trevor stepped into the elevator with him, his heart began to trip lightly in his chest.

'Dinner party tonight. Jan and Lucia. You going to make that?'

It all seemed so petty to him now, so bland, so *small*. 'Bored.'

'I hear that. Gets so it's the same thing, day after day. Same people, same talk. But you've got to do something. Could use a little excitement though, something different. Something unexpected.'

Trevor smiled as they stepped off the elevator. 'Careful what you wish for,' he said and laughed and laughed as Dix unlocked his door.

Eve screeched to a stop outside Dix's building. She was out of the car with her badge held up before the doorman could sputter an objection.

'Chad Dix.'

'He just came in. About ten minutes ago, with a companion. I'm afraid you can't park—'

'I'm going to need a blueprint of the building and of the apartment.'

'I can't help you with—'

She cut him off simply by holding up a hand, and looked over as Roarke pulled up. 'I need the blueprints, and I need your security to shut down the elevators, block the stairwells on every floor. Roarke.' She jerked her head, knowing he'd get results quicker. 'Talk the talk. Peabody, let's get that backup.'

She yanked out her communicator to contact her commander and apprise him of the situation.

By the time she was finished, she was ready to confer with McNab and Feeney in the security office. The diagram of the building was up on screen.

'We send a uniform up to the other units on this floor. We determine what other tenants are in residence and move them out quick
and quiet. Then we lock down the floor again. Make that happen,'
she said to Peabody.

'Yes, sir.'

'Emergency evac in Dix's unit, here.' She tapped a finger on the
screen. 'Can that be sealed from this location?'

'Sure.' Feeney jerked a thumb toward McNab to put him on that
detail.

'He won't be going anywhere,' Eve stated. 'Got him locked, got
him boxed. But that doesn't help Dix. We wait and Whittier remains
unaware of our presence, maybe he just walks out, but odds are
he kills Dix, takes his prize, then tries to walk. That's his style,
that's his pattern. We move in, we've got a civilian in the crosshairs.
We let Whittier know we're here and he's sealed in, he's got a
hostage.'

'Has to be alive to be a hostage.'

She met Feeney's gaze. 'Yeah, but he doesn't have to stay that
way. Big place,' she continued, studying the diagram of the apartment. 'Chad's got himself a big-ass place. No telling where they
are in it.'

'They came in chummy,' Feeney reminded her. 'Maybe he takes
the toy, leaves Dix alive.'

She shook her head. 'Self-preservation comes first. Dix is too
big a risk, so he has to eliminate him. Easier to do it now. He's
killed twice before and gotten away clean.'

To better absorb the whole of it, she stepped back from the
screen. 'We seal it up, we seal it up tight. Isolate him. Let's go
with decoy first. Delivery. See if we can get Dix to open the door.
He opens it, we get him out, move in. He doesn't, we assume he's
dead or incapacitated and we take the door.'

She pushed at her hair. 'We work on getting eyes and ears in
there, but we try the decoy now. This turns into a hostage situation, you take the negotiations?' she asked Feeney.

'I'll get it set up.'

'Okay, somebody get me a package. McNab, you're playing

messenger. I want three of the tactical team up, positioned here, here, here.' She tapped the screen again. 'Feeney, security and the coms are on you. McNab, let's move.'

She looked at Roarke. 'Can you ditch the locks on the door without letting anyone inside know?'

'Shouldn't be a problem.'

'Okay.' She rolled her shoulders. 'Let's rock.'

Chapter Thirty-One

Inside the apartment, Dix suggested another drink. 'Since I'm blowing off the day, I might as well make it worthwhile.'

Calculating, Trevor watched him get out a martini shaker. The doorman had seen him come inside. Security disks would show him entering. If he needed a little extra time, it might be wise to set the stage for an accident. Alcohol in the bloodstream, a slip in the bathroom? He could and would be gone before they found the body. Gain a little more of a buffer while they investigated what would appear, on the surface, to be a drunken fall.

My God, he was clever. Wouldn't his grandfather be proud?

'Wouldn't say no to a drink. I'd really like to see the piece.'

'Sure, sure.' Dix waved him off while he mixed drinks.

He could send a text message from Dix's 'link to his office, Trevor decided. Set it to transmit ten minutes after he left the building. Security and the doorman would both verify his exit if need be, and the message would appear – until they dug deeper – to have been sent by Dix himself, alive and well, and alone in his apartment.

God was in the details.

He could knock him out, anywhere, then cart him into the bath, angle him, let him fall so that his head hit the corner of the tub, say.

Bathrooms were death traps, after all.

'What's the joke?' Dix asked as Trevor began to laugh.

'Nothing, nothing. Little private moment.' He took the glass. His prints wouldn't matter. In fact, all the better that they show up on a glass. Nice, companionable drink with a friend. Not trying to hide a thing.

'So, what's wrong with your father?'

'He's an anal-retentive, stiff-necked, disapproving asshole.'

'A little harsh, seeing as he's dying.'

'What?' Trevor cursed himself as he remembered. 'Being dead doesn't change what he is. I'm not playing the hypocrite over it. Sorry he's sick and all that, but I've got to live my own life. Old man's already had his, such as it is.'

'Jesus.' With a half laugh, Dix drank. 'That's cold. I've got issues with my father. Hell, who doesn't? But I can't imagine just shrugging it off if I knew he was going to kick. Pretty young for taking the slide, isn't he?' He squinted as he tried to remember. 'Can't have hit even seventy yet. Guy's just cruising into his prime.'

'He hasn't ever been prime.' Because it amused him, Trevor spun out the tale. Lying was nearly as fun as cheating, and cheating came very close to stealing. Killing didn't give quite the same rush. It was so damn messy. It was more of a needs-to-be-done kind of chore. But he was beginning to believe he'd enjoy ending Dix.

'Some genetic deal,' he decided. 'His mother passed it to him. Son of a bitch probably passed it to me. Some brain virus or happy shit. He'll go loony before he kicks. We'll have to put him away in some plush cage for mental defectives.'

'God, Trevor, that's really rough.' A glimmer of the man Samantha Gannon had enjoyed eked through the haze of gin. 'I'm sorry. Really sorry. Look, forget the money. I didn't know it was something like this. I wouldn't feel right taking money for the loan when you've got all this on your head. Just to keep it clean, I'll draw up a paper, a receipt, but I can't take any money for it.'

'That's big of you, Chad.' It got better and better. 'I don't want to trade on sympathy.'

'Look, forget it. Your father's got a sentimental attachment to the piece, I get that. I'm the same way myself. I couldn't enjoy owning it if I thought about him being upset, under the circumstances, that it was sold off. When, ah, the rest of the collection comes to you, and you want to unload any of it, just keep me in mind.'

'That's a promise. Hate to cut this short, but I really should get moving.'

'Oh, sure.' Dix drained the last of his drink, set the glass aside. 'Come on back to the display room. You know, the reason I took this apartment was for this room. The space, the light. Samantha used to say I was obsessed.'

'She's your ex, what do you care what she used to say?'

'Miss her sometimes. Haven't found anyone else who interests me half as much as she did. Talk about obsessions.' He stopped, blocking the doorway. 'She got so wrapped up in that book she couldn't think about anything else. Didn't want to go out, barely noticed if I was around. And what's the big deal? Just a rehash of family stories, and that bullshit about diamonds. Who cares? Could it be more yesterday?'

Yes, Trevor thought, it would be a pleasure to kill this tedious moron. 'You never know what'll juice the unwashed masses.'

'You're telling me. The thing's selling like it was the new word of the Lord. You were pretty interested,' he remembered. 'Did you ever read that copy I passed you?'

'Scanned through it.' Another reason to snip this thread, he reminded himself. And quickly. 'It wasn't as compelling as I'd thought it would be. Like you said, it's yesterday. I'm a little pressed for time now, Chad.'

'Sorry, sidetracked.' He turned toward the wide etched-glass door. Through it Trevor could see the floating shelves, the glossy black cabinets all lined or filled with antique toys and games. 'Keep it locked and passcoded. Don't trust the cleaning service.'

The lock light continued to blink red, and the computer's voice informed him he'd entered an incorrect passcode.

'That's what I get on three martinis. Hold on a sec.'

He reentered while Trevor stood vibrating behind him. He'd spotted the shining yellow bulldozer, parked blade-up on a wide, floating shelf.

'You're going to need a box for it,' Dix commented as he rekeyed.

444

'I keep some stored in the utility closet off the kitchen. Some padding there, too.'

He paused, leaned on the glass door until Trevor imagined bashing his head against it. 'You're going to have to promise to return it in the same condition, Trev. I know your father's careful, and you've got a decent collection yourself, so you know how important it is.'

'I won't be playing in the dirt with it.'

'I actually did that when I was a kid. Can't believe it now. Still have a couple of trucks and one of the first model air-buses. Bunged up pretty bad, but sentimental value there.'

The light went to green, and the doors slid open. 'Might as well get the full effect. Lights on full.'

They flashed on, illuminated the nearly invisible shelves from above and below. The brightly painted toys shone bright as jewels with their ruby reds, sapphire blues, ambers and emeralds.

Trevor's gaze tracked across, and he noted the wide curved window, without privacy screen. Casually, he crossed over, as if studying the collection, and checked the windows on the building next door.

Screened. He couldn't be sure, not a hundred percent sure there wasn't someone on the other side looking over. He'd have to make certain Dix was out of view when he put him down.

'Been collecting since I was ten. Seriously since I was about twenty, but in the last five years I've really been able to indulge myself. Do you see this? Farm section. It's an elevator, John Deere replica in pressed steel at one-sixteenth scale. Circa 1960. Mint condition, and I paid a mint for it, but it was worth it. And this over here . . .' He took a few steps, swayed. 'Whew. Gin's gone to my head. I'm going to grab some Sober-Up. Look around.'

'Hold on.' That wouldn't do, not at all. Trevor wanted the alcohol, and plenty of it, in his system. Added to that, the impairment of it would make it simpler to kill him. 'What's this piece?'

It was enough to draw Dix's interest, to have him shift direction and move just out of the line of sight of the side window. 'Ah, game department,' Dix said cheerfully. 'It's a pinball machine, toy-sized version, baseball theme. Circa 1970. Be worth more in the original box, but there's something to be said for the fact it saw a little action.'

'Hmm.' Trevor turned around, grinned broadly. 'Now, that's a hell of a piece.'

'Which?' Dix turned as well. 'In the military section?'

Trevor slipped his accordion baton from his pocket. 'The tank?'

'Oh yeah, that's a jewel.'

As Dix took a step, Trevor snapped his wrist to extend the baton. He swung in up into an arch, then brought it down across the back of Dix's skull.

Dix fell as Trevor had positioned him, away from the shelves and out of the line of sight of the unprotected window.

'Spending this much time in your company,' Trevor said as he took out a handkerchief and meticulously cleaned off the lethal wand, 'I've discovered something I only suspected previously. You're an unbearably tedious geek. The world's better off without you. But first things first.'

He stepped over the body, toward the toy that had once been his father's. As he reached out, the doorbell buzzed.

His heart didn't leap, but stayed as steady as it had when he'd fractured Dix's skull. But he spun around, and calculated. To ignore it – and how he wanted to ignore it, to take what was his and see it at last – would be a mistake.

They'd been seen coming into the building, riding up in the elevator. In a building like this there would be security cameras in the halls outside. He'd have to acknowledge whoever was at the door and dismiss them.

More irritated than uneasy, he hurried to answer the summons. He engaged the security screen first and studied the thin young man in an eye-searing pink shirt covered with purple palm trees. The man looked bored and was chewing what appeared to be a fist-size wad of gum. He carried a thick zip-bag. Even as Trevor watched, the man blew a bubble the size of a small planet and hit the buzzer again.

Trevor flicked on the intercom. 'Yes?'

446

'Delivery for Dix. Chad Dix.'

'Leave it there.'

'No can do. Need a sig. Come on, buddy, I gotta get back on my horse and ride.'

Cautious, Trevor widened his view. He saw the purple skin pants, the pink airboots. Where *did* these people get their wardrobes? He reached for the locks, then drew his hand back.

Wasn't worth the risk. There'd be too many questions if he accepted a package, if he signed Dix's name, or his own, for that matter.

'Leave it with the downstairs desk. They'll sign. I'm busy.'

'Hey, buddy—'

'I'm busy!' Trevor snapped and disengaged the intercom. He watched, just to be sure, and sneered as the messenger flipped up his middle finger and walked out of view.

Satisfied, he switched off the screen. It was time he accepted his own special delivery, long overdue.

'Shut down the coms and screens,' Eve ordered Feeney through her communicator. 'We'll have to take the door.'

'Shutting them down.'

She turned to McNab. 'Nice job. I'd've bought it.'

'If that was Dix and he wasn't under duress, he'd have opened the door.' McNab drew his weapon from the base of his spine and holstered it at his side.

'Yeah. Take care of the locks,' she told Roarke. 'Weapons on stun,' she ordered the team. 'I don't want a hostage taken down. Hold fire until my command. Peabody and I go in first. You take the right. McNab, you're left. You, you, you, fan out, second wave. I want this door secured behind us. Roarke?'

'Nearly there, Lieutenant.' He was crouched, delicately disarming locks and alarms with tools as thin as threads.

She squatted beside him, lowered her voice. 'You're not going in.'

'Yes, I don't believe I heard my name in today's lineup.'

She suspected he was armed – illegally – and that he would –

probably – be discreet about it. But she couldn't justify the risk. 'I can't take a civilian through the door until the suspect is contained. Not with this many cops around.'

He shifted his gaze and those laser blue eyes met hers. 'You don't need to explain or attempt to quell even my infamous ego.'

'Good.'

'And you're in.'

She nodded. 'You're a handy guy to have around. Now step back so we can take this asshole.'

She knew it was hard for him to do just that, to stand aside while she went through the door. Whittier was almost certainly armed, and he would kill without hesitation. But Roarke straightened, moved away from the team.

She'd remember that, she thought – or she'd try to remember that – when things got heated between them as they tended to do. She'd remind herself that, when it mattered to her, he'd stepped aside so she could do her job.

'Feeney? Emergency evac?'

'It's down. He's boxed.'

'We're on the door. Peabody?'

'Ready, sir.'

With her weapon in her right hand, Eve eased the unsecured door open with her left. With one sharp nod, she booted it, went in low and fast.

'Police!' She swept, eyes and weapon, as Peabody peeled to the right and McNab came in from behind and shot left. 'Trevor Whittier, this is the police. This building is surrounded. All exits are blocked. Come out, hands up and in full view.'

She used hand signals to direct her team to other areas, other rooms as she moved forward.

'You've got nowhere to go, Trevor.'

'Stay back! I'll kill him. I have a hostage. I have Dix, and I'll kill him.'

She held up a closed fist, signaling her team to stop, to hold positions, then eased around the corner.

'I said I'll kill him.'

448

'I heard you.' Eve stayed where she was, looking through the open glass doors. Light glittered on the toy-decked shelves and on the blood smeared on the white floor.

Trevor sat in the center of it, the prize he'd killed for beside him. He had an arm hooked around Dix's neck, and a knife to his throat.

Dix's eyes were closed, and there was blood on the otherwise spotless floor. But she could see the subtle rise and fall of Dix's chest. Alive then. Still alive.

They looked like two overgrown boys who'd played just a little too hard and rough.

She kept her weapon trained and steady. 'Looks like you already did. Kill him.'

'He's breathing.' Trevor dug the point of the knife into flesh, carving a shallow slice. Blood dribbled over the blade. 'I can change that, and I will. Put down that weapon.'

'That's my line, Trevor. There are two ways you can leave this room. You can leave it walking, or we can carry you out.'

'I'll kill him first. Even if you stun me, I'll have time to slit his throat. You know it, or you'd have hit me already. You want to keep him alive, you back out. You back out now!'

'Kill him and the only thing I put down is you. Do you want to die today, Trevor?'

'You want him to die?' He jerked Dix's head back, and stirring slightly, Dix moaned. 'If you don't clear this place, that's what's going to happen. We start negotiating, and we start now. Back out.'

'You've been watching too many vids. You think I'm going to deal with you over a single civilian who's probably going to die anyway from the looks of things? Grab some reality, Trev.' She smiled when she said it, wide and white. 'I got pictures in my head of the two women you killed. It'd just fucking make my day to end you. So go ahead, finish him off.'

'You're bluffing. Do you think I'm *stupid*?'

'Yeah, actually. You're sitting there on the floor trying to talk me into negotiating when you're holding a knife, and I have this handy little thing. You know what they do when they're on full?

It's not pretty. And I'm getting a little tired of this conversation. You want to die over a toy truck, your choice.'

'You have no idea what I have. Clear the others out. I know there are others out there. Clear them out, and we'll talk. I'll make you the deal of a lifetime.'

'You mean the diamonds.' She gave a quick, rude snort. 'Jesus, you *are* stupid. I gave you too much credit. I've already got them, Trevor. That's a plant. Set you up. I set you up and used that clown for bait. Worked like a charm. It's just an old toy, Trevor, and you fell for it.'

'You're lying!' There was shock now, and there was anger, clear on his face.

As his head whipped around toward the bright yellow truck, and his knife hand lowered a fraction, Eve shot a stream into his right shoulder. His arm spasmed, and the knife fell from his shaking fingers.

Even as his body jerked back in reaction, she was across the room, with her weapon pressed to his throat. 'Gee, you caught me. I was lying.'

She was glad he was conscious, glad she could see it sink in. Tears of rage gathered in the corners of his eyes as she dragged him clear of Dix.

'Suspect's contained. Get medical in here!' It gave her a dark satisfaction to flip him onto his belly, to drag his hands back for the restraints.

She'd lied about the diamonds, but not about the pictures in her head. 'Andrea Jacobs,' she said in a whisper, close to his ear. 'Tina Cobb. Think about them, you worthless fuck. Think about them for the rest of your miserable life.'

'I want what's mine! I want what belongs to me!'

'So did they. You have the right to remain silent,' she began, and flipped him back over so she could watch his face while she read him his rights.

'You got all that?'

'I want a lawyer.'

'There you go, being predictable.' But she wanted a few moments with him first. She looked over her shoulder where the medical techs were readying Dix for transport. 'How's he doing?'

'Got a good chance.'

'Isn't that happy news, Trev? You may only get an attempted murder hit on this one. That's no big after the two first degrees. What's a few years tacked onto two life terms anyway?'

'You can't prove anything.'

She leaned close. 'Yes, I can. Got you with both murder weapons. Really appreciate your bringing them both along today.'

She watched his eye track over to where Peabody was bagging the baton.

Leaning back again, she laid her hand on the bulldozer, rolled in gently back and forth. 'You really figure they're in here? All those shiny stones? Be a joke on you, wouldn't it, if your grandfather pulled a fast one. Maybe this is just a kid's toy. Everything you did, all the years you'll pay for it would be for nothing. You ever consider that?'

'They're in there. And they're mine.'

'That's a matter of debate, isn't it?' Idly, she worked the lever that brought the blade up and down. 'Pretty freaking arrogant of him to pass this to a kid. Guess you take after him.'

'It was brilliant.' There were lawyers, he thought. His father would pay for the best. 'Better than a vault. Didn't they do exactly what he told them? Even after he was dead, they kept it.'

'Got me there. You want me to tell you where you weren't brilliant? Right from the start. You didn't do your homework, Trevor, didn't dot all your *i*'s. Your grandfather wouldn't have been so sloppy. He'd have known Samantha Gannon had a house-sitter. Those diamonds slipped through your fingers the instant you put that knife to Andrea Jacobs's throat. Sooner really. Then killing Tina Cobb on your father's job site.'

She enjoyed watching his face go gray in shock. It was small of her, she admitted, but she enjoyed it. 'That was sloppy, too. You just needed a little more forethought. Take her over to New Jersey, say. Romantic picnic in the woods, get what you needed from her, take her out, bury her.' Eve shrugged. 'But you didn't think it through.'

'You can't trace her back to me. No one ever saw—' He cut himself off.

'No one ever saw you together? Wrong. I got an eyewitness. And when Dix comes out of it, he'll tell us how he talked to you about Gannon's book. Your father will fill in the blanks, testifying how he told you about your grandfather, about the diamonds.'

'He'll never testify against me.'

'Your grandmother's alive.' She saw his eyes flicker. 'He's with her now, and he knows you left his mother, the woman who spent her life trying to protect him, lying in the dirt like garbage. What would it have cost you? Fifteen minutes, a half hour? You call for help, play the concerned, devoted grandson. Then you slip away. But she wasn't worth even that much effort from you. When you think about it, she was still protecting her son. Only this time, she protected him from you.'

She lifted the bulldozer, held it between them. 'History repeats. You're going to pay, just the way your grandfather paid. You're going to know, just the way he knew, that those big, bright diamonds are forever out of his reach. Which is worse? I wonder? The cage or the knowing?'

She got to her feet, stared down at him. 'We'll talk again soon.'

'I want to see them.'

Eve picked up the truck, tucked it under her arm. 'I know. Book him,' she ordered, and strolled away while Trevor cursed her.

Epilogue

It wasn't what she'd call standard procedure, but it seemed right. She could even make a case for logical. Precautions and security measures had to be taken, and paperwork filed. As all parties were cooperative, the red tape was minimal.

She had a room full of civilians in conference room A, Cop Central. Plenty of cops, too. Her investigative team were all present, as was the commander.

It had been his idea to alert the media – that was the political side that irked her, even though she understood the reasoning. Understanding or not, she'd have a damn press conference to deal with afterward.

For now, the media hounds were cooling their heels, and despite the number of people in the room, it was very quiet.

She'd put names to faces. Samantha Gannon, of course, and her grandparents, Laine and Max, who stood holding hands.

They looked fit, she thought, and rock steady. And unified. What was that like? she wondered. To have more than half a century together and still have, still need that connection?

Steven Whittier and his wife were there. She hadn't known exactly what to expect by mixing those two elements, but sometimes people surprised you. Not by being morons or assholes, that never surprised her. But by being decent.

Max Gannon had shaken Steven Whittier's hand. Not stiffly, but with warmth. And Laine Gannon had kissed his cheek, and had leaned in to murmur something in his ear that had caused Steven's eyes to swim.

The moment – the decency of that moment – burned Eve's throat. Her eyes met Roarke's, and she saw her reaction mirrored in them.

With or without jewels, a circle had closed.

'Lieutenant.' Whitney nodded to her.

'Yes, sir. The New York Police and Security Department appreciates your cooperation and your attendance here today. That cooperation has, in a very large part, assisted this department in closing this case. The deaths of . . .'

She'd had very specific, very straight-lined statements prepared. She let them go, and said what came into her mind.

'Jerome Myers, William Young, Andrea Jacobs, Tina Cobb. Their deaths can never be resolved, only the investigation into those deaths can be resolved. It's the best we can do. Whatever they did, whoever they were, their lives were taken, and there's never a resolution to murder. The officers in this room – Commander Whitney; Captain Feeney; Detectives Baxter; McNab; Peabody; Officer Trueheart – have done what can be done to resolve the case and find justice for the dead. That's our job and our duty. The civilians here – the Gannons, the Whittiers, Roarke – have given time, cooperation and expertise. Because of that, it's done, and we move on.'

She took the bulldozer from the box she'd unsealed. It had been scanned, of course. She'd already seen what was in it on screen. But this, she knew, was personal.

'Or in this case, we move back. Mr. Whittier, for the record. This object has been determined to be your property. You've given written permission for it to be dismantled. Is that correct?'

'Yes.'

'And you've agreed to do this dismantling yourself at this time.'

'Yes. Before I . . . I'd like to say, to apologize for—'

'It isn't necessary, Steven.' Laine spoke quietly, her hand still caught in Max's. 'Lieutenant Dallas is right. Some things can never be resolved, so we can only do our best.'

Saying nothing he nodded and picked up the tools on the conference table. While he worked, Laine spoke again. Her voice was lighter now, as if she'd determined to lift the mood.

454

'Do you remember, Max, sitting at the kitchen table with that silly ceramic dog?'

'I do.' He brought their joined hands to his lips. 'And that damn piggy bank. All it took was a couple whacks with a hammer. Lot more work involved here.' He patted Steven's shoulder.

'You were a cop before,' Eve put in.

'Before the turn of the century, then I went private. Don't imagine it's all that different. You got slicker toys and tools, but the job's always been the job. If I was born a few decades later, I'd've been an e-man.' He grinned at Feeney. 'Love to see your setup here.'

'I'd be glad to give you a personal tour. You're still working private, aren't you?'

'When a case interests me.'

'They almost always do,' Laine put in. 'Once a cop,' she said with a laugh.

'Tell me about it,' Roarke agreed.

Metal pieces clattered to the table and cut off conversation.

'There's padding inside.' Steve cleared his throat. 'It's clear enough to get it out.' But he pushed away from the table. 'I don't want to do it. Mrs. Gannon?'

'No. We've done our part. All of us. It's police business now, isn't it? It's for Lieutenant Dallas now. But I hope you'll do it fast, so I can breathe again.'

To solve the matter, Dallas lifted the detached body of the truck, reached in to tug out the padding. She laid it on the table, pulled it apart and picked up the pouch nested inside.

She opened the pouch and poured the stones into her hand.

'I didn't really believe it.' Samantha let out a trapped breath. 'Even after all this, I didn't really believe it. And there they are.'

'After all this time.' Laine watched as Eve dripped the glittering diamonds onto the pouch. 'My father would have laughed and laughed. Then tried to figure how he could palm a couple of them on his way out the door.'

Peabody edged in, and Eve gave her a moment to goggle before she elbowed her back. 'They'll need to be verified, authenticated and appraised, but—'

'Mind?' Without waiting, Roarke plucked one up, drew a loupe out of his pocket. 'Mmm, spectacular. First water, full cut, about seven carats. Probably worth twice what it was when it was tucked away. There'll be all sorts of interesting and complicated maneuvers, I imagine, between the insurance company and the heirs of the original owners.'

'That's not our problem. Put it back.'

'Of course, Lieutenant.' He laid it with the others.

It took Eve more than an hour to get through the feeding frenzy of the media. But it didn't surprise her to find Roarke in her office when it was done. He was kicked back in her chair, his elegantly shod feet on her desk while he fiddled with his ppc.

'You have an office of your own,' she reminded him.

'I do, yes, and it has a great deal more ambiance than yours. Then again, a condemned subway car has more ambiance than yours. I watched your media bout,' he added. 'Nice job, Lieutenant.'

'My ears are ringing. And the only feet that are supposed to be on my desk are mine.' But she left his there, sat on the corner.

'This is tough on the Whittiers,' he commented.

'Yeah. It's a hard line they've drawn. I guess it's not easy, whatever the circumstances, to turn your back on your son. Junior's not going to sponge off Mom and Dad for his legal fees. He's going down, all the way down, and they have to watch it.'

'They loved him, gave him a good home, and he wasted it. His choice.'

'Yeah.' The images of Andrea Jacobs and Tina Cobb held in her head a moment, then she put them away. 'Just answer one question, no bullshit. You didn't switch that diamond, did you?'

'You wired?' he said with a grin.

'Damnit, Roarke.'

'No, I didn't switch the diamond. Could have – just for fun, of course, but you get so cross about that sort of thing. I think I'll buy you a couple of them though.'

'I don't need—'

456

'Yammer, yammer, yammer,' he said with a wave of his hand and had her eyes going huge. 'Come sit on my lap.'

'If you think that's even a remote possibility, you need immediate professional help.'

'Ah well. I'm going to buy some of those diamonds,' he continued. 'They need the blood washed from them, Eve. They may only be things, as Laine Gannon said, but they're symbols, and they should be clean ones. You can't resolve death, as you said. You do what you can. And when you wear the stones that cost all those lives, they'll be clean again. They'll be a kind of badge that says someone stood for the victims. Someone always will. And whenever you wear them, you'll remember that.'

She stared at him. 'God, you get me. You get right to the core of me.'

'When I see you wear them, I'll remember it, too. And know that someone is you.' He laid a hand over hers. 'Do you know what I want from you, darling Eve?'

'Sweet-talk all you want, I'm still not sitting in your lap in Central. Ever.'

He laughed. 'Another fantasy shattered. What I want from you is the fifty years and more I saw between the Gannons today. The love and understanding, the memories of a lifetime. I want that from you.'

'We've got one year in. Second one's going pretty well so far.'

'No complaints.'

'I'm going to clock out. Why don't we both ditch work for the rest of the day—'

'It's already half-six, Lieutenant. Your shift's over anyway.'

She frowned at her wrist unit and saw he was right. 'It's the thought that counts. Let's go home, put a little more time into year two.'

He took her hand as they walked out together. 'What's done with the diamonds until they're turned over to whoever might be the legal owner?'

'Sealed, logged, scanned and locked in an evidence box that is locked in one of the evidence vaults in the bowels of this place.'

She slanted him a look. 'Good thing you don't steal anymore.'

'Isn't it?' He slung a friendly arm around her shoulders as they took the glide. 'Isn't it just?'

And deep, deep under the streets of the city, in the cool, quiet dark, the diamonds waited to shine again.

b